BIG BAD WOLF

SULEIKHA SNYDER

sourcebooks
casablanca

Published by Sourcebooks Casablanca, an imprint of Sourcebooks
P.O. Box 4410, Naperville, Illinois 60567–4410
(630) 961-3900
sourcebooks.com

Printed and bound in the United States of America.
SB 10 9 8 7 6 5 4 3 2 1

For Frank, of course

1

THE MAN WHO SAT ACROSS from her looked like he wanted to eat her, and Neha Ahluwalia had no doubt that he could. In great big bites. Laying her to waste with swipes of his claws.

Would it be kinder than what he'd done to land himself behind bars? *That* she had no inkling of. But she did know he was guilty. Guilty and a killer. One was a legal distinction, the other largely genetic, but they were both equally true. It wasn't just the look in his eyes. Not just speculation or suspicion or her overactive imagination. It was the facts. Spelled out in fine print, looped in strands of altered DNA. Joe Peluso was the monster in the closet, the creature you were warned about in fairy tales...and still, somehow, not the scariest white man Neha had encountered while doing her job. What passed for humanity these days terrified her far more than the things that went bump in the night.

His first trial had dominated the headlines for months. "Unknown Sniper Spurs Gangland Chaos." "Brutal Killer Caught!" "I Did It: Queens-Born Shooter Confesses." You couldn't walk by a newsstand or flip past the local news without seeing Peluso's face. His police mug shot. Broad features spattered with cuts and bruises. Ears that stuck out in almost comical contrast. He looked dangerous. He *still* looked dangerous. Like someone who would absolutely cut down four members of a Russian drug ring while they were eating dinner—leaving them facedown in their borscht—and then stab another two guys in close combat in the parking lot.

"*Yeah, I fuckin' did it! Is that what you want me to say?*" he'd shouted in court, according to the transcripts. "*Let's just get this bullshit over with!*"

What the transcripts hadn't said was that he'd almost *transformed* while raging on the witness stand. It wasn't that much of a surprise to people in law enforcement, like her—all kinds of new species had inched their way into the light since the Darkest Day in 2016, and she had more than a few in her own family—but the ripple of fur across his body, the *fangs*, had been enough to throw the court into a tailspin. Pun fully intended. That he'd shot people, stabbed people, but hadn't turned berserker—hadn't *devoured* his victims—had put a whole different spin on his case. Instant mistrial. Instant cover-up…at least as far as the press and the public were concerned.

Neha should've been terrified at the prospect of this new client *and* of the reality of him sitting across from her right now. And, sure, maybe she'd freaked out a little that morning at the firm. She'd spilled coffee on her second-best blazer and asked her favorite senior partner to repeat himself. "*I want you to sit in, Neha,*" Nate had obliged. "*I think you could learn a lot on this one…and I think we could learn a lot from your take. I want your profiling skills on full display.*"

As a junior associate, she was practically begging to log some more billable hours and hack away at her law-school debt. But the Peluso case? *Not* one she'd been expecting to have land on her plate. *Not* high on her list, since it wasn't exactly going to help pay the bills. But she'd said yes anyway. Because how did you turn something like this down? A vigilante shape-shifter in a Sanctuary

City? It was the kind of opportunity that could make or break her career…even if it didn't break the bank in the process.

Now here they were at the table. Her, Nate Feinberg—the first chair on the case—and his second chair and partner in defending crime, Dustin Taylor. With Joe Peluso himself staring back at them. His bruises were fresh. Probably from a recent tussle in jail as he waited for the new trial date. But everything else was the same as in his picture. His dark-brown hair chopped short in a blunt cut. A harsh-featured face only a mother could love. Those ears. And his dark, cold eyes. Meeting them, acknowledging his blatant perusal, Neha knew without a doubt that he was capable of taking lives. Professional. Efficient. Ruthless. But there was something else there, too. Not vulnerability. Not softness. Nothing like that. Just…depth? A hint of something below that chilly surface, something charismatic or compelling. A mystery waiting to be solved. Was it the monster? Or was it the man? Either way, Neha couldn't—*wouldn't*—take her eyes off him.

There were too many things about him, about this case, that didn't add up quite right. Like Peluso's heavily redacted military files. Like how he had only gotten caught because, of all things, he'd called in a tip after his hit. A two-minute, forty-second phone call telling the cops about a shipping container full of "goods" scheduled to arrive later in the week. While one set of law-enforcement officials had tried to trace the burner-phone call and cross-referenced the security cameras and drone footage from nearby, another had intercepted the drop. The shipping container in question hadn't been full of drugs or bootlegs or weapons. It had been full of people—mostly human women—slated for sex trafficking.

Joe Peluso had cut down six criminals without blinking…but spared one thought to save dozens of lives. A man who'd clearly done his homework about the security drones that circled the city, he'd figured out their patterns. Even though they were supposedly on a randomizer and changed circuits every day, he had chucked all of that—risked being recorded—to make a call. What she didn't know, and didn't remotely understand, was *why*. And she hoped that the why would help them win their day in court, despite all the odds that were stacked against them. Not the least of which was the fact that this guy had taken out a bunch of Russian nationals, and all of the current president's New York-based cronies were calling for Peluso's head. So that the Russian government didn't retaliate. So they didn't lose all their cushy connections. Add in the supernatural factor—which called into question rights and personhood and whether he was even *entitled* to a new trial—and it was a mess.

There was buzz around the firm that the rest of the senior partners had balked at Nate taking this case, fearing public backlash. *"Sanctuary fucking City,"* he'd reportedly said in response. *"Last I checked, mobsters, pimps, and white supremacists were still the bad guys, and all Americans are still entitled to due process. No matter what's going on in Washington with birthright citizenship and humanity verification legislation, Joseph Peluso is still a citizen."* And that was that. As long as the mayor and the governor kept fighting the dark curtain that had dropped across the United States over the past few years, the legal firm of Dickenson, Gould, and Smythe would keep holding the line.

How Nate managed the other partners so efficiently was a secret well above Neha's pay grade. And, frankly, she didn't want to know. The enigma sitting across from them was more than enough to deal with. She just had to trust that both Nate and Dustin knew their shit. As for herself…? She'd come into law after doing a doctorate in behavioral psych. It was her job to know Joe Peluso's shit.

"Get him talking, Neha. Find out what his public defender missed. We don't want to repeat those mistakes."

Too bad the man across the table didn't seem particularly inclined to talk at the moment. His posture was closed-off, sullen.

He answered questions in monosyllables. It was no wonder that first trial had been an epic disaster. Peluso screaming he did it. Gavels banging. Everybody and their mother shitting their legal briefs. The presidential cronies and right-of-center government officials calling for oversight on sanctuary-city legal procedure. That made the governors and mayors who were part of the nationwide Sanctuary Alliance push back and cite the Sanctuary Autonomy Act of 2019. All of it had kept Peluso on ice in prison for months without even a question of retrial. Nobody at DGS wanted a repeat of that three-ring circus.

And on a more local level, nobody really wanted to mess with Aleksei Vasiliev, the Russian mafia *vor* whose underlings Peluso had eliminated so ruthlessly. Vasiliev owned a string of clubs and bars in the old-school Russian enclaves across Brooklyn and Queens, but it was fairly common knowledge that (a) they were a cover for drugs and sex trafficking and (b) he was just one cog in a larger operation run by a criminal network that both local authorities and Interpol had been watching for years. Plus (c) his potential supernatural affiliation—there was no confirmation in the legal community, but rumors had him as everything from werewolf to sorcerer. Oh, and there were also (d) his ties to several Aryan militia groups. The overlap between white supremacy and organized crime was such that the Venn diagram was practically one circle.

Aleksei Vasiliev was a nightmare. It was just Neha's luck that Joe Peluso had messed with him—and then some—by taking out a bunch of his pals. Peluso had basically kicked over six hornets' nests. And, looking at him now, it certainly seemed like he did not give a single fuck about it. He was slouched, almost bored. Staring at the table or the wall more than paying attention to his lawyers. There was a slight tension to his shoulders, to the lines of his mouth, but that could be attributed to any number of things. A problem with authority. General surliness. Constipation.

Dustin's smooth baritone betrayed not one bit of annoyance

that their new client wasn't playing ball. "Would you say you were under duress when you left Queens on the night of September 14?"

"'Under duress?' What kind of bullshit phrasing is that?" Peluso rolled his eyes. "No one forced me anywhere. Lone-ass gunman, remember?"

Nate offered his most charming smile in response. "Was it a full moon?" He knew the answer to that already. The date of the hit was well documented. But he wasn't fishing for calendar confirmation. "Were you perhaps driven by...impulses?"

This, too, met with disdain. And zero acknowledgment of what Nate was referring to. "Do I look like the Weather Channel?" Peluso sneered. "The fuck do I know if it was a full moon?"

Neha struggled not to laugh, to not give him the satisfaction of a reaction, and applied herself to taking notes while Nate and Dustin went over the prelims again. But mostly she just watched their client. Studied him. Recorded what questions made the veins on his neck stand out. When he clenched his fists. He didn't like talking about his past. Bristled when asked about motive. On the surface, he seemed like the classic alpha male with authority issues. Push the wrong button and he would blow.

But then you added in the shifter factor...and she was stumped. From all reports, Peluso hadn't changed forms, or attempted to change, since his outburst in court. The medical staff at Brooklyn Detention had done as much blood work as their limited capability allowed, monitored him for weeks afterward, and only logged a few minor signs of supernatural ability. Bursts of increased aggression at certain times of the month—something she could actually relate to. But he hadn't gone full wolf or bear or whatever he was. He'd done nothing that required putting him in solitary. Aside from being a surly asshole who clearly got in a few dustups here and there, he was a model prisoner. Not so much the model client.

It was the world's most personal *Law & Order* rerun—movie-star handsome Nate and suave and serene Dustin trying to get a bead on the chillingly charismatic killer they'd agreed to defend. The contrast was almost comical. Their suits probably cost more money than Joe Peluso would ever see. Hell, Neha knew without a doubt that their suits cost more than her entire wardrobe. They were almost incongruous in the spare, utilitarian, private visitors' room. Two shining beacons of Armani hotness surrounded by cinder block and reinforced steel—an ad for a fashion house versus the Brooklyn House of Detention.

Halfway through the meeting, she realized Peluso was looking right at her. Leaning back in the chair bolted to the floor, chained fists on the table before him like he'd been ordered to pray. There was something like a smile on his face. A glitter in the black ice-chips of his pupils. *Oh. Of course.* She knew what was coming. She'd worked as a grunt in the DA's office for two years before DGS fished her out of the shallow end. This was when the client said something like "Who's the bitch?" or "She a perk?" or "Can I see your tits?" The veritable sexual harassment buffet.

She braced for it. It never came. Peluso just flicked his gaze back to Nate. "Why's *she* here?" he demanded. "You trying to soften me up or something? It ain't gonna work. I know what you think I am, but you can't bribe me into good behavior like a dog."

He was angry. And she wasn't sure what to unpack first—that he thought she was a bribe, or that he'd compared himself to a dog. There was definitely a chunk of the public who thought he was a rabid monster off the chain, even without knowing his true nature. There were certainly people at the firm who thought she was just a diversity hire with great legs and a pretty face—a showpiece. But he was wrong. Nate hadn't brought her here to soften him. Just to get to him. And the fact that he'd noticed her meant she was *in*.

She leaned forward, folding her hands on the metal table in a parody of his. "I'm here to learn, Joe," she told him. "Nothing more, nothing less." The skin around his left eye was black and blue. His right cheek looked like someone had taken a cheese grater to it a week ago. But it was his gaze she focused on, his intensity that held her fixed.

Nate's hand settled on her knee. A warning squeeze, not a stolen grope. He was in no way interested in any of her body parts besides her brain—not just because he was gay, but because he didn't subscribe to the toxic male posturing that seemed to permeate most law firms. He'd likely brought her on board because she'd profiled his boyfriend a few months back over Friday night drinks. His now *ex*-boyfriend.

"Tread carefully," he was saying with the squeeze. "Tread carefully but work it." She was thirty-five. Older than a lot of her fellow junior associates. She didn't need the warning. She knew how to be careful.

"Bullshit," Peluso pronounced, that almost-smile returning to his face. Bizarrely, she kind of wanted to see the real thing. "It's never 'nothing less.' You want something from me. And good luck with that, 'cause I got nothing to give."

He was guilty, but he didn't seem to have any guilt. Not about what he'd done. That much was clear. And he wouldn't stand for *more* bullshit. So, she told him the truth as she knew it. "Okay. Here's the bottom line, Joe. They're here to defend you. I'm here to break you down. Get inside your head. Find out what makes you tick."

It amused him. He tilted his head, sizing her up with his good eye. "I'd like to see you try."

The way he said it—a cocky, casual threat—should have sent a chill down her spine. It didn't. It just got her back up. "That's the beauty of it, Joe," she told him. "You won't see it. You'll be halfway there, looking around and wondering why you told me every secret you've never told another soul."

She'd tried that line on a few clients here and there. Most of them laughed, because they didn't believe her. They didn't realize that she'd been cracking people like safes since long before the psych degree. When one of her older brothers had held her Malibu Barbie for ransom, she'd gotten the doll's location out of him in four minutes. She'd been eight.

People told her things. Whether they wanted to or not. People connected to her. Whether she wanted them to or not. It was a blessing and a curse. Maybe it was *her* supernatural gift.

"You'll give me everything," she assured.

Joe Peluso didn't laugh off the challenge. Instead, he seemed to mull it over. His brows winged together. His eyes went distant. He interlaced his fingers, cuffs clinking against the tabletop. He watched her watch him. Nate shifted beside her, obviously unsettled by the standoff, but he wouldn't have asked her along if he hadn't thought she could handle it.

She could handle this. She could handle *him*.

She knew Joe was guilty…and she knew she was just that good.

His new lawyers were slick talkers in expensive suits. Fine by him, since the public defender who fucked up his last trial was a dumb shitbag who couldn't string a sentence together, much less a defense. And he knew these guys were in it for the headlines. It sure as shit wasn't about the money, because he didn't have any to pay them with. The woman, though, he couldn't figure out. Secretary? Paralegal? They'd introduced her at the beginning. First name Neha, last name something with a lot of syllables. She'd spent most of the hour scribbling on a yellow pad, occasionally looking up at him and tapping her lips with her pen.

They were good lips. Full. She wasn't wearing lipstick. Someone probably told her to wipe it off before coming out to the jailhouse in case the sight of Posy Pink incited a prisoner riot. The problem was, she couldn't wipe off that she was hot. Black hair pulled back into a prim ponytail. Huge doe eyes. Smooth brown skin. What he could see of her above the table was bangin'. Her tits looked like they'd be a perfect handful. Makeup or no, the woman was a total fox. Enough to start a riot all on her own. Which was why he figured it was a play. Nobody brought a beautiful woman into a prison unless they wanted something.

"You'll give me everything."

Problem was, Joe didn't know what he had to give. Blood? Sweat? Been there and fucking done that. He had nothing left. She wasn't going to break him. She wouldn't even come close. But he liked hearing her say it. So serious. Intense. Like she wasn't a Disney princess who'd stumbled into the wrong movie. Like he couldn't snap her in half with one hand. She probably teased tigers for fun. Poked bears on Sundays after church or temple or whatever. Maybe that was why they thought she could tangle with him. Just another animal for the circus tamer.

"You're a shrink," he concluded out loud. "I get free therapy with this gig now?"

Her big, dark eyes narrowed. The fancy suits—Feinberg and Taylor—looked uncomfortable but curious. They were waiting to see how it all unraveled. He'd played worse games. Hell, he'd won a round of hoops with some punk asses in the showers last week— and his head was the ball.

"I'm a lawyer," she said, all snotty and self-assured. She thought she had him pegged already. "I also have a PhD in psychology and am here to utilize my skills as a profiler. But any official psychological evaluation you require will be handled by someone not affiliated with our firm. We don't cross the streams. We won't risk contaminating your defense."

Fuck. If she looked like a princess, she sounded like a phone-sex operator—all husky-voiced and pitched low for the bedroom. And Joe could imagine just how she would "contaminate" him. How she'd "utilize her skills." That mouth on him. Sucking him down. It wouldn't be because he was in control. No. It'd be because *she* set the rules. Because having him in her mouth meant she literally had him by the balls. He sprang wood pretty much instantly at the thought, and he was glad for ugly orange coveralls and chains. A con's equivalent of a coat to button up over your junk.

The irrational lust raged through him like someone lit him on fire, burning him down to the bone. And there was a whisper at the back of his brain, a low growl he couldn't make heads or tails of. It didn't make sense...but then again, not a lot had made sense since the military docs shot him up full of shifter juice. *"There may be side effects,"* they'd said during one of those early debriefs. *"Some species have reported instances of imprinting."* The fuck was imprinting? Like he was a damn duckling except with the urge to bone a complete stranger?

One thing was for sure: he couldn't remember the last time he actually had sex. He'd killed people more recently than he'd fucked anyone...and he could just imagine what his not-so-sainted nonna, who'd spent every day in church, would say about his life choices. Fortunately, she was dead—and hopefully rotting in hell. He wondered if he needed to say all of this to this lawyer-psychologist. She'd probably find it significant that he associated his sex life, or lack thereof, with a formative female relative. The shrink he'd seen before the Corps approved his fancy upgrade and handed him over to his new unit sure had.

He stared at his panel of would-be saviors until they started to fidget. It was a game of chicken he never lost. He could stay quiet for hours. Days. Years. When they started shuffling papers and making to wrap things up, he cleared his throat, tapped the table with his knuckles. The white-haired guy, Feinberg, looked up first. His sharp-dressed wingman next. The woman didn't have to...because she hadn't taken her eyes off him this entire time. She caught him staring and gave it right back. *Fuck you, too, buddy.*

"Did you need something, Joe?" she wondered.

He needed a lot of things. A Heineken. A decent burger. A room with an actual door. A flight outta this joint. He rattled off the list just for kicks. "And a 1963 Corvette Stingray. Can you get me that, too?"

"Right after your trip to Disney World and a massage from a supermodel," she said, like he'd asked for the most reasonable things in the world. Smart as a whip and cool as a cucumber, this one. But there was fire there, too. Burning close enough to the surface that it wouldn't take much for it to rage. That interested him. More than anything had interested him in a long-ass time.

"Okay, I'll talk to you," he told her. "Whatever you want. You and me, we'll chat."

And maybe they'd do more than just chat. Maybe they'd get to be alone. Sitting real close as he spilled his guts to her. Braiding each other's hair and shit…or unbuttoning each other's buttons. He knew which option she'd prefer, and which one sounded better to him. She didn't pick up on what he was already imagining…which was a good thing, because he'd be slapped with extra charges so fast. Whatever the opposite of "contempt of court" was.

He had absolutely no contempt for this hot shrink-who-wasn't-*his*-shrink whatsoever. Probably because he'd never been able to resist a woman telling him what's what. Because it had been too long, and he'd missed someone talking to him like she *saw* him. Sure, she didn't *like* what she was seeing, but he didn't much like himself either. And his dick did not give a good goddamn that he was facing twenty-five to life. It only cared that he was facing someone beautiful. It only wanted to listen to that growl coming from deep inside him. He hadn't understood the growl before, but he heard it clearly now. Saying "take" and "have" and "mine." *Imprinting. Quack, quack.* His beast and his brain and his body all plotting together, because it beat the alternative: remembering why he was actually here.

Of course, his brain had to go and ruin it as the lawyers walked out and he got yanked out of his chair by the guard. *You really think she's going to do more than talk to you? Knowing what you've done?*

Knowing what you are? You're a killer, Joe. A thousand times over. And maybe he wasn't all that sorry for all the things he'd done, but it was a lot to ask of anybody else. Especially a woman like the doc. Somebody with a brain and a heart and morals. Murder didn't tend to curl a lady's toes, did it? And shifters weren't exactly prime dating material. Fuck. He was one deluded motherfucker, wasn't he? *She's not for you, buddy. She's never going to be for you.*

He could just imagine what Kenny would have to say about that *"Joey, since when do you have troubling getting laid? Shit, if you can't get pussy, where's the hope for the rest of us?"*

"You watch your mouth, kid," he'd say back. *"There's more to women than pussy. Don't disrespect 'em that way."* Kenny Castelli, the closest thing he ever had to a brother, who fucking hero-worshipped him and probably died because of it. Joe was always great at giving him advice that he'd never actually taken himself… and that Kenny didn't take either. And now here they were. A dead man and a dead man walking.

The trip back to his cell—if it could be called that when he was being shoved most of the way—stripped the rest of the swagger right out of him. Every ounce of attitude he'd displayed for Feinberg, Taylor, and the doc just faded away. He couldn't afford to forget why he was here, a "guest" of Kings County. He'd taken human lives without an ounce of regret. Too many lives. And he wasn't supposed to add one more spectacular body to the count.

2

HER KNEES SHOULD'VE BEEN WOBBLING when they collected their things and left the correctional facility. Her guts should've been in a twist. But she walked out onto Atlantic Avenue on steady legs, with a serious craving for chicken and dumplings from the soul-food place just up the block. That it still existed despite rising rents and weekly ICE and Supernatural Regulation Bureau raids was one of the world's small miracles.

"Damn, Neha! You've got balls!" Dustin gave a low whistle of admiration and shook his head. "Glad we brought you in on this."

"Ovaries," she corrected. "I believe the term you're looking for is 'ovaries of steel.'"

He laughed while Nate suppressed a smile, his eyes serious. "You did good today, Neha. Keep it up."

"Don't worry; I will." She was pretty confident—you didn't get through law school without at least a little bit of a high opinion of yourself—but the validation still felt good.

Papa and Ma had wanted her to go into something "safe" and high-paying, expecting her JD to land her a legal-eagle husband and not a stack of alleged criminals to defend. Now, one of their biggest nightmares was that she would pick up a man in Kings

County Criminal Court. To be fair, they also thought that if she opted to hang her shingle out as a therapist, she'd be bound to fall in love with a patient. They watched a lot of Indian soap operas on satellite—their respite from a far-more-bonkers reality.

Joe Peluso was a character they could never dream up. The basics were easy to check off. He was forty-two years old, Italian-American, with a blue-collar upbringing in Queens. What they could access of his military service record was spotless. He'd had tours in both Iraq and Afghanistan and never faced disciplinary action of any kind. He seemed like the typical white American male who liked beer and guns and his country. But there were so many unanswered questions. From what little she knew about shape-shifters, they were born, not *made*...and yet there was no indication that Joe's family were anything other than human. When had he been turned and by who? Why hadn't he killed Vasiliev's men in his supernatural form? Why hadn't he taken on that form during almost a year in a jail? She would have to dig for the truth...and the challenge made goose bumps break out on her skin even though it was a perfect autumn in Brooklyn. What had turned this guy into a murderer? What could they use to reduce his sentence or, miracle of miracles, put him back on the street?

Yeah. Okay. Maybe they should have had a few moral qualms about setting a killer loose. But he hadn't exactly gone after six Girl Scouts. He hadn't committed *carnage*, letting his beast run wild all over New York. She was going to sleep at night by reminding herself that a few dead sex traffickers were no great loss to society.

It was depressing to put it into words, but from a purely PR standpoint, they were infinitely lucky that a decent percentage of the country still believed Nazis were bad. That Joe Peluso had kind of done a public service by taking out guys who sported Wolfsangel and swastika tattoos and sold young girls into sexual servitude. There was, of course, still a percentage who thought Joe's victims were "very fine people." Very fine people who had cats and helped old white ladies across the street when they weren't stuffing teen-agers into shipping containers and yelling slurs at anyone brown. God bless America.

Theoretically, you weren't supposed to put the victims on trial. But more often than not, that was the job. Arguing why certain people deserved to live and others deserved to die. Sometimes you just had to park morality at the door and look at the shades of gray. It didn't help that the world had changed in the past few years. Practicing law in America, practicing medi-cine, practicing *basic humanity*...none of it was like it had been when Neha was growing up. There were more shades of gray than anything else.

Yeah, she would've made a lousy wife to a nice, well-adjusted guy her parents approved of. To that staid L-school son-in-law they were still dreaming about. Maybe she would've been safer, but safety was overrated. Hell, when you had darker skin—no amount of Fair & Lovely skin cream could turn her into a white girl—safety was a flat-out lie.

Nate and Dustin grabbed a private car back to the office. It was only a ten-minute walk, but Neha wasn't surprised they wanted to keep the dust off their Ferragamos...and avoid the drone sweeps that had become part of daily American life these past few years. Part of the deal that kept the Sanctuary Cities running was manda-tory surveillance. The footage was flagged for criminal activity by algorithms and then pored over by a joint federal-state task force. Ostensibly impartial, the group was composed of humans and a few warlocks who'd been cleared for intelligence work. There were countless task forces and bureaus these days. They all amounted to the same thing: control. She was probably on multiple watch lists already, and her serviceable DSW pumps had seen better days and many a block. Even cell blocks. And they'd be seeing a lot of Joe Peluso in the weeks to come.

She'd had a choice back in that visitation room. She could've called him "Mr. Peluso." She'd gone with "Joe." For all the classic reasons. It created kinship with the person, established power dynamics, blah blah blah. She also knew herself. She'd just wanted to hear how it would sound. How it would feel to call a merciless brute by his first name. It felt powerful. *She* felt powerful.

For someone who had to speed up on the sidewalk and curl her fingers around her keys when she heard a noise behind her, that was a heady feeling. Addictive. She couldn't do anything about the assholes on the street, or safe in their places of power, but the ones on the inside…? For just a little while, she held their fates in her hands.

That was fucked up. She was aware. She'd had friends tell her that fifty percent of a psych degree was a "heal thyself" thing. They were not altogether wrong. But she'd take empowerment where she could get it. She sure hadn't found it with her last two boyfriends. One had kept bugging her to learn to cook saag paneer and be more Indian—a rich request from a guy named Brad who grew up in Connecticut—and the other one tried to make erotic choking a thing…a *surprise* thing. No thank you. She preferred to negotiate her kinky play beforehand. A man like Joe Peluso probably didn't ask first, either, but she'd find details like that out. She had to. How he treated women would help set a baseline for how he viewed humanity in general. Mass shooters, for instance, often had a history of domestic violence. Joe Peluso didn't—or at least he'd never been arrested for it—and one violent act didn't necessarily mean he was a violent person overall. They needed to prove he was a victim of circumstance, or someone who had acted irrationally for the first time in his life, not point to a pattern of behavior.

Ugh. Neha wasn't sure she was up to the challenge. Human behavior was a specialty of hers. Human misbehavior was her job. *Supernatural* misbehavior… Well, it was about to become her new field of expertise.

It wasn't something little girls dreamed of. Not something *she'd* dreamed of. She'd wanted to be a princess or a fireman or a princess who fought fires. But she was good at this. At the mountains of paperwork and equal amounts of legwork. She wouldn't have made it through L-school and the DA's office otherwise. She'd make it through this case, too. Nate, Dustin, and Joe Peluso were counting on it.

By the time Neha got back to the firm, it was mostly deserted. Some of the first-years were milling around. Assistants, too. But the partners were all gone. Nate and Dustin had likely turned their hired car toward the city. They loved knocking back shots with hedge-fund bros. She couldn't say she shared the fascination. Most men of that set thought she was a ballbuster, a bitch, and had an overly high opinion of how hot she was. In a guy, that kind of attitude was just considered confidence. In a woman, it was somehow the worst thing in the world. Women needed to be modest and subservient and accommodating. *Fuck that.*

She wouldn't have survived long in criminal justice without some steel in her spine. She wouldn't have made it through that first meeting with Joe Peluso either. If she were the good and sweet Neha Ahluwalia, with coconut oil braids and a terminal case of the blushes, he would've been the wolf to her Red Riding Hood. And, sorry, but she refused to walk through the woods unprepared.

Sure, she was little bit fucked up...and she refused to be fucked over.

———

There was nothing bearable about being in prison. Anyone who said they liked the rec room or the yard or, hell, even the three squares a day was a damn liar. The nights were the worst. Everything echoed. Joe was in a max-security unit with a bunch of repeat offenders who were looking at first or second degree and would probably end up at Sing Sing or one of the border camps after their trials. There were a handful of other supes on the block. A yaksha who accidentally killed someone during a bank robbery. A vamp who took out some MTA workers in a frenzy.

Having a bloodier rap sheet than the rest of the pop didn't make anybody feel all warm and fuzzy. And *being* a little fuzzy, or at least furry, didn't earn any friends either. Especially with the Emergency Service Unit boys breathing down your fucking neck. You heard someone getting beat, someone crying into their pillow, someone busting a nut, and nobody looked anybody in the eye in the morning. You tried to keep out of ESU's way but still ended up getting shoved into a wall. And a floor. And the bars of your cell. Knowing that if you let the monster out, it would just be an excuse for them to put you down. It wasn't survival of the fittest, just survival.

Joe had always been good at that. Surviving. After he enlisted in the Marines, he figured he'd get through boot camp on a prayer, but it turned out he thrived in the Corps. He made a good grunt, an even better sharpshooter. And a "truly exemplary" shifter on an elite team of military operatives. He managed to come back from multiple tours alive. He'd get through this, too. Unless he got life in prison, courtesy of the State of New York, or a death penalty courtesy of anyone who didn't like his altered DNA.

"We're aiming for a reduced sentence," Feinberg had told him during one of his weekly visits. *"And, of course, we're fighting for your rights as a supernatural as well. But there are no guarantees."* Joe had to admire that. No bullshit. No promises that he'd walk free.

There was blood on his hands. He *shouldn't* be allowed to walk free. But then again, there were a whole fucking lot of other people who shouldn't have been on the street either. And they were all still out there—while he slid his arms behind his head and stared up at a concrete ceiling. Decorated with dried gum, graffiti, and hash marks no one ever bothered to scrub clean. The Brooklyn Hilton got a fancy upgrade way back in 2012, but it hadn't taken long for it all to go to shit, especially with the new governor shutting down Rikers Island in 2020 and the rest of the prisons in the area still scrambling to pick up the slack. Jails were overcrowded. Everybody was overworked. Nobody was about to come by and fluff Joe's pillows. They were too busy cursing Governor Nixon's name and telling the mayor where to fuck off to.

He was no stranger to less than five-star accommodations. He'd slept in muddy trenches. On rock and stone and concrete. Hell, he could catch a power nap standing up. When he got back stateside this last time, he'd crashed in Mrs. Castelli's spare bedroom—his old high-school haunt—and that was like fucking luxury. After he landed a steady gig on a crew working out in Long Island City, he'd rented a cheap efficiency off the E train. Shared bathroom and a pay phone in the hall. No lease. No questions. They'd probably tossed his shit out on the curb the minute the cops took the yellow tape off the door. It'd been almost two years since he last saw that place, and he wasn't exactly dreaming of going back. The NYPD had confiscated anything worth a damn. All he had left was himself. Stuffed into a six-by-eight cell.

Sometimes they let him have books. A guy came by with a cart. Paperbacks falling apart and falling off it. He'd snagged a couple Patricia Cornwells and some medical thrillers by Tess Gerritsen. Not for nothing, but lady crime writers did love themselves some gory shit. He got creeped out—and wouldn't *that* crack up the guys from his old team—but he read them anyway. Squinting at the pages in the dim light of his cell.

He didn't really sleep. Because sleeping meant letting his guard down. Because sleeping meant dreaming, and he wasn't a huge fan of that picture show these days. He didn't wanna see Kenny. All fresh-faced and awkward, that cowlick from when he was a toddler still sticking up at nineteen and twenty-two and twenty-six. He didn't wanna see that fucking dive in Gravesend he'd visited a couple times when Kenny was on shift. With the saddest strippers he'd ever seen, making the saddest tips. Which meant even less for the bartenders. *"It's still extra money, Joey. Better money than any-place else. Don't ride me on this."*

"You wanna work for a buncha Russian assholes, it's your funeral, kid." That was what he'd said. And of all the bullshit pronounce-ments he'd made in his life, that was the *one* that came true. Gravesend dug Kenny's grave. He never should've left Maspeth. At least there they knew all the meth-head devils.

So, no, Joe didn't sleep. He didn't want to see the kid he'd loved like a little brother dead on a slab, four slugs in his chest because some Russian fucknut had a grudge with another fucknut and thought a titty bar was the place to settle it. Four people had died besides the fucknuts in question. One of the girls. Two regulars. And Kenny. All of them forgotten in the twenty-four-hour news cycle. It was bullshit then and bullshit now, playing on Joe's eyelids on a loop even though he was in another damn borough at the time.

And he didn't want to see Afghanistan either. Because that was the other option, right? The other matinee special at the Peluso Theater. All the things they'd done over there for god and coun-try. The literal monsters they became in the name of patriotism and heroics. He could wash off the sand, wash off the blood, but there was no washing off the stain of those years, those souls. He was a damn good Marine. He fucking made corporal. He followed orders. He never missed a shot. He never left a man behind… unless it was one of the men he was putting down. He wasn't sure that made him a good human…but they hadn't *wanted* a good human, had they? They'd wanted a beast. They'd created a beast.

It's hotter than balls. Worse than a subway platform in August. And Joe has a hostile's brains splattered all over his cammies. The ring-ing in his ears just won't stop, but neither will the shells. It's been hours, and he can't stop tasting the meat…

Fuck. *No.*

So Joe turned to fantasies instead. It wasn't always sex... No, who was he kidding? It was *mostly* sex. He didn't wrap his hand around his dick, though—didn't try to get off—because the cellblock didn't need a show. It was just him and the double feature on his eyelids. Silent. Fists curled on the thin mattress. He remembered Tasha in the back seat of a borrowed Impala. His first. She was Kenny's babysitter back in the day and still came around the Castellis' house all the time. Gorgeous. Legs for miles. Then there was Mishelle, practically his common-law wife...if you didn't count all the time he'd spent deployed.

They'd had five good years together and two pathetic ones. And luckily no adorable Haitian-Italian babies to show for it. Because what kind of shit father would he have turned out to be? Thank Christ, Mishelle wasn't tied to him and his bullshit for life. But when they were good... Yeah, they'd been pretty amazing. He could've happily died in her pussy. And now...? Probably in any pussy. He didn't have a type or anything. He loved all kinds of women. Loved their minds and their bodies. Loved how they tasted and smelled.

That doctor-lawyer-whatever. Neha. He knew she'd smell real good. Like that first gulp of air whenever he walked out of lockup. And she was soft under those clothes even if she pretended she was made of cast iron. She'd melt for him. Black hair all loose and wild. Honey on his fingertips and his tongue. Thighs spread. Begging. But she wouldn't need to beg for it, not really, because he'd give it for free.

While all the other dipshits at Aviation High were pressing their girls for blow jobs, Joe had learned how to make girls scream. He aced every lesson, got a 4.0 in eating out. He was a doer, Mishelle told him once. He didn't bother protesting or arguing or trying to negotiate reciprocity, he just went for it. Why waste time when he could be knuckle-deep in a woman, licking her while she yanked at his hair and said his name like he was a god?

If the death penalty were an option, if they gave him the chair, he knew exactly what his last meal would be. "An hour with her," he'd say, and point to the doc.

3

"WHY IS JOSEPH PELUSO NOT dead yet?"

"Boss, I—"

"—have no excuse."

When her brother was angry, the whole world knew it. Not because of the volume of his fury, but because of the silence. After eight months in his employ—and twenty-six years in his life—Yulia was more than used to the malevolent absence of sound that marked Aleksei Vasiliev's displeasure. The moment after his interruption stretched to infinity, growing darker and more threatening with every passing second. She knew better than to cross the threshold into his office and, instead, pressed flat against the wall just outside. This wasn't the first time she'd done so, and it was far from the first time she'd heard something sensitive. Such was the life when your family was Russian mafia…and a clan of bear shifters. You were far more likely to overhear your brother planning violence than discussing birthday gifts.

"Our men have tried, Boss. On multiple occasions. Peluso is… formidable."

Yulia winced. There was no "trying" in Aleksei's world. You either succeeded or you failed. This flunkie was either terribly new or terribly clueless. Perhaps terribly arrogant, for that was also a rampant disease in this place. Either way, he would learn the lesson that she had as a cub: One did not upset or disappoint Aleksei without consequence. Nearly fifteen years her senior, he'd won his control of Little Odessa coldly and ruthlessly—without even one swipe of his massive paws—in the wake of Hurricane Sandy, indebting struggling businesses in South Brooklyn's Russian community to him with a huge influx of cash. He'd rebuilt their restaurants, their family groceries, their shops…and bought so many souls. He was forever expanding his territory into different neighborhoods, different aspects of illegal activity. Some Ukrainians had pushed back more than a year ago. This Joe Peluso person… he'd become her brother's obsession when he placed himself in the middle of the conflict. She'd seen some of it on the news. There was only so much she wanted to know. Only so much she could bear…so to speak.

There was a human woman who'd often come into the Confessional, the bar where she'd worked before. A writer bent over notebooks, drinking Moscow mules—which would be funny, perhaps, in any other situation. *"Russian mafia heroes are huge in romance novels right now,"* she'd confided once. *"Hot Russian billionaires. Hot Russian hit men. Is that even a thing?"*

Yulia had laughed and laughed. *"No,"* she'd managed to gasp out. *"This is not a thing for us."*

Fear was a thing. *Forced respect* was a thing. Hiding outside your brother's office and praying you did not catch him in a terrible mood was a thing. But she'd taken the time to explain to her clueless patron that not all Russians were billionaires or hit men. That she knew plenty of hard-working average Russian-Americans who did their jobs and went to church and did not even jaywalk. They just didn't happen to number among her family members. And she had not mentioned her family's *other* truth at all.

She drew in a shaky breath, made to step away and head back

toward the main floor of the club. But Aleksei's laughter stopped her in her tracks. The sound was like icicles breaking away from frozen window ledges in midwinter. So cold. So sharp.

"I admire your balls, Anton. But I expected better from you. I expected results. Shall I call Yuri?"

"You may call Medvedev if you like, but I will deliver," the underling—Anton—assured Aleksei. He smelled not of bear but of bird. "I can be trusted to serve your interests as well."

Medvedev. *Yuri.* Yulia shuddered. Another cub she'd been raised with. Another killer. The most valued of her brother's enforcers and the most lethal. She had no desire to see him darkening their doorstep once more. A visit from him was like a visit from Death. She hadn't always thought so. As a silly young ursine shifter, she'd thought him glamorous and powerful and handsome. The light to Aleksei's darkness. She knew better now. And she knew better men now. Men with sweetness in their eyes, warmth in their touch… warmth that could have so easily been heat, fire, if she'd allowed it.

"Hey. Hey, you know you can call me any time, right? I'm here for you."

"You don't understand. Danny, it's too dangerous."

"Not for me. Never for me. Yulia, I can handle it. I have connections, too."

He was not for her. *He* was never for her. But Yulia still hugged the image of Detective Danny Yeo close as she fled back to the hostess station, her reason for seeking out her brother forgotten. There was the light in *her* darkness. Golden-skinned and brown-eyed. Slight and slender but still so strong. A beautiful man she could never have. Not if she wanted him to live. After all, if her brother could so easily, thoughtlessly, order the death of someone like Joe Peluso—someone he did not even know—what could he do to a human police officer that his sister held affection for? The possibilities were endless, each grislier than the last.

She knew it was cowardly to just go back to her job like she'd heard nothing of consequence. Cowardly to paste on a smile and pass out menus and continue pretending Kamchatka was nothing more than an upscale supper club and bar just steps from the boardwalk. But cowardice had kept her, and the people she cared for, alive thus far. Perhaps there would come a time when she would need bravery. It could be tomorrow, or next week or next month. Right now, in this moment, Yulia Vasilieva was content to simply survive.

Danny Yeo swiped away the pictures on his tablet, tossing the device down on his desk with a clatter and a huff of frustration. Neither noise made much impact in the cavernous space that was the open floor of Third Shift Security. But, then, he was *used* to not making much impact, wasn't he? Both at this job and his primary one at the NYPD.

To say that the years after the Darkest Day hadn't been kind was a gross understatement. New Patriot Acts. Travel bans. Increasingly isolationist policies that benefited the very rich and took advantage of the already struggling working class. The rolling back of LGBTQ rights and women's rights that had been protected for decades. New sanctions against classes of supernaturals who'd been living quietly among human populations for centuries until all too recently. It was, as Danny's bosses liked to say, a total clusterfuck.

Growing up thoroughly geeky, he and his sister had frequently boggled at how things could go so completely to shit in the eighteen years between *Star Wars: Revenge of the Sith* and *Star Wars: A New Hope*. "It got so awful that Ewan McGregor turned into Alec Guinness! Damn!" Sarah would laugh. They didn't laugh like that now. Because it had taken less than five years for the same thing to happen to the United States of America. That rapid descent into dystopia was why a lot of people had started calling the turning point in 2016 the Darkest Day…which was particularly ironic considering the even darker times that had followed.

Danny scowled, waking his desktop computer from sleep mode and calling up the interoffice messaging system. Two new chat windows awaited him. One from the higher-ups about a team meeting at 2200 hours—10:00 p.m. to a civilian like him—another an automated reminder from their admin about updating his personal information with any relevant changes to name, address, or other occupations. Third Shift might operate by their own set of rules, but they still had to answer to the government at large. And the government's questions had only gotten more personal since the 2016 election cycle. More personal and more dangerous.

The most popular rumor about the "outing" of supernaturals in December of that year was that it had been a controlled leak from the NSA. Spilling the secret before the new POTUS could blurt it out at a press briefing. It was one of those "keys to the kingdom" things, like the existence of aliens and the Illuminati, that probably went back to the very founding of the nation. Danny had every confidence that various government agencies and the military had known about supernaturals, and used their talents for warfare, from the very beginning. The only reason the country hadn't descended into utter chaos when the news hit the media sites was that several key members of Congress and the Supreme Court had stepped into the light as supes, too. Both Democrats and Republicans. So, deals had been made across the aisle. Senate subcommittees, a hastily formed Supernatural Regulation Bureau. Detention centers, too, of course. They lined both the northern and southern borders now. Though people of color seeking asylum and aid were still the primary target, the camps had more recently been outfitted for superhuman occupants as well.

The Resistance still rallied, both in the streets and behind closed doors. What remained of the free press still spoke out as much as they could. Sure, the *New York Times* had finally come out publicly as a propaganda machine for the ruling party, but the *Daily News* had survived to shit-stir, hiding behind its shield of tabloid-worthy headlines and over-the-top graphic design. Large metropolitan centers like New York, Chicago, Atlanta, and Los Angeles had taken the concept of "sanctuary" one step further, almost operating as city-states to protect their vulnerable citizens. They were capital-letter Sanctuary Cities now, offering shelter to humans and nonhumans alike. And, somehow, America trudged on. The TV shows hadn't changed that much—aside from a major uptick in '80s–'90s nostalgia and paranormal content—and gas prices were manageable. The day-to-day for the average white human citizen was as it had been a few years before. Most people got out of bed in the morning without thinking about how the Empire was in charge.

Danny wasn't most people. His family and friends weren't most people. As an idealistic kid, he'd thought joining the NYPD would be enough. That changing the system from the inside was the best way to fight it. Now, just shy of thirty and wearing a detective's shield by day, he knew better. Because he'd learned quickly that idealism and reality were like oil and water. And he'd nearly quit the force a dozen times. It was his sister, Sarah, who'd talked him out of it. *"Think of how much good you can still do, Bro. They need people like you to de-escalate situations. You can't let it be a white, human boys' club."* And she was right. As much as it hurt to deal with all the racist crap behind the impenetrable blue line, being able to advocate for minority citizens and keep an eye on his pale police brothers was invaluable. Too many Asian-American cops were complicit in police brutality. He refused to be one of them. If his efforts to be the change he wanted to see in the world didn't do nearly enough to fix a shitty system... Well, that was where moon-lighting paid off. He could use his investigative skills and his inside knowledge of the NYPD's operations for bigger things.

That was where Third Shift came in. For all intents and purposes, it was a PI and security firm, staffed primarily by people who needed a second job in a gig economy. Several military veterans. A few lawyers. Cops like him. IT pros. Doctors. They were a ragtag crew who moonlighted fixing other people's problems. Except the ragtag crew included some werewolves and vampires and sorcerers. And, these days, many of their clients happened to be highly placed government officials sympathetic to the Resistance—and their problems involved weapons smuggling, petty dictators, and circumventing global crises. And, oh, putting down supernaturals who were aiding in those endeavors.

One such supernatural crisis was occupying the team now: the ever-increasing Russian shifter foothold in American politics and the criminal underworld, and the blurring of lines therein. Danny would be lying if he said it wasn't personal.

"Hey. Hey, you know you can call me any time, right? I'm here for you."

"You don't understand. Danny, it's too dangerous."

"Not for me. Never for me. Yulia, I can handle it. I have connections, too."

Eight months. It had been eight terrible, nerve-wracking months since he'd last seen Yulia Vasilieva in person. The surveillance photos from a few days ago didn't really count as anything but proof of life. And they were only transmitted to his personal tablet because Finn thought he was "helping." Third Shift's founders, Elijah Richter and Jackson Tate, didn't exactly approve of using company resources to track women you had a thing for, but rules had never stopped Finian Conlan. Neither did rope. Or a gag. The vampire was impossible. He'd somehow secured shots of Yulia outside her brother's club, Kamchatka. *"We've our eye on Vasiliev anyway. What's a few extra pictures?"* he'd reasoned. *"Consider it an early birthday present!"* As creepy a gesture as it had been, Danny cherished the photos. Because they told him Yulia was alive.

Tired-looking. Too pale. Perhaps a bit thinner. But alive. Her dark-blond hair longer than he remembered, well past her shoulders. Poured into a sparkly cocktail dress that overemphasized how hot she was...but made him miss the Yulia who'd dressed how *she* liked to dress, just as gorgeous in long-sleeved T-shirts and jeans as she pulled pints and filled cocktail shakers.

Elijah's voice cut into Danny's sentimental ruminations. A lion shifter, Elijah had one of *those* voices. What Danny's sister would call "panty-melting" in a romantic context, but what was just plain authoritative and, if need be, scary in a professional one. He'd just walked off the elevator from the public-facing floor to this one, the secure inner sanctum. A burner cell phone was practically surgically attached to his ear as he growled into it, "Four weeks? I want in. Get me on the detail for the event." And then he snapped the flip phone shut and raked his gaze across the rows of cubicles. Until his dark, penetrating eyes landed on Danny.

"Heard you got a present today?" It was less a question and more of a statement. Because of course. Nothing happened around here without Lije's knowledge. He stopped by the short wall of Danny's cube, leaning one thickly muscled arm across the top. "You know how we feel about misappropriation of resources."

Yeah. It was why he didn't even steal pens from the office—just in case they turned out to be spy pens or something. But this was different. This was about Yulia. "Finn's a regular Santa Claus," Danny acknowledged with a sigh and a what-can-you-do shrug. "But I can't say I'm sorry he broke protocol. I'm glad to know Yulia Vasilieva's okay."

"For now," Elijah said grimly. "Vasiliev's days might be numbered. Our contacts abroad tell us that his friends are none too happy with him at the moment. Mirko Aston, especially. He's been increasingly dissatisfied with Vasiliev since Peluso hit that club last year and got in the way of that shipment of women. He's up to something even worse now, so the pressure is on for Aleksei to handle Peluso once and for all and prove his worth."

Joseph Andrew Peluso. Age 42. Depending on who you asked, he was a hero or a hoodlum. Former Marine turned construction worker, he was the kind of headline-grabbing vigilante that gave a lot of people hope…but turned others into cynics. Danny fell somewhere in the middle. He knew full well what could happen if someone who looked like him or like Elijah shot at a bunch of white guys. And throw in the fact that Peluso was, according to their contacts, a turned shifter from an elite intermilitary unit…? In the same position, he and Lije probably wouldn't have lived to see a first trial, much less a second. As for Peluso's impact on the local shifter-controlled Russian mafia…well, that had the potential to blow back on a woman that Danny cared about. That was a fear he would never be able to shake.

He didn't really give a rat's ass about Joe Peluso himself. But Elijah and Jack were invested in the case for reasons at least two levels above his pay grade. As far as he could tell, they considered Peluso another piece of the larger puzzle they'd been putting together for years. Human-shifter alliances. Government corruption and conspiracy. Peluso taking out Vasiliev's men and dropping a dime on their trafficking plans had messed with something much more complicated. Something involving a Slovakian arms dealer who went by the name Emeric "Mirko" Aston. So many people, so many crimes, so many wrongs to right. Whatever the bigger picture was here, it wasn't a pretty one. But Danny wasn't in this for watercolors, was he? The past few years in the Divided States of America had fixed his path more securely than his time at the police academy or his experiences on the beat in Flatbush and Kensington.

He was going to fight for freedom and equality in the only ways he could—and protect innocent shifters like Yulia, or die trying.

4

NEHA HAD NO SOLID EXPLANATION for why she was walking back into Brooklyn Detention just a week after Nate and Dustin had introduced her to Joe Peluso. There were other cases on her desk; she had plenty of other things to do. It wasn't strictly necessary to do a follow-up visit this soon. And yet here she was. Because there was a puzzle to solve, and she hadn't even started cataloging all the clues.

"So, what's your assessment of our client?" Nate had asked a few days ago as they doctored their respective coffees in the DGS break room.

"He's an asshole," she'd said simply. Because it was the truth. The rest of it… That was much harder to piece together. *"But something about this just doesn't feel right. I know he says he did it, and the forensics back it up, but…he held himself back. He didn't tear them to shreds. Everything we've heard about monsters, and he proved it all wrong. That has to count for something."*

Her favorite senior partner had stared at her for one beat. Two. Those ice-blue eyes seeing entirely too much. *"So figure out what it means. That's why we brought you in. Because his life could depend on it."*

The directive had haunted her. And overachieving Indian-American that she was, she'd been unable to resist taking another crack at the mystery. At the man tilting back his chair legs as far as his cuffed hands would allow.

"Back so soon?" Joe Peluso arched a dark brow at her, looking just as uncooperative and bruise-mottled as he had upon their first encounter.

"I don't want you to think DGS is ignoring you," she said as she took the chair across from him and dropped her recorder and notepad on the table. "We take our clients very seriously."

Especially when all sorts of city movers and shakers were calling for said clients' heads. Dealing with this kind of tricky political bullshit was new for her, but Nate and Dustin were used to it. They'd sat next to her last week like they were holding court, firing off questions like nothing big was at stake. For them, maybe that was true. They were basically two of the city's best criminal attorneys, working largely with the underprivileged population—usually those impacted by the new Patriot Acts instituted in late 2019. Immigrants, LGBTQ citizens, low-level supernaturals accused of petty crimes. But thanks to good looks and boatloads of charisma, they were also veritable rock stars, minor New York celebrities. The kind of men who got shout-outs in gossip columns and took models out to dinner at the trendiest Greenwich Village hot spots. Dickenson, Gould, and Smythe also handled big-money corporate litigation and high-profile divorce, which was why Nate and Dustin could afford to be pro bono *and* pro boning. Between the two of them, they had twenty-five years of trial experience and a mind-blowing number of successes.

Neha had barely a quarter of that. She was still making a name for herself. How she handled assisting on this case, how she handled Joe Peluso, could either be the most promising career move she'd made in years…or her biggest disaster to date. And *her* good looks and charisma? Well, those things weren't seen as assets in women. Neither was a healthy sex life. All she could count on was her dedication and her skill.

It was already clear where Joe's interest was. Not in those things. He paid little attention to her introductory chatter and answered her in monosyllables whenever possible—the same act he'd pulled with Nate and Dustin that first day. All while making sure to focus on her mouth. On the high collar of the blouse she'd chosen to wear today—buttoned all the way up—and the loose fit of her suit jacket. He certainly hadn't done *that* with his male lawyers.

If this was how all their meetings were going to be, Neha was already over it. But she knew better than to let him see her frustration with his games. "Why don't we talk about your military service?" she suggested. "The prosecution won't overlook your time in the Marines, so neither should we."

He rolled his eyes and made a dismissive hand gesture—or at least a truncated one, since his hands were secured to the table. "I know what this is all about, you know. You and your Brooks Brothers buddies, you want me to get up there and talk about what it was like over there. Paint me as some kind of wounded war veteran who went 'off' because of PTSD. That ain't me, Doc."

"Then who *are* you?" She followed up with the obvious question.

He gave her another one of those long, slow clothes-stripping looks. "You haven't figured that out yet? Babe, I'm a guy who can't stop thinking about you."

After seeing her once? Yeah, right. And hell was experiencing a polar vortex. Neha understood what he was going for now. It wasn't so much sexual harassment as distraction, distraction, distraction, "Cute. Flattery will get you absolutely nowhere, Joe."

Her shutdown didn't even faze him. "You think this is flattery? I barely know you. It's been, what, a week since you walked your ass in here with Feinberg and Taylor? This ain't flattery. It's obsession."

His dark eyes glinted. No, they *smoldered*. And if she hadn't guessed it was mostly an act, it would've been a damn good smolder. As it was, the back of Neha's neck prickled uncomfortably and she had to flip through her notes to refocus herself. "It's unproductive, is what it is," she said. "Can we please stay on topic?"

"You *are* my topic," he insisted. "What if *you're* my real way out of here, Doc? What if you're my only hope?"

"Bullshit." Neha snorted at the dramatic intensity in his voice. Intensity that she didn't buy for a minute. "You've been watching too many prison movies."

Joe immediately dialed back the swaggering jailhouse Romeo act, relaxing in his seat and huffing out his annoyance. "Yeah, because I've got nothin' to do in here but Netflix and chill."

"I'd suggest switching to *The Great British Bake-Off*," she said, dryly. "It might keep you from hitting on your lawyers, and you'll learn how to perfect a Victoria sponge to boot."

He laughed at that. A genuine laugh, not something manufactured for her benefit. It wiped some of the years from his face, took away a little of the smarm and the menace, too. "You old enough to remember that guy who used to host his cooking shows drunk? Graham Kerr? My nonna loved that guy. Him and Julia freaking Child."

It was a surprisingly personal detail for someone pretending he didn't want to share a single thing with her besides bodily fluids. Neha's fingers itched, but she let the digital recorder capture what she didn't dare write down, lest Joe become a semi-silent sleaze once more. "*Yan Can Cook* and Ming Tsai," she murmured instead. "We were all about the Asian solidarity in my house."

She waited for him to say something blatantly flirtatious in response. Or something gross and racist. But the moment stretched between them like their reflective smiles. It was…*nice*. A real connection, an honest one, over something as simple as cooking shows. It didn't do a damn thing for Joe's case…but it made all the difference to her. It reminded her that there was a *person* at the center of this. Joe wasn't a gentleman. He didn't say all the right things and observe all the social courtesies. He clearly didn't give a damn what anybody else thought. And he didn't seem to care if he lived or died. He was still entitled to the strongest possible defense, still entitled to basic human decency.

Maybe it reminded him that *she* deserved decency, too. Because he made another little motion. A go on "So, what else you got for me, Doc? And I don't just mean TV suggestions."

Neha tried not to let the thrill of the small point in her favor show on her face—and she tried to ignore the goose bumps on her arms telling her it was equally thrilling when his gaze eventually drifted back to her lips. Not deliberately. Not provocatively. Naturally. Like it wasn't an act at all.

It's obsession, he'd claimed.

No. It couldn't be. There was way too much at stake.

He *liked* her. The doc. He didn't want to like her. That was totally different from wanting to get in her pants. From wanting to eat her like a meal. It made things complicated. The last thing Joe needed right now was anything complicated. So he couldn't let her know it. Couldn't let anyone see that side of himself. He repeated the pep talk to himself several nights in a row. While in line for chow. While watching his back in the showers. And it was the pep talk he gave himself when she came in for a third time. A week or two after the second one…which, in prison, felt like months ago. The one where she'd suggested he watch *Bake-Off*. Funny how that was what he came away remembering from the visit. Not any of the legal shit she'd had for him. This time, though…this time there was no getting away from the legal stuff.

She was already waiting for him when the guards brought him in. Dressed in one of her cute little suits, hair all tied back. Sitting up straight, with her hands folded on top of her notes. Ready for any crap he might throw at her. Asking him about the night he hit the club. About the tip he called in to the cops. Making him go over things he'd already gone over way too many times with Feinberg and Taylor. He let her hammer it all at him until he just couldn't handle it anymore.

"What's the point?" he blurted out, shocking her into silence. "How long do you think I got in here, Doc? Be real. Odds are, I ain't even gonna make it to my trial. There's gonna be another 'accident' in the shower. Or someone's gonna take me out during a transfer. This ain't the movies, you know? No one's getting an Oscar for my story."

She'd flinched when he mentioned getting taken out. But her response was light. Joking. Trying to "reestablish rapport." "Well, damn," she said huskily, her pretty eyes twinkling. "I was hoping they'd get a Bollywood actress to play me!"

"No Bollywood actress could come close," he assured her. And then immediately wished he could take it back. That he wasn't all cuffed up so he could hit himself upside the head. *Way to act like she doesn't mean shit to you, jackass.*

Her cheeks went a little pink. Not so anyone human would notice. But he could sense the blood rushing beneath her skin, hear her pulse skipping. She was flattered. *Fuck.* And that made *him* feel flattered. Like when Tasha Vega had let him get to second base in the Aviation High auto shop. But falling for Tasha hadn't had consequences beyond teenage fuckheadedness. Beyond a breakup after she caught him going down on a senior girl at a party. He didn't remember the girl's name—Melissa, Melanie, Mel-something—but he sure as shit remembered the four-letter words Tasha had thrown his way when she hauled him off the bed and hit him with whatever brick was in her purse. More than twenty years ago, and he could still feel that blow. Worse than any bullet he'd ever taken in the desert.

This doc, Neha, she'd hit him with more than her purse if he didn't watch himself. So he *had* to watch himself. Wanting her was fine. But liking her? Caring about her? *Actually* being obsessed with her like he'd pretended to be the last time she was here...?

Fuck, no. He had to draw a line. There was way too much to lose if he didn't.

5

HER APARTMENT FELT LIKE A furnace even though it was relatively cool outside, so Neha positioned her ancient box fan a few feet from her couch as she settled down to work. Central air was a luxury most New Yorkers could only dream of, especially since older buildings weren't built for it, but she wasn't about to complain. Her one-bedroom in Kensington, just blocks from the F train, was $1,300 a month—practically a steal in this neighborhood, where you couldn't even get a studio for under $1,000 anymore. The window AC unit in her bedroom had been a splurge, and a welcome one given the humid city summers, but she wasn't about to curl up in bed to work. Not *this* kind of work. It felt wrong to be that cavalier and casual when she was swiping through the mug shots and rap sheets on her tablet. A veritable rogue's gallery of ugly.

If she'd thought Joe Peluso had a face only a mother could love, it was only because she'd discounted his victims. Six brutes she wouldn't want to meet on the street. Each with a record longer than her legs. Drugs. Assault. Domestic violence. None of them had spent more than a few years in prison, though—which told her they worked for someone with deep pockets and high connections. Autopsies had revealed that four of them were bear shifters, just like Aleksei Vasiliev was rumored to be. The other two had "as-yet undetermined supernatural characteristics." They could be anything from sprites to goblins to god-only-knew-what.

"It would be an open-and-shut case if they were humans," Nate had said when he approved her signing out the docs. *"Joe Peluso wouldn't have a chance in hell. Neither would we. We're…lucky."* Five years ago, that would have struck her as an extremely fucked-up thing to say about his own client. Now, given the United States' new alliances, and given the kinds of powers supernaturals had, it made sense. Russian criminals, no matter their white-supremacist or violent shifter ties, were still a political minefield. Even in a Sanctuary City like New York, law-enforcement and government officials had to worry about the national and global implications. Because some terrible people mattered more than others. And factoring in that the victims were supes meant they could have defended themselves in ways that humans couldn't. That added a whole other level of complication.

Joe Peluso hadn't considered any of that when he'd opened fire. She had to think about it now. *What are you doing, Neha?* A small part of her felt guilty. A small part of her was sick that she was trying to rationalize six deaths, six cold-blooded murders. They lived in a country where a Black man could be choked to death for selling cigarettes and a Sikh like her papa could be beaten for his turban…and here her firm was defending a white shape-shifter who'd been apprehended with nothing more than bruises. But it was the job she'd chosen. And you couldn't pay rent with ideals, could you? So, she needed to know what made Joe tick. And what made six other men better off dead. If she sold off a piece of her soul in the process, it was just a by-product of her profession, right?

Bullshit. You are so full of it. The tablet fell to her lap, and Neha tilted her head back against the arm of the couch. She could make excuses all day long, but she knew what this angst was really all about. *Who* this was really about. Joe.

She couldn't get him out of her head. Two weeks had passed since that first meeting, and he'd already moved in. With his bruise-mottled skin and chains and jumpsuit. And those icy, cynical eyes that burned hot when he turned them her way. Profession be damned, she knew she'd be conflicted about crimes committed by almost anyone else. But something about Joe Peluso flipped her inside out. As determined as she was to get to him, he was getting to her, too. After just two more meetings that had lasted maybe fifteen minutes apiece. After jokes about cooking shows, for fuck's sake.

It was disgusting. *She* was disgusting. She shoved off the couch and stalked to the tiny kitchen just off her living room, searching for the wine she'd uncorked two nights before. It was thick and red, like the blood that was likely on her hands now. She filled a stemmed glass to the brim with it.

She'd been a nice girl once. The kind of girl who wore a kara around her wrist and went to the gurdwara regularly and spoke fluent Punjabi—plus a smattering of Bengali and Urdu picked up from some of her papa's cabbie friends. It wasn't like she'd forgotten the languages, but she'd forgotten how to be her—the girl who'd never seen crime-scene photos, who'd never held the hand of a woman beaten nearly to death by a spouse or looked into the eyes of remorseless killers. The girl who still thought the best of people. That Neha wouldn't be fascinated by a monster like Joe Peluso, who put his worst on display. That Neha would want to laugh with one of Dustin and Nate's hedge-fund buddies and make a good impression. Sometimes she felt like she'd killed that Neha when she went to work for the DA's office. That death was on her conscience, too. Maybe *she* was a monster, too.

The morbid thought made her toss back two more glasses of merlot and chased her to bed later that night, kept her tossing and turning for hours.

"You think making a phone call about those girls makes me

sympathetic? It was a call. The goddamn bare minimum. Don't turn me into a saint, Doc. Don't look for something that ain't there."

Their third meeting—only the second without Nate and Dustin. His bruises are healing, his black eye almost back to normal. He still won't win any beauty contests, and his walls are still sky-high. She tries sneaking around them. She tries the direct route. He refuses to let her in.

"What's the point?" he asks after minutes of her attempts to reason with him. *"How long do you think I got in here, Doc? Be real. Odds are, I ain't even gonna make it to my trial. There's gonna be another 'accident' in the shower. Or someone's gonna take me out during a transfer. This ain't the movies, you know? No one's getting an Oscar for my story."*

"Well, damn. I was hoping they'd get a Bollywood actress to play me!"

She'd made a joke of it. Laughed it off. But curled up on her side now, with one hand clutching her pillow, all she could imagine was the scenario he'd sketched out coming to pass. His blood circling a drain. His body battered in the back of a police van or slumped on a sidewalk. All because she'd failed him. Because she hadn't fought hard enough.

She already had blood on her hands. She already had deaths on her conscience. She couldn't, *wouldn't*, let Joe's join the list.

───────────

The one-on-one with his lawyers' "official psychiatric consultant" was a total waste of time. "A formality," Taylor had called it. "To create a baseline assessment and establish that you show no signs of sociopathy." It was really an hour with some bored, big-money baby boomer from Connecticut who just wanted to tick off a bunch of boxes, say "hmm" a couple times, and then half-heartedly pitch him on copping an insanity plea. He'd look really good on the stand, credible expert witness for the defense, all that jazz. Joe was no dummy. He got what was going on. So he also got that the real work was being put through the pretty doc. After all, she'd said it herself, right? *"You'll give me everything."*

He barely remembered his mom, but he still missed her. He liked to read. He loved dogs. That was the kind of shit they wanted Joe to confess in his little meetings with the doc. How he was really a sweet and fluffy guy on the inside, and he had a sweet little pittie named Sadie growing up. Somebody who loved puppies couldn't be all bad, right? In fact, that was why he'd decided to volunteer for the Apex Initiative and undergo the turning. On account of his affinity for animals. *So, Your Honor, Joe Peluso most certainly does not deserve to spend the rest of his unnatural life behind bars.* The hell of it was, he really did love Sadie to pieces, and he'd bawled his eyes out when his old man drove out to Long Island and dropped her off at the side of some road. He'd been around six or seven. After that, he'd quit crying about much at all. Then his pop had the good grace to die, leaving Joe at the mercy of his nonna—and the foster-care system every time CPS got a bug up their ass.

He'd never killed anyone who didn't deserve it. That was another thing the lawyers wanted him to say. That he'd never shot a man in Reno just to watch him die. Joe had never been to Reno, but he'd shot plenty of men before playing target practice in South Brooklyn. Tore 'em apart, too. And who was he to judge if they deserved it or not? Judging wasn't his job. Questioning it wasn't his duty. What he'd done over there, he did under orders from his superiors, in the service of his country, like generations of brave men and women before him. But he wasn't about to split political or moral hairs…especially since the country had changed so damn much since he was deployed the first time.

And as for what had gone down here in the States? It had fuck-all to do with his military background. Everything to do with Kenny being in the wrong place at the wrong time and getting caught in some shit between a Russian shifter outfit out of Brighton Beach and some human Gravesend Ukrainians. Four

Russian bullets laid him out. Fucking *four*. How did you wave that off as an accident? Just getting "caught in the cross fire"? But that was what all the news stories had called it, and why the local cops just wrote it off and padded their pockets with bribes. Joe had gone with Kenny's pop to the morgue to make the ID. Mrs. C couldn't. She just couldn't. She wouldn't leave her bed for days for crying. Two of her sisters had to hold her up at the funeral. And the clawing in Joe's gut—the closest thing he'd felt to grief in a long damn time—made him go looking for payback.

"You think making a phone call about those girls makes me sympathetic? It was a call. The goddamn bare minimum. Don't turn me into a saint, Doc. Don't look for something that ain't there."

"Don't hide something that is. If you were a killer without conscience, you wouldn't have spared a thought about dropping that tip. You would've gone straight home and dined on steak without a care for the blood on your hands. Hell, you would've dined on your targets."

"What makes you think I didn't still do that?"

"Besides the autopsy reports?" She'd just stared at him. With those Disney princess eyes. He hadn't given her any reason to believe in him. Hell, he'd been a belligerent asshole. But it felt like she saw him that night. Crawling into the bottom of a bottle of cheap whiskey to drown out the *hiss-punch* of silenced shots. Waking up a day and a half later to the cops pounding on his door. Going with them without protest, without struggle, because he knew exactly what he'd done. The taste of it was just as stale as the booze.

That didn't make it okay. Fuck, no. He was raised Catholic enough to know that an eye for an eye didn't play. But that was the excuse they'd want to use in court if he started talking. They'd want to call in Mr. C or Kenny's mom as character witnesses, hear stories from Zizi Teresa about how he sang in the church choir until he was eleven. They'd want to hear how Kenny was just a baby when Joe moved in with the Castellis a couple years later. How Joe helped him learn to walk and ride a bike. The whole heartbreaking sob story about how he was really a good man and he just had to avenge his family after a horrific tragedy.

Thing was, Joe couldn't sit there in a cheap borrowed suit, in front of all those people, and listen to that lie. He wasn't a good man. He wasn't even an okay man. Hell, by some definitions, he wasn't a man at all anymore. Yeah, he'd never laid a hand on a woman. He'd never run with a gang or dealt in drugs. And he didn't go around snacking on people even though he was an apex predator now. But he was no hero. Not even some comic-book vigilante like Batman. He put down those motherfuckers, and he'd fucking loved it. Hell, he'd *excelled* at it. Because killing people was something he was just that good at. A pro. A gold-medal-worthy killer in the Murder Games.

What would the doc say if he told her that? Dr. Neha Whatshername. Ahluwalia. Neha Ahluwalia. All those pretty vowel sounds for a pretty girl who'd never taken joy from taking a life.

He'd seen her three times so far, and they had another meeting set for tomorrow. A week ahead of his prelim hearing, where his options were accepting a plea deal or saying those two ridiculous words: "not guilty." And Joe could barely sleep for thinking about it. Not the hearing—fuck that—but *her*. What she would wear. What she'd smell like. If she'd have her hair up or down. If she'd hand him over her panties if he just asked nicely enough…

"*Fuck.*" He exhaled, and it sounded like a gunshot ricocheting across the cell.

Yeah, he loved dogs. He thought cats were freaking adorable, too. But his biggest problem right now, stuck in the dark with nothing but hours to kill, was how obsessed he was with one particular pussy. More obsessed with it, with *her*, than with his own defense.

Feinberg and Taylor wanted to put his former XO on the list of character witnesses right off the bat. Joe shut that shit down immediately. He hadn't talked to any of the guys from his old human unit since his arraignment almost a year and a half ago. That was on him, not them. No way did he want any of this shit touching the Corps. And Apex…? He couldn't risk anything casting a shadow on their military service or putting their supernatural statuses into question. Stevens. Buchanan. Hawk. Drake. Even the newer members of the Apex Initiative that he'd barely gotten to know. They didn't deserve to be pulled into this shitshow.

And if the SOBs in charge had anything to say about it, that wouldn't even be an option. They'd let Joe twist in the wind before risking public exposure of the whole program. They made that crystal clear for every Apex soldier before deactivation. *"We will disavow all knowledge. We will take every necessary measure to protect the integrity of the unit and the program."* Translation: "We won't hesitate to put you in the ground if you breathe a word of who we are." So, he'd leaned into the lone-gunman narrative the minute he got hauled in. *Lone wolf. Ha.* Fuck yeah, it was just him and his guns. Nobody else. He'd never needed anybody else. Until now. Until *her*.

6

HE WAS ALONE IN THE room for ten minutes before the doc showed. Long enough to sweat it. It was a little joke the guards loved to play—especially since they'd figured out that he wouldn't shift and wasn't that much of a threat. Moore, this ancient fucker who was one step from a mall security guard, had pulled the "gotcha!" on him a few days ago. Kept him cooling his heels for nearly a half hour before he said, *"Whoops! My bad! No one's here for you after all!"* Asshole. So now the possibility of that was always in Joe's head. Under his skin. Hanging on to the hope of seeing Neha only to have it yanked away. But then the door opened, and it was one of the other guards, Miller—thank fucking Christ—and he had the most gorgeous company in the world.

Oh, fuck. She was wearing a damn miniskirt. Sure, it was masquerading as a business suit, but the only business that came to mind was the kind transacted horizontally. Joe tried not to moan when she walked in and sat down across from him. He'd had a bitch of a night. A worse morning, getting hassled by the guards and knocked into walls as they moved him up the block. But it all faded away with Neha in the room. Her hair was down. Loose around her shoulders. And she was all buttoned up again—a row of 'em down a prim-and-proper black jacket and skirt that stopped inches above her knee. His eyes and his imagination should've stopped there, at her fucking knee, but it was too late.

She was maybe five foot seven or five foot eight tops, and she had legs for days. And he wanted nothing more at this point than to get between them. To grab her knees, press them apart, tear her tight little skirt at the seams. The fantasies had been torturing him all week, because thinking about her was better, sweeter, than thinking about everything he'd done. Twice he'd nearly broken his own jailhouse rules and wrapped his hand around his dick. But, fuck, there was no releasing this tension. Especially with her trying to get into his head, all serious and full of questions, while he just wanted to bury himself in her. His tongue. His dick. His fingers. Whatever he could get inside her. He'd make it so good.

"…and I was in touch with Nate and Dustin this morning. They're keeping things close to the vest, of course, but they seem upbeat about your chances for a plea agreement."

He had to force himself to quit staring at her mouth—so soft and so pink, he'd kill to fuck it—and actually focus on the words. "I'm glad they're upbeat. I ain't holding my breath," he said with a snort.

"You're also not being helpful," she pointed out. "You stonewall them in every meeting. You don't listen to me either. Your meeting with the independent psychiatrist was, by all accounts, a complete travesty. You seem wholly uninterested in your own defense, shooting down every logical strategy. You won't agree to character witnesses. You refuse to address your upbringing. You won't talk about your supernatural abilities. You're resistant to *anything* that might make you sympathetic to judge and jury. Why is that? What is it about your background that you want hidden? Are you afraid to be seen as a decent person who snapped? Is it just that—"

Oh, hell no. She needed to knock this shit right off. He couldn't have her digging into his psyche or whatever the fuck, trying to get him to spill all the things he'd never talked to another soul about.

It was like seeing him naked. No, like seeing him shift. "Doc." He leaned forward, cuffed hands on the table in front of him like he was praying to the goddess of legal miracles.

"Yes?" She blinked. All long lashes and parted lips. Shocked that he cut her off midspeculation about using his childhood as a defense strategy.

"You ever slummed it?" he wondered, tacking a sleazy grin on the question. Testing her fences. Like one of those *Jurassic Park* raptors. "Ever fucked a blue-collar guy?"

"What?" Oh, she got good and pissed just like he wanted. If she was angry, she wasn't curious. She sat up straight, her jaw going tight and her dark eyes spitting nails. He couldn't help but smile wider as he smelled the anger rolling off her skin.

"You heard me." Maybe she felt this thing, too. This wild, dark, impossible chain tying them tighter than his handcuffs. But she'd never do anything about it. Women like her never did. Except maybe under the sheets, a naughty book in one hand and her vibrator in the other. "Ever had a dirty hand down your pants? Grease-stained nails getting you off? I can't figure if you're the type of girl who might go slumming once in a while in between all those fancy dates uptown."

"That's enough, Joe." The doc didn't yell at him. She didn't haul off and slap him. She just sat there, still as a statue, getting a handle on her temper, getting a handle on her breaths if not her heartbeat. Until the nails in her eyes were more like sharp little pins. "I know what you're doing," she assured him. "Trying to change the subject. Trying to make me so uncomfortable that I'll stop asking you questions you don't want to answer. You can stop, because it didn't work before, and it won't work now."

No. He couldn't stop. Because *he* hadn't had enough yet. Not enough of the pulse beating wildly at her throat, of the scent of her outrage and what she probably didn't even realize yet was arousal. Maybe he couldn't turn, but he *could* turn her on. Anything to turn her away from the truth of him. "What about a supe? Ever done one of us? Had someone slide their fangs into your throat while they dick into you? Grabbed on to a wolf's ruff when he's nosing between your legs? Does that idea get you hot or disgust you? I can't tell."

"Does it get *you* hot or disgust you?" She turned the question around on him, startling him out of the nasty little daydreams and making him register that she was leaning so close they were almost forehead to forehead. So close that he could smell the floral notes in her shampoo. "Why would you think to ask me these things if they weren't on *your* mind?" she wondered. "Maybe we should talk about *that*? Do you have some sort of residual guilt about being a supernatural? Is that why you killed those men? Because you hate yourself?"

Christ. She was good. And too good for him. But Joe didn't want to talk about his "residual guilt." Or any guilt at all. What did it matter how he felt? They were all still dead. Kenny. All the people he took out overseas. Those fuckers in the club. None of that was going to change if he gave Neha a sob story. And did he hate himself? The fuck did that even mean? "What would you know about hating yourself? Pretty little PhD with your fancy legal degree? You don't know what it's like to be me, Doc. And you definitely don't know what it's like to be a supe. You can try and shrink your way into my head, but you'll never understand it."

"Are you seriously implying I'm classist *and* racist?" Her palm slapped down on the table. "You don't know anything about me, Joe," she told him in no uncertain terms. "My immigrant father drove a New York City cab for thirty years. He never had his own medallion. My mom worked two jobs and raised three kids. My collars are only white because I learned how to bleach them. I have snake shifters and yakshas in my extended family—and in many Indian cultures, they hold those beings *sacred*. More well-respected than you'll ever be. So, I'll say it again: that's enough!"

Whoa. Color him totally surprised. He'd had her pegged as some Upper East Side trust-fund diva. Not an outer-borough brat like him. "Sorry!" He lifted his bound hands in a gesture of surrender, glad they weren't bolted down for once. "I was just…curious." It was true, albeit not completely honest. He knew better than to admit he'd just wanted to mess with her a little, or that he wanted to distract her from getting too close to all the shit he kept locked down.

And the half-assed excuse didn't unruffle her feathers. "You shouldn't be curious about me, Joe," she said in a severe tone that would make a nun proud. Or whatever the Indian equivalent of a nun was.

He shrugged. Tried to find a way to respond that wasn't going to set her off again…though, hell, she was fucking gorgeous when she was mad. "But I *am* curious, and I can't do a thing about it except ask you all the questions I've got," he explained. "Sorry, Doc. Blame all the time in jail if you want. It's not like the social scene here's anything special. A man's mind gets a little one-track, you know? It can't be all *Great British Bake-Off.* I've got needs." He still didn't know what a Victoria sponge was, but everything his imagination came up with was X-rated.

"I'm trying to help your defense, not improve your love life." Neha's voice went even lower than its natural sex-hotline level. She wasn't impressed with his Netflix callback. "Right now, it sounds to me like you've got shit chances at both."

Maybe it sounded that way to her. It didn't look that way to him. Not when her body was still canted toward him. Not when she hadn't broken eye contact since she'd come in. There was a faint tinge of pink across her cheekbones. And there was the tiniest little catch in her voice when she warned him, "Joe…Joe, stop it."

"Stop what?" He leaned in as close as the table between them would allow. And he didn't have to go all that far, because she'd already met him halfway. "What am I doing, baby?"

The breath she took was shaky. The words she said were even shakier. "You're calling me 'baby,' for one. This is so inappropriate," she reminded him. "And, as I told you before, changing the subject won't work on me."

"Then maybe this will." Baby. Honey. Sweetheart. Sugar. Fuckin' beautiful. He hadn't even started with the names. He could come up with a dozen more with his dick buried balls-deep inside her. Joe memorized the tilt of her nose. Sent the tiny mole at the corner of her lips to his mental spank bank. And then he did what any desperate, deranged asshole in this situation would do: he kissed her.

It lasted all of two seconds before the guard started yelling for them to break it up and stormed over, waving his Taser, to yank Joe back and nearly off his feet. But what a goddamn glorious two seconds. Soft mouth under his. Lips parting in shock. A taste of her skin. He knew a real kiss would taste even better. And kissing her *everywhere* would taste the best.

She knew it, too. He could tell from the sharp bark of her voice as she assured the guard that she was fine and could handle her client. He could see it in how she got all gathered and composed, radiating prissiness and disapproval, but fumbled when she tried to collect her notes. *Oh shit, yes.* She could glare all she wanted, but she couldn't cuss *him* out for this without including herself in the rant. He wasn't the only one who sensed her arousal. She wanted him, too. The electric current that zipped through him then was a billion volts more than any Taser. He'd been wrong about her. About what kind of woman she was. She took no prisoners in court, but she'd take him anywhere else. Maybe she'd even take him inside her. Joe almost groaned with relief. Maybe she wouldn't be his last meal. Maybe she'd be the first decent one he'd had in years.

She was a bleeding heart. She was going off the deep end. She was becoming a furry—not that there was anything wrong with that. She knew a few really nice furries. No, it was more like she was becoming one of those women who turned prison pen pal to guys like Bundy and Richard Ramirez. There were a dozen explanations going through Neha's head when she left lockup and returned to the real world, but there was only one image. Joe Peluso, right before he kissed her. That brutish face, still a little bruised and cut. And his eyes. Looking too far. Seeing too much. She'd dealt with plenty of sexual overtures, but she'd never, *ever* had anyone look at her that way. Like she was the beginning, middle, and end.

He *wanted* her. No, more than that, he *craved* her. She'd never been the subject of this kind of desire. The men she'd dated… She'd had to work them to arousal, convince them to do the same for her. Usually in exchange for a blow job. They'd never been turned on just by being near her. She'd never been out of her head just being around one of them. It was overwhelming…and it was exactly whelming enough. Like a drug in her veins. She'd had one hit and she was spoiled. *I want, I need to be wanted like that.*

It was unprofessional. A complete breach of ethics. She needed to tell Dustin and Nate ASAP and recuse herself from any involvement with Joe's case. But she didn't reach for her cell when she hit the sidewalk on Atlantic Avenue. Instead, she slumped against a lamppost, her fingers going up to her lips. It was ridiculous that she could still feel him. It had been over before it even began. But she traced the kiss anyway. Gentle. A surprise. But not a demand. What was that Katy Perry song? *I kissed a prisoner, and I liked it…* no, worse…*I kissed a werewolf, and I liked it.* Oh god, she was a fucking head case.

It took Neha the entire walk back to the office to get ahold of herself…and once she was there, safely ensconced in the Brooklyn Heights brownstone that Dickenson, Gould, and Smythe had called home for more than a decade, she'd somehow already convinced herself to not say a word about the line that Joe had crossed. The line that she *let* him cross because she was already way too invested in him.

And because she'd learned he was smart—that his brooding silences hid a sharp mind that missed nothing. And he was funny. Sure, his humor generally skewed toward lewd, but he made her laugh with those pervy quips more often than not. And all the dry facts she'd absorbed when DGS first took his case were personal now. They had context. She understood why he was a loner. His mother had an aneurysm when he was two and never recovered. His father crashed into a guardrail seven years later in a fatal DUI. He'd been shuffled back and forth between foster homes and the care of an elderly grandmother, crunched through the system for years. Only finding stability when family friends in Maspeth took him in until he was old enough to enlist in the Marines. Papa and Ma drove her up a wall sometimes, but she couldn't imagine not having them in her life. Or her older brothers, who'd taught her how to be tough and scared away entirely too many potential high-school boyfriends. She knew instinctively that Joe would be that kind of brother, given the chance. But kids like him didn't get chances. Most grown men like him didn't either. And somehow, in what was probably the most imprudent decision she'd made in a long time, she wanted to give him one.

She wanted to *save* him. Like those gullible, idealistic heroines in movies. *"Don't get too involved,"* Nate had warned her. *"I know the guy's got charisma, but we need to use that against the prosecution, not weaponize it against ourselves."* But it was too late to point Joe Peluso elsewhere. He'd zeroed in on her. And she was a willing target.

No. Stop it. Neha looked around her cubicle, using basic grounding tricks to snap herself out of her head. Four things she could see—the Lord of the Rings action figures on her desk. Three things she could hear—two of the paralegals discussing their superior, the hum of the copier, the crackle of the aging light fixtures. Two things she could smell—someone's Italian lunch and the nail polish her fellow associate, Tania, was applying in the next cube over. And one basic bit of truth: this wasn't a noble campaign for Joe's rights; it wasn't some touchy-feely Lifetime movie. It was lust.

A raging case of it, blotting out everything rational. She'd had a copper IUD for a while to prevent pregnancy and regulate her cycle, but she remembered what it was like to get completely rattled by her hormones—the ticking biological clock. Being in heat. In season. That irrational week of her period where all she wanted to do was stroke a puppy, hold a baby, and get laid. Somehow, Joe Peluso had turned into the puppy, the baby, and the jones for sex wrapped into one. Everything she craved. Nothing she could actually have. The beast in him calling to the wild animal in her.

She had to get over it. Mind over matter, and all of that. But she didn't dare talk to any of her friends about him. She'd committed enough questionable acts in the last few weeks, and she didn't need to add breaching client confidentiality to the list. But she needed to put *some* of it into words, to at least have one person confirm she was off the rails while also being terribly sympathetic to the desperate state of her vagina. Neha whipped her phone out of her purse and typed out a quick message to her cousin Tejal, who was bound by the rules of family to be on her side even while criticizing her choices…and who knew the world of supernaturals all too well.

Hey. You around this weekend?

Tejal was half-Punjabi, half-Gujarati, and wholly a Naga—a snake shifter. Fully inherited from her Gujarati side, as the Punjus in their family never failed to point out. Thanks to thousands of years of intermarrying with humans, and being hunted to near-extinction by enemies, their particular breed of shifter was dying out. Tejal's twin sister, Toral, was a genetic researcher out in the Bay Area—working on a database project to help keep the world's tiny Naga population alive. Tejal was doing her own part for their people as an ob/gyn at a fertility clinic in North Brunswick. It didn't escape Neha that her cousin's entire life involved holding babies. And she had an adorable black Lab. Whether she was getting laid at the moment was something Neha would, no doubt, find out after spilling her own personal soap opera.

Minutes went by like hours before the three little dots signaling her cousin's reply appeared. For you? Always. Chaat and chat at the usual place?

YES, PLEASE!!!

It was enough to unknot some of the tension in Neha's shoulders, to help her get through the rest of the day and night without making any more questionable decisions. At least not *conscious* decisions. Because, of course, Joe followed her back home to Kensington and into her dreams, where he did more than just steal a quick kiss across a table. He touched her and held her and wrangled her body into impossible circus-performer positions, all while whispering the filthiest suggestions in her ear. Not to rile her up, not to distract her, but to make her feel good. *So damn good.*

"Neal and Nitesh are going to kill you," Tejal said the next day, before Neha even finished sketching the picture of a tough-as-nails jerk who'd lasered her clothes off with one look. "No," she corrected herself. "They'll kill this guy and then they'll kill you."

Her brothers, Neha knew full well, would only murder her in the metaphorical sense. "Shh!" she cautioned. "It's bad enough white people assume all desi girls get forced into marriages or honor-killed. No need to put that out into the world."

Besides, she was pretty sure Joe Peluso could break Neal and Nitesh in half. A cardiologist and an IT guy, respectively, they probably couldn't bench-press 100 pounds between them.

"Do you see any white people here?" Tejal rolled her eyes, scooping samosa chaat onto one half of her paper plate before arranging a few pani puri shells on the other.

Not a one, actually. Just a mix of various desi folks. From all across South Asia. She and her cousin were surrounded by the comforting hubbub of conversations in Urdu and Gujarati and Tamil and Bengali. The benefit to meeting at their favorite hole-in-the-wall Indian restaurant. Neha had taken a Jersey transit train out from Penn Station in the morning. Since that involved swiping through at checkpoints and having her entry and exit from New York City recorded by drones, she'd fully expected to spend the entire day with Tejal and then probably pop in on her parents for dinner. She might as well make all the hassle worth it. Cue plastic trays heaped with delicious street food—and a side of carefully edited gossip.

There was no chance of anyone from the firm, or the other side of the case, finding her here. Her conscience and her libido, however, had no problems tracking her across the river. She could feel the prick of one and the burn of the other as she shifted on the bench seat and tried to focus across the booth. Tejal looked unbearably pretty. Traditional. She wore her long hair in one thick braid. Her clothes were bright and flowy. Thick kohl lined her eyes and her nose piercing was a simple red jewel. On the surface, she represented everything Neha no longer was. Below it… Well, that was a different story. There were painful chapters. Secrets. Things Tejal couldn't shed like her skin.

Tell her. A part of Neha was itching to spill every last detail. To open up to her cousin about Joe Peluso being a supernatural, a shifter. Tejal was guaranteed to understand that part, even if the "Oh, and he killed six people" bit was a deal breaker. She'd have insight. She'd have advice. *She'd be dragged into this.* In the end, it was that thought that kept Neha reined in.

She exercised the same kind of restraint as she gently tapped the shell of one of her pani puris, breaking a wide enough hole to add the chana and aloo filling. "It's not like I haven't dated bad boys before," she pointed out with a heavy sigh. Mr. Fifty Shades of Nope came to mind. And the guys in high school who'd spent more time smoking stinkweed behind the football field than going to class. And the L-school douchebag who now worked for the Republican Hindu Coalition. *Gross.*

"But this is a different kind of bad boy," Tejal countered, infinitely practical…and more on target that she could possibly realize. She filled her own puri and then pushed the dish of tamarind water across the table at Neha. "Your type was always…*wrong* for you. Slackers. Stoners. Conservative assholes. I was always like 'What is Neha *thinking*?' every time you'd tell me about who you were dating. And you may not be hooking up with this guy yet, but he sounds like someone you actually *click* with. Is he worth the risk?"

"Are *any* of them worth the risk?" Neha laughed.

Tejal winced, acknowledging the point…and lifted her pani puri in a toast. It was filled to the brim with tamarind water like a crispy, spicy, shot glass. Mere seconds from collapsing. Much like their lives, it seemed, the snack's structural integrity was shaky at best. "Cheers," she said wryly.

Neha quickly prepped her own and echoed the sentiment— "Cheers"—before popping the one-bite treat into her mouth. Tart-sweetness exploded in her mouth…and it almost overpowered the taste of her guilt.

At least she had the luxury of making shitty choices. Both of the twins dated sparingly, knowing that they'd have to factor in their responsibilities to the Naga. Falling in love with someone who couldn't, or wouldn't, help propagate the species was practically a betrayal.

And what's falling for a criminal? Is Joe worth that risk? Because what would that even *mean*? He was behind bars…with absolutely zero guarantee he would be set free. He wasn't even *interested* in being set free. She'd compared herself to women who wrote to serial killers…but what if that wasn't a tired joke but her actual reality? How could they possibly make a relationship work when all the beats would be played out over monitored visits? Was she ready for that?

The questions stayed with her for the next hour, pushing her back to the city instead of to see Papa and Ma. *Is he worth the risk?* It haunted her for the rest of the weekend and chased her into the office on Monday morning. *Is he worth the risk? And why am I willing to take it?*

7

JOE'S NEXT HEARING WAS IN a couple days. But his hearing wasn't the problem. No, it was his seeing. All the damn visions he was hoping Neha would keep away. The Peluso Theater was up and running, playing the Technicolor feed across his eyelids instead of letting him sleep.

It's hotter than balls. Worse than a subway platform in August. And Joe has a hostile's brains splattered all over his cammies. The ringing in his ears just won't stop, but neither will the shells. It's been hours, and he can't stop tasting the meat...feeling the tear of skin under his teeth, the acid-sharp spurt of arterial blood painting his face, his throat. There's a second when their hearts stop beating, where their weight shifts. The physical journey from life to the lack thereof. It's a heaviness. He tastes that, too.

The first time he killed someone, he was twenty-two years old. Didn't even see a face. Just the kill zone in the sight of his rifle. It was like something out of one of those single-shooter video games. An internet-trolling incel's basement wet dream. He thought he was such hot shit. Swaggered around collecting back slaps from his brothers, his friends. But that buzz wore off real quick once he got out of the high corner and down into the villages, into the desert camps. Once he started seeing their eyes. Real men. Real people. Who'd signed up for service just like he had. It was nothing like bagging CGI targets to rack up points. He quit swaggering. But he still said yes to Apex ten years later. Made it even more personal. Took the guns out of it, added fangs and claws. It took months for the man to stop throwing up what the monster tried to eat.

Twenty years on, he hadn't forgotten a single kill, even though he wanted to. He carried every death on his conscience, even though he liked to think he didn't have one. And there were so damn many deaths. All in the name of duty and honor. He pretended he couldn't judge what he'd done, but he judged himself plenty. Again and again and again. For every time he'd watched the life drain out of an enemy combatant. The doc and his lawyers... they thought what he did to those Russians was bad but defensible. They had no fucking idea.

Joe gave up trying to sleep somewhere around 3:00 a.m. By that point, he wasn't dealing with nightmares so much as memories. Afghanistan. Iraq. That shit was all on the books. But he'd been to a dozen more places he couldn't pick out on a map—because why *know*, right? Why *care*? As far as the brass were concerned, too much information could lead to questions and regrets and hesitation. To insubordination. They'd dropped him into the brush with nothing but a pack for his gear and a couple of other Apex predators. Lions, and tigers, and bears, oh fucking my.

The powers that be, the suits and scientists in charge, they'd called it Phase Three of the program. Joe had no clue what Phase One or Phase Two involved. Tinkering with born supes? Getting supes and humans together and making superpowered babies? He'd tried to ask a couple times, throwing all that creepy sci-fi shit in there, but got shut down with the government's favorite sentence: "That's classified." *He* was classified. The Phase Three group was all handpicked for their "highly specialized skill sets." For their "spotless service records." All fancy ways of saying that they were really good at killing whoever they were told to kill without asking too many questions. Perfect weapons in human form. Just point 'em at a bunch of hostiles and let 'em loose, right? Who cared what the consequences were? Those Brooklyn mafia goons…? Those motherfuckers who hadn't cared if Mrs. C's baby boy and some innocent women got caught in their cross fire? They were the first people Joe had taken out without being under orders…and the only deaths he carried that he didn't regret one damn bit.

Maybe *that* was how he could force the "not guilty by reason of insanity" bullshit to leave his lips. Because he had no guilt about it. Because he had to be insane. Because the craziest thing about all of this was that he had more feelings about a woman he'd just met than he did about what he was going on trial for. Feelings about making her laugh. About touching her, taking down her hair and digging his hands into it. About kissing her again. Jesus Christ, did he have feelings about kissing her again. Longer, harder, for days. This time with no interruptions.

Best-case scenario, maybe Dr. Neha Ahluwalia's mouth would wipe the taste of blood off his tongue once and for all. Worst-case scenario, maybe she'd just be the next person he ripped up and devoured. The latest in a long-ass line of casualties he wouldn't, *couldn't* forget.

The one who'd haunt him all the fucking way to his own early grave.

———

It was close to four o'clock when Neha finally made it over to Brooklyn Detention for her weekly check-in with Joe Peluso. For her last attempt to get through to him before his hearing. She'd put it off as long as possible, donned as much protective armor as she could find. As if smoky eyes and a bold lip would make her forget that he had kissed her. That she had liked it. As if blasting hard rock on her iPod during the walk over would drown out the sound of his voice whispering seductive filth.

Neha was proud of herself for the first ten minutes of the visit. She kept to the last few items she wanted to touch on before he entered his plea. Made a final effort to crack his backstory. "Your military records have been heavily redacted. We could only glean so much. Can you tell me anything about your time in the Marine Corps that might be helpful?"

Joe clearly hadn't gotten the memo about the tone of their meeting. He was slouched in his seat, arms as loose as his cuffs would allow and his eyes smoldering with some emotional tempest she couldn't identify. "What does my time in the Corps have to do with anything, Doc? Why do you keep coming back to that question?"

"You tell me." She shrugged lightly, shuffling her notes. "Is that where you became a shape-shifter?"

A crack of lightning appeared in his stormy gaze. "This ain't a road you wanna go down," he warned.

"Yes, it is." She was already going down roads she didn't want to go down. There was definitely no turning back now. "Especially if it'll help your defense."

"Fuckin' hell, Doc." Joe's anger seemed to dissipate. He leaned awkwardly so he could scrub at his face with one of his hands. "It won't. Nothing I did over there will pretty up what I did over here."

At least he was acknowledging he'd done things. That was a place to start. But Neha knew better than to harp on those details. It would just make him aware that he'd let something slip. "Are there a large number of supernaturals in the military?" she asked instead.

"I don't ask, and I don't tell," he said dryly.

Oh, so funny. A regular joker, this guy. She huffed out her frustration, sitting back in her chair. "You know the government's pushing for a supernatural registry? Just like the Muslim registry they were pulling for a few years back?" Nate, who was Jewish, had hit the *roof*, practically shouting the DGS walls down when the AP wire broke the story. *"This is bullshit! We are not going to let this happen again!"* He'd gotten on the horn to the ACLU immediately about filing an injunction, joining in on any large-scale lawsuits, etc. The case, like the legislation, was still pending.

"Yeah? And?" Joe made a motion like "go on," his handcuffs rattling with the gesture. "What does that have to do with me right now?"

"I think legislation like that is racist, dangerous, and unnecessary. And I don't personally care if there's an entire elite unit of wererabbits in the U.S. Navy. Law-abiding American citizens should be allowed to live their lives—and the ones who don't abide by the law deserve due process. *You* deserve due process."

"Wererabbits? Really?" He bypassed her last assertion entirely, brows pulling together in a mock-frown. "Wouldn't Navy Seals be better?"

She couldn't stop the laugh this time. It burst out of her like a shot. Was it better or worse that Joe had gradually decided to trade surliness for silliness? Not that his delivery was all that much different...still gruff, raspy, like his throat was an unevenly paved road. The variation was in the tilt of his lips, the faint twinkle in his eyes. It was charming. And it was charming *her*.

But he quickly turned serious once again. She watched him work out just how much he wanted to say next. The thoughts flickering across his face. The set of his jaw. "My unit was a cooperative project across Army, Navy, Air Force, the Corps," he said finally. "No wererabbits. What I can tell you is that every soldier was there voluntarily. Most were fully human to start. None of us were human by the finish. And that had nothing to do with shapeshifting. That had everything to do with war."

PTSD, she thought, even though he'd dismissed that idea weeks ago. He shook his head, like he'd already guessed she'd go that route again. "Don't even try it. I've said all I had to say about PTSD."

"Joe, you won't let us try *anything*," she pointed out, unable to keep the reproach out of her tone.

He grinned then. The same lewd grin that had gotten them both in trouble the last time she visited. *"You ever slummed it? Ever fucked a blue-collar guy?"* What he said this time wasn't nearly as problematic, but it got to her just the same. "Not true. I'd let you try whatever you want on me. They've already got me chained up. You can do the rest."

Neha's imagination immediately ran wild—too wild and too far for her to call it back. *Pinning him down. Gripping those thick wrists. Riding him hard until he begged to come.* Would an alpha male like him really let her try that? Oh god. She dropped her head into her hands, hiding not from him but from her own thoughts. What *was* this? Why couldn't she stop? Why couldn't she shut him out?

On paper, there was nothing that indicated Neha was susceptible to such poor decision-making. Her parents hadn't been abusive. Papa had never touched a drop of liquor in his life and subscribed wholeheartedly to Sikh tenets. Ma was never particularly strict, and her brothers were awesome. Their upbringing in Woodside—just twenty-five minutes from Manhattan via the 7 train—had been damn-near idyllic. Her parents had given them choices from the beginning. Easy-to-pronounce names that danced on the edge of assimilation, forgoing traditional Sikh naming conventions. Not pressuring them to follow religious laws. Especially after 9/11. They hadn't even been out of their teens, but the hassles for covering their hair, for "concealing" ceremonial daggers, had been endless.

Her brothers had picked totally opposing ways to cope. Nitesh, who now worked at a tech firm in Jersey City, was totally clean-shaven. Short-haired. He barely admitted he was Punjabi. Neal, meanwhile, had a beard that would make a Brooklyn hipster cry with envy. His hair was glorious, too. Longer than Neha's and almost always covered by an array of bright turbans. He'd officially been baptized in the Khalsa and legally changed his name to Indrajit Singh Ahluwalia. He was *Dr.* Indrajit Singh Ahluwalia. *Fancy*. This had yet to stop the immediate family from still calling him Neal—because your house name stuck with you *forever*.

She fell somewhere in the middle of her siblings. She respected her heritage, cooked desi food when she had time on the weekends, still had salwar kameez in her wardrobe and a picture of Guru Nanak on the wall. But she wasn't devout—her version of a commitment to service meant doing her own thing and working in criminal law. And she wasn't some kind of rebel either. She hadn't stripped to help pay for law school like some of her friends had. She hadn't turned to drugs or alcohol when classes got too stressful. She didn't party. She didn't hang out with rogue vampires. She'd had a few shitty boyfriends, but who hadn't? There was no sob story to explain why there was suddenly a direct link between Joe Peluso and her hormones.

All she knew was that his voice was enough to make her squeeze her thighs together under the table, and his dark eyes made her bite down hard on her lower lip so she wouldn't show him an ounce of the weakness he'd brought out in her. She had to turn it into strength. She needed to use it as a tool. Lust was a weapon that could be bent and turned around. If it freed them both, all the better.

"I'm not going to blow this case," she told him, leaning forward and low so her neckline gaped and the slope of her breasts grazed the tabletop.

He followed the motion, his mouth giving a tiny quirk. And then his eyes flicked back to hers. "Yeah? You got any plans to blow anything else, Doc?" he mocked.

Yes. No. *No way in hell.* "You still think you can scare me away with that kind of talk? Haven't we moved past that, Joe?" She tilted her head, offering him her best angle. A face that could launch a thousand ships. "Isn't it time you told me why you killed those men in human skin instead of shifter fur and helped us mount a solid defense?"

Fuck. She realized her verbal error too late. One wrong word choice gave him back the upper hand. "You want me to mount you?" His laugh... Oh hell, it was wicked and full of promise. "Kinda hard to do that in here, but let's see what I can manage in court."

The images slammed into her again. Brutal. Gorgeous. Wrong. *Joe bending her over the jury box. Seating her on his cock in the witness chair. Doing unspeakable things with a gavel. Taking her on all fours as the fur rippled across his body.* She had to close her eyes against the full-color pictures. Against him. She almost conceded the point to him...the entire damn round...but spared from visual proof of his charisma, she could hear him. His breaths. How they came sharp and jagged. He was just as turned on. Just as affected. Joe Peluso was as connected to her as she was to him. They were in this together. Damned if they did, damned if they didn't. And it didn't make sense at all.

"Did you...did you *do* something to me?" She forced herself to give voice to the ridiculous question, but she couldn't force herself to look at him while she asked it. "Did you *make* me feel this way?"

One moment passed in silence. And then another. When Joe finally replied, it was softly...almost *wounded*. Like she'd hurt him somehow with the accusation. "What exactly do you think I did to you?"

"I don't know," she admitted. "I have no idea what kind of supernatural powers you have. Maybe you put some kind of whammy on me. Put me in thrall. So I sympathized with you. Felt for you. *Dreamed* of you." *Fantasized*, really. Writhing in her sheets. Trying not to touch herself and failing miserably. If that wasn't some sort of spell, what could she blame except her own bad judgment?

He laughed. The caustic, self-loathing laugh that she already knew all too well. "Doc, if I had that power, do you think I'd be *in* here? Don't you think I would've whammied my way to freedom? Anything you feel…anything you dream…it's no different than what you've been doing to me."

Neha's chest tightened. Her breath caught somewhere between her throat and her rib cage. "We shouldn't be doing this at *all*. This is insane." The irony of her declaration wasn't lost on her. His plea hearing was set for tomorrow. Nate and Dustin had been coaching him to go with "not guilty by reason of insanity," but there was no guarantee he'd follow through. A court-appointed shrink could pretty easily substantiate the claim if he did—on paper he read like a sociopath—but sitting across from Joe now, shuffling notes like she wasn't flustered and hot and confused, she knew he was as competent to stand trial as she was. Not that her own mental state was really much of an endorsement. After all, she'd become totally obsessed with him…advocating for him and flirting with him and *wanting* him when he'd killed six men with no regrets. The only regret he seemed to have was for her.

"Doc…" He made the nickname sound like a tormented groan. Not impersonal. Not a jab. "Doc, you gotta look at me," he urged.

So, she did. She looked at his broken nose and his faded bruises and his scars. At his pouty mouth, not just swollen from a punch he took but also because it was asking to be kissed.

"I know a guy in ESU," he whispered, too low for the guards to hear. "He can get us a few minutes tomorrow. Before I go in."

There was a crashing sound in her ears that she recognized as her heartbeat. And a lurch in her stomach that she knew was the union of elation and fear. "Why do you want that, Joe? What do you hope to accomplish?" She almost sounded professional. Rational.

He saw through it, of course. Right through the table and her clothes to where her panties were damp. "I hope to get my arms around you," he said, like it was the simplest thing in the world. "I just want to feel you close."

If he'd said "because I wanna fuck you," she could've resisted it. That was what Neha told herself later. If he'd made it crass and vulgar, she would've said no. The tenderness in his voice destroyed her. All she could do was nod "yes."

8

"I JUST WANT TO FEEL you close." What kind of dumbass bullshit was that? Long after he was back in his cell, cooling his heels and waiting to hear if his bribe went through, Joe kicked himself for saying it. For wanting it. For daring to hope she'd show. For daring to hope at all. He had no use for sentimental crap. Especially in here. It was a weakness. And with the assholes who'd jumped him last month just itching for Round Two, he could not afford any kind of weakness. But he was the walking dead anyway, wasn't he? He was gonna meet Kenny on the other side any day now. So, what did it matter? He knew he had no right to do this to pretty little Neha Ahluwalia. To ask her to meet him. To make her face up to this thing they had going between them. He didn't care. It was the first time in years he'd felt something, *anything*, besides anger and grief. Besides empty.

Wanting her... It was this clawing thing inside him. It was alive. White-hot and hungry. Just like the beast. He had to see it through before it burned him up worse than the fires of hell ever could. He'd never wanted a woman this damn much. He'd never wanted *anything* this much. Fuck, he'd only been with three people since high school. He hadn't been a player in a long time. And maybe that was part of it—that he'd just gone without for too long. Or maybe it was just her. Just Neha. With that smoky sex-goddess voice and the mile-long legs and those eyes that saw too much of him. Or maybe…just maybe…it was a supe thing. The animal inside him recognizing a mate.

The military doctors at Apex had warned them time and time again that there could be side effects depending on their species. Imprinting. Increased appetite for meat. Inherent urge to maintain pack hierarchy. *Powerful biological imperative to mate.* He still remembered Dr. Fredericks, this pasty little motherfucker sweating like a sixth-grade science teacher trying to explain the birds and the bees. *"We tried to synthesize that element out of the serums you've been given. There is no guarantee we succeeded. You may still experience an overwhelming pull toward a sexual partner."*

Fuck. Joe scrubbed at his face. Slumped on his bunk. He could practically hear Mishelle in the back of his head. The way she'd laugh when he did something dumb and try to make up for it. *"Don't think you're going to get out of this with your moves, boy. I'm not here for your pants feelings. Button it up."* She wasn't here at all anymore. And his pants feelings were for someone else. So fucking powerful that he had to press the heel of his hand down on his cock and will his semi-permanent hard-on to behave itself. Except his dick didn't take the cue. No, it throbbed against his palm. And he got the fucking shakes just thinking about Neha's fingers replacing his. About her mouth…her gorgeous mouth opening up on him. He had to bite back a whimper. He didn't bite back the prayer.

"Please, Doc. Please be there tomorrow."

─────────────

She was nuts to even consider it, beyond help for actually agreeing. Why had she said yes? The moment haunted Neha for hours afterward. What kind of woman, what kind of psychologist, what kind of lawyer, agreed to a stolen rendezvous with a violent shape-shifter going on trial for murder? She was failing this on every level. And for what? Because he turned her on? Because she'd been buzzing herself to orgasm every night for weeks thinking about his head between her thighs?

It was just sex, for fuck's sake. An attraction. And she wasn't some sheltered fourteen-year-old in a Shakespearean cautionary tale. She'd occasionally had questionable taste in men, but she'd never been this reckless. She was always practical, always rational…yet she was suddenly killing the hell out of a bottle of Riesling on a weeknight while burrowed under a throw on her couch, streaming but barely watching a *Law & Order* marathon.

This Neha was not the kind of woman that made a bold impression…and she didn't give a rat's ass. Her hair was ponytailed. She hadn't bothered with makeup because she wasn't leaving the house. She wore a ratty law-school sweatshirt—you could barely make out the letters for "Pace" anymore—and Old Navy leggings. The cushions were littered with paperwork for cases she'd been ignoring in favor of Joe's. Her *own* cases. She had a client going to trial in two months, and aside from a few phone calls and one check-in meeting, she'd all but forgotten about it. She was letting her fellow associates and their shared paralegal pick up her slack. That was not normal for her. This was not how she operated. And to be falling apart, chucking her principles, because of a *man*? It added insult to injury.

"You ever slummed it? Ever fucked a blue-collar guy?"

And that was only the half of it, wasn't it? Because he wasn't *just* a man, *just* a blue-collar guy.

"What about a supe? Every done one of us? Had someone slide their fangs into your throat while they dick into you? Grabbed on to a wolf's ruff when he's nosing between your legs?"

Neha composed a half-dozen texts to various friends and then deleted the drafts. Olivia and Mika, her sorority sisters from undergrad—who she kept in touch with mostly via

Facebook—weren't the best audience for a crisis like this, especially since it would involve breaking client confidentiality. Breathing one word to Nate—who was more her boss than he was a friend—would result in her getting tossed off the case and probably losing her job. And telling Tejal about her moral crisis? No. No, she couldn't put her sweet, funny, cousin-sister in such a terrible position. It had been all well and good when they were discussing the theoretical. The reality…? The reality was that she couldn't drag Tejal into a battle between ethics and family loyalty, couldn't involve her in the dangerous shifter politics that surrounded this case. She was on her own with her bad decisions. Until tomorrow. When she would be alone with Joe and his.

"You want me to get up there and talk about what it was like over there, don't you? Paint me as some kind of wounded war veteran who went 'off' because of PTSD. That ain't me, Doc."

"Then who are you?"

"You haven't figured that out yet? Babe, I'm a guy who can't stop thinking about you."

"Cute. Flattery will get you absolutely nowhere, Joe."

"You think this is flattery? I barely know you. It's been, what, a week since you walked your ass in here with Feinberg and Taylor? This ain't flattery. It's obsession."

"It's unproductive, is what it is. Can we please stay on topic?"

She'd talked such a good game. Pretended to be objective. Only to have the entire act destroyed by one press of his mouth against hers. Was she really so weak? Was she really so naive and lust-addled that she was willing to start something with Joe Peluso that they probably couldn't finish? *Am I a terrible person?*

There was only one person she could think of to ask for the truth. One person she could trust to not hold back. Not Tejal. Not this time. Her hand shook as she reached for her phone and hit the speed-dial button for her mother. Jasminder Kaur Ahluwalia picked up on the second ring, with a too-loud and immediately rapid-fire "Beta? What's happened? Are you okay? You don't sound good!"

The last bit was truly remarkable, considering she hadn't even said "hi" yet. Neha was glad she'd picked voice instead of video chatting. Guru-ji only knew what Ma would make of how she looked right now. "Hi, Ma. I just…I had a silly question." A silly, Riesling-fueled question. And that lead-in alone earned an instant "Chee!" of disapproval.

"There are no silly questions, beta," her mother chided. There was distortion on the line —presumably as she bustled around the kitchen making roti or paratha. It was her Monday-night ritual: rolling out a week's worth of flatbreads while watching Punjabi soap operas on the iPad propped against the blender. "Now what is all this nonsense? Tell me!"

Neha forced herself to put the fears that were currently clawing at her guts into words. "Am I a bad person? Do you and Papa wish I was…better?"

This elicited one of those emphatic tongue-clicks that her mother excelled at. One click of the tongue from a traditional desi mom was like a paragraph-long diatribe from a white suburban soccer mom. And then Ma launched into the actual response. "Better than what?" she demanded in Punjabi. "Better than who? We've never compared you to anyone else. We love you as you are. We love your brothers the same."

Her brothers weren't flirting with confessed killers, with shifters. Nitesh was making it his mission to date every twentysomething blond human in the Tri-State area, and Neal was working on getting his girlfriend, Gurpreet, over from Amritsar on a fiancée visa—something that had become exponentially harder in the last few years. They were good sons, decent men, with solid jobs. Neither of them on the verge of making a gargantuan mistake.

Neha tried again. "But I'm not a good desi girl," she said, refilling her wineglass. "Don't you wish I was sweet and nice and on track to marry some perfect Punju husband and give you a bunch of grandkids? Or that I had a safer job?"

"What will wishes do? We are thankful for what we have, beta." A sigh came across the line, and Neha could picture her mother standing there in the kitchen, shaking her head. In about twenty-five years, Neha was going to look like her. Soft and round. Gray-streaked hair pulled back in a bun. "Do I think you should care for yourself more? Of course. You could stay out of the sun. Lose five, ten pounds." *There* was the unflinching desi honesty Neha had been searching for. "But you care for others so much. We know you became a lawyer to help people. Your papa and I are so proud of that."

The vote of confidence made tears spring to Neha's eyes, and she had to blink them back. "Even if I'm helping people who are guilty?"

"Especially then. Serving the good is easy, Neha. Serving the troubled, the bad, the lost without becoming lost yourself? That takes strength. That takes sacrifice."

"How do I know I'm not losing myself?" How could she want Joe Peluso and still be the daughter, the woman, the lawyer that her parents had raised so lovingly and faithfully?

"You called your mother, didn't you? That's how I know my Neha is still here. I believe in you."

That made exactly one of them, Neha realized as she finished up the conversation with hollow pleasantries and promises to chat again in a few days. She had no more clarity than she'd had before the call. If anything, she felt worse. Like a fraud.

"I just want to feel you close."

A fraud who was going to get dressed up for court in the morning and step into the arms of a guilty man and an admitted monster. A fraud who was going to grab those minutes with both hands and cling to them.

9

IT HAD TAKEN NEARLY A year, but Yulia had slowly adjusted to her new terms of employment—if "employment" was even what strict, unquestionable loyalty to her brother's endeavors could be called. Working the hostess stand of Kamchatka several evenings a week was easy. Mindless work. It was the other nights of hostessing, presiding over the club's most lucrative enterprise into the wee hours, that took a toll. The Bear Pit. Aleksei's vicious little joke. The basement arena, two levels below the restaurant, with its massive steel cage, where those of their clan and outside it met in their fur and claw and clashed for sport. It was a sport Yulia did not understand. Not when immigrants and supernaturals alike were being caged along both borders now. To lock oneself behind bars voluntarily, to spill sweat and blood for money and entertainment... What horror was this?

"*You were always too stupid to appreciate our business,*" Aleksei had laughed during her first shift in the Pit, when she'd been foolish enough to cringe at the first strike of fist against flesh. "*Do you not understand that this is* mine? *The American government can do what they wish to whomever they wish, but this is* my *rule. Here, I am king.*"

How exactly that made him different from the tyrant in Washington, Yulia could not begin to guess. And she certainly did not wonder such a thing aloud. She'd armored herself after that first night. Now, she no longer shook when she passed through the security doors into the arena. She no longer flinched when fighters collided. The sounds of snarls and grunts and screams were white noise. Buzzing in her ears. She was stone, she was earth, she was water. Elements that did not feel, did not hurt, did not do anything but weather over time.

She thought often of Danny. His soft laughter. His hand curled around hers, squeezing and offering strength. This Vision Danny of hers was not shocked by her family's secrets. Not frightened away by the cinder-block walls, the rows of leather banquettes, the rapture and the glee of half-shifted bears cheering for more blood, more broken bones. He didn't call it in. He didn't order squad cars to converge on the premises. No, he simply held her hand and carried her through each night. *You'll survive,* he told her. *You have to survive.* Why? *So I can see you again.* Perhaps it was childish to cling to a fantasy the way she'd clung to her mother as a cub, but Yulia was happy to be a child if being an adult meant reveling in pummeling one another to pulp.

The Pit was a study in excess. Cash changing hands, bottle service, too loud, too violent, too male, too *everything.* Yulia navigated it with something near a smile. A taut tilting of her lips that upon close inspection would reveal itself to be a grimace. Her stiletto heels clicked against the terrazzo tile floor. The full skirt of her dress whipped around her thighs. Yulia Vasilieva, ice princess. Murmuring polite greetings, gesturing for empty tumblers to be refilled, taking vodka shots for the glory of Kamchatka. No one looking at her would know that she was anything but calm, cool, collected, professional. No one knew just how badly she wanted to run screaming out the door.

Out of the corner of her eye, she watched Aleksei. Sitting on his throne—an ornate chair in his box, a cordoned-off VIP area in prime view of the cage—boasting and bragging, in a much better mood than a few days ago. Perhaps he'd solved his Joe Peluso situation. Perhaps he was so confident now in his successes that it did not matter. He was entertaining some contact from one of his many illegal operations. From what little Yulia knew, the man had arrived from overseas just that morning. He'd been plucked from JFK and taken to a luxury hotel in Dumbo. No expense was being spared. He was important, and Aleksei was showing off.

Yulia filed away details as though she were remembering a regular's order. Thinning blond hair. He looked older than her brother, which would put him in his late forties or early fifties, but men in their business often aged poorly. He could be in his twenties for all she knew, wearing the violence in the lines on his face. She'd yet to come close enough to hear his voice, detect an accent, but his scent was easy enough to pick up. Rank and aggressive beneath a layer of expensive cologne. He smelled like a bear, but not of their clan. Not a brown bear shifter she recognized. But a better question, a more dangerous question, was this: Was he a big fish or the biggest fish? The boss or the boss's right hand?

"Yulia!" Aleksei's voice carried across the arena. A sharp slap that cut through the pleasant fog of three shots of Mamont. "Come!"

She detoured just long enough to pick up another chilled bottle of vodka from the bar. *You'll survive*, Danny reminded her again. *You'll get through this.*

She was stone, she was earth, she was water. She would weather this night, just as she'd weathered everything else.

The display on his smartphone read just a few minutes until midnight. Joe Peluso's pretrial hearing was tomorrow. Almost today. Nate knew his arguments backward and forward. And he had every confidence that they wouldn't matter one tiny bit.

"You know we're fucked, right? There's no way this case is gonna go our way."

Dustin's low voice rolled across Nate's skin like a rumble of thunder. Appropriate, since a storm was about to hit them both. "Aren't you supposed to be the optimist?" He scowled, slumping back in his chair with his tumbler of scotch, tempted to just swap it out for the bottle. He really had no business drinking at all…but wasn't that what law school prepared you for? All the vices and all the functionality rolled into one ruthless package? "One of us has to believe in the greater good, remember?"

His best friend laughed, crumpling up his empty Red Bull can. "I didn't realize it was my shift on the rah-rah squad. Sorry. I left my puppies and rainbows at home, man."

Nate didn't even have a supply of puppies and rainbows anymore. The greater good. *Ha.* What did that even mean now? In a country where presidential term limits had vanished, abortions had been criminalized in more than half the states, and being different in any significant way got you sent to detainment centers? He'd grown up with "never again" echoing in his ears, learning his family's history over his bubbe's brisket, knowing firsthand what devastation creeping fascism could result in. He'd naively thought it couldn't happen here. And yet here they were.

In the past few years, their pro bono cases involving supernaturals had skyrocketed, coming just about even with their work with undocumented immigrants and those seeking political asylum. A decent percentage of their clients were innocent, railroaded by authorities who were basically acting like bullies— factions of NYPD, ICE, the SRB, all playing secret police for the modern age. But the firm had plenty of clients who'd committed actual crimes, too. Peluso *had* killed people. He'd taken justice into his own hands. The odds of getting him off, or even brokering a decent deal, were slim to none. Sure, Nate and Dustin were the Wonder Twins—the best at what they did—but there was only so much their powers could actually activate. "Are we doing the right thing?"

"Fighting for this? Fuck yes!" D exclaimed without hesitation. "The Peluso case might not be ideal, but if we sit around waiting for the ideal case, it'll be too damn late to do anything. Our client did the planet a *favor* by taking out those assholes. The least we can do is make sure he gets a fair trial. It may not go our way, but we're *trying*. The minute we stop trying, it's over."

It was nothing Nate hadn't already said to himself, to Neha. Neha, who was already too close to this case, to this client. But Nate couldn't help the unease that washed over him. There was no guarantee that he was *right* to feel so off-kilter. He wasn't psychic, couldn't boast any particular supernatural identity or ability. He'd been asked, sure. The "What are you?" questions for anyone who didn't fit into neat little boxes were more frequent now—and no less rude. But being gay and Jewish, while both marginalized identities, was a completely different thing than sprouting fur or conjuring magic. He trusted his instincts, though. They'd seldom let him down.

Something was *wrong*. About this case. About this client. About this whole entire world. Nate had devoted most of his life to making things right...and he had the sick sense, the ever-growing suspicion, that he was doing it in vain. That tomorrow's hearing didn't actually matter in the grand scheme of things. That nothing was ever going to change for the better, no matter what they did or who they fought for.

Dustin slid a can of Red Bull in front of him, shaking his head and sighing. "Still need those rainbows and puppies, huh?"

"No," Nate admitted grimly. "What we need is a global miracle."

10

___

JOE'S COURT SUIT WAS THE one he'd worn to Kenny's funeral. Maybe it had fit once, but now the jacket was too tight across his shoulders, the pants a little too short at the ankle. Almost as restrictive as the handcuffs they'd slapped right back on him after he changed. It wasn't a good look for someone desperate to steal time with a woman he was obsessed with. He felt like a kid playing dress-up. Or the Incredible Hulk about to bust out of his clothes.

It was ridiculous to be this nervous. To feel this sweaty and out of control. And not over what was going to happen in the courtroom. He didn't give a shit about his plea and the judge and whatever the hell Feinberg and Taylor wanted him to do. It was all about her. Neha. And that damn voice deep inside him that couldn't seem to say anything but "mine." He could hardly sleep for thinking about it. Fuck, his priorities really *were* for shit.

Of course, he didn't really think she'd show. Why would she? How could he ever be that lucky, right? So, when the anteroom door clicked shut behind her, he went a little light-headed. Like she was a hallucination. A beautiful fantasy in a fitted gray suit and beige heels, she looked so much better than he ever could. "We don't have much time." She stayed there, in the doorway, staring at him with those big doe eyes. "They're going to call you in soon."

"I know." He couldn't stop drinking her in. Minutes. Hours. It didn't matter because she was *here*. For him. For this. She was so damn hungry for it. Just as ravenous as he was. Maybe she hadn't been kissed right in months. Probably hadn't been fucked good in years…and, hell, neither had he. He felt the want rolling off her in waves, masquerading as caution. But she wasn't afraid. Not of this. Not of him. Not of the creature beneath his skin. And she came closer when she should have backed up.

"God, this is *so* unethical," she said with a weary little laugh. He could see the faintest circles under her eyes. Like she hadn't gotten much sleep either. Like maybe this had kept *her* up, too. "I'd throw a book against the wall for pulling this shit. Walk out of a movie theater."

"You can walk outta here, too, Doc." It was the last thing he wanted. But he had enough kindness in him, just the tiniest bit, to make the offer. "You can leave. Pretend this never happened. You were never here."

She just shook her head, pink lips pressing tight before she spoke. "You know I can't do that. You wouldn't have asked what you asked if you thought that was an option."

Wouldn't he have? Wasn't he just enough of a mess to ask for things he couldn't have? He was a guy used to hand-me-down shoes and dollar slices and military programs that would feed you and clothe you in exchange for playing Dr. Frankenstein. She could've said no. She could've blown him off today. He'd *expected* her to blow him off today.

Instead, she made the first move. "Joe?" She wasn't asking what he was going to do. She was telling him what *she* was about. And she did it better than he did back in the jail. She walked up to him nice and slow. She even fucking looked to him for consent. "I'm going to kiss you now. Is that okay?"

Is that okay? Sexy, smart goddess in her short skirt and fuck-me shoes. He wasn't going to tell her no. He wasn't going to do anything but lift his cuffed hands so she could slip into the loop of his arms. It was like she belonged there. Fucking cliché, but true. Soft and slight, almost level with him thanks to her heels. Smelling like that flowery shampoo and something earthy and elemental that the wolf inside him recognized. Maybe all he needed was this. Maybe he didn't need more. But she'd said she was going to kiss him, and she kept her word.

She did it with her eyes open, still careful, still checking in, and it was so damn sweet he could have been at the prom instead of a holding room with a cop outside the door. Except he'd spent most of the prom going down on his date in the band room, hadn't he? So Neha really didn't have to go through all the formalities. She didn't *have* to be sweet. He didn't need wooing or courting. And if they only had minutes, he wanted to make the most of them. He kissed her back hard and fierce, until she quit looking and started feeling. Until he was losing himself in the heat of her pretty mouth and her eager tongue.

Neha slipped her arms around him, getting in as close as she could with their clothes on. Chest to chest. Thigh to thigh. They were making out like dumb kids after sunset in the park—kids who'd said "fuck it" to prom and to each other—and he couldn't get enough of it. *Fuck. Yeah.* He angled his head, tasted her jaw, and licked a trail down her throat, and she ground against his hip, rubbing all over him. He grabbed her ass, because he couldn't hold on to much else with the damn cuffs on, and she moaned, telling him, "Yes, Joe. Yes." Jesus fucking Christ. He could come in his pants just from this, but he wanted to get her off a dozen times first.

This woman was something. Maybe she was everything. He wanted to find out.

But all he did was slam her to the floor. Because a burst of gunfire blew through the door, the window, and the wall, sending shards of glass and drywall raining into the room.

Neha curled into him, ducked her head, a scream dying in her throat. His fur rippled under his clothes, claws and teeth straining to pop. *But he couldn't change. He couldn't. Fuck.* They rolled together, still caught in the circle of each other's arms. He bit back the pain of his interrupted shift, knocked the table over and forward so it shielded them. And the bullets kept coming…until they didn't. Until everything went quiet except for the alarmed shouts outside. *Shit.* No wonder the uniform at the door was happy to take a couple of greenbacks to leave them alone. He'd already been on the payroll for a hit.

"Let me… I…" Neha wriggled out from their enforced clinch, so they were each as free to move as they could be, given that someone had just been shooting at them. And even though that improved their chances of survival, he couldn't help but miss how she'd felt plastered against him. Hell, if he was gonna die right now, why not die inside her?

He entertained that thought for about a split second. Then he levered them both up. Told her to run. But there was something in their way. The guard, slumped over the threshold. Riddled with bullets. A victim of the assault he was probably in on. Joe didn't waste any tears on him, instead quickly rifling through his pockets for the handcuff keys. Precious seconds. Anticipating more bullets. Shouting at Neha, "Go!"

And then they were both out the door. Down the hall. Through the crowds of people already getting the hell gone. She tugged him to the fire stairs. Nothing fueling them but *go* and *escape* and *now*. They made it two blocks, maybe three, before she stumbled in those ridiculous high heels. *Goddammit, Doc.* He hauled her to her feet. His grip on her wrist was like a match on the side of its box. She cried out his name. Half in pain and half in relief. Maybe an extra half in lust. Need. Tension. Whatever this thing was between them.

Before he knew it, they were ducking into the narrow space between two buildings. Hands roaming everywhere. Checking for wounds. He already felt like shit. Looked it, too. Wasn't anything new to catalog. But she tried anyway, touching him with those clean little fingers. His touch wasn't as innocent. He patted down her breasts and lingered. Grabbed on to her hips and her tight butt. He couldn't hear much over the rush of blood in his ears. But he was still gonna wait for a yes. A sign. Another match to the flame.

"Joe?" This time when she said his name, it was permission. And when she tilted her face up and kissed him, that was permission, too. Permission and a demand. Pushed by adrenaline and need and fear and things she would probably regret later.

He wasn't going to regret them at all.

"Yes, ma'am," he said before he unbuckled his pants.

It was hard and nasty and frantic. Getting into her clothes. Finding her wet. Still smelling gun oil and smoke as he pressed her thighs apart and sank into her. He licked the corner of her mouth. Tasted the blood on his own bitten lips instead of her beauty mark.

It wasn't romantic. It wasn't kind. It was rutting knowing you were inches from dying. The only thing he could offer a woman anymore. And she took it. All of it. Tugging at his hair. His ears. Going wild. Crying and cussing him out and sinking her teeth into his throat. Adding to the scars he would never count. They didn't have time for this. They took it anyway. Stole it. Owned it. Rubbing all up on each other. Sticky and sweaty and dirty.

He could feel her everywhere even though they were both still mostly dressed. Hear her breath and her heart and even the blood racing through her veins. In pace with his. This beautiful, sexy woman keeping up with the wolf's hunger, the man's appetite. Joe had never had a quick fuck like this…one that felt like hours packed into a few filthy minutes. When she went over, it was like her whole body caught fire. So hot. Melting. Burning his cock so hard that he barely remembered to pull out before he shot his load.

Fuck, man. Fuck.

He asked her for time while he was barely done spilling all over the bricks. Leaning his forehead against hers. Breathing her in. Ass bared to anybody who wanted to look into the alley, to any cops who might want to shoot him in it. "Just a little time. Let me figure this out. Let me figure out what I'm gonna do. And then I swear I'll contact you. I'll find a way."

Her eyes were huge. Glassy. Like a doll's. She nodded. Clutched him. Let go. Clutched him again. Shock. Yeah, of course. She just got shot at and then fucked raw against a wall. Her skin was ice-cold. He had ideas about how to warm her up, but no time to put them into action. It was too dangerous. They'd risked too much already. And he couldn't be weighed down. No ties. No baggage. No matter how prettily she came around his cock. They'd write this fuck off as a one-time thing. Adrenaline. Stress. A mistake. Something they had to get out of the way because it was too deep under the skin.

"I'm sorry, Doc," he whispered, rubbing her hands. Kissing them, too. "I'm sorry it has to be this way. Thank you for giving me one last good thing to remember."

––––––––––––––––

The bricks dug into her back. She was winded and dirty, and she'd just fucked a shape-shifter in an alley. A shifter. A criminal. A killer. Unprotected. Sure, he'd pulled out, but she was still wet from both of them. From insanity and adrenaline and the need that had been clawing in her since the day they met. Maybe it spoke to just how screwed up she was that, in that moment, she didn't give a flying fuck. All she could register were Joe's hands rubbing hers, trying to coax some warmth back into her numb fingers. His mouth, so mean a few minutes ago, was sweet and soft against her palms. And he told her he was sorry. So, so sorry. Not for the sex but for leaving her afterward.

No. Awareness, reality flooded back to Neha in one sharp slap. She didn't need a grounding trick this time. "No, you can't go," she gasped, lurching forward so fast that their foreheads knocked together. "Your case is shot if you leave."

Joe let go of her fingers, chuckling as he touched the spot where they'd bumped. "We ran, baby. My case is already shot because somebody shot *at* us. And my only chance is if I get to the motherfuckers that did it. If I hit them before they can hit at me again."

She knew with every fiber of her being that he was wrong... which was funny, considering her complete lack of moral fortitude five minutes ago, when she was scratching at him and biting and taking him so deep that she could still feel him inside her. But facts were facts. If he went off on his own right now, he'd really be screwed. No third chances. He'd be hunted by the motherfuckers *and* the law. Every cop in the New York metro area. State troopers. Feds. Sanctuary City rules would not keep him safe.

She could already hear the sirens. Fire trucks, too. The courthouse was still in chaos, but that didn't mean they had time to waste. Neha hurriedly tugged up her underwear, put herself to rights. It was a miracle her brain worked after having so much of it fucked out of her, but she heard herself spitting out words that made a lot of sense. At least to her. She couldn't account for them making sense to anybody else. "I'm coming with you. I can help you, and I can hide you while we work through this together."

"Doc..."

"*No.* You're not going off on your own right now." She didn't give him time to disagree. She wrapped both arms around one of his and tugged. "Come on."

Joe could have easily shrugged off her grip, pushed her away with no effort at all. Instead, he let her hustle him toward Jay Street–MetroTech. She thanked their collective lucky stars for the lack of drones overhead and swiped them both down into the bowels of the New York City subway system, while the howls of the emergency crews got louder and uniforms started converging in doorways. With any luck, the cops would focus on Hoyt Street and the 2 train because it was closer to the courthouse, not realizing they'd wandered further—in more ways than one.

Neha was wholly conscious of how undone she was, how completely obliterated. Luckily—though they both looked disheveled—in their court suits, they were just three-martini-lunch casualties instead of persons of interest. No one gave them a second glance as they caught the Downtown F. Especially when she draped herself across Joe's lap, turning them into one of those obnoxious PDA pairs that was a bigger eyesore than the rats and graffiti. Neha's hair spilled around them, hiding Joe's face for the duration of the ride.

It was only fifteen minutes, maybe twenty, but it felt interminable. His eyes locked on hers. The bulge of his erection under her thighs. How was he still hard? How was *she* still craving him despite finally giving in to her wildest impulse? It didn't make any sense. But he was and she was. Damp for him, turned on, still slick from her last orgasm. She didn't know if she'd have time to shower once they got to her place. Or time to fuck him again. But she desperately needed both.

"Why?" His voice rasped along her ear like sandpaper. It was a lot of questions packed into one, but Joe plucked out the most interesting to him in this moment. "Why'd you let me do it?"

There was no "letting." Any more than you "let" a volcano erupt or a tornado wipe out your house. She said as much aloud. He made a sound low in his throat and threaded his fingers through her hair, cradling the back of her head. "Baby, you are so fucked," he groaned before kissing her.

She wanted to stay like that forever. Fused to his lips. Safe in his arms. But the automated announcement for their stop pulled her away. Another cold-slap reminder that this night was not over. That they'd made their bed but they didn't have time to sleep in it.

Neha's place was five blocks from the subway station, on the ground floor of a two-story house, with her own entrance off the side. Even with the uptick in surveillance across all the boroughs, there was no one to see her tug Joe inside. No one to see him press her against the closed door and kiss her again.

She clung to him then, climbing him like a vine. Because she was still afraid he'd let her go, shove her away, and ruin any chance they had of getting him out of this alive.

He was right. She was *so* fucked.

11

THE COURTHOUSE WAS A FUCKING zoo for hours after the shooting. Nate had spent the initial moments afterward facedown on the courtroom floor, trapped beneath Dustin, who'd hit the deck with him on instinct. And he'd been thankful to feel that weight on top of him—terrified, unable to breathe, hearing the echoes of gunfire even after it stopped, but so thankful that Dustin was there, with him, and not somewhere in the line of fire. They said your life was supposed to flash before your eyes at times like that...but it wasn't *his* life he'd seen. Just D's. *Please don't be hurt*, he'd begged. *Please don't be shot.* Because they couldn't be the Wonder Twins if one of them was dead.

Three minutes after that, Nate had realized that Peluso was the target of the hit...and that Neha had been with him. And the shit had really hit the fan. The ADA on the case had cornered him, along with an NYPD detective and two uniforms. An agent from the Supernatural Regulation Bureau wasn't far behind. The questions had rung in his ears just like the gunfire. *"Did your client plan this?" "How much did you know?" "Can we assume your client took your associate against her will?"*

They couldn't assume anything, despite the APB that had gone out within twenty minutes of Peluso's vanishing act. Nate had a hard time believing that the moody loner they could barely convince to cooperate would be capable of arranging a breakout from the Kings County Criminal Court—and he said as much while pinned under Detective Hudson's shrewd gaze.

"I'm inclined to see this as another instance of retaliation from the Russian mafia," Dustin added. "Peluso incurred numerous injuries while in lockup, and while he didn't say outright that they were courtesy of Vasiliev's organization, our sources told us exactly who was walking around with bruised knuckles afterward."

Dustin had a way of putting people at ease. And it wasn't a supernatural talent either. He claimed it came from being six foot four and built like a linebacker. He'd learned to balance his size with his honeyed voice and an even temper. "I'm a gentle giant," he insisted, dark eyes always twinkling. Nate had no illusions that the act was easy. Growing up in Bed-Stuy, D had encountered his fair share of trouble with people who wanted to pick a fight with a warrior poet. And coming over the bridge to play with the straight WASPs of the Manhattan elite wasn't exactly a cakewalk. Nor was dealing with law enforcement. They were both very, very aware of the uniforms. Two young white men barely out of diapers had their hands hovering over their holsters.

Detective Hudson made a noise of disgust, shaking his head. "I'm going to want statements from both of you," he barked. "And don't leave town."

"But I had a pressing engagement in the Hamptons on Wednesday." Nate couldn't help himself. "Tennis with Alec Baldwin."

Hudson scowled. The ADA—a skinny Princeton grad who'd been on the floor with him just a short time before—looked disgusted. Nate wasn't particularly concerned about making a good impression with Carter Beckinsale. The guy would never, *ever* relate to someone like Joe Peluso—and his goal would be making sure a jury had the same deficiency. *See Peluso as less than. See him as an animal.*

"Nathaniel." Dustin frowned at him, playing the disciplinarian for their audience's benefit. "I think you're overwrought—which is understandable, given that we were all in the vicinity of a shooting." He turned his body so he was half shielding Nate, easily creating a barrier between him and the esteemed employees of the City of New York. "If we hear anything from Peluso or our associate Ms. Ahluwalia, you will be the first to know," he lied in the velvet-smooth tone that had disrobed countless people across the Eastern Seaboard.

Dustin always protected him. Without fail. Together, they would protect Neha and their client.

The sound of shattering glass could've meant anything. A clumsy moment. A raucous toast. The angry torrent of words that came after it was unmistakable. Aleksei had fucked something up. His pleasure and pride from the night before, in the arena, had vanished into utter fury. Yulia winced, flattening against the wall outside his office door, hearing only his side of the conversation. Hell, they could probably hear his half of the conversation all the way at the top hill of the Coney Island Cyclone. Now it was a steady stream of suddenly deferential Slovak punctuated with curses. It was a talent to cover one's ass and display one's rage at the same time, but Yulia was no stranger to her brother's many skills. The self-proclaimed king of South Brooklyn's Russian and Eastern European enclave was desperate to hold on to his empire even as it slipped through his fingers.

His anger woke the beast inside her, making her fur ripple over her skin and her claws pop. But she forced back the turn, swallowed the urge to shift. The hit went bad, she surmised, once she'd heard enough. Her Slovak wasn't great, but she understood what was important: the Maspeth Mauler, or whatever silly name the news was calling him this week, had somehow escaped. Now Aleksei had to explain himself to the big monsters on top—the monsters no one *ever* wanted to disappoint. If her brother had named himself king, then it was safe to say that the men he answered to thought themselves gods. Yulia had never been happier to be a nonbeliever.

She hurried away from the offices, back to the front of the club, shaking the ice crystals from her skin. Yes, she could melt the chill…but she could never be rid of the stain of the business. Her phone burned a hole in the back pocket of her jeans, begging to be plucked out and used. *Call Danny*, said the little voice in her head she'd been ignoring for months. *Call him and tell him what's happening.* But she'd sworn—*sworn*—loyalty to Aleksei, hadn't she? Wasn't that the deal she made with him, with herself, when she wiped down the bar at the Confessional on Church Avenue for the last time and came back down to Kamchatka? No more contact with Detective Danny Yeo. No more looking outside their family, outside their world. *No more humans.*

That foolish vow didn't account for what she saw when she closed her eyes. Because Danny was always there. Strong, steadfast, kind, and funny. Quick with a light for her cigarettes, giving of warm end-of-shift hugs. Despite discovering her connection to one of Brooklyn's most notorious crime rings, he'd never pressured her to turn on her brother. He'd never asked for any information. Even when she'd itched to give it to him. And now…now that they never spoke, all she wanted to do was spill everything.

My brother is a killer, she'd say. *And I never should have left you to be by his side.*

———

Danny was on shift at 3S when the call came in, when their scanners went wild. *Shooting at Kings County Criminal Court. Police and Fire on the scene. Suspect at large. Possible rogue supernatural unaccounted for.* It wasn't his precinct, but he half expected his personal phone to light up, calling him back into the station where he'd already clocked a full shift. It stayed silent. Unlike Elijah and Jack, who slammed out of the glass-walled conference room set against the back wall, voices raised.

"I told you we should've kept a closer eye on him!" Lije was saying, his eyes going shifter-gold with anger.

Jackson, who normally looked like a poster boy for white Republican chic, had lost his suit jacket sometime in the last hour. His tie was unknotted and his usual perfectly styled brown hair was a mess. "Oh, you did, did you?" he spat. "When exactly was that? When you were cleaning out the tabloid shelf at the Duane Reade?"

"Sod off, Jack!" Elijah roared. Like *literally* roared.

Heads went up across the sea of cubicles, like meerkats popping up out of their little meerkat holes. Not that they had any meerkat shifters on staff, as far as Danny knew. He locked eyes with Joaquin Serrano, Third Shift's best surveillance expert, who already had their wall of monitors syncing in with drone coverage of the area. Finn Conlan and Mack Wilson both had quarters on premises and therefore tended to be around for all major Third Shift events. They slipped out of their desk chairs and into the aisle. Like they could intercept and subdue their bosses before things got too out of hand. *Ha.* A vampire and a human against a lion shifter and a sorcerer? Fat chance. But Danny admired the initiative. Maybe he envied it a little, too.

Finn and Mack were both senior field operatives with decades of experience—it was possible the decades were all on Finian's side, since he bragged about being ninety-something years old—and risked little blowback for shouting. "Hey!" and "What the hell is going on here?" at the two powerful men who'd created 3S.

As if only just realizing they had an audience, Jack and Elijah seemed to immediately deflate. The shadow of Elijah's lion vanished. The faint glow around Jackson that meant conjuring was imminent disappeared, too, and his pale face reddened with embarrassment at having lost his cool patrician facade. "I'm sorry," he said, in a milder tone better suited for the workplace. "That dig about the tabloids was uncalled for."

"Accepted. Forgotten." Elijah offered a curt nod. "Now what the hell are we going to do about Joe Peluso doing a runner?"

Was *that* what had happened at the courthouse? Danny felt a surge of dread followed by confusion. "Why do we *have* to do anything about him doing a runner?" He was like a high-school kid again, raising his hand in class. But the question had to be asked. For his own edification if nothing else. "Isn't it better for the bigger picture if he just vanishes and the Russians are left chasing their tails? If we just let the local precinct clean up the mess?"

Jack made a face, and then scrubbed the expression away with the palm of his hand. "There are things you don't know," he admitted, though it clearly pained him to do so. "Things we haven't told all the operatives."

"Like what?" Finn's near-black brows rose, and then wiggled in speculation. Because there was nothing he couldn't turn into innuendo. "He an ex or something? Did you have a threesome and not invite me? I'm insulted, honestly."

"Shut it, Finian," Elijah said, not entertaining the digression even a little. "We *do* have a past with Peluso, but it's not that sort of past. He's one of us."

That told Danny absolutely nothing. "A shifter? A supernatural? We knew that already."

Elijah and Jack traded an indecipherable look. One that resulted in Lije slumping against a cubicle divider while Jack straightened his tie and cleared his throat. Lecture mode, activated. "The Apex Initiative—the cooperative military program that created supernatural soldiers like Peluso—began with a team of born supes. I was on that team. So was Elijah. We were the first wave. Phase One.

When the project was deemed a success, they decided to pursue a new avenue: making their own supes via genetic manipulation. Joe, and others like him, are results of that experimentation."

Holy shit. Danny had known, of course, that they'd met during wartime and dreamed up Third Shift for when they weren't active duty anymore...but he'd never figured *this* was part of their origin story. That the intermilitary unit Peluso was a part of had started with them. "So, Third Shift wouldn't even exist without Apex. And you still feed into each other, don't you?"

Elijah nodded. "We pull recruits from that pool, yeah. And they keep us informed of ongoing developments with the program. Sometimes they'll kick us an op they need done off the books. Sometimes we watch their retirees. Like Peluso. *Especially* if they stumble into one of our active missions. So, we can't just let him vanish."

"Not even if he wanted to," Jack added. "He's too valuable. And too dangerous. The public has just started accepting supernaturals in their midst. If word gets out that the military's been *making* supe-soldiers for decades, the tiny bit of progress we've made will get buried in a shitshow."

Danny flinched. To think, he'd written off Peluso as unimportant, unworthy of his attention. Too caught up in what that hit last year had meant for him and Yulia on a personal level to link it to what Third Shift was trying to do overall. He'd sworn to fight for freedom and equality in the only ways he could. That meant fighting for Joe Peluso, too.

"We'll find him," he said, even though it was a promise he couldn't be sure to keep. "I know we'll get this back on track."

Elijah's roar this time was one of weary laughter. "Then you know more than me, Danny. You know a whole bloody lot more than me."

12

THEY WENT AT IT AGAIN right there by Neha's door. The lights were off. It was all touch and taste and scent, no sight. And he couldn't not have her. Because, fuck, the cops could bust in on them right then, guns blazing, and if he was gonna die, Joe wanted to die like this. His fingertips sinking into her hips. His cock sinking into her softness, the way eased by that first round against the bricks. He should have been halfway across town by now. Not here, fucking her, swallowing her little moans, letting her believe that she could save him. He wasn't supposed to be getting off on how she clutched fistfuls of his shirt and bit at his throat. Like she was the supe, not him. Like she wanted to drink him dry.

Vasiliev was behind the hit. No question. The beatdowns in lockup were just foreplay. Joe knew his best bet was to go to ground for a couple days and then get the fuck out of Dodge. There was no shaking that kind of target on his back. But there was no shaking Neha either, even though he needed to walk the fuck out right now. Instead, he shoved her jacket down her shoulders, trapping her arms at the elbows, and he ripped open her blouse, sending the buttons flying. And he took and took. Tonguing her pretty throat and her jaw and her tits. As heavy and full against his lips as he'd imagined they'd be.

He knew the minute she stopped being into it. She went still under his mouth. There was a break in how she was panting for him. "Don't like having your tits sucked, Doc?" he wondered, trying not to laugh and accidentally bite her beautiful brown nipple right off.

"Doesn't do a damn thing for me," she confessed, her shoulders lifting in a shrug that just scrunched her gorgeous rack together like an invite to fuck it. He wanted to slide his cock right into that valley and die there...except for the part where she was like, "Have at it if you want. Just remember we're in a rush."

Joe couldn't help it then. He did laugh. Lowering his head and cracking up right there against her chest. And his damn fool cock didn't even feel insulted. Still hard as a rock. "Nah," he told her, once he'd gotten himself in hand. Literally. "I think we can work out a compromise." He grinned up at her before he slid down her body. So soft and hot and sweaty from everything they've already done. "I ever tell you that I was the pussy-eatin' champion of Aviation High?"

"We're still in a rush," she reminded him.

"Time me," he said before he put his face between her thighs.

The reality of that first taste...*fuck*. It beat every fantasy in his jailhouse spank bank. Salty. Musky. His come and hers combined. So fucking filthy. He had to brace one hand on her hip so he didn't go all in like the rabid animal everyone assumed he was. But he wanted to. Fuck, he wanted to. Because she was so wet and so into it. Making little hungry noises, reaching down to tangle her fingers in his hair and tug. He used his tongue. His thumb. Pressing into her clit while he licked into her. And, fuck, hell, god, it was everything. Everything and too much. His fur bristled under his skin like a thousand pinpricks. His balls drew up tight. He was gonna spill again without even touching himself. Just from touching her. Devouring her.

Her orgasm hit fast. No slow build. No tiny tremors. Her whole body went over the edge. And it was beautiful. Wrecked him. Wrecked her.

"Three minutes." It was barely a whisper. It was enough. For the first time in a long-ass time, Joe actually felt a little smug... and a little safe.

————————

She'd just had the best sex of her life—*twice*—and she couldn't even stop and linger in the afterglow. The clock was ticking. Neha managed to yank herself away from Joe at some point after he'd pulled two more orgasms from her with just his mouth. She practically had to crawl, her knees were so shaky. It was a miracle she could move at all, leaving him there by the door as she willed her limbs to propel her to the bathroom for the world's fastest and hottest shower. She made sure to clean every nook and cranny—no sense in getting a UTI while on the run with a wanted criminal, right? And when she emerged a few minutes later, dressed in loose cotton Indian clothes, it was to find Joe up and prowling her living area.

"The shower's all yours," she offered. She didn't have to tell him twice. He set down the family photo he'd been studying and made a beeline down the short hallway.

He didn't take long. She'd barely managed to gather up some toiletries and extra clothes when he came out bare-chested and damp-haired, wearing just his suit pants, a sheepish grin on his face. "I hung the jacket up in the steam. The shirt's kind of a waste, though."

Because she'd ripped it open at some point. Just like he'd shredded hers. And she wasn't at all sorry. Joe's chest was a thing of beauty. Like something carved from rock and hewn further by the elements. Suntanned, hairy but not furry, his was the body of a man who worked outdoors. His abs hadn't come from a gym. They weren't six-pack, but she knew from close perusal that she'd hurt her fist if she tried to hit him in the gut. God, she wanted to just stand there and stare at him for an hour. But she couldn't.

"I have some oversized T-shirts somewhere. Go check in the bottom drawer of my dresser. You can borrow one," she assured him before moving from her first bag to the second one she'd grabbed from the top shelf in her closet. Her go bag. She'd packed it for the first time on November 9, 2016. The day after the Darkest Day.

He reemerged from the back of the apartment, pulling a generic promotional T-shirt over his head, as she checked the contents. And his dark eyes went wide as she laid out the inventory. The steel bangle kara she no longer wore. Her American passport. Her U.S. birth certificate. Protein bars. A couple of water bottles. A first-aid kit. Two burner phones. A slick and shiny Apple iPod Touch. A Taser. A sweet little handgun. Extra bullets.

"Is that a—?"

"It's a .22," she confirmed, running her thumb across the hammer. "I worked in the DA's office. And half the country hates people who look like me. Probably more than half. You think I'm going to take any chances?" It wasn't a choice she'd made lightly. She'd spent most of her life hating guns. Hating anything wielded in violence. But as the nation had changed, so had her stance. Out of sheer practicality if not actual principle. Her first few months at the DA's office, she'd spent as many weekends as she could at an NYPD firing range with a guy she was dating. The target shooting had proved to be way more useful than the guy, who got transferred to a precinct in Staten Island for coking up on the job.

She didn't know how much longer she'd be allowed to carry. There was legislation being circulated in Congress right now to restrict Second Amendment rights to humans of a Caucasian persuasion. They were pretending the intent was something less malevolent, but anybody with half a brain knew it was just one more step on the road to a white-supremacist, humans-first America. And Neha wouldn't be allowed on that road. Countless people would be happy to leave her corpse on the side of it. So, she and Joe had to keep moving while they could.

Still, her hands shook as she finished inventorying her bags and then zipped them up. All the practical preparation in the world didn't ease the tension brewing in her gut and tightening her shoulders. "What are we going to do, Joe? What are our choices?"

He sighed, shoulders sinking as he gripped the back of his neck with one hand. "I know what I was gonna do. Go after Vasiliev and then get the hell outta Dodge. Fuck if I know what to do now."

The reminder stung a little. He'd meant to leave her after taking her against the bricks, and she'd kept him from going off without her. "So, it's all up in the air because I'm with you. It'd be easier if you could go it alone, but I messed that up for you by insisting you stay with me."

"You didn't mess anything up. I messed up *your* life. I dragged you into my bullshit." Joe sighed again. His dark-brown gaze flicked over her face and then away, toward the picture frame he'd picked up earlier. "I know you're worried about my case and shit. I'm not. They were probably going to give me life anyway. So, I could get gone. Duck out of sight. Never come back here. But you? You *can't* run," he pointed out. "You have family and shit, right? People who'll miss you."

Ma. Papa. Her brothers. The twins. Those were only a few of the faces that flashed through her mind. A few of the faces in the photo he'd studied. "People will miss you, too."

Joe's laugh was short and sharp like a bark. "Yeah, like who?"

"Me," she said simply. Because after kissing him, getting shot at with him, and having sex with him, that was something she couldn't deny. Good or bad, Joe Peluso was a part of her life now, a part of her history and memory. There was no going back to a no-Joe existence.

Maybe he saw that in her face. Because he shook his head in disbelief, the set of his jaw a little grim. "That's some Stockholm fucking syndrome, Doc."

"Well, it's a fucking syndrome alright," she cracked, a little bit exhausted and a little bit hysterical…and a lot determined.

Because if they were both caught up in this *thing* with each other, she couldn't let him go off alone. But there was no way in hell she would allow him to regret, or second-guess, staying. She was an asset, not a liability. Maybe her skill set was different from his badass military shifter powers, but she knew how to protect herself, and how to protect people she cared about. They'd survived decades in an increasingly hostile America, after all. Her community had taught her the value of strength in numbers.

Her *community*. *Oh.* Neha's tired brain grabbed on to the word like a life raft. The word, the concept, the *place*. No one would think to look for Joe Peluso amid a bunch of Indian people. It would give them a chance to breathe, to regroup, to come up with a real plan. Her immediate instinct was to hide him in Edison or Rahway or North Brunswick, surrounded by desis for miles. But they couldn't risk going across state lines. Hell, putting aside the risk of hitting an SRB or ICE checkpoint, she didn't even want to leave Kings County.

Joe had already fucked the chances for a plea deal. The last thing they needed was extra charges piled on top of multiple counts of Murder One and jailbreak—however mitigating the circumstances of said jailbreak might be. But New York was a Sanctuary City, a haven. That still counted for something. And even if he was a supernatural, Joe was first and foremost a white cisgender heterosexual man. That counted for even more. She just needed to get him somewhere safe before she could take advantage of that privilege with regard to all his charges.

"We need to go to Queens," she concluded grimly as she patted the packed go bag and set it aside. "Jackson Heights is probably our best bet for a temporary hideout. We can reassess things from there after the search for you has died down."

Though most of the area's Punjabi population had jumped ship to Jersey, like her own family, she still had two aunties who lived right off Seventy-Third Street, smack in the middle of dozens of Indian restaurants and clothing stores. They were unrelated to each other and not at all related to her, but the community bonds were thick nonetheless. Elders were *always* your aunties and your uncles…and always happy to help.

"I'm *from* Queens," Joe pointed out. "First place they're gonna look, sweetheart."

Sweetheart. Cute. Was that a step up or down from "Doc"? "It's called 'hiding in plain sight' for a reason," she fired back. "It'll take the drones hours to sift through footage…and facial recognition will be harder if I'm surrounded by other brown people. Even computers can't tell us apart."

"Okay." He sighed, scrubbing at his jaw with the back of one hand. "Okay," he repeated, as if he'd grudgingly convinced himself to go along with her. And then he looked at her for a long moment…the kind that spanned sweat-drenched hours. "So, uh…we gonna talk about what we just did? I kinda fucked the hell outta you, babe. *Twice*."

Four times if you counted oral separately, and Neha definitely did. She wasn't sure she had the energy for an Oprah Winfrey heart-to-heart about sex in stressful situations, but it was best to just get it all out of the way. "I get tested for STIs every year. And you don't have to worry about telling Joe Jr. we conceived him against a wall. I have an IUD."

"Hell. So do I." He barked out a laugh at what she was sure was an expression of utter bewilderment on her face. It was close enough to an actual bark that it made her wonder, yet again, what kind of shifter he actually was. "Why do you think I haven't changed since I've been a guest of the Brooklyn Hilton? I'm chipped, Doc. Chipped and snipped."

"You *can't* shift forms?" An implant preventing him from going full supernatural explained so much…and yet not nearly enough. She gave his phenomenal body another once-over, wondering where it was.

"I get the prickles, but it hurts like a bitch and I can't shift *fully*," Joe confirmed. If he was discomfited by her staring, by her obvious curiosity, he didn't show it. "Not since I was oh-so-honorably discharged. They weren't about to let us Apex boys run around unchecked. And, all apologies to Joe Jr., I can't get you pregnant either. Mandatory vasectomies. They didn't want to risk us passing on our altered DNA or some shit. But that ain't what I'm asking about, and you know it. You fucked me. You bagged yourself a supe. How does that make you feel?"

He gave the classic psychiatrist question a mocking edge as he turned it back on her. It was all there in the set of his shoulders. In the way his darkly cynical gaze cut from her back to the family photos on her mantel and to the picture of Guru-ji on the adjacent wall. He was waiting for her to panic. To backpedal. To say she was sorry for what had just happened between them. He would have to wait a very long time.

Neha sighed, dragging her hands through her still-wet hair. "What do you want to hear, Joe?" she asked, coming around the couch to where he stood. "That I'm disgusted with myself? That I fulfilled some sort of weird fetish and I'm done now? Neither of those things are true. I don't have any regrets. I know who and what you are. I knew what you wanted from me the first time I saw you…and if I'm honest with myself, I wanted it, too. And I want it again. As many times as you're willing to give it. I like sex and I like you. But more than that…? I want to help you. I want to keep you alive."

Was that enough for him? God, she hoped so. But he didn't confirm or deny. He just stared at her for a long, charged moment. And then he reached for her duffel and slung it over his shoulder, ready to go.

13

THEY TOOK THE LONG WAY to Jackson Heights, walking to the F train at ass o'clock in the morning, her go bag in her hand and a duffel filled with clothes and other shit slung over his shoulder. It was full dark, with drones buzzing in the distance like wasps. They picked a nearly empty subway car toward the back, and Neha pretty much immediately dropped her boss superhero act, taking up two seats and half his lap.

"You manspreading now?" He laughed, tucking the backpack between his knees and laying one arm across the back of the beat-up red-and-orange plastic seats. So much security shit had gotten upgraded since 2016…but the MTA was still chugging along old school, put together with duct tape, spit, and prayers.

"You gonna stop me?" She mimicked his tone with surprising ease. He could almost believe she grew up down the street from him, dodging pimps and meth-heads.

"No, baby. You can spread for me anytime," he leered, reaching down to squeeze her thigh.

The jokes were easy. Even when everything in him hurt and he was constantly glancing around the train as it lurched up through Brooklyn and into Manhattan. Jesus, fuck, how did it all get to this place? And he knew that was a fucking laughable question. *He* got it to this place. With a licensed 9mm and a KA-BAR he bought at a trade show upstate.

Fucking a woman…fucking Neha…was about feeling everything. Skin and sweat and come and your heart pounding in your ears. Killing someone, at least for him and at least in the moment, involved feeling nothing at all except the rush. He'd taken out those six motherfuckers with an empty space in his chest and ice behind his eyes. And they weren't the first people he'd put in the ground. Just the first he did for personal reasons. For him and not for his country.

The lawyers thought the why mattered. They thought the why could get him a plea deal. The why didn't matter. And copping a plea was definitely off the table now. He'd be lucky if he made it to the end of the week without getting shot by the cops or the Russian mafia. Maybe cops who *were* Russian mafia. Wouldn't that just be fucking poetic?

Somewhere around Midtown, Neha sighed and turned her face into his neck. She wasn't asleep like he'd figured, just quiet. Thinking. Maybe thinking the same things as him. "I'm going to get you out of this," she said softly.

"I like sex and I like you. But more than that…? I want to help you. I want to keep you alive."

It was hilarious that she thought she could. And kinda fucking beautiful, too. He kissed the top of her head before he could think better of doing something so mushy. "And who's gonna get *you* out of it, huh?" She'd probably watched a lot of cop and lawyer shows growing up. *Ally McBeal* and *SVU* and all that shit. Where the case got solved in an hour and everybody hit the bar after to celebrate. That didn't happen in reality. Not his reality, anyway. "You're not gonna walk away clean, Doc. They'll get you, too. All because you came with me."

"I'm not scared of the legal consequences," she assured him, pulling back to scowl at him—or at least what passed for a scowl on a face too pretty for mean mugging. "They can hold me in contempt and disbar me, but they can't deport me or my family. We're all citizens."

Like that had ever stopped the government or the mob from disappearing people they wanted disappeared. Yeah, she'd definitely watched a lot of TV growing up. Like Kenny. You couldn't tear that kid away from his phone or his iPad. Always streaming some ridiculous escapist comic-book shit that had him thinking he was indestructible, too. He wasn't.

None of them were bulletproof.

The train started to fill up a little at Rockefeller Center. More people got on at Sixty-Third. Night shifters getting off the clock. People walking over from the 4, 5, and 6 trains. Neha rearranged herself, sat up. She'd put on some kind of Indian outfit before they left, soft but brightly colored. Her hair was braided. She looked sweet and… What was the word he was looking for…? *Wholesome.* Not like the woman he'd eye-fucked across a table almost a month ago.

He wasn't really sure this Neha 2.0 helped him look less suspicious. If anything, she made him look worse. A hulking thug with a ball cap tugged low over his eyes, wearing a suit with a generic radio-station T-shirt that he found in the back of a drawer. He looked like someone who beat his family on the regular. Or someone who kidnapped kids into his white van. Shit, maybe it wouldn't take a week for them to get caught. Maybe there would be a whole crew waiting for them when they got off at Seventy-Fourth Street in Queens. Guns blazing.

"You're tensing up." Now it was Neha's turn to squeeze *his* thigh. "Try not to brood so loudly, okay?"

He couldn't even argue with that. Instead, he turned in his seat, because looking at her was way better than looking in at himself. "Just what are we gonna do when we get where we're going? Call the ACLU?"

"I prefer the Southern Poverty Law Center myself," she said with a hefty dose of fake high-and-mighty. "But, no, 'we' are not going to do anything." She wagged her finger at him like his nonna used to do. Except it was a thousand times hotter coming from her. "*You* are going to lay low. Tomorrow, when things have cooled down a little, I might make a few calls and assess the situation."

She wasn't the only one who was going to be making calls. Or assessing things. Joe had work to do, too. Hail Mary passes to throw. Sure, he was on board with Neha's way for now…but he *had* to go after Aleksei Vasiliev eventually. Or it would never stop. Russian mafia would always be looking for him. And they'd probably go after everyone else he'd ever cared about. The Castellis. Mishelle. Neha. Vasiliev's people would dig up all the intel and pick them off one by one. So he had to hit them on their turf. Harder than he hit them before…but not without putting a few safety nets in place.

He'd had the digits in his head for years. One of his Apex brothers had passed the intel to him on their last night in Helmand. When they were outnumbered by a pride of Taliban shifters and hunkered down in the brush. Nothing like surprise lions to mess up your evening. "*By all reports, white lions are no longer native to the area,*" the fancy zoologist advising their unit had told them in the initial mission briefing. "*If there are insurgent groups of supernaturals, they should be foxes or Pallas cats.*" Yeah, that was a negative, Chief. Their team got incontrovertible—and indigestible—proof that night.

While they were regrouping, plastered against a rock wall, Drake had started giving out his last will and testaments. Just in case it all went FUBAR. He'd bequeathed Joe a phone number. "*These are the guys you call to unfuck things. You hear me? Word has it, they're like us.*" Like *us*. It could've meant anything. Military. Supe. Fucked in the head. Drake hadn't gotten the chance to elaborate because they had to go back out into the fray. Joe was now clinging to hope that it was all of the above. Enough to help him with this epic shitshow. To give him some backup or Neha a safe route out. And if it wasn't? Well, the lone-wolf narrative still fit him to a T. He'd take off. Promises to Neha or no.

She wanted to save him. Maybe the best thing he could do for her was save her from himself.

━━━━━━━━

Aishneet Auntie handed over the keys to her rental, some of her husband's clothes, and a Wi-Fi password without a single question. Comments about how Neha needed to stay out of the sun and perhaps lose a few pounds, sure, but no interrogation about why she needed to crash in the studio the couple rented out for extra income. Sikh generosity was truly a blessing. And though she'd long since given up on praying, Neha sent up a thank-you to Guru-ji as she collected Joe from the side of Auntie's house and they made their way to a tiny apartment above a kebab shop.

Neha's phone had started blowing up with texts while she and Joe were still at her place. Mom. Papa. Her brothers. She hadn't realized her parents were so up on their emoji game. She'd shot off vague reassuring replies that implied she'd been nowhere near the courthouse when the shooting began. What else could she say? She'd packed down *her* worry about *their* worry and focused on the immediate problems...and then she'd copied a few numbers into her burners and iPod Touch, powered down the smartphone, and shoved it in a drawer so she couldn't be tracked. In the bright light of day, Aishneet Auntie was her best shot of getting a real message to her frantic loved ones.

It had only taken a quick exchange in Punjabi to make her meaning clear. *Bas. Done.* Auntie Network activated. It would probably filter through two more aunties before someone rang her mom with a greeting of "*Sat sri akal!*" and gushed about how wonderful it was that Neha was off on a big business trip for her law firm and maybe she'd meet a nice man and settle down. Virtually untraceable by the feds *or* Vasiliev's goons. Maybe after all of this was over, she'd write a book: *A Desi's Guide to Going on the Run.* Item 1: Aunties get shit done.

It was early yet. The neighborhood was quiet. Metal barriers were still down over most of the storefronts, which had signs in English, Bengali, and Hindi advertising everything from gold jewelry to cell-phone plans to homemade sweets. Neha felt safer in neighborhoods like this than on the Upper East Side of Manhattan. No one here would follow her around a store to make sure she wasn't shoplifting or assume she couldn't afford the merchandise. Sure, she might get dinged on not speaking fluent Bengali, but that level of passive-aggression was something she was more than capable of handling. And she had an arsenal of Punjabi just waiting to be deployed.

"So, that was your aunt?" Joe wondered as she fit a key into the lock of the third-floor walk-up.

She had to laugh. "No. Just my auntie. One of Papa and Ma's friends from the gurdwara we used to go to when I was a kid. Indians call everyone 'uncle' and 'auntie' as a sign of respect—and it pretty much gives all your elders free rein to boss you around and harp on all your shortcomings." And to love you and care for you. She was lucky that way. There was a cross-country network she could count on if she and Joe *did* have to leave the state. "Never underestimate a desi auntie," she told Joe as they walked into the studio one after the other. "They're probably more connected than the Bratva or the Cosa Nostra."

A grin split his craggy face. "Reminds me of my old neighborhood. Everybody always in your business. My nonna's friends would be shouting from window to window if they saw me out smashing parking meters with the bigger boys, and I'd have the switch waiting for me by the time I got home." Neha couldn't check her flinch, or swallow the lump that suddenly rose in her throat. Joe dropped their bags, his hands coming up to cradle her cheeks. "Hey. Don't feel sorry for me. That kid *needed* his ass beat."

"Bullshit. No child deserves to be beaten." She covered his wrists with her fingers, barely able to circle them. "You deserved to be loved, Joe. To trust that you could come home and be safe."

"And then what? I would've turned out okay? I wouldn't have iced those fuckers?" He shook his head. "You know better than that. Plenty of kids get beat and *don't* become killers. And I saw guys with two parents, a dog, and a picket fence practically getting off on 'accidentally' shooting noncombatants in the 'Stan. My backstory doesn't change what I did, Doc. Don't try to make it my defense."

It was too late for that. Neha had built up every defense in the world for Joe Peluso. And she had none left for herself. "Joe…" she began, letting Aishneet Auntie's keys dig into the fleshy part of her palm. "Joe, you have to stop."

"Stop what?" He shook his head, kicking her duffel bag a few feet in, further from the door. "Believing I'm trash? 'Cause, babe, that ain't about to happen. Not now and not ever. I've earned every bit of the hell raining down on me right now. *You* haven't. You shouldn't be a part of this."

But she *was* a part of it. She'd chosen this. Chosen *him*. There was no going back.

14

IT WAS ASTONISHING HOW HER brother's mood could flip from elation to rage on a dime. Literally overnight. Yulia had come into Kamchatka for the morning shift and found it looking like a tornado had struck. Glass everywhere. Water and flowers scattered from the broken vases. The top-shelf liquors behind the bar all emptied, with the bottles broken. By all accounts—and the amount of new barware she was directed to order by the club's general manager—Peluso and the lawyer woman had vanished into thin air. Aleksei had not emerged from his office since his tirade.

Yulia wanted to cheer, wanted to throw cash into the secret betting pool that the Kamchatka servers and kitchen staff had going, but she knew better than to make her feelings on the subject public. Be seen and not heard. Tight skirts and even tighter lips. It was Yulia's job to play hostess, not just of the club but of her brother's entire enterprise. And should she fail in that endeavor... well, the Confessional could always fall victim to faulty wiring and go down in flames during happy hour, couldn't it? So tragic, how fragile these old Brooklyn buildings were.

Her brother excelled at casual threats, spoken over thick bowls of Austrian goulash, the extra syllables sopped up with crusty bread. Yulia wished he'd been there the day that Peluso shot up the dinner meeting. How much simpler her life would've been if Aleksei had been among those breathing their last in their borscht. But she couldn't subsist on such dreams, couldn't survive on those fantasies. So, she spent months drifting through the hallways of Kamchatka, a ghost in a sparkly dress and black eyeliner, catching cig breaks in the alley when she could, shifting into fur late at night to draw comfort from her braver beast. She haunted doorways, was the smoke slipping through keyholes—and she slowly fashioned herself as the specter of Aleksei's doom.

And now she was ready. She had no *choice* but to be ready. Her brother was vulnerable, behaving erratically, upsetting the men he answered to. There would not be a better time to put his downfall, and her own bid for freedom, into motion.

Yulia tucked into one corner of the kitchen storage room, dug her phone from the depths of her purse, and texted Danny five words.

Smoke break. Got a light?

———————————

Smoke break. Got a light?

It was the text Danny had been dreading and praying for at the same time. Proof of life. Contact. An opening into Vasiliev's organization. And Yulia putting herself in harm's way. *Fuck.*

For you? Always. Just tell me when.

He typed out the reply quickly and then put his smartphone down on the table, knowing he had to update the team regardless of his personal feelings. That was how Third Shift worked for the most part. Everything on the table. One hundred percent cooperative. Elijah and Jack had put together the organization with a single goal in mind—meting out justice outside strictly legal channels—and he'd joined up just a few years ago determined to do his part, to help in ways he couldn't while he wore a badge. He was one of the newer recruits to a twenty-member team—in the half that stayed stateside while others embedded themselves in Eastern Europe or South Asia or Brazil—and still earning his stripes. And now Yulia needed his help, was *asking for* his help. It was more than a stripe. More than on-the-job training. It was everything.

And as he finished explaining the implications of Yulia's message to Lije, Jack, and his fellow operatives around the conference table, he couldn't keep the worry from his voice. "She's giving us a direct route to her brother. But I don't want anything to happen to her."

"She's already *in* harm's way, bruv." Elijah, ever practical, glanced up from the dossier he was studying. Far from a normal 411, it had clips from the few grocery-rack gossip magazines that still existed, screenshots from Twitter and Instagram, and news stories pulled from Google Alerts. As if knowing what kind of nail polish Meghna Saunders favored and who she hung out with in the Hamptons might help him on his next op. Maybe they'd exchange fashion tips as Elijah tracked down whatever secret bioweapon her arms-dealer boyfriend was trying to sell.

"These women…" Danny's boss tapped the folder with two fingers. "They know they're up to their necks in it. They're not collateral damage standing on the sidewalk. Your girl grew up in a Bratva family. In a supernatural family. And this one…?" He looked back down at a photo of a beautiful South Asian woman with thick black hair and a full face of makeup. "No way she doesn't know her boyfriend's rotten to the core. But power's attractive. Addictive."

He had a point. Yulia had always been aware of her brother's criminal ties. She'd been as honest about them as she could when Danny admitted to being a badge. And she hadn't run far enough from the family before Vasiliev pulled her back in. But this was different. This was bigger. NYPD, the feds, Ukrainian and Russian gangsters, supernaturals…all converging on the same clusterfuck.

Plus the people in this room—so off the books that only a few high-level officials in strategic government positions knew what they did. Yulia didn't remotely know the scope of it all. And that could get her killed. Just like whatever Elijah had planned could get Meghna Saunders killed.

"They're still innocent," he pointed out. "They didn't ask for this."

"Yeah, well, we didn't ask for six dead Russians to fuck up our month and yet here we are." Trust Finn to make Joe Pesci's hits sound like a minor inconvenience. Up there with a 4 train going local instead of express. The Irishman rolled his eyes…and then immediately looked contrite. Presumably because of the icy look Grace shot him across the conference table. The cocky vampire wasn't afraid of sunlight or fire or garlic. Just Gracie's glare. And Danny couldn't blame him one bit. Dr. Grace Leung, their resident physician and all-around science wonk, was formidable. Biracial Black and Chinese, movie-star gorgeous, and a total badass. "Where do we go from here? What's our next move?" Finn asked, rubbing the back of his neck and fidgeting.

"We keep it small. Secure. Everyone in this room. Mack on transport. Joaquin on tech. No need to pull in more operatives. Elijah and I will be taking point on the situation, obviously, but we have our own projects in play, too." Jack gestured to the Saunders dossier. "We still have to focus on the bigger picture."

Elijah and Jackson had always been on the bigger picture, ever since putting the firm together in 2010—and that partnership was more than a little strange, considering how different they were. It was common knowledge in-house that they'd met after 9/11, around the time of the Iraq War. The rest of the whys and hows had been a mystery until recently—when they revealed the truth about their ties to the Apex Initiative. They still made for an odd couple in Danny's book. Lije was a brawler at heart, and not just because he was a shape-shifter. Former British Army, all Cockney accent and Premier League games on satellite. He played in a rugby league between ops and taught one term a year at a military academy just north of the city.

Jack was a sorcerer whose family magic went all the way back to the Salem witch trials. He had family money, too. He was whiter than white, as American as apple pie, and he dressed like a high-end model. With his commendation-laden military record and DoD ties, it wasn't hard to imagine him taking his initial Third Shift marching orders from POTUS himself. Something that was definitely not possible under the new administration, with the man who barely deserved the title of POTUS. Danny wasn't sure who dotted the *i*'s and crossed the *t*'s for Third Shift now, but it certainly wasn't anyone at the White House.

"So how do we proceed?" he asked as Jack's searchlight gaze swung around the conference table and landed on him.

"Go ahead and set up a meeting with Yulia Vasilieva," the sorcerer said sharply. "Keep her and her secrets safe. And yourself, too. Finn, I want you to see what Peluso's legal team knows. There's no way Neha Ahluwalia hasn't looped them in."

"I'd be delighted to pick Nate Feinberg's pretty little brain... and his pretty everything else." Finn flashed his fangs before leaning over to remind Gracie, "He looks like Anderson Cooper, you know." It was the verbal equivalent of yanking on her hair for attention. "Positively dreamy."

"I *do* know. You may have mentioned it five, six, or seven hundred times." The lone medical professional in their current group—a trauma surgeon, at that—Grace had nerves of steel. So, it was no wonder Finn couldn't rile her. She refused to give him an ounce of her jealousy and turned to Jack. "What about me? Am I just on hand to patch up the inevitable GSWs and claw marks?"

"Definitely not," he assured. "Right now, we need you on medical records. Access Peluso's records from Brooklyn Detention. See if we can match the pattern of his beatings to any of Vasiliev's

known associates. That might narrow down who they're sending after him. And check the redactions against what we have—
because the last thing we need is the city having access to classified
intel."

Danny tuned out the rest of the briefing. Rude, yes, but Yulia
was his bigger priority. The last time he'd seen her at her bar,
she'd been bone-thin, dark circles weighing down her pale-blue
eyes. *"I have to quit,"* she'd told him, worrying the dish towel she
used to wipe down the wells. *"Aleksei…he wants me to go back to
Kamchatka and work for him."*

He'd tried to talk her out of it. To no avail. And now she was
caught in the center of something that eclipsed them both. Her
brother's vendetta against Joe Peluso. And Third Shift's overar-
ching mission. After all, neutralizing and netting Vasiliev would
lead them one step closer to undoing the whole criminal network.
To nabbing the next person up the food chain. Mirko Aston was
allegedly a sorcerer and definitely hoarding a massive cache of
weapons that he sold to the highest, and most lethal, bidders.

Word on the street was that he'd secured his most valuable
weapon yet sometime in the last month. A biological agent of
some kind. It was anybody's guess as to where he would unload
that sucker—Russia, North Korea, ISIS, potentially their own
government—and 3S needed to get a bead on it before he could
broker a deal. Elijah had vowed to chase the leads to the ends of
the earth if necessary. Danny's missions were local, less with the
tactical assaults and more with the research and legwork, utilizing
his skills from years with the NYPD. Local…but never personal.
Not until now. And it terrified him.

Got a light? Yulia had texted him.

What if all he could give her was darkness?

15

HIS FIRST IMPRESSION OF NEHA as a damn Disney princess was right on the money. And he was the damn Disney villain. That had never been clearer. Joe flattened his palms on the tiny bathroom counter, like that would steady him or maybe lock him down. Like he was in an interrogation room with two-way glass instead of a mirror. He couldn't fucking breathe. No. That wasn't true. It was more like all he could breathe was her. Her skin and her hair and the salty tang of her pussy on his fingers and his tongue.

They'd gone for another round two seconds after walking into her little safe house. He couldn't help himself. He had to have her again. He'd crushed her up against him and stumbled with her to the bed at the end of the room and just gone at her like an animal. *Because you are one, remember?* He couldn't remember the last time he'd had sex three times in less than twenty-four hours. The last time he'd had sex at *all*. But Neha was a drug and he was addicted. He couldn't stop touching her. He couldn't stop wanting her. The creature under his skin, twisted into his blood and his soul, had her marked. *Mine*, it kept telling him. *Mate*, it kept insisting. And that was bullshit, because he had free will. He had *choice*. And he'd made the wrong one. Again.

Fuck. Fuck, he'd fucked this up so bad. Letting her come with him. Letting her come *on* him. All over his cock. *Letting. Ha.* Okay, so she'd encouraged it. Demanded it. 'Cause digging bits of grit out of her shredded palms after she got plowed in an alley by a criminal and a monster was apparently her idea of a good time. 'Cause this whole damn thing was apparently turning her crank. 'Cause she had no regrets and no questions and nowhere near enough sense to stay away from a man like him. 'Cause she'd made *her* choice.

Joe stared at his reflection. At hers as she walked up behind him. They couldn't have been more different. She was all golden and beautiful and perfect. He was a walking bruise. It was like somebody had locked a cheetah in with a retired circus bear... except that wasn't what they actually were, right? She was human. Completely human. And he'd been something else for years. Something so much worse.

"Why are you here?" The question came out raspy, like he needed to shave his voice along with three days of scruff. If he accidentally cut his damn throat in the process, it would be doing them both a favor.

"Why are *you* here?" she asked. She was bare-assed. Unselfconscious. And, hell, with her slammin' body, he couldn't blame her. He could only blame himself for staring. For forgetting to answer her question or prompt her for one to his. "You didn't have to come with me. You could've ditched me at any time. I have no power over you."

She had *every* power over him. And the worst one was her belief that he was decent. He could still see her face when he let slip about Nonna hitting him. So much sympathy. So much understanding. For someone who was a shrink *and* a lawyer, she was pretty fucking naive. And it gutted him. It scratched up his insides and shredded whatever was left of his heart and soul. The same way he'd scratched and shredded enemy combatants on his country's command. He was no hero. He didn't deserve her faith. He didn't deserve her beautiful body pressed up against his back. Her lips on his neck. Her sweet whisper of "Come back to bed."

But he took it all anyway. He clung to her as she walked him backward toward the queen-sized bed, now all nice and domestic with the flowered sheets she'd just put down. He hung on tight. Because he was greedy and selfish and he might die tomorrow. That was all this was. That was all it could be.

Neha had never seen Joe so naked, so vulnerable. And not just because he *was* naked. He was wrecked emotionally, shaken to the core. Like *she'd* somehow shaken him. This big, powerful brute of a man. She saw it in the set of his shoulders and his jaw as he followed her back to bed. She read it in his haunted gaze. "What is it?" she asked softly, even though she knew the answer. "What's got you so twisted up inside?"

"Do you feel the blood on my hands, baby? It's all over you now." He leaned back, slouching, a thumb across his lips, eyeing Neha like he'd left handprints across her breasts, her belly. Impressions of his meaty fists on her hips and thighs. "But maybe you like that, huh? Maybe that's what this is all about." He tried to sound disgusted with her, but the look in his eyes told her that the loathing was really aimed inward.

"No," she murmured, pushing aside the comfortable cotton sheets and climbing into the bed. The sheets were pristine. And there were no stains on her that she hadn't asked for. "You don't get to accuse me of slumming again. Not after yesterday. Not after last night." A stuck-up princess having a fling with a thug didn't jeopardize her career by leading him *away* from the courthouse and the cops. By bringing him home. "We're in this now," she told him as she leaned back against the headboard. There was a space next to her if he wanted it. And she hoped he wanted it. "You tied me to you the first time you kissed me. And I'm not walking away until you walk free."

A laugh burst out of his throat. Tired and cynical but still a laugh. "Ah, Doc. I ain't ever gonna be free," he said. But he joined her on the mattress, sinking to his knees in front of her. "You still shouldn't be here." It wasn't the first time he'd said it—and it probably wouldn't be the last—but it was the first time it really stung. "You should've let me go."

"So where should I be?" she asked, sitting up, letting the sheets pool around her hips. "Forgetting I met you? Going to the office every day? Filing motions? Drinking lattes and moving on?" There was no normal now. She'd accepted that the minute his lips touched hers. Apparently, he was still having problems adjusting. "You want me to just walk away? So you can go on some one-man mission against Aleksei Vasiliev? And you think I'm going to comply? What the fuck, Joe? What the *actual* fuck?"

He flinched, and she wondered how she'd ever thought his face blunt and brutish. Because his eyes were soft and his mouth was kiss-swollen and his broken nose against her clit had made her come harder than her favorite vibrator. Joe was not as cold as he pretended to be, not as cold as he *wanted* to be.

That was part of why she was still here. She couldn't really address the other part, the part where her feelings were getting involved. Not yet. So, she shoved it deep down inside, somewhere dark and protected behind the cage of her ribs. "I'm not leaving," she assured him as she climbed atop him, throwing one leg over his hip. The world's least believable cowgirl. But he didn't buck her off as she rolled a condom down over his length. Instead, his hands closed around her waist and he pulled her just the slightest bit forward. So he could nudge his cock into her. Inch by inch and then an easy slide home. "I'm not leaving," she said again on a gasp. "You can't make me. You told me that, remember?"

"So, what *can* I make you do, Doc?" he growled against her neck. "What power do I have?"

"The most important power." Her arms came up to cradle his head. She leaned into the piston motion of his cock, rising and falling with each snap of his hips against hers. "You can make me come."

A tormented groan tore from his throat. "You're damn right." And he swept her back with him, keeping her on top as he sprawled against the pillows. She'd demanded he do the work, but he let her set the pace…so she reveled in it, drawing out her pleasure and his. They fucked slow, without the frantic heat of their first few times together. Like they had all the time in the world and weren't racing a clock. Like lovers and not a lawyer facing disbarment and a shape-shifter on the run. He kissed her face, her throat, her breasts. He took handfuls of her hips and her ass and squeezed, urging her to go faster, to take him harder. Neha did. She took and took and took. This wasn't how she'd expected her life to be, but this was how it was playing out. Dirty, sweaty, sticky, unapologetic…and good. So fucking good.

Afterward, they flopped back onto the mattress, side by side, out of breath, connected by a strange, new intimacy that she couldn't define. Neha could safely say this was the closest she'd been to any man in the borough of her birth. All the other sex she'd had in her life had occurred in Brooklyn and Manhattan.

"That's right…" Joe turned onto his side, brows furrowing as she repeated this thought aloud. "You said you were a Queens girl, didn't you?"

"Woodside born and bred, baby." She laughed. "Does that surprise you?" Her parents had moved across the Hudson a few years ago, only after Papa retired from driving city cabs. He was a Lyft driver now, mostly for fun. At seventy-two, he'd had no desire to revisit the civil engineering he'd studied in India. And who could blame him?

"All we've got left are surprises," Joe pointed out, echoing her laugh with a rueful chuckle. "I don't even know what your favorite color is. You ain't got a clue that my first concert was the Boss."

He was right. Between the prison visits, the going on the lam and the marathon sex, they hadn't left a lot of room for small talk. They'd skipped the getting-to-know-you steps and gone straight to the serious part of a relationship, where counting on each other was a matter of life and death. Like they were in an action movie with a compressed timeline. Two days in their world was like two years.

"Think we passed each other on the 7 train and didn't know it?" he wondered.

"Probably." According to her quick mental calculations, Joe would have been in his twenties while she was in high school. Home between deployments. "I bet you manspread across three seats and little teenage me had to stand."

"Doc, I'd *always* have a seat for you," Joe said with an exaggerated leer, gesturing to his crotch.

Neha rolled her eyes at him. She'd had enough of that particular express train for one day, thank you very much. "It's funny, isn't it? How New York's such a giant small town. You cross paths with the same people over and over and don't even realize it."

"You ever grab a burger at Donovan's?" It spoke to Joe's level of cultural awareness that he followed that up with "I'm sorry, I don't even know if you eat meat."

Neha couldn't help herself. She echoed the same lewd gesture he'd made just seconds before. "Do *I* eat meat? What do you think?" Both Joe and his, er, *meat* reacted to the innuendo—the former with a barked laugh and the latter with a hopeful swell. Since she was temporarily vegetarian, at least until she regained her strength, she focused on his actual question. "You bet I've been to Donovan's. It's a requirement. Most famous burgers in the borough! Nothing beats the food in Queens. Thai, Chinese, Indian… but my friends and I mostly hung out at a pub on Skillman. Killer happy-hour martinis."

It was kind of absurd to be lying here talking about neighborhood hangouts. This wasn't normal. They weren't on a first date. Somewhere outside were a ton of people who wanted them dead. And in here…in here, Joe wasn't just a guy she could've run into at her local. He was a military operative, a genetically altered shapeshifter who'd absolutely killed more than just the six men she knew about.

And as if Joe realized it, too, he went quiet. "I still don't get it," he said after a while. "Why you're taking up for me. Why you're here. Why you even looked at me in the first place."

"Why do you need an explanation? We're *both* here. Mostly because someone took a shot at you. And *you* started this thing between us," she reminded. "I don't generally pick up men in lockup."

A tinge of red flushed his cheeks. "I don't usually pick up women in lockup," he assured her. "I know better than that. If there's one thing I learned from my nonna, it's how to mind women, how to treat them nice. Thanks to all the shit I got for running with the boys as a kid, I basically went the other way and only hung around girls until I left for boot camp."

"And that, ladies and gentlemen, is how Joe Peluso became the 'Pussy-Eating Champion of Aviation High.'" She cracked up. She couldn't fault his skills. He'd certainly picked the right vocation in vocational school.

Joe reached across the few inches between them and threaded his fingers through hers. "I'll be any kind of champion you need," he whispered. "I got you into this. I'll be damned if I don't get you out."

Huddled in the dark, cocooned away from the rest of the world, Neha could almost believe him.

16

TWO DAYS AGO, HE'D BEEN in the midst of a courthouse shooting. Now, today, Nate was fairly certain he was party to some elaborate spy game. What were the odds? To his credit, it didn't take long for him to realize he was being played. He couldn't say he minded. It was an impressive attempt. The man was stunning, like an actor or a model. Dark hair. Blue eyes. A pouty mouth that looked like it told dirty lies and fulfilled even filthier wishes. He was dressed head to toe in basic New Yorker black but somehow managed to make it look like a designer original from Planet Fuck Me. The whole presentation was masterful, but Nate couldn't quite figure out the man's angle. He wasn't media. Reporters were obvious in a different way. Predictable. People with a professional grudge... Well, they tended to be outright hostile. And while Nate was definitely being cruised, he was fairly sure that sex wasn't the priority. *A* priority—one he was receptive to—but not the main event.

"So." He took another sip from his G&T. "What is it that you want from me, Mr....?"

"I didn't say." The man was Irish, and the lilt in just three little words of deflection were charming as hell. He would be absurdly hard to crack on the witness stand. And, Nate imagined, a total firecracker in bed.

Too bad he didn't have time for this dance. Not with his most high-profile client still AWOL with his favorite associate, and a dozen state and federal agencies breathing down his neck. There was so much shit on the fan that the other partners at the firm wanted to nuke the house said fan was in and move on. But Nate Feinberg didn't abandon people. That was not how he worked. Not how he lived. Neha was going to need him, and Joe Peluso still deserved a defense.

That had to be it. This meet-cute at the corner of the bar was about *them*. Stranger things had happened than being shaken down by a mob henchman in the middle of a trendy Fort Greene wine bar. Hell, this was an average Tuesday in his world. "Whose payroll are you on?" he demanded. "The Russians? Ukrainians?"

The stranger laughed. Nate had been on the hookup scene for more years than he cared to count and didn't consider himself easy prey, but his boxer briefs felt distinctly singed by the sex of that sound. "I've been in bed with a few Russians in my time, but no. Not at the moment," the man assured him. He hadn't even touched the fancy cocktail the mixologist had placed before him ten minutes ago. "Let's just say I represent certain interested parties. And we've no issue with your client."

That was a new one. Even *Nate* had issues with his client. And he suddenly wished Dustin were there instead of nailing down the brass tacks on a bitter WASP divorce. It was amazing how much he missed his better half when they were working on separate projects. His better half. His wingman. His Wonder Twin. Though the legal community had far less complimentary terms. Ebony and Ivory. Black & White Cookie—sometimes just "Cookie" hissed across the aisle of a courtroom. There were worse things they got called, of course. Dustin took the obvious hits. For Nate, it took them a minute, but then they were ready with the slurs. Racism and anti-Semitism all shaken up in one disgusting cocktail of hate. It paired poorly with the apples and honey he'd had for Rosh Hashanah last month.

People also thought Nate was the brains and Dustin the brawn, but they were wrong. D was the tactician, carefully measuring every option and plotting out every strategy. Nate was the performer, the showman, and he did all the talking. The carnival barker prepping everyone for the show. He employed that skill now, toying with the swizzle stick in his drink and then pointing it like a conductor's baton. "If you have no issues, why are you here? I know I'm something of a local celebrity, but you must need something besides my admittedly wonderful company."

His new friend nodded before grinning in a way that needed to be illegal in all fifty states and U.S. territories. "Your company's the bonus," he practically purred. "But, yes, my associates and I simply want a bit of information. Have you heard from that wandering friend of yours? How's her vacation going?"

Danger, Will Robinson. It was in that moment that several things fell into place. The play. The players. The untouched drink. *Vampire.* It would explain the off-the-charts charisma. And the lack of issues with Peluso's actions. Nate settled back in his barstool, infinitely glad it provided back support, and gestured to the bearded barkeep for another gin and tonic. If he was dealing with a supernatural, he was going to need more fortification. "Who says she's sending me postcards?"

His caginess won him points. "You don't trust me yet. Good." Blue eyes darker than his own twinkled. "I was prepared to be underwhelmed, but what they say about you is true. You're good-looking *and* smart." The compliments were nice, but Nate still wasn't giving up any details on Neha's whereabouts...not that he had any as of yet. So, he just bided his time, waiting for his new drink and any incentive to keep engaging. It came in the form of a conspiratorial whisper. "How about a little round of 'I'll show you mine and you show me yours,' then?"

Nate knew better than to look down as the vampire rifled through a pocket. Moments later, a small white business card slid across the wood grain of the bar. *Finian Conlan* declared the tight black script. *Third Shift Security.* There was a stylized 3S in the upper-right corner and a 718 phone number across the bottom. Local. If Conlan was a PI, Nate would eat his nonexistent hat. And that name was probably an alias. But he pocketed the card anyway just in case.

Conlan took that as a good sign. His smile was radiant. Lethal. "You can ring that number any time," he assured Nate. "With any little bit of intel that strikes your fancy."

It was a very, very good thing that Nate had no bits of intel to deliver. Because at that particular moment, he was certain he'd willingly tell Finian everything he knew.

"Is this"—he waved his hand in a wide circle to indicate everything Conlan had going on—"a supernatural thing, or just *you*?"

If the smile had been radiant, the laugh that followed it was positively incandescent. "A little from Column A, a little from Column B, I'd wager."

Nate had no plans to wager anything. But he couldn't help but feel like he—and Dustin and Neha—still had everything to lose.

———————————

The back of the club is dark. Then again, so is the front. Nobody here gives a shit about ambiance. And he's glad. It lets him move through like a ghost, listening to the soft chatter, the deals being made and the threats, too. He's just another guy in black. Just another guy with the bulge of a piece under his jacket. Seen one, seen 'em all. They're so fucking blasé about all the bullies and beasts passing through that he stashed his sniper rifle out by the dumpsters with no problem whatsoever. He can't wrap his head around that kind of arrogance. He wraps his hand around his gun instead. Easing up on the back room, folding into the thick velvet curtain and peering out through a gap so he can assess the situation.

His Russian's not great. Slovak's even worse. But he can make out snippets, voices. Something about an important shipment. Enough to know they're distracted and won't know what hit 'em when he bursts out of the curtains. He has his piece out and trained before anyone clustered around the six-top can reach for their own weapons...but they do start to shift. Fuck. Who needs guns when you have teeth, right? Big bear motherfuckers, instinctively hulking out in their dinner jackets and coming for him in a blink. So he squeezes off four head shots in quick precision. Bam, bam, bam, bam. Four guys down just like that. He vaults across the table just as one goon rushes in from the front and starts to return fire, hitting the floor on the other side on a roll. The inhibitor chip may be doing its thing, but his reflexes ain't suffered a bit. His speed's optimal, too.

Fuckers don't even care about cover on the back door. It's clear for egress. For him to hightail it through and into the back parking lot. With a few seconds to himself, he pulls his serrated KA-BAR from its ankle sheath. Damn fine auxiliary weapon. Not so long ago, his auxiliaries would've been his teeth. His claws. He doesn't even need 'em with these assholes.

Fucking amateurs. No wonder Kenny and those girls died. Fury and disgust and adrenaline propel him toward the short fire escape up to the roof. From there, it's a fifteen-foot jump to the next building. He can make it with no problem and get the fuck out of here the same way he came in.

But then two more targets spill out from the club into the lot. Their guns are drawn. They're shouting. One sprouting feathers, the other conjuring some sort of energy ball. They're not going to let him go so easy.

Fuckers, he thinks again, before he springs into action.

Joe bolted upright still tasting the kickback. Still seeing the blood spatter from the bird shifter's slit throat. *Shit*. It'd been a while since he'd dreamed about that night—not since Neha had provided a whole new reel for his eyelids—but it hadn't quite gone away. It would *never* really go away. No matter how hard he tried to ignore it…or to claim he didn't regret it. And, fuck, he wasn't going to think about that. He *wasn't*. Because if those deaths weren't justified, then what right did he have to even *be* here, lying next to Neha, breathing in the sweet clean smell of her skin instead of gun oil and blood?

Hell. He had no right to be here at all. Especially when every second he stayed was putting her in more danger. He couldn't afford to keep dragging this out, to trust that lying low and waiting were going to take the heat off him. Maybe…just maybe…he needed to put the heat *on* and turn it up all the way. And there were a few things he had to do to make that trash fire happen.

Neha was still asleep—fucked into oblivion—when he slipped from the bed and grabbed a burner phone from her go bag. It took him three tries to key in the right number from memory, and he watched her the whole time. A mound under the sheets. Only her mass of dark hair visible. She was curled up tight. So vulnerable and small. The total opposite of the take-no-shit Amazon she was when she was awake. It made him hurt inside, and he rubbed the hollow spot beneath his sternum as the line connected and started to ring.

It was amazing that the number was even in service after all this time. The male voice on the other end didn't bother with a greeting or an ID. Just a "Yes?" Good thing Joe hadn't expected pleasantries. Hell, he hadn't expected much at all. He could still hear Drake, though. So confident as he passed him the slip of paper with the usual warning to memorize the intel and then flush it or eat it. *"You ever get into a jam or need an off-book gig, these are your guys. Mostly supes. Like us. They'll unfuck shit. No questions asked."*

"I hear you help unfuck things" was all he said to the mystery supe's single, terse word.

"We offer many services. Unfucking falls under the very large umbrella." The guy's tone didn't change, but Joe could tell he wanted to laugh. It was weirdly reassuring. He had a pulse. He was more than a random voice in the void.

They barely exchanged ten sentences after that, but they were significant ones. The bare bones of the situation. A pickup spot. Another phone number. When Joe was done, he deleted the call from the log and put the phone back where he found it. Instinct, he told himself. Not a deliberate decision to keep Neha out of the loop for now.

But if it *was* deliberate, so what? This gorgeous woman had put herself in enough danger for him already. Didn't he owe it to her to keep her safe and shielded from whatever he could? Fuck. He was such a fucking piece of trash. He didn't deserve to slide back into bed with her, didn't deserve to pull her back against his chest, but he did it anyway. Because he'd already accepted that he was just that selfish.

He'd always looked after his own needs first. As a kid, with his nonna, it was a matter of survival. But after that...? Maybe if he'd been any kind of a good man, Kenny would've followed in his footsteps and enlisted instead of tending bar at some shitty mob-backed dive a whole-ass borough away from where they grew up. This was all on him. Every last bit of it. Every drop of blood spilled. Every tear Neha would stubbornly blink back after he was dead and gone. Joe had done this. Maybe the people on the other end of the call could fix it. Maybe they couldn't. But they were insurance. For *her*. To get his girl out of this alive.

His girl. Now *that* was a real joke. Like he was writing home to a sweetheart while deployed. Except he never had written to Mishelle, had he? She'd broken it off when he was in Kandahar and married some Irish kid who could give her more than fast hard fucks while on leave. Neha would find someone like that, too. She'd put this whole mess behind her, go back to her nice little family and her Sikh temple and her battles for the underdog.

It was a nice story. Neat. A happy ending. Joe hated it. And he muffled a groan against her hair. There was no part of him that wanted to give her up. Especially not his dick, which was hard as steel against the curve of her ass.

"Joe…?" She drowsily nestled into him, into his cock. "Is everything okay…?"

"Shhh…it's fine, babe," he said. "It's all okay for now."

"That's not what your penis is telling me." Her laugh was a more woken-up one. And the way her hips moved was its own message.

"My penis needs to shut up," he said, pressing a gentle kiss to the back of her neck. "'Cause we could both use the rest."

She was always so hot for him. So in tune with him. Like some higher being had made them perfect for each other. But even just holding her like this, splaying his palm across her belly as he played big spoon to her little one…it was more than he ever thought he could have. It was the closest he'd ever felt to a religion, to any god. It didn't make sense to be falling for her so hard and so fast, but he couldn't stop. Like he was destined to from the minute they met.

You started this thing between us…

Yeah. He'd eye-fucked her good that first day. Imprinted on her like a kinky duckling. Flagged her as *his*. And it was all going to end soon enough…but, until then, he was going to savor this. He was going to drown in her for as long as he could. And maybe, just maybe, he'd break the surface and come out washed clean.

17

"I HEAR YOU HELP UNFUCK things..."

She'd heard snatches of the strange conversation. Sure, Joe had fucked her insensate before and after, but Neha had always been a light sleeper. Couple that with a very tiny apartment in a prewar building where everything echoed and...yeah, secrecy was a concept, not a given. She waited for Joe to address the phone call the next morning. She got cleaned up, changed into another set of Indian clothes, and waited. To no avail.

Joe was a vault, locked up tight, as they navigated the oddities of sudden and forced domesticity. They couldn't hide out indoors indefinitely. Not with an empty fridge and limited supplies. And Neha was fairly certain she needed to buy stock in cranberry juice after the amount of sex they'd had. Some sort of chafing balm for her thighs, too. A quick check via the basic web browsers on her devices revealed that there was an APB out for Joe already, and constant news bulletins coming through on social media about the courthouse hit. No casualties besides the one guard, thank goodness—not that it was much of a bright spot. One death was a death too many, even if the guy had likely been on the take.

And Joe may not have pulled the trigger, but the blame was

falling squarely on his shoulders. Making his capture even more of a priority. They'd have to move on soon, find him another place in the five boroughs to hunker down while she snuck back into Manhattan to work out his legal problems—but, in the meantime, Neha knew that Joe had to blend in.

"Doc…I ain't so sure about this."

The borrowed kurta was too tight across his shoulders. Aishneet Auntie's husband, Saravpal Uncle, wasn't built like a dock worker. It was a miracle the shirt fit at all. But Neha fiddled with the plain brown shawl, pulling it across Joe's wide torso like a Highlander's tartan, until he looked as he should. Olive-skinned, of indeterminate ethnicity, vaguely threatening and more than vaguely brooding. If he kept his mouth shut, it was entirely possible they could pull off this ridiculous charade for another day or two.

"I feel like I'm in fucking pajamas," he grumbled, while she finished poking and prodding and double-tying the drawstring of his cotton pants.

"You *are* in fucking pajamas. The word came from India," she pointed out. "And if anyone asks, you're my cousin from Punjab. Fresh off the boat. No English."

"Babe, no one's going to believe we're cousins." The way he looked at her then, all bedroom eyes and filthy promises, certainly ensured his words. They were more like kissing cousins. Okay, cousins who fucked against brick walls. But it was no less ridiculous than anything else they'd already been through. A lawyer and a shape-shifting vigilante who was awaiting trial on the run together from the Russian mob? Who would believe that outside of a Hollywood producer?

"Fine," she snapped. "You can be my fiancé. Arranged. A nice, healthy Punjabi farm boy who does whatever I say."

He laughed, the sound more genuine now than it ever was while he was behind bars. "No one's gonna believe that either. And not just because I'm as white as fuck. You really think you can push me around, Doc? On what planet?"

It was funny that he tried to posture, to pretend he was some kind of alpha male dick, when they both knew he *did* listen to her. More than that, he listened to what she *didn't* say. What her body told him. What her soul screamed out for. This was a man who valued her input, her opinion, her pleasure. And just thinking about that made her breath catch, her limbs go languid. She was turned on as hell, and she wished she could tear off the trappings of desi disguise that she just painstakingly put him into. She wanted to bite all the places she hadn't yet discovered. Mark them all as hers like he'd marked her.

He felt it, too, of course. They'd only known each other a short time, but he was already able to sense when she needed him inside her, when the craving for sex and connection was too much to control. Maybe he sensed more than that. Like how they were in too deep, too fast. Like how she needed *more* than his dick; she needed his brain and his heart as well. She needed all of him. She wanted all of him. "Why push you around when I can pull you toward me?"

His eyes went heavy-lidded; his tongue flicked across his lower lip. He huskily warned her, "Doc..." before he grabbed the pallu draped over her shoulder and tugged her close. Despite all the complicated folds and tucks, saris were easy-access outfits. One piece of continuous cloth that could come off with a few quick motions. But Joe didn't undo her work. Instead, he slid his wide palm around her bare midriff, claiming the skin there. He leaned his forehead against hers, breathed her in. They stood like that for a dozen heartbeats. His fingertips stroked the base of her spine, dipped beneath the border of her petticoat to the cleft of her ass. She was in disguise, too. Undercover as a Hindu. Not that he would know that Sikh women didn't generally wear saris. And, in this moment, telling him wasn't high on her priority list.

"Doc," he whispered again, lips feathering across her forehead, her temple, her jaw. "Ain't no one gonna buy that a woman like you would marry a thug like me. There's only one thing I'm good for." The words were as cruel to him as his touch was gentle to her. "Everybody out there's gonna take one look at us and know that my dick's been inside you. You can only be in it for the ride."

She wasn't naive. What he was saying had a ring of truth to it. On paper, there was nothing about them that worked—he was white, she was Punjabi; he was a shifter, she was a human—but that didn't make it any less hurtful. To her. To him. To everything they'd just experienced over the last few days. And she would never let a friend say such a terrible thing about themselves. From someone she'd been to bed with, the sentiment was even more unacceptable.

"It's a hell of a ride, Joe. But it's *not* the only thing I need you for." She slipped her hands into his hair, gripped the short, bristly strands. "We can make this work. We *have* to make this work. To keep you safe from whatever they're blasting out on the news wires. And if that means I have to pretend I dragged you to a gurdwara and traded vows with you to make it believable, I will."

She would never *really* take Joe to a gurdwara. No. After the 2012 massacre in Oak Creek, she couldn't even conceive of bringing the threat of violence into a place of peace. Yes, they would gladly offer shelter…but all Neha had to offer in return was death. She valued her family's faith—and basic common sense—enough to know that the option was totally off the table. And she valued Joe, too.

He was quiet for a long time. Kissing her. Touching her. Having an entire conversation in silence. And then he spoke against her lips. Muffled. Gruff. "Neha, I'll make a vow to you right now: I will do anything to keep *you* safe."

"Neha, I'll make a vow to you right now: I will do anything to keep you safe."

His words rang through his mind while they made their first trip outside since getting to Queens, ducking drones as best they could. Or at least Neha was ducking drones. Maybe he wasn't so careful. Maybe he lingered a little when they split up for a bit to pick up basic supplies for a few days in hiding. Maybe he was a little late meeting back up to grab some bomb-ass Indian food. Because the whole time, the vow echoed. Along with the battle cry of his plan: *Come and get me, you motherfuckers.* He'd put the first part into motion last night, with that phone call. Now he had to play out the rest. No matter how much it sucked, how much it hurt. How risky it was. He had it all hammered out by the time they made it back to base. Back to their little sex oasis. *Fuck*, he didn't want to leave it. It was the most peace he'd had, the happiest he'd been in…ever. But he had free will, he had choices, and he knew what choice he had to make next.

"What are you planning to do with all of that?" Neha's face paled when she saw him take everything out of his bags and start to arrange it for immediate use. Scalpel. Forceps. Disinfectant. Bandages. Medical tape. A fifth of whiskey. A thick rawhide chew from the janky pet store off Thirty-Seventh Avenue. He'd grabbed that last thing while she was in an Indian clothing shop a few storefronts over. He didn't blame her one bit for being weirded out.

He whipped her uncle's shirt over his head. Stepped out of the soft white pants, too. "It's not me who's gonna do it, babe. My hands won't be steady enough. I need *you* to take out the implant. My werewolf collar's gotta go. I can't *not*-shift right now. We need me at full capacity in case everything goes sideways."

He gave her massive credit for not immediately turning tail and running the hell out the front door. For just laughing a little and rubbing nervously at her throat. "Joe, I hate to shatter stereotypes here, but being Indian doesn't mean I'm a doctor. Not *that* kind of doctor, anyway."

"You got into my head just fine," he reminded her. "So, I can probably trust you to cut into my thigh."

"That makes one of us. Because *I* don't trust me at all." Neha shuddered, looking a little green around the gills at the prospect. "What if I nick your femoral artery? There is no way we could stop a bleed like that."

"You know where the femoral artery is?" He scoffed as he finished getting ready for their impromptu game of Operation. "That already puts you ahead of most of the guys I served with."

"No." Neha was still pale. Still shaking her head. She was not into any of this at all...and he needed to get her on board ASAP. "I've watched a lot of *Grey's Anatomy*. That doesn't make me an expert. And definitely not an expert in supernatural physiology."

"Could've fooled me." Joe grinned, gesturing not so subtly down to the bulge in his shorts and winking at her. "But I'd switch to some of those vampire soaps, if I were you. And read some urban fantasy. Then you'd know that shifter healing ability should kick in the minute you get that thing out of me. It'll slow any bleeding. Anything that doesn't heal right away will get taken care of while I sleep."

Her eyes lit up. The change of topic obviously fascinated her—and, even better, distracted her from her nerves. "*You* read urban fantasy?"

"Uh-huh. Urban fantasy, thrillers, paranormal romance." He was almost kind of offended by her surprise, except he got it. No one looked at him and saw the guy hunched on his bunk, squinting in the dark, tearing through books to get his mind off all of the shit in the world. They just saw his ugly mug and his fists and figured that fighting was all he was good for. The U.S. government sure as shit had that impression, and he'd let them fly with it for twenty years. But he didn't need to rehash any of that right now. No, he just needed to get Neha to relax enough to play doctor.

"Here's the real kicker: I've seen all the Twilight movies," he told her. "Wasn't much to do in those first weeks at Apex while they were doing all their sciencey shit. They thought it'd be a stress-reliever to 'educate' us through books and movies. Made us watch a ton of movies while they were poking and prodding and assessing. Most of us ended up Team Jacob, 'cause I don't know if you know this, but vampires are *assholes*."

She laughed at that. "I can't say that I've ever had the pleasure of meeting one. At least not that I know of." Her voice was still wobbly. No sign of the ballsy broad who'd strutted into Brooklyn Detention with "fuck you" in her eyes. But she was getting on board with him now, for better or worse. She took a breath, ruefully shook her head. "The supernaturals I *have* encountered were born, not made. Families living quietly in plain sight for generations. And none of them prepared me for you."

"I know, babe. And I'm sorry." Nothing could've prepared him for this either. For today. For now. For *her*. "Just tell me: Are you prepared for this? Can you do this for me?"

She answered by shimmying out of her pretty Indian clothes and slipping on the T-shirt he'd worn yesterday. Then she grabbed a bunch of towels from the linen closet and layered them on the bed before putting down a trash bag from the kitchen cabinet for good measure. And she added the first-aid kit from her go bag to his pile of supplies. *Atta girl.*

He'd undergone—and performed—worse field surgeries. She probably wouldn't find that reassuring, so he kept it to himself as he settled onto their makeshift operating table with the chew toy.

"No belt? Maybe a stick?" She made a face, slapping on latex gloves from her kit.

He'd had worse things shoved in his mouth, but he wasn't about to tell her that either. "My bite could get pretty bad—especially if I start shifting," he explained instead. "I'd probably snap a stick in half. And why ruin a good belt? A canine chew toy is a safer bet."

She wrinkled her nose, obviously still grossed out by the idea, but totally willing to roll with whatever. In for a penny, in for a pound and all of that. "Keep this up, and we'll have to get you a leash and a collar."

He waggled his eyebrows. "You say that like it's a bad thing."

The kinky joke worked. She laughed again, some of the tension draining from her features as she lined up all the supplies on the nightstand. She looked at the last item with suspicion. "Is the whiskey for you or for me? 'Cause I have to tell you, Joe, I'm not sure getting me drunk is going to help this procedure."

"It's for both of us. After."

After. Felt like eight hours instead of what was probably twenty minutes. He talked her through where to cut. How deep to go. And then he gagged himself. The rest of it was a blur of pain. Of her swearing and apologizing for hurting him. Of her soft hands on his skin, balancing out the bite of the scalpel. When she started to dig out the inhibitor, the blur turned sharp. Everything slipped into focus. Her huge, dark, wet eyes. The smell of her fear.

Fur rippled across his skin. His mouth filled with teeth, and he tasted rawhide and blood. He started to turn. He couldn't stop. He didn't want to. He thrashed against the mattress, back bowing.

"Joe!" It was a whip-crack command befitting a military commander. Cutting right through the haze, the frenzy, the beast wanting to run free. "Joe, you have to let me work. It's not all the way out, and I won't be able to find it if you change. Stay with me."

Stay. Stay with her. That was all he wanted. All he'd ever want. His woman. His mate. Safe. Joe clung to it like a rope, pulled himself back along the tether. He held on as tight as he could...until everything, mercifully, went black.

18

JOE STAYED PASSED OUT FOR hours. Dead to the world…but not dead to her. The steady rise and fall of his chest assured her that he was more or less okay. Neha eventually paused her bed-side vigil to clean up the surgical tools, toss the bloodied bandages and garbage bag, and steady her nerves with a strong cup of chai. Aishneet Auntie hadn't stocked the tenant-less apartment with much, and the kitchenette was minuscule, but you could always count on a desi auntie to keep some tea on hand for emergencies. After two doses of cultural curative, she felt more or less grounded again. As grounded as she could be, given the circumstances. Circumstances *so* wildly out of her control.

She wanted to call someone. Anyone. Everyone. Tejal, or her mom, or Nate. Someone who could serve as a touchstone, bring her back to reality, ground her in what was important. *You know what's important. Staying alive is important. Joe is important.* The inner voices that had been steering her—in directions both right and wrong—kept her hands off her burner phone and safely knot-ted in her lap until Joe finally began to stir.

"Doc?" The word was a low rumble. His eyes seemed to gleam in the darkened room.

She leaned forward in the chair she'd dragged over to his bed-side. "I'm here. You're here, too. Guess all the *Grey's Anatomy* binges did their job after all."

"Glad to hear it." He winced, rising halfway and leaning against the headboard. "I knew you'd get it done."

Like she'd said to him earlier, that made exactly one of them who'd believed in her abilities. And it still baffled her that he'd had to even ask her for help. "Why didn't you do this long before now? You could've gotten anybody to take the implant out for you at any time, right? Why wait?" *Why use guns on those Russian thugs instead of claws and teeth?* Wasn't that fundamental question what had led to him getting a second opportunity at trial?

"Nah. Wasn't that simple." Joe shook his head and slowly swung his legs over the side of the bed, bracing his palms on the mattress. "I was trying to behave myself. Trying to stay out of trouble. As a condition of my military discharge and my deactivation from the Apex Initiative. Can't really have supercharged supes running around unchained, can they?" he pointed out. "So, they inhibit us and LoJack us. Do periodic check-ins like we're on parole. Wouldn't be surprised if they're tracking me right now and just keeping out of it until I really fuck things up."

Neha could almost feel her eyebrows climbing into her hair-line. "Getting arrested for multiple homicides and making a scene at trial doesn't count as a fuckup?"

Joe met her disbelief with a shrug. "I didn't break my NDA for anybody but you. As far as anybody knows, I'm just a lone gunman, a loose cannon. If I take their secrets to my grave, we're square."

He'd broken so much more than his nondisclosure agreement for her. She couldn't fathom it. And now? Now, he'd changed the game entirely. "They'll have to know you took the chip out. Won't they come after you?"

"Add 'em to the list." His eyes twinkled with dark humor. "The Russian mob, the cops, the feds... Might as well throw in Apex, too."

Neha shook her head, wrapping her arms around herself as if that could ward off shivers that had nothing to do with feeling cold. "You have a death wish or what?"

"No." Joe chuckled like he didn't quite believe his negative reply. And then he looked up at her, his gaze searching and seeking and searing her to the bone. "All I've ever done is survive. And since I met you, the only wish I've got is to *live*."

She was no stranger to romantic declarations. Had heard plenty of platitudes from all kinds of men. Joe Peluso, with his gruff voice and blunt Queens accent, put them all to shame. She didn't know what to say in response. So, she didn't say anything. She just scrambled out of her chair and into his lap and pressed her lips to his.

His mouth opened beneath hers, wet and hungry. She could taste the growl building at the back of his throat. His bare arms tightened under her grasping hands…and bristled. Stiff hairs brushed her palms. The musky scent of animal rose from his hot skin. Not unpleasant. Just…different. Like a wine description at an upscale bar. He was earthy, rich, smoky. Like the forest floor. She'd always wondered who went around licking the forest floor in order to make such a comparison…and, as her tongue tangled with his, she completely understood the compulsion.

"Doc…" Breathing raggedly, he moaned the endearment—because that's what it was; it had long since stopped being just her title. "It's been too long. Too fucking long. You ready for a show?"

Was she ready for the truth of him? For as much as he'd already shown her, and what she'd glimpsed while extracting the inhibitor, this was a different kind of intimacy. This was his choice. This was hers. Seeing the mouth that had been between her legs turn to muzzle. Watching the fingers that had stroked into her become claws. What if it was too much? What if it was terrible and horrible and gross?

Neha didn't hesitate a second longer. "Yes," she said against his jaw, which was already shaded with several days' growth of beard. "I'm ready. Show me who you are."

"Okay. *Okay*." The repetition of the word, exhaled in a huff, was like permission granted. The last bit of tape ripping away from his control. He gently set her aside, letting her claim his spot on the mattress, and then stumbled backward into the studio's open area, every inch of his body exposed to her gaze.

She would never get tired of seeing him naked. His powerful, work-hewn form stole her breath. But watching it contort— watching him change—was something else entirely. A theft of not just her air but her reality, her perception, her understanding of the universe.

His back bowed like it had while she was working on him. Then his bones cracked. Nails elongated. Hands became paws. Hair became fur. She tried to avert her eyes from his cock, but she was human and woman and curious. Fascinated by how his genitals drew up and morphed.

Something like a laugh escaped Joe's vocal cords. And what sounded like "You're killin' me, Doc."

"You'd look, too!" she pointed out as her cheeks heated with embarrassment.

His reply was a defensive bark. Because, all of a sudden, what stood before her was a massive four-legged beast that could barely be called a wolf. Five feet at the shoulder. Sleek black coat and amber-gold eyes. It would've been strange to see Joe's very human chocolate-brown eyes looking back at her out of this face, she realized. More disturbing than his overall transformation into this ginormous canine creature. He was likely triple human Joe's fighting weight. One lash of his tail could probably take out an opponent.

His tail. Neha giggled. She couldn't help herself. Chalk it up to stress-induced hysteria. But the man she'd gotten to know over the past few weeks had a tail, and he was roughly the size of a pony, and what exactly was she supposed to do with that? "Nice doggy?" she offered, as the laughter drove her back against the bed.

Joe woofed softly, showing his teeth in what would probably be an expression of aggression in a real wolf but was clearly just an exasperated smile from him. He stalked forward, the ripple and shift of his muscles mesmerizing, silencing the last of her mirth.

She wasn't afraid. She'd never been afraid of him.

"*Nicest* doggy," she said this time. "You are *such* a good boy."

Joe gave her a toothy grin—a very bad boy's grin—and then his body began to bend and break with transformation once more.

―――――――――――――――

He'd never shown anyone outside his unit the change before. Or the change back. When it was all said and done, he was standing there before her shivering and sweating like a motherfucker. He felt...*small*. Like being human again had diminished him somehow. And his brains were rattled. Half-wolf, half-human. The thoughts still coming in bursts. Mostly in English, partially in instinct. Instincts that told him it was all different now. That he was back at square one...that place where he was nothing and she was everything. *She's not for you, buddy. She's never going to be for you.*

"Joe? Are you okay?" The smile she had on her face was gone. No more "nice doggy" for him. "Is everything alright?"

No. No, it wasn't alright. It wasn't okay. None of this was okay. "Do you still want me? Knowing what I really am? Seeing it?"

Neha looked at him with her heart in her eyes. *Yeah. Fuck.* Here he was, Joe Peluso, fearless special operative, shape-shifter, ruthless executioner of mafia thugs, terrified of rejection. After everything they'd already been through.

"I kissed you in the courthouse knowing what you really are," she reminded him. "I took you into my body knowing you took lives. Eyes wide open. What makes you think *this* is the deal breaker?"

She moved toward him slowly, palms out, like he was still the wary wolf. "Your fur is beautiful, Joe. Seeing you shift into it doesn't make it ugly. And I don't want you any less than I did before." She took one of his hands in both of hers, brought it to her face and nuzzled into his palm. "I still want you to touch me. I still want you to kiss me. And I still want you to fu—"

He cut her off then. With a growl and the hot press of his mouth on hers. The kiss was fierce but gentle. Claiming but exploring. He brought her fully against him, cradling her cheek with one hand and her hip with the other, encircling her in the cage of his arms and the wall of his chest. A better prison cell than Kings County could ever offer.

"Doc. Jesus, Doc, I don't deserve you," he whispered into her lips.

"Then become the man who does."

19

ALMOST THREE DAYS WENT BY before Yulia and Danny could meet in person. Seventy-two of the longest hours of Yulia's life. Seventy-two hours that she spent either hiding from Aleksei's rages or bearing witness to them. Or tossing and turning with fantasies that she dared not make reality. *Shifting to her purest form and tearing out her brother's throat. Stripping to her skin and pressing her lips to Danny's.*

And then she took the F train just long enough to shake one of her brother's hired spies before transferring to the G all the way out to Williamsburg, to a hipster whiskey joint where they paired every shot with a kind of grilled cheese. Just another girl with dirty-blond hair, too much makeup, and her yoga mat hooked below the bar. Nothing to see here. Danny, however, stood out in any crowd, even though he wore the Brooklyn uniform of flannel shirt and beanie cap. He was clean-shaven, golden skinned, and stunningly handsome. *"You should model,"* she'd blurted out the first time he came into the Confessional. *"NYPD Hunk of the Month calendar, Mr. October,"* he'd said without skipping a beat.

Her heart skipped at least two when he walked toward her. Because it felt like it'd been years, not months, that they'd been apart. And a very significant part of her just wanted to fall into his arms and sob. Silly. She'd never sobbed a day in her life. She could not start now. But she did lean in for the obligatory hug and air kiss, breathing him in as her lips barely brushed his cheek. This was what safety tasted and smelled like, she thought. Crisp, clean, and a hint of soap.

"Yulia." His hands came down on her shoulders, and his dark eyes were stern as he stopped her from pulling away. "Are you okay?"

No. Yes. How to answer such a loaded question? Instead she turned and ordered a shot of Buffalo Trace, neat, from the harried man behind the bar. Danny followed her lead, even though he must have been on duty—there was the telltale lump of his badge on a chain beneath his shirt—and asked for an old-fashioned with Bulleit rye.

It was like they were on a date. A very awkward first date. With the topics of murder and mafia and betrayal between them. It was never silk. It was never skin. She'd never fucked this man, only fucked him over by involving him in her problems. Yulia prayed she wouldn't do the latter again. At least not until she had a chance to do the former. It was silly, now that she thought about it, for them to have waited. Played such tame and tender games of flirtation instead of taking what they wanted that first night, or the second, or the third. He could've gone home with her then. He could not go home with her now.

They spent a half hour making idle chatter and finishing their drinks. Yulia perched on the edge of a stool. Danny stood angled toward her, one elbow resting on the wood grain of the bar. For a short time, the fiction of the date worked. His eyes twinkled. She joked about the classes she was no longer taking, the dog she left with a roommate in Windsor Terrace. He swept up her yoga mat on their way out, slinging it over his shoulder as though he did so every day. And she told him the truth like she did so every day.

"Things are out of control, Danny. I need your help."

He slipped his hand into hers and squeezed. "I'm listening."

As he walked her back toward the G train, she told him every-thing she knew. About Aleksei's rage. About the man he'd hosted in the Pit. About the person he took orders from on the phone. They didn't speak for long after her revelations, didn't dare linger…but she didn't want to let go of his hand, of the sense of being steadied and protected by the simple press of his fingers. How much safer would she feel under the press of his lips? It was reckless, utterly irrational, to wish for that, to lean in for that in public. Where anyone could see and report back to Aleksei. Yulia was so tired of being smart.

She pulled him aside and in toward her, just a few steps from the subway. Under the shade of a bodega awning. Years of long-ing, of wondering, of denying…she molded them into one stolen moment. Licking the hints of whiskey and sugar from his full bottom lip.

"Yulia…" He groaned her name quietly, as if chiding her for the epically bad idea. But he also pulled her closer, hand to hip, mouth to mouth, kissing her back with heat and tenderness. *Yes.* This would sustain her in the days ahead. It *had* to.

It was over too quickly, practicality forcing them apart once more. Leaving her with a gossamer memory to stow in the vault, like all of the precious things in her life. "It's okay," he whispered once they reached the top of the station stairs. "You did the right thing. And I'll keep you safe."

Oh, Danny, she thought, as she took one last look at him. His face, his hands, his silly hipster hat. It was not her own safety she worried over but the safety of everyone else. The men her brother hated. The girls who waited tables at Kamchatka and the boys who worked in the kitchens and tended bar. The city at large. Anyone who got in Aleksei's way.

Her phone rattled in her bag a mere three stops from Williamsburg.

Just once. A text message, courtesy of the MTA's unreliable Wi-Fi. She unearthed the mobile, balancing her yoga mat and trying not to hit the person in the seat next to her. And then she swiped to the message, and the bourbon she'd consumed with Danny sloshed sickly in her stomach. The smartphone felt cold and slippery in her palm. Come to work. Now. Aleksei. As if he'd sensed her fears, known she'd set out to thwart and betray him.

No. No, she could not let him learn what she'd done. Or what else she might do.

The club was practically dead when she stepped through its doors some thirty minutes later. She'd wanted nothing more than to go directly home to the one-bedroom she leased in her uncle Stanislav's house. Go home, and then cradle Danny's words close to her chest as she slept. But the sharp text from Aleksei had forced her to detour. There were only a few people on the main floor, picking at appetizers and drinking martinis. A handful more in the VIP area. It was after eight, prime drinking hour on a Thursday, and she'd specifically asked Ana to cover her shift because it would be too busy for one of the waitresses to balance hostessing along with her tables. But it wasn't busy at all. *Strange.* Stranger still was the chill of the staff hallways, and the hair on the back of her neck prickled with awareness just as goose bumps broke out on her arms. Something was *wrong*.

Admittedly, something was *always* wrong at her brother's place of business, but this was different. Specific. Before Yulia could even process that it was specific to *her*, affirm that his text message had triggered the correct instincts, it was too late. She was in front of Aleksei's open office door and facing the gleaming muzzle of his gun.

"Did you enjoy your date, rybka?"

How appropriate that he called her "little fish," trapped as she was in his precious nightclub like it was a barrel. So easy to shoot. Had it only been an hour ago that she was safe by Danny's side? It seemed like lifetimes now, as the man before her—the man she'd always known to be cruel and humorless—flipped his weapon around and around like it was nothing more than a quarter dancing on his knuckles.

"Well?" he prodded. "Nothing to report, sister mine?"

Yulia's hands clenched and unclenched around the strap of her purse. Air trapped itself between her throat and her lungs. She couldn't give up Danny so easily. All her risks would be in vain. She did the only thing she could in that moment. She donned a shaky smile and prepared to show her most important customer the best table in the house. Aleksei wanted the truth. What he'd get was a song and dance.

"I did not think you'd find out," she confessed, her Russian deliberately breathless and high-pitched with nerves. "I just *had* to see him, Aleksei. I could not take the distance anymore."

"I could put so much distance between you. Earth. Ocean. Fire. Whichever element I choose to use, I could." He barked out a laugh, his eyes like chips of ice. Their entire lives, people had told them they looked alike, but she couldn't see it. Yes, they were both fair-haired and pale-eyed, but violence had warped her brother's features at an early age. There was a coldness to him. As if he generated a deep freeze like a superpowered villain. This was not like looking into a mirror. It was like gazing into a void.

"Why? What does it matter to you? You have everything, Aleksei. Everyone at your service. You cleared the club on a Thursday, when we turn a good profit, and for what…? To wave your gun at me because you do not like the man I love?" She made a light noise of confusion, even though her heart thudded in her chest with perfect clarity. "I do not understand. Why must you keep us apart?"

"As if you are Romeo and Yuliet?" he scoffed. "You do know how that story ends, yes?"

Yes. She'd always known that. But there was one important

thing her brother was forgetting. She inhaled. Exhaled. Said the words with as much sweetness as she could muster.

"Tybalt dies, too."

———————

Third Shift was not a nine-to-five operation—not with most of its operatives pulling double duty as private citizens with regular day jobs. Team meetings could happen at six in the morning, two thirty in the afternoon or, like now, a little after eleven. Danny had been at the office for hours, going straight from Williamsburg to Hell's Kitchen and into the conference room, which was now in command-center mode with its windows opaque. His third can of Red Bull was parked next to his laptop, which was streaming both Yulia's location and a live audio feed—courtesy of the spider he'd slipped into her purse.

God, it had terrified him to hear Aleksei call her out. His first impulse had been to commandeer one of the motorcycles from storage downstairs and ride to her rescue. But then he'd kept listening. Kept breathing. She'd managed her psychotic brother nicely, putting him in his place without arousing suspicion of what she was really up to. Still, Danny hadn't really been able to unclench until he heard the telltale sounds of her leaving Kamchatka and going home…and, by then, the spider had done its work.

It was one of Joaquin's most ingenious inventions—more than just a bug. It "crawled" across all available networks once activated, providing monitoring across all channels. And they could kill the original as needed. So, the inside of Yulia's purse would offer up no more intel…while Aleksei's phone, computer, and surveillance cameras were open to their hack. It was virtually untraceable and kept Yulia in the clear.

"Report?" Elijah had been doing his homework on pretty cele-butantes with shitty taste in men for weeks now, but that didn't put a crimp in his full-on boss mode. When he looked around the conference table, everybody knew that single word meant business.

Danny sat up a little straighter in his chair, closing the lid of his laptop. "Vasiliev knows that Yulia and I met. He had someone watching her. But per our surveillance feed, he hasn't made me as an operative. He just thinks she and I are sneaking around. Brooklyn's own Korean Romeo and Russian Juliet."

Finn made an "aww" noise, because the bastard just couldn't help himself. Danny was relieved that he wasn't the only one to respond with a scowl. He took a swig of Red Bull before continuing. "According to Yulia, Vasiliev's a much happier camper than he was directly after the courthouse hit. He's sitting pretty right now, slinging threats left and right. He's smoothed things over with his higher-ups for the moment. Even gearing up for another trafficking run. And they've narrowed down Peluso and Ahluwalia's location. They're set to move on them before the week's out."

"And what *is* that location? Apex is playing it close to the vest, keeping their bloody hands clean, but they let us know that Peluso's implant shorted out. Last known ping on his whereabouts was Queens. So, we need to be piggybacking on Aleksei's intel." Elijah swung his piercing gaze to Finn. "Anything from the lawyers?"

Naturally, Finn wasn't one bit intimidated. "Feinberg's cagey, too, but I think he'll come to me if she makes contact," he said with a shrug.

"You *think*? We need better than hypotheticals, people." Their fearless—and fear-inducing—leader made a sound of disgust, shoving at the folders in front of him. But then he grinned. "Luckily, while you lot were sitting round with your thumbs up your arses, we got a call on Jack's emergency line. It was none other than the man of the hour, one Joseph Andrew Peluso. He's been given coordinates for a rendezvous point that we'll be monitoring. If he can't get there himself, he's going to get the woman there. He's indicated that's his priority. He sees himself as expendable."

Elijah's smile fell away then. And Danny could relate. They could *all* relate. Each one of them was prepared to sacrifice their lives for the greater good. You couldn't be involved in any form of law enforcement or covert operations without knowing the risks. Even though Joe Peluso was presently on the wrong side of the law, he clearly had a working knowledge of those risks as well.

"So where does that leave us?" Danny wondered. "What do you want us to do?"

Elijah sighed, dragging his hands over his smooth-shaven head before knotting them together in front of him. "Jack's on his way back from DC. He's been making arrangements for Peluso in the event that he *does* get out of this alive. For Neha Ahluwalia, too. What I want is for you jokers to close in on your marks. Danny, enlist a couple of our freelancers to watch Vasiliev the old-fashioned way. I know Joaquin's on the hack, but it might take hours we don't have. We need eyes *and* ears on Aleksei in the meantime. Finn… turn all that thinkin' into some action. Put the screws to Feinberg and Taylor. And not with your sodding cock."

"What about Gracie?" Finn's favorite person to needle wasn't even at HQ at the moment, but that never stopped him from bringing her up. It was almost cute, Danny thought. The closest thing the unrepentant pansexual playboy had to a crush.

Lije wasn't as charmed. He glowered. "Grace is more useful than you and, therefore, done with her role in this little party if she wants to be. She discovered that Peluso's jailhouse beatings were administered by a particularly nasty crew of Vasiliev flunkies. Two of the leaders are still on the streets. Yuri Medvedev and Anton Sokolov. Ten to one that's who they've got on Peluso's trail right now."

Medvedev. *Fuck.* Danny knew that name. He knew the face, too. He'd picked him up a year ago on a drunk and disorderly call at a flower shop/bar combo down on Cortelyou Road. That drunk and disorderly had quickly turned into assault. He hadn't relished discovering what a broken flower vase could do to a person's face. There was no telling what a man like Yuri Medvedev would do to Joe Peluso. Or to any woman in his vicinity.

They had to wrap this up ASAP. Before Yulia ended up in more danger.

"Tybalt dies, too." That was what she'd told Aleksei. So fucking brave.

The problem with a Shakespearean tragedy, though, was that by the end, *everybody* died.

20

HE SHOULD'VE GUESSED THE MYSTERY man, the virile vampire, wouldn't just leave it at a drink and a business card. Then again, Nate had a *lot* on his mind. A client still AWOL. Cops and the DA breathing down his neck. Other cases piling up like mid-December snow—he'd finally had to farm several out to hungry associates. It was perfectly reasonable to be thrown for a loop to discover Finian Conlan waiting outside when he got home after a strategy session with D.

"Y-you," he sputtered, the keys to the converted firehouse slipping from his suddenly nerveless grasp.

Conlan grabbed them before they could hit the pavement, mischief bright in the blue of his eyes. "Me," he confirmed. "I could've let myself in, but I thought that might be rude."

"Rude, illegal. Potay-to, potah-to." Nate recovered his composure quickly—and his keys, too. He snatched them back and fit the right ones in the regular lock and the dead bolt. "Thank you for showing restraint."

"I'm bad at restraint," Conlan admitted with entirely too much cheer, slipping inside before he could be invited. "Though I do enjoy being tied up. Bound. Cuffed. I'm terribly good at that, or so I've been told."

The modicum of gravitas Nate had achieved vanished in a puff of smoke, replaced by the extremely vivid image of this man spread-eagled on a bed. Dark hair, dark beard, acres of sun-starved Irish vampire skin. *Fuck.* He shook his head, forcing himself to think of the unsexiest things possible. The law-school debt he'd only paid off a few years ago. The 6 train during rush hour. The Jersey Turnpike. The night of the shooting…when he could've lost his best friend in the world. He stashed his coat in the hall closet, and by the time he joined his unwelcome guest in the open-plan living area, Nate felt marginally more in control. He crossed to the antique beverage cart that held a selection of his favorite liquors, splashing a healthy amount of gin into a tumbler. "Why are you here, Mr. Conlan? What do you want?"

A dismissive noise tore from the other man's throat. He stopped prowling across the hardwood and laid claim to the leather sofa, sprawling on it like an indolent king. "Oh, please," he said with a huff. "It's likely that we're going to fuck tonight, or at some point in the near future, so there's no need to be formal. Do call me Finn."

Wow. A cosmetics company could make a fortune bottling his confidence and selling it by the ounce. Nate was too impressed to be unsettled—and definitely turned on. "Are you always this cocky?"

"Mm-hmm. I'm terribly good at that, too." Finn waggled his eyebrows and tilted his head like he knew it was his best angle—though if he had a bad angle, Nate hadn't found it yet. "But to return to your first question…I'm here because our timetable has seen some changes. Making contact with Neha Ahluwalia is of the utmost importance. Her life could depend on it."

As if he hadn't been worried enough about Neha before. Nate tried to suppress a shiver of fear. The vampire could probably sense it anyway. "I told you: I don't know where she is. She hasn't been in touch."

"Shame. Someone should always be touching you." Finn's gaze

cut to the picture frames on a side table. Him and Dustin when they graduated L-school. And a goofy shot from some DGS Halloween party where they'd dressed up as Paul McCartney and Stevie Wonder from the "Ebony and Ivory" video. "Is *he* touching you? Because that's an idea I will certainly wank off to in the near future."

Nate choked on a mouthful of gin. He had to sit down. But not on the sofa. Not next to this walking one-man orgy. "Dustin is my partner. Not my *partner*," he said emphatically. "There is nothing like that going on between us." Not for lack of wondering. There had been times over the years—*no*. No, now was not the time to go down that road. He wasn't going to lay his private life bare for a gorgeous, filthy-mouthed operative with an agenda. Especially if Neha was in danger. Maybe his dick didn't have a sense of priorities, but his brain definitely did.

"As I said, Neha hasn't contacted me. She probably thinks whoever is after her and Peluso is watching me. She's probably right," he admitted. And another bolt of fear, combined with unease, skated down his spine. Was someone outside right now, in an unmarked car along the curb? Were his phones tapped? How could he have been so careless as not to think about that?

"Nah." Finn waved his hand. "They have someone monitoring your law-firm offices and your business line, but your personal phone is clean. As is your lovely home. Nary a bug to be found."

Nate frowned, retrieving his iPhone from inside his jacket and staring down at the screen. As if there would somehow be a Post-it note on it declaring that it had been inspected by Shady Agent No. 2. He'd had it on silent all day. It definitely hadn't left his custody. As for his house… "I thought you said you didn't let yourself in."

That earned a laugh. Another wicked look. "I thought you said your 'partner' didn't touch you?"

"You're exhausting." Before the obvious retort could be made, Nate added, "I have no doubt you'd tire me out sexually. It's not going to be tonight."

Finn let out a sigh…which brought up all sorts of questions about vampire physiology that they didn't have the luxury to address. He leaned forward, up and out of his insouciant sprawl. "It pains me to say it…but you're right. We simply don't have time to shag properly—and why do it at all if you don't put in your best effort? I have a reputation to uphold, after all. And, besides…" He gestured with a tilt of his head. "Your mobile's ringing."

Sure enough, the screen was lit up with an incoming text from an unknown number.

We're okay. For now.

Nate felt dizzy for reasons that had nothing to do with Finian Conlan's overt sexuality. "Are you a psychic, too? Did you *know* she would reach out to me tonight?"

"No. Psychic ability is not on the list of my many talents. My life would've turned out far differently if I'd been born with the Sight." For a second, the flirtatious mask fell away, and Nate saw something in the man's face that made a shiver skip down his spine. Then it was gone, and the wolfish grin returned. Finn reached across and plucked the gin from Nate's hand, gesturing for him to focus on replying to Neha. He lifted Nate's glass in a toast. "But I *was* gifted with impeccable timing. Slainte!"

To his health. To their collective health. Somehow, it felt more like a harbinger of doom than a blessing.

21

WE'RE OKAY. FOR NOW. BUT I'll need your help.

Joe was asleep when Neha sent the message. He'd been out cold for hours, likely slayed more from the effort of changing for the first time in years than from her impromptu impression of Meredith Grey. His breathing was even, pulse steady. He'd reopened the incisions when they'd made love this last time, so she'd checked his bandages, and the cuts were nothing more than thin red lines, nearly healed.

The iPod Touch sat in Neha's palm like a live grenade, pin pulled. Texting Nate was a bad idea. Even with the secure messaging app and Auntie's Wi-Fi, it was risky. That wasn't how this was supposed to work. Not how it went in the movies. You were supposed to be totally off the grid, right? But she wasn't a fictional character, not some suspense-thriller badass who couldn't rely on the system—even if she did own a .22 and a Taser. She was a real person. And real people called those in their lives who might be able to help when they were in trouble. Or they messaged them from a device their tech-head big brother had tricked out with a VPN and all sorts of hacker doodads.

The text sat there. Unread. Then read. But with no dots

popping up to signal that Nate was composing a reply. *Fuck*. That just made her second-guess her decision. After all, there was no handbook for being on the run with a wanted criminal. Jason Bourne movies definitely didn't count. So, she had no idea if she was doing this right or if she was just putting them in more danger. All she could be sure of was that there was no way she and Joe could get out of this on their own. There were too many variables, too many moving parts—too many people she couldn't control. And they could only hide out for so much longer. Hiding wasn't a plan. Going to Nate and Dustin and trying to work something out with the DA and the feds was a plan. Joe would hate it, but it was the most sensible, practical option.

Five minutes went by. Ten. She watched the bed and her screen in turns. What would happen first? Nate responding or Joe waking up?

She was at least eighty percent certain that their cover hadn't been blown yet. The flimsy disguise of Indian clothes had actually worked when they'd test-driven it the day before. Slouching in the back of a dosa restaurant with cellophane shopping bags at their feet. Because New York City was the biggest small town in the world and you couldn't go out without running into someone you knew, one of Aishneet Auntie's neighbors had been in the same restaurant.

"Neha Ahluwalia…is that you? And who is this…? Do we know him? Who are his people?"

"Namaste, Auntie-ji! This is just a friend. Visiting from abroad."

"'Friend'? Chee! At your age, you should have more than friends. You need a husband and two-three children."

"Three? Auntie, who has time for three?"

Her hypothetical children had occupied the nosy neighbor so thoroughly that Joe didn't have to say a single word to authenticate his identity. Meena Auntie had gone away clicking her tongue about "modern girls today" and not even questioning the suspicious fellow Neha had been keeping company with. *"Shit,"* he'd joked later, *"I think I'm more scared of your aunties than I am of Vasiliev's goons."*

Fortunately, there'd been nothing more on the news, no chatter on social media when Neha had done a quick check via the apps on the Touch. That didn't make it any easier to wait. Someone— several someones—had tried to kill Joe. And her by extension. Each time he walked out the door, it could be the last time. And then what? What did that make her? An accessory to a dead man? A fool?

Her iPod buzzed with a message just as Joe stirred on the bed with a rusty groan.

We've got your back. Where are you?

"Doc?" Joe sat up slowly, squinted at her in the dimness. "You okay?"

She didn't know which question to answer first, so she tackled both simultaneously, thumbing out a quick "can't say yet" and assuring Joe "Yeah, I'm fine" aloud.

Fine was one of those filler words that meant nothing. That you said out of habit. Joe didn't buy it for an instant. "Don't bullshit a bullshitter," he said as he gingerly climbed off the mattress. "You ain't fine. Nothing about how you're looking at that phone right now says you're fine."

"I'm worried," she admitted. That wasn't the whole truth, but it would suffice until Nate texted again. "I think we've probably been here long enough and it's time to move on. Maybe out to Long Island or up toward Tarrytown…though both of those options could leave you vulnerable to an SRB pickup, since they're outside the city limits."

Joe pulled a pair of Saravpal Uncle's drawstring pants over his hips, gaze flicking to the iPod still sitting silent in her hand. "Did someone tell you to go out to Tarrytown? Or you just got a jones for Sleepy Hollow all of a sudden?"

"I reached out to Nate," she said, cautiously setting the phone down beside her. "I didn't give him any indicators of our location. You know I'm not that incompetent."

A humorless smile pulled at the corners of Joe's mouth. "It's probably one of the only things I know about you. Besides how you taste."

He was right. They still barely knew each other. A few minutes of fanciful pillow talk about subway seats didn't a couple make. Trust took longer than that to build, didn't it? Neha felt the unease in every pore as Joe began pacing the living area, alternating between working out the stiffness in his limbs and dragging his hands through his hair in obvious frustration. "Doc, telling Feinberg *anything* could put us in danger," he growled. "They could be watching his every move! You can't just do shit because you feel like it!"

What the hell? Neha's jaw practically hit the floor. "Because I *feel like it*? Like this is a fucking lark for me? I *left my life* to keep you safe," she reminded him, wrapping her arms around herself even though the studio was far from cold. No, the chill was between them. A box of ice that had materialized despite all the heat they'd generated. "Are you being one hundred percent honest with me, Joe? I doubt it. I know I'm not the only one who used this phone."

"You don't want my total honesty, baby. Trust me." He laughed, scrubbing at his mouth with the back of his hand. Like he needed to get rid of the sour tinge of his own words. "I've seen things, I've done things that you can't even imagine. Things you'd never *want* to imagine. I'm not a hero. I'm not even a good man. Hell, depending on who you ask, I'm not even a man at all."

Oh, they were *not* playing this self-pitying game. "I don't care about what anyone else thinks. And I'm not naive. I read the police reports. I read the first trial transcripts. And I still came with you! Because I believed in you. Because I wanted you." When she said it out loud like that... Neha winced. It was her turn to scrub at her face. "God, maybe I *am* naive."

But that didn't mean she was going to lose sight of their priorities. Staying alive rated far higher than figuring out the action-movie-meets-Bollywood laugh riot that appeared to be her love life. She pushed off from the small sofa, grabbing her jacket from where she'd tossed it after their last supply run. "I'm going to do a walk around the block. See if anything looks suspicious."

Joe laughed again. "The most suspicious thing around here is me."

He wasn't wrong. She ached to protest, but he wasn't wrong. "Who did you call the other night when you thought I was asleep? What if *that* puts us in danger?"

"It won't," he said tersely. "I called people who might be able to help."

"Nate might be able to help, too. He and Dustin can work something out with the DA's office and the FBI, if they're involved already. Don't strip me of that choice. Of the chance to get us out of this. I have just as much right as you do. We're in this together, remember?"

She wanted to fight him just as much as she wanted to fuck him. To push back and push forward and push sideways until he cracked open. Until *they* cracked open. It had to be the forced proximity—the stress of hiding that they'd ignored in favor of marathon sex. Or maybe it was the lies. She was still keeping things from him. He wasn't being entirely honest with her. They'd bathed in each other's spit and come, but their belief in each other was fragile, made of wishes and dreams and not reality.

Maybe he saw a hint of those wishes and dreams on her face, because he stopped pacing and parked himself before her, crossing his arms over his massive chest. She'd braced her palms against that chest. Now it was an impenetrable safe with his heart locked inside. "If we do make it out…how do you think this is gonna go, Doc? You gonna introduce me to your family? Marry me in that Sikh temple? Live happily ever after?"

The last few words were sharp and bitten off, like expletives.

He made it all sound completely absurd…but hadn't they already survived the unbelievable? Wasn't this entire situation already bordering on big-screen action-adventure ridiculousness? "Why *can't* we have a future?" Neha demanded. "You have *no* idea what my parents are like," she pointed out. "Ma and Papa taught me to help people, Joe. To stand up for myself. I am the woman they made me. You think they'd turn you away because you're white? Because you've killed men? Did I?"

He flinched. "You should have! You should've told me to fuck off and get the fuck away from you. I'm poison, Neha. Why the hell did you pour yourself a cup of it? I don't deserve you. I never deserved you, and you *knew* that."

The condemnation hit her like a fist to the gut and infuriated her all at the same time. Neha shoved at his shoulder. "Bullshit! You can't pull that noble crap on me now. Not when you stripped me naked with your eyes every time I walked into Brooklyn Detention. You don't get to rewrite how we started just because you don't know how it will end."

Joe swore in a mix of English and rusty Italian, his fists clenched so tight that the whiteness radiated out from his knuckles like spikes of infection. "I had to have you," he said thickly. "I wanted you so bad I couldn't think about anything else. That's on me. I know it's on me."

And she knew that her own lust was on her. She'd walked into this with eyes open. All she was trying to do now was *keep* her eyes open. "I get it. I was a distraction. An easy prison fantasy. But we're back in the real world now, and I'm a real person. With my own needs and my own thoughts. I'm complicated, Joe. And messy. And angry. I want to fix all of this as much as you do. The difference is…unlike you, I still have hope."

"You think hope is that easy? That fixing this is that easy?" He turned as if to punch the wall, and she had no idea what held him back. Certainly not any concern for Auntie's property. "You think I wanted to be mixed up in this?" he growled. "Fuck. I work construction. I keep my head down and my nose clean. Maybe I go grab a beer at the Knights of Columbus once in a while. But then…those shitheels dragged Kenny into the middle of their turf war. Just a dumb kid who liked to smoke up and chase skirts. Never hurt a fly in his life." Instead of his fist, Joe's head hit the wall—with a dull thump, like he was taking the pain that this Kenny had never caused anyone else. "Kenny Castelli," he ground out, as if he'd heard the question in her mind. "Basically my baby brother. You know they didn't even spend a day on the hit that killed him and the others in that strip club? Twenty-four-hour news cycle… Fuck, it wasn't even twenty-four minutes. And I bet he wasn't in any of those files they gave you about my case. Like he didn't matter. Like he never existed at all.

"And, Neha, all I could see for days after was red and cold. There was no insanity. No PTSD. I didn't shift. I didn't attack out of animal instinct. I *planned it*. I took out those motherfuckers because I wanted to. Because I needed to. Because I couldn't think of anything else. And you still think you can get me a deal? Now? After all of this?" He waved around them indistinctly. At the mess their lives had become. "Christ."

This was what she'd wanted to hear for weeks. His "why." She ached for having learned it. And he was right: It wasn't a motive that would get him knocked down from Murder One to manslaughter. Neha didn't care about that, though. She cared about the smudges under his eyes, the shadows within them. She cared that his shoulders were slumped and his body was angled away and he might never touch her again. That he might never be kind again. That he might never know kindness from anyone else. That was what she was fighting so hard for.

"I do think hope is that easy, Joe," she told him gently. "Because, right now, it's all we have to get us through this."

Hope. Fuck, he didn't even know what that word meant anymore. Unless you counted the hope that she'd kiss him back, the hope that he'd get to have her one more time before he had to leave her.

"What're you hoping, exactly? That I'm a decent person?" he wondered. "You want to believe that, don't you? That me not tearing up those Russians is some kind of proof? That me leaving people alive at the courthouse is evidence? You think that's some proof of my conscience, my self-control?" Joe had to laugh again. And again. "I said it before, and I'll say it again. I'm not a good man."

He was shit at being good. At protecting people. He'd always known that. Seeing Kenny on the slab had made it crystal. Looking at Neha now just hammered in the point. Of course she didn't trust him. Of course she was mad. And he couldn't blame her. He'd eye-fucked her in that visitors' room over and over again. He'd played on her compassion and her interest. He'd manipulated her into meeting him before his hearing. Sure, it felt noble and romantic and frantic at the time, but he wasn't kidding himself. None of this would have happened to her if it hadn't been for him thinking with his dick. She should've been back in Brooklyn, advocating for people who actually deserved it, instead of riding said dick. She should've been anywhere else but here. This wasn't about having hope. It was about being realistic. She didn't belong here with him. And he didn't belong here with her.

It was time to go. Time to draw out Vasiliev's men and end this.

"It wasn't self-control, babe," he told her. "The only reason I didn't do more damage is because I literally couldn't. That's it. And now, thanks to your little game of Operation, I can. That should scare the fuck outta you."

Neha's arms were still crossed over herself like a shield. She shook her head, pretty mouth tight with disappointment. "The only thing that scares me is the prospect of you dying before we can fix this."

"Then you're a fool," he ground out, before grabbing the rest of her uncle's clothes and getting dressed as quickly as possible. Wrapping the shawl around himself like she'd showed him. "You stay here. *I'll* go out and do a sweep of the neighborhood." He'd do more than that. But she didn't need to know that yet. She'd figure it out soon enough after he was gone.

When she'd played dress-up with him the other day, he'd asked her about wearing a turban to help with camouflage even more. She'd looked horrified, before explaining to him how offensive that was. *"These are just clothes. Turbans are part of a religion—of my family's faith. I know it might hide you better, but there are some lines I'm just not going to cross."*

That was who Neha was. A woman who had lines she wouldn't cross. Joe's entire life was about erasing the lines. Kicking dirt over them. Covering them in blood.

Fuck, he was going to ruin her. Maybe he already had. He swiped her iPod Touch from where she'd set it aside. Opened up the secure messaging app and keyed in the number that was burned into his brain. "If I'm not back, if something happens, I want you to call this line. Call it before Feinberg. Before anybody else. Call it. Text it. Whatever. They're expecting it."

"You sound like you're not *planning* to come back," Neha looked at him with that intense scrutiny she'd been laying on him since the beginning. Like she was seeing right through him. "You can't escape me that easy, Joe."

Escaping her, running from her, was impossible. She'd dug too deep under his skin. Buried herself there with his damn DNA. But he had to be practical. There was a giant motherfucking target on his back—a target he'd made purposely bigger by making himself visible in Jackson Heights. And every minute he stayed with her was a minute she was in danger, too. "I might not have a choice."

Maybe the cops or the feds would show up before the Russians did, but they were stretched thin, with resources in use all over the city. Plus, they had to wait for the drone footage to be analyzed. Vasiliev's guys had nothing but time for vendettas. And any one of their shifters could pick up the traces of his scent. That was what Joe was counting on.

Neha shook her head slowly, the disappointment on her lips traveling up to her eyes. "Was that your plan this whole time? Stay with me just long enough for things to die down and then leave anyway? And now's as good a time as any?"

He couldn't answer that. He wouldn't. Because he couldn't say for certain it was true. Somewhere in the past few days, being with her, he *had* fantasized about hunkering down here forever and telling the whole goddamn world to fuck itself. But a fantasy was all it could be. "Doc…it ain't like I *want* to leave you. I'm just saying I can't control what's gonna happen out there."

Neha moved around the studio, restless, frustrated with him, hurt. *Alive.* And that was what mattered most. "Half the city is looking for you," she said as she knelt by their bags and started rifling through them. "It's not safe out there. Even with you in disguise. You should never have gone out with me for supplies."

"It's not safe anywhere I am," Joe pointed out. "But I was trained for this. For stealth. For recon. You weren't."

"Do you want to take this with you?" Resigned to his decision, or at least pretending to be resigned to it, she stood up with her gun and its holster. Which was in no way going to fit him.

He raised one hand. The ripple-burn of the change flowed through his fingers as they turned into claws. The partial shift was one of the first skills they'd mastered at Apex. For those times in which they might need a human brain and a monster's strength. Joe would've been lying if he said it didn't feel fucking fantastic to be able to do it again. "I got my own weapons back, remember?"

Just like when he'd changed before, she didn't look grossed out. Didn't look judgy. "Oh, *that's* a nice trick," she said, managing to sound impressed and a little sarcastic. "You're practically one of the X-Men."

"Always did love me some Wolverine," he admitted.

For just a second, the tension between them drained away. He could've ruined it in two seconds by telling her what he'd used to take out the Russians in the club—a nine-millimeter. By talking about how it was important to minimize the glare on the sight of a sniper rifle. By explaining to her how ripping out someone's guts with your own claws wasn't like a comic-book panel or a movie. Violence was purely theoretical for this gorgeous woman in front of him. She'd never really known the practice of it. Not until he'd brought it into her life.

She claimed to not be that religious, but he saw how it was still in her. All of that faith. All of that goodness. "Keep your gun," he told her, trying to be gentle after the harshness of earlier. "Keep your phone. Keep everything that makes you feel safe."

He hadn't earned the way she smiled at him then. Or how she crossed the room. Or her lips on his cheek. He *had* earned the salt her whisper poured on his wounds. "You make me feel safe, too, Joe. That's why I'm keeping you."

When he slammed out of the apartment a couple of minutes later, that whisper dogged his heels. Haunted him like a damn ghost. Got in his veins and his head and distracted him in ways he had no business being distracted. Because he didn't pick up the tail for nearly ten blocks. Just north of the Sixty-First Street–Woodside station. As he was cutting through a construction detour—closed in on two sides by flimsy green walls, with his six totally vulnerable and his twelve, too. *Fuckfuckfuck*. This was what he'd wanted. What he'd asked for. But he'd already lost control of it.

The flap of wings coming at him. The flash of black in his peripheral vision. Footsteps behind him. Cologne and animal musk. Danger. *Danger*. Joe tried to shift, but it was too late.

He'd had the shit kicked out of him. He'd been shot. Knifed. Bitten. Blown back fifteen feet by an IED. He'd never been tased. His second-to-last thought before he hit the pavement was that a gazillion volts hurt like a sonofabitch. His last thought was... *Neha*.

22

YURI MEDVEDEV WAS AS DARK as her brother was fair, with the sort of dangerous good looks that belonged on the cover of one of those mafia romance novels that Yulia's Confessional regular had once talked of. But the sight of him in the halls of Kamchatka did nothing to inspire romantic thoughts. Just cold, clawing fear. Yulia wanted to keep on her path to the Pit's hostess station, wanted her feet to continue steering her in the slightly safer direction, but her mind refused the easy way and guided her instead to the basement bar, where Yuri nursed a vodka and tonic…and a grudge. Something had tightened his shoulders. Something had him surveying the arena floor like a threat could emerge at any moment. She owed it to Danny, and to herself, to try to find out what that threat was.

Aleksei's mood had turned uncharacteristically cheerful that morning. He hadn't barked unreasonable orders at Elizaveta or Minka, hadn't scowled at the busboys. Yulia could only surmise that his operations were going well. But Yuri's arrival in the Pit, and the fury that he radiated, spoke of anything but positive turns in the Vasiliev family business. As she closed the space between them, his glower deepened. So, it was *she* who'd warranted this thundercloud? Dread crept up Yulia's spine like a spider. More spiders skittered along her back and upper arms as Yuri spoke.

"You have been busy, little girl." People who did not understand Russian often thought the language harsh, coarse and unpleasant to the ear. They could not possibly understand what it was like to hear true violence in simple words. In a tongue that had always been like music to her.

"It's always busy here," she said, deliberately misunderstanding his meaning. "You would know this if you came to visit more than one or two times in a year."

He scoffed, not buying her deflection, and slammed his glass down on the bar. "This is not a 'visit.' This is business. *You* are business now."

Don't panic. Stay calm. She thought of Danny's steady hand on her arm. His warm gaze giving her strength. "Me? Don't be ridiculous, Yuri."

"I am never ridiculous. Only serious. You should remember that, little fish." From any other man, such a statement might be flirtatious. Yuri Medvedev was not any other man. He was not any other bear.

As if she'd ever forgotten that. Yulia was proud of herself for not betraying a single hint of her inner turmoil as she reached for the ever-present bottle of Mamont and poured Yuri a shot. Tonic be damned. It was easier still to swipe a glass from the stack just beyond a human patron's reach and pour herself one as well. "What are you so serious about today, then? What have I done that requires your attention?"

"It is not what you have done. It is what you *will* do." Yuri could have said more. Explained. But that would ruin the suspense. Ruin these moments where he held so much power. The pleasure of it was in his voice, in the flirtation that was not with her but with death.

Perhaps her hand shook just the tiniest bit this time, as she

poured again. Because the things that her brother and his henchmen could make her do… That list was endless, was it not?
Endless like a scream. Was she to wake up tomorrow in a shipping
container with a dozen other women? Would she be gifted to that
man who'd held court with Aleksei just days ago? All the blood
she'd given, all the loyalty and time, and it would never be enough.
Her body, her soul, her life were all still commodities.

"Your games will not work on me, Yuri," she murmured,
buoyed by the sweet burn of vodka sliding down her throat. "Tell
me what you intend, deliver your punishment, but this cat and
mouse grows tiresome."

His dark eyes glinted with an emotion that might have passed
for respect. "No punishment. Consider this…a promotion. We are
expecting a very important package today, and you will be tasked
with its care."

A package. She'd been embroiled in this family nightmare long
enough to understand what that meant. A prisoner. Someone they
did not trust to be handled by just any guard…but would gladly
hand off to someone they could also control. For what was Yulia
but a prisoner, too?

I'm here for you, her imaginary Danny reminded her. *I will set
you free.*

But Yulia could not truly count on fantasy rescuers, could
she? Her fate, and this mysterious package's fate, was solely in *her*
hands. So, she smiled. And she sat down next to a killer and met
his brutal gaze like she'd meet a lover's. "Oh, thank you, Yuri, for
this momentous news," she purred. "I am so happy for the extra
work."

"*Are* you?" Yuri bristled, both literally and figuratively, not
appreciating her tone. "It sounds to me like you aren't grateful at
all, little fish."

She lied as if her very existence depended on it. Because it did.

After an hour, Neha had no choice but to go looking for Joe. Especially after their argument. Neha couldn't trust—especially given his lack of assurances—that he wouldn't leave her and go after Aleksei Vasiliev and his men on his own. Maybe that had been his private plan all along. Joe Peluso had a strong streak of self-sacrifice in him, whether he realized it or not. And it was probably going to get him killed.

She changed out of her desi clothes, tossing on a T-shirt and cargo pants from her duffel and tying back her hair. Her burner phones and iPod went into an oversized pocket. She slipped on her holster and a jacket, too. It was amazing how one presidential election had set her on the path to becoming Lara Croft or one of the X-Men. Neha Ahluwalia, action hero. She'd always tried to be careful, hypervigilant. But now…all that care and all of that vigilance was crystallized, focused. Driving her as she locked up the studio and headed out.

There was no sign of Joe in the immediate vicinity. Nothing about that was comforting. Especially when she picked up on the signs that *did* exist. The neighborhood was teeming with people from all walks of life, all cultures and faiths. But even so, one particular white guy didn't quite fit in. He stood a head taller than most of the people making their way down Thirty-Seventh Avenue, and his posture was predatory. He wore all black, but there was no mistaking him for waitstaff getting ready to go on shift or a trendy Manhattanite about to hit up an art gallery. Aggression rolled off of him in waves. *If you see something, say something*, the MTA's old ad campaign had urged. This was the kind of person who made you want to say something. No. To change subway cars or cross the street to avoid him.

He was here for her and Joe. She knew that as surely as she knew her own name. Somehow, Vasiliev had found them. Maybe the goons had started out on McDonald Avenue first, searching all the brown parts of central Brooklyn, but they'd eventually made their way here to Jackson Heights. And maybe they'd already grabbed Joe. Maybe he hadn't just left her. Maybe, like he said, he'd had no choice. *Fuck.* She ducked into a sari shop, digging into a pocket for her burner and the iTouch app where Joe had logged his emergency number. *"If I'm not back…if something happens…I want you to call this line."* Joe had filed the number under Donovan's. She took two seconds to appreciate the private joke as she dialed it and waited for the line to connect.

"Yes?" It was a low, masculine voice. Clipped. Polite. "Can I help you?"

Neha felt suddenly ridiculous. What did one *say* to a mysterious voice on a phone line connected to god-only-knew-where? "I have a problem. I've heard you can solve it."

"Potentially." The reply was pleasant, with no trace of regional accent. "What's the nature of this problem? Pest control? Search and rescue?" Whoever these people were, they were *good*.

She peered out the shop's display windows, toward the sidewalk. "Approximately six foot four. Two hundred and ten pounds of solid muscle. Russian gang tattoos visible on his neck. Sound familiar?"

"Intimately." The pleasant tone hardened a little. Just enough that Neha could detect frustration. "We have operatives in transit already. Can you evade the problem until then, or has the situation already escalated?"

Operatives in transit already? Had they been monitoring Nate's phone? Been in the room with him? Somehow traced the call that Joe had made the other night? Or had she and Joe managed to land on drone footage despite their efforts to duck the surveillance? The thought would be creepy as hell, except that Neha had bigger things to worry about than Big Brother. She couldn't hide out in the sari store forever. The clerks were already giving her hard looks.

"I don't think I've been spotted, but I can't say that will stay the case for long," she admitted, pretending to look at a rack of colorful lehengas.

"Understood. Your friend gave us a pickup location. Can you meet us there?"

When the man rattled off the meeting spot, Neha was surprised to realize she knew it all too well—one of the Woodside parks, easily walkable from where she currently was. "Sure. I can do that."

"Good. Keep this line clear. Keep your head down. We will find you."

The line went dead before she could end the call. She didn't know whether to be reassured by the efficiency or chilled by the ominousness. But Neha *did* know that she had to be prepared. So she carefully made her way back to Aishneet Auntie's apartment, packed up her and Joe's stuff, and then hurried away from the safe haven of Jackson Heights.

23

3S HQ WAS BUZZING EVEN before Jack ended the call from Neha Ahluwalia. The monitors that lined one wall were already cued up with CCTV and drone footage from around the Jackson Heights subway hub on Seventy-Fourth Street. Various angles. Crowd coverage. The six-foot-four Russian gunman that Neha had mentioned on the phone was easy to pick out. Worse yet, cycling back through the footage showed the same man and a few of his pals getting the jump on Joe Peluso and hustling him into a dark van.

Fuck. In a matter of hours, everything they'd been monitoring had gone from status quo to clusterfuck. Third Shift's contacts on the street in Brighton Beach had fallen just a half step behind Vasiliev's flunkies…and that half step was enough to put Anton Sokolov in Queens before they could set a tail on him. And Yuri Medvedev—arguably the most dangerous of the crew—was off the grid, too. Leaving 3S chasing their tails while Peluso was grabbed and taken off to parts unknown.

Danny's first instinct was to contact Yulia. Text. Twitter DM. Even carrier pigeon. The spider he'd planted hadn't picked up anything specific to her in hours. *Fuck.* Though it *had* given up some valuable intel for Elijah's mission. A few phone calls between Aleksei and upper-level mobsters about an upcoming VIP party and some sort of big-deal weapons auction after that. Lije had already handed off oversight of current events to Jackson so he could dig deep into Phase one of his project. No time for the little fishes like Vasiliev when you had your eye on the sharks, right? It made Danny feel small and powerless, even with all the resources at their disposal.

His phone buzzed before he could even touch it. Rattling on the table like a wakeup alarm. Number unknown. He swiped across his screen without even second-guessing it. We have a guest. Yulia. Every fiber of his being knew it was Yulia. Using a new burner phone. Contacting him before he could reach out to her. Jesus. Christ. Vasiliev had Peluso. Or Neha Ahluwalia. There was no other way to interpret the message. His fingers flew across the tiny smartphone keyboard ahead of his brain cells.

Hope you're treating them hospitably.

Amenities are not the best. The client should book new accommodations as soon as possible.

Oh, shit. Whoever the Vasiliev organization had in custody was in grave danger. Danny wasted no time saying that aloud… and received dark, knowing stares in response.

"It's Peluso," Jack confirmed crisply. "The timeline matches up from when he was snatched off the street. So this situation is officially off the rails. I've sent Finn and Grace to bring Neha Ahluwalia in."

"And then what?" Danny glanced around the busy conference room turned command center. Joaquin was bent over their laptop, monitoring the spider hack and sifting through the archived drone footage from the last hour. Elijah was pulling up hotel plans on his own computer, no doubt working out something for his impending undercover operation. The bulk of the active team was out living their first-shift lives. Nothing about the office tonight telegraphed that some big takedown op was in motion. "We have a tea party?"

"Danny." Jack sighed. It wasn't quite chiding. More weary than anything else. "It might not look like it to you, but we have just as much investment in this as you do. We will protect Yulia Vasilieva and Neha Ahluwalia, and even Joe Peluso, to the best of our ability. You know that. You wouldn't be here if you didn't believe that."

The list of things he wouldn't be doing if he didn't believe was as long as his arm. Danny looked down at his phone and inhaled. A steadying breath. Let us know if we can upgrade your guest's rooms, he typed.

He waited for the three dots signifying a reply was imminent. He hoped he wasn't waiting in vain.

―――――――――

He was probably only in the hole for a half hour when he started losing his mind. His head was pounding like a motherfucker. His whole body, really—he could check "how it feels to be tased" off his Shit I Never Needed to Know list—and he couldn't see more than a few inches in front of him. They'd tossed him somewhere dark. Cold. Damp, too. Right out of the gulag playbook. There was a faint smell of oil. Like a refinery or a machine shop. He'd explore, but he couldn't move. Not just because everything hurt, but because they'd cuffed him to a damn pipe. *They.* The Russians. Vasiliev's men, he assumed. There were no introductions made. Except between his face and a couple fists. And his arm and a wicked needle. They'd shot him full of something that had him sluggish, that was keeping the beast out of commission.

He flexed his wrists. Felt the tension all the way up in his shoulders. And a tingle, too. Like the cuffs and chains had been charmed or hexed or whatever. *Nope.* There was no getting out of his restraints. Or this room. Not anytime soon. So, of course, that was when his company arrived. Not the goons again. He wasn't that lucky. Instead, it was ghosts. Every man he'd ever shot. Kenny's body on the slab. Those four guys in the back of the club, clinking their ice-cold vodka before he iced them. The corpses piled up in the darkness.

It was like this at Apex. Exactly like this. His first month in the program. When they'd pumped him full of their supernatural juice and sat back to watch the results. Leather restraints, not cuffs. But the room was tiny. Dark. And haunted. There hadn't been any physical pain from the initial changes. No, it was all in his head. That was where it hurt the most.

The door rattled then, shaking him out of his circular thoughts. He expected a couple of the goons who'd tossed him into the holding room. Fucking extras from central casting who stank of unwashed fur and cheap cologne. But when the reinforced steel door opened inward, it was a woman. A girl, really. Dark-blond hair, rail thin in her fancy formfitting cocktail dress. Pretty. At least from what he could tell with his enhanced vision in this shitty light. Not human. He could tell that, too. There was a musky smell rolling off her skin—probably undetectable to nonsupes—and it reminded him of the men who'd jumped him and dragged him into a van. She was some kind of shifter. The sense memory hit him as she shut the door behind her, moving in slowly and carefully, holding something in her hands. Meat. Meat to feed his beast. *The motherfuckers at the club. Falling facedown into their soup course. They stink of the wild.* Whatever they were, she was, too.

"You need to keep your strength up," she murmured as she dropped something a few feet from him. "Eat." The tray clattered, echoing off the four walls. The sound grated on his ears. Not like her accent, which was so fucking beautifully New York to him. Faint Russian plus heavy Brooklyn.

"Why? Ain't they gonna just fuckin' kill me?" When captors wanted to feed you, it was shady shit. No point in wasting resources on someone you were going to off, right?

The woman actually laughed...and not at his expense. Her shoulders slumped just the tiniest bit. Her gaze flicked up toward the corners of the room, confirming his suspicion that there were probably cameras or bugs. "Oh, no. Death...death is too easy," she assured him. "We are a practical clan. We have plans for you, Mr. Peluso."

Yup. Shady shit. Joe tested his cuffs again. Shifted along the pipe. There was no give. No possibility of escape. Until he looked into her eyes. Pale blue. Despairing. Determined. *There.* There was the escape. He didn't dare voice it aloud. He was smarter than that. She was smarter than that, too. She didn't keep the conversation going. She just fiddled with his shackles long enough to undo one of his hands and wrap the short chain so tightly around his other one that there was no chance of undoing it or breaking it. He could've fought her in that span of seconds. Bucked her off him. Strangled her with the chain. But he didn't. Because of her quiet whisper, the barest sound against his ear. "*Don't.* Not yet." Then, she backed toward the door, not falling into that rookie mistake of turning away from him. She may have looked like a human woman, but she was a predator like he was. A *prisoner* like he was.

"I will return shortly for the plate. Keep your strength up," she repeated. "You must prepare for what lies ahead."

Torture? He could handle that. He'd been trained for that. Getting his ass kicked? Yeah, he'd been trained for that, too. Joe waited until she was gone before he reached out for the food tray. He hooked it with his foot and then pulled it the rest of the way with his free hand. Beef. Cabbage. Solid basics. Energy and farts. Just call him silent but deadly.

Joe shoveled the nutrients in as fast as possible...tasting the underlying tang of some sort of sedative and not giving a damn. So they wanted him incapacitated, unable to fight back, unable to change. Being knocked out for a while was the least of his problems. On the bright side, when he was forced into another bout of shut-eye, the nightmares were quieter. His head hurt less. The

Taser effects were all but gone. The danger...? Still there. Always there. Never going away.

Christ, Neha. Stay away. Don't get anywhere near me. Please be as far from this as possible.

He wasn't deluded enough to think *that* was going to happen.

24

WHEN SHE'D PLOTTED OUT HER life's trajectory over stale nachos and tequila one night in law school, it hadn't included getting shot at in a courthouse. Or going on the run with a shapeshifter. Or meeting up with mysterious operatives at a community park. Really, it had been more along the lines of the old *Buffy the Vampire Slayer* movie: "All I want to do is graduate from high school, go to Europe, marry Christian Slater, and die." Swapping in L-school for high school and George Clooney for Christian Slater. But here she was. One hand on the snub-nose pistol in her bag. Dread crawling up her spine. Two people in dark clothes walking up to her. Europe and Clooney were off the table. Dying was still very much an option.

Neha shivered even though it was nowhere near cold...and then she shoved the fear deep down inside her. Joe was missing. He *needed her*. He didn't think he did—didn't think he deserved her or had any kind of future—and here was her chance to prove him utterly and completely wrong. By pulling his stubborn ass out of the fire. So, she put her analytical skills to work, cataloging all the surface details about the new arrivals. A movie-star handsome white man and an equally striking woman of color. They both wore suits with detectable bulges under the jackets and kept their hands at their sides as they stopped just a few steps away. As wary of her as she was of them. Not inclined to shoot first and ask questions later.

"Ms. Ahluwalia? We're here to help."

She blinked, rocking back a little at the woman's words. That they knew her name shouldn't have shocked her, but it did. She'd given so little information over the phone…and they probably already knew everything about her, didn't they? Whoever these people were, they'd likely gathered all the intel they needed about her and Joe. Down to the contents of her underwear drawer. "Wh-who *are* you?" It was a silly question, but the only one she could manage at the moment, the only thing that would give her back a measure of power.

Sympathy flickered in the woman's dark eyes, quickly replaced by a cool detachment that matched her voice. She was the kind of beautiful that wouldn't look out of place on a Paris runway… tall, her thick, black hair barely tamed by a bun, with warm brown skin a shade or two darker than Neha's own. "I'm Grace," she said. "My partner is Finn. I know you have no reason to trust us, but I recommend you do so anyway."

Did Neha have a choice? Probably not. But she'd known that when she made the call to that mysterious number, when she'd spoken to the equally mysterious man on the line. Bringing other people into this meant having to trust someone besides herself. "Okay." She nodded wearily. "Okay, I guess that's the best offer I'm going to get right now," she said before following the duo back the way they'd come, past the doughboy statue that loomed over the park's entrance and toward the street, where a huge, black SUV sat waiting.

The man, Finn, opened the back door for her. "Only the best for our gentlewoman callers," he said in a lilting Irish accent, capping the words with an impertinent little bow before he gestured her inside.

Grace made an all-too-relatable sound that telegraphed her impatience with her flirtatious coworker as she slid into the front passenger seat. It seemed to rein him in as much as was probably possible, and he hopped into the driver's side without any further flourishes.

As the vehicle pulled away from the curb, taking her to god-only-knew-where, Neha couldn't help herself. "No blindfold?" she asked while buckling her seat belt.

Finn chuckled. The sound was rich and deep, almost annoying in its blatant appeal. "Someone's been watching too many movies."

A strange echo of what she'd once said to Joe—that he'd watched too many prison movies. And funny, considering she suddenly felt like she hadn't watched *enough* movies to get a proper feel for this whole clusterfuck. Maybe, like Joe and his unit, she needed to marathon a bunch of werewolf flicks and horror films? And spy movies, too. Neha scowled at the bright-blue eyes that met her gaze in the rearview mirror. "Pardon me for not knowing proper secret-agent protocol."

"The improper protocol's far more fun." He waggled his eyebrows at her, back in full-wattage charmer mode and not the least bit contrite.

The memory hit her fast, without warning, and she clutched the handle above the door to steady herself. *"Sorry, Doc. Blame all the time in jail if you want. It's not like the social scene here's anything special. A man's mind gets a little one-track, you know?"*

"I'm trying to help your defense, not improve your love life."

This agent was nothing like Joe—stylish, suave, aware of his own beauty—but they sure had impropriety in common.

"*Behave*, Finn." Grace twisted in her seat, shooting a scowl of her own at her colleague before she weighed in. "We don't have a secret lair, Ms. Ahluwalia," she assured. "We're just taking you to the offices of our private security firm. It's public record. You can even google us. 'Third Shift, here for your personal security and investigative needs at any hour.'"

Hunh. Neha knew a fair amount of the private investigative firms across the five boroughs, but she'd never heard of Third Shift. Did they have an Insta? A Twitter account? She seriously doubted there were Yelp reviews for their park-pickup skills. And all of the other shady things they probably handled. The hysterical giggle started to build in the back of Neha's throat and she swallowed the sound, staring out the tinted windows at the storefronts on Queens Boulevard as they headed west toward Manhattan. She didn't have to be a superspy to know that Finn would pick the Queensboro Bridge over the Midtown Tunnel. The bridge was out in the open. The tunnel could box them in.

The last thing she wanted to be was boxed in. Unless it was with Joe, like they had been for those blissful few days in Auntie's rental. "I don't want to just sit on the sidelines in some safe house. Or drink lukewarm tea in your conference room. I need to be a part of this."

"You shouldn't be a part of this." Finn looked back at her, equal parts exasperation and sympathy. "You don't have the training for this, love."

What was it with attractive, dangerous men assuming she couldn't handle herself? Neha resisted the urge to kick the back of his seat. While it would feel immensely satisfying, it would do nothing to solidify her argument that she was competent enough to be involved in whatever happened next. "You don't have the *knowledge* for this. You don't know Joe like I do." She ignored the tiny voice in the back of her mind that suddenly wondered *How much do you know him, really?*

Finn's eyes met hers in the mirror again. Like he'd heard that quiet question. Maybe he had. She didn't know if he was fully human. For all she knew, he could be some sort of psychic sorcerer. But she wasn't about to ask. "What are you?" was just as rude to a supernatural as it was to a person of color. Just as rude as if she asked Grace where she was *really* from.

"Ms. Ahluwalia. Neha." His tone was gentler this time. She half suspected Grace had kicked his ankle or squeezed his thigh… giving in to the impulses that Neha had to rein in. "We know the sort of people he's mixed up with. The sort of *beings* he's mixed up with. Have you ever dealt with any of them without a visitor's table between you and guards in the room?"

For all his efforts at placating her, she still bristled. "Would you ask your partner a condescending question like that, or am I just the luckiest woman in this SUV?"

Another ridiculously charismatic laugh rolled up from Finn's chest. Practically filling the car like an aphrodisiac being pumped through the vents. "I would never presume to condescend to Grace," he assured Neha, still chuckling. "She frightens me far too much."

"Besides, they come to me *on* the table," Grace added, something like a smile playing at her lips. "In that room, *I* am the guard. Between life and death."

"In more than just that room," Finn murmured, his admiration obvious.

Oh. She was a doctor. Surgeon, judging by the matter-of-fact yet utterly confident declaration. Neha wasn't sure if she ought to be comforted by the revelation, but having a guard between life and death was somewhat reassuring nonetheless. "First, do no harm" and all that.

The rest of the drive went by in relative silence. Her temporary handlers would occasionally say something to each other, Finn's undertone unmistakably flirty and Grace's responses endlessly patient. Were they dating? Fucking? Pining for each other like the private investigator version of *The Remains of the Day*? She couldn't tell. They seemed like polar opposites. The inveterate flirt and the über-professional ice queen. But, then again, what were she and Joe? Not exactly Couple of the Year.

"Ever fucked a blue-collar guy? What about a supe? Ever done one of us?"

All of her expectations were being laid to waste lately. Three decades' worth of ideas about who she was and what the world around her was like…turning on a dime. For example, Neha didn't know what she'd expected a black ops organization's HQ to look like. It was disorienting, disconcerting, to climb out of the SUV into an underground parking garage on the city's west side. It sat beneath a dark, sleek building that spoke more to hedge-fund management than a secret base of operations.

Grace and Finn led her to Third Shift without any acknowledgment of real estate disparities. Not even blinking as they used fancy biometric palm scanners to let themselves into what could have easily been a Midtown office building. They did the same scans before ushering her into an elevator. When they emerged on the firm's floor, it could have been any high-end law office or decently budgeted magazine. There was an empty reception area with a black marble desk and a stylized 3S on a fancy wall marquee behind it. What she could see beyond the curved entryway was an open floor with a few desks and some offices lining the walls. It looked like a model office, not something anyone actually used.

So it wasn't much of a surprise that it wasn't where Finn and Grace took her. No, they detoured toward a second elevator. Unlike the first one they'd used in the garage, it had no number buttons. Only three more strange-looking scanner panels. Grace put her palm on one and leaned in for a retinal scan on another set slightly higher up. Red lights on each square turned green in almost no time at all. It was then that Finn tapped his card against the third panel and pressed something on the touch-screen display.

"Triple-factor authentication for me," he explained, though it didn't really explain anything at all. "Can never be too careful these days. All sorts of riffraff might get in."

"What kind of riffraff are you?" she asked, since he'd given her the opening to appease her curiosity on that front.

"Worst kind," he said, shaking his head in mock seriousness.

"Lapsed Catholic. Former altar boy. *Vampire*. It's why I get a card, too. Because they can't rely on my bio scans."

Vampire. That made all kinds of sense. Though Neha suspected he'd been born with the charm and the good looks. No supernatural help needed in that department. But... "What happens if you lose the access card?"

"I keep backups," Grace answered before Finn could. "And I make him beg for them," she added in a tone that would make a dominatrix proud.

Wonder of wonders, the vampire's pale cheeks reddened. Neha suppressed her laughter as the elevator took them up in a swift journey that barely felt like a minute. She had no sense of how many floors they'd traveled, only that the doors were opening again with a metallic whir. Like the floor below, this one had an open floor full of cubicles and some offices. Unlike the floor below, there were flat-screen monitors practically everywhere. A long conference room—the one where she assumed she'd be parked with tea and condescending head pats—sat along the back of the space, the glass panel walls revealing a flurry of activity within.

"If I'm not back...if something happens...I want you to call this line."

"Welcome to Third Shift," Grace said, gesturing her forward.

"Welcome to Wonderland," Finn corrected as the walls ahead dimmed and frosted over for privacy. "You may not think you fell down the rabbit hole, but you well and truly did."

No, Neha had fallen into a far deeper hole than that. One she was terrified to label...and even more scared to lose.

———————

"So now what?" Neha Ahluwalia demanded, her dark-brown eyes flashing fire at nearly every person in the room...and probably a few beyond the frosted glass in the cubes, too.

Danny watched the woman pace the command center like an

angry tiger as Jackson and Elijah tried to field the question that had more answers than she could possibly guess. She was human, he knew, but he'd been around enough cat shifters to recognize and appreciate the similarities. The barely leashed frustration. The curled fists, like she was resisting scratching something or someone. He fully understood the inclination. He wasn't particularly thrilled to be here either. Relegated to the desk work while Yulia was miles away in South Brooklyn, at her brother's club, putting herself at risk. But even he, a cop, knew better than to suggest involvement from law enforcement.

"I don't understand why you can't just tip off a police raid or something…especially if you know that Vasiliev is up to his eyeballs in illegal activity," Ms. Ahluwalia exclaimed. "Just get in there. Blow it all wide open!"

"Would you want your man Peluso caught up in a police raid? Really?" Elijah was due to leave eventually for an engineered meet-cute with Meghna Saunders. Turning on the charm, creating a bond with her, all in the name of the mission. Maybe this was a practice run. The role of peacekeeper. Tamer of fellow lions. "Think about it," he urged. "I understand you're frustrated, but you know we can't just go in guns and claws ablazin'."

Danny winced. Because Elijah was right about what the NYPD would do in this situation. Too bad the voice his sister got starry-eyed over did little to calm Ms. Ahluwalia. Though she stopped pacing, she rubbed her arms as though she were cold. Her gaze continued to dart around from Lije to Jackson to Grace and Finn to him and Joaquin. "Then what do we do? Just let Vasiliev execute Joe? How's that any different than letting the state do the same?"

New York had abolished the death penalty in 2007. Plenty of states were rushing to tweak the laws in light of the supernatural come-out in 2016, but that wasn't what Neha was talking about. No, they all knew too well what she was talking about. From "accidents" as a result of excessive force to being secreted away in some detention facility never to be heard from again, there was no shortage of things that could be done to someone like Joe Peluso. That had *been done* to so many others before him.

"Peluso is *alive*." It was Jack's turn to weigh in. And he did so in a tone that brooked no argument. As if that wasn't enough, he added some minor theatrics. Magic prickling across his skin, dancing across his fingertips in tiny balls of light. "No one's executing anybody on our watch…and we *are* watching."

Joaquin had been on it for hours, using the spider to hack the phones, computers, and security cameras in Kamchatka. They were a bona fide Dark Web wizard—no magic needed—so they'd eventually succeeded on all fronts. Now the team had audio *and* visuals on the space. Danny turned to their guest again, watching her focus on the wall of monitors and the sound that was piping in on the speakers on low volume, like the most depressing streaming playlist. Even with Jack's little show, Third Shift didn't look like much right now. A few people in an office with an overly secure elevator. He understood why she was so wired, so impatient. But that was the thing about hiding in plain sight, about developing shields and defense mechanisms… It was all so you didn't notice what was right in front of you. The multiple angles on Kamchatka flashing across the screens. The bursts of Russian and Slovak that they were running through translation apps on a thirty-second delay. The fact that this room, this boring-ass conference room, currently hosted a lion shifter, a sorcerer, a vampire, and a hotshot doctor who was probably scarier than all the others combined.

Jack and Elijah were explaining some variation of that very thing when Danny's phone vibrated, dancing across the tabletop a few inches. His heart knocked around his chest at roughly the same rhythm.

Our guest is not scheduled for checkout yet. He might appreciate a mint on his pillow from a nice maid. Can you arrange for a service?

Yulia. Finally texting him back. She'd been on-camera a handful of times. Navigating the hallways. Smiling and soothing and ducking grabby hands in the fight pit below the club. Going through one private door twice. To a place where there was no surveillance. One guess as to where *that* was. The barest of details followed the initial message. A big show of some kind planned two nights from now. From which Joe Peluso might *permanently* check out.

"Uh. Hey. Everyone." Danny cleared his throat. "Yulia's saying she can get at least one of us into the club." And if one of them were in... Well, that meant *all* of them were in. He quickly recounted everything she'd texted him. "It'll be a tight window, but she's willing to make it happen."

"Me," Ms. Ahluwalia said before Jack or Elijah could make any kind of call. "If anyone's going in there for Joe, it's going to be me."

The bosses looked at her. Looked at each other. Some sort of eerie silent communication passed between them. Probably *not* psychic, probably just the shorthand of two people who'd worked together a long fucking time, but Danny had learned a while ago not to make assumptions about anyone at 3S. Maybe there was a whole mental conversation going on there between the lion, the male witch, and their wardrobe.

"It's not going to be you *alone*," Jack assured her, the steely resolution in his voice offset by the thrill of the chase gleaming in his eyes. "We're pulling together an op. They want to put on a show? We'll give them audience members. A few of the city's finest and not-so-finest."

The knot of tension that had been sitting in Danny's chest for days loosened just the tiniest fraction. He caught Finn's grin across the room and felt an answering smile spread across his face. Third Shift was about to go on the hunt.

25

THE LOCKER COULD HAVE BEEN at the top of the midrise building or at the bottom. Neha really had no idea. Up was down, and down was up. Finn was right: she'd stepped through the Looking Glass into Wonderland. A place where the rule of law didn't matter as much as the rule of claw did. Grace had whisked her back into the elevator just moments after Jackson had made his big pronouncement about putting together a mission. Before Neha could even voice a protest about that or anything else—not that there was much protesting would do versus Grace's surprisingly firm grip on her arm. And now here they were in a cross between a weapons locker, a gym locker, and a Foot Locker...all decorated in dark, dour colors and easily cleanable tiles.

Neha didn't want to think too hard about how much blood had been cleaned off the floors she now walked upon. Hell, she wanted to turn her brain off entirely...except that Joe needed her to be on her A game. He needed her mind, her tenacity, her fighting for him.

Grace looked up from a tablet she'd drawn from inside her jacket. "Jack's already got the bare bones laid out, as per Yulia's messages. We'll be going in as waitresses, extra hires for the big event. So we should look the part. Off to the costume closet we go," she said wryly.

Neha blinked. It hadn't even been five minutes since they'd gotten off the lift. She was still in the middle of the nickel tour. Staring at grenade launchers in a reinforced glass case. There were operation specs *already*? Third Shift looked simple on the outside...but they were far from it once you got past the surface. Maybe she could trust her decision after all. Maybe she could trust *herself*. "And then what? What do we do once we're in?" she prompted. "Because I need to see Joe. I need to know he's okay."

They'd had visuals on every single thing in Aleksei Vasiliev's club up on those screens in the conference room. Every single thing except Joe. He was, no doubt, behind the door that Yulia and a few brutish guards had periodically been vanishing through. It felt like he was millions of miles away.

Grace didn't answer right away, instead leading Neha down a narrow hallway toward what was, indeed, a clothes closet. A really *big* closet, illuminated once Grace flipped the studio lights on. Poles heavy with hangers ran the length of the room on either side, while shelves and drawers made up the middle. Most everything was in shades of black or blue. *To hide bloodstains*. Neha again had the disturbing thought, and she had to shake it off as the surgeon-spy waved her over to a rack toward the back. Here was a splash of color. No, more than a splash. Like Picasso and Cyndi Lauper's sartorial love child. Neon. Fuchsia. Leopard print.

"I'll be assessing the hostiles," Grace said as she flipped through jackets and skirts, each louder than the previous. "We already have a head count on the regulars going in and out of Kamchatka, but there will be a massive uptick on Friday night. Joaquin has already hacked in and added one of Finn's aliases to the digital guest list. One of his disreputable ones," she added with a slight smile.

Could anything be more disreputable than Finn already was?

The bit of humor was enough to relax Neha just enough to rifle through clothes herself. "And then you go all superhero team and take the bad guys down?"

"No." Grace grimaced…and the expression did nothing to make her look less beautiful. "We prefer to be a little less big-budget than the Avengers. Our extraction of Joe Peluso will be dependent upon exactly what they have planned for him. We may have to let Vasiliev's show play out and *then* take action."

Neha didn't like the sound of that. Because it meant Joe could be collateral damage during his own rescue. He could get *hurt*. "He'll need to know. That's why I need to see him as soon as possible. So he can be warned, prepared."

"Is that the only reason?" The other woman's gaze was too keen, too penetrating…but her voice was gentle. Low and comforting, not the don't-fuck-with-me tone she seemed to default to around her male colleagues.

Was it that obvious? What Neha and Joe had been up to these past few days? Could the shifters smell it on her? Could they all see the desperation on her face? Neha swallowed hard and drew on her composure as she drew some items off their hangers and slung them over her arm. "It's the only reason that's relevant."

"Okay." Grace nodded, accepting the evasion for what it was and letting it go. She shifted gears seamlessly. "Is there anything else you need before we check back in with the bosses and find you someplace to bed down for the night?"

And just like that, Neha's composure wavered. Because she needed dozens of things. Hope. Strength. A bottle of wine. Pani puri with Tejal. Ibuprofen. Joe's arms around her. And… "Do you think I could call my mother? I promise it'll be secure. She thinks I'm on a business trip."

The grip on her arm was soft this time. A squeeze. "Sure," said Grace. "You can let her know you'll be home soon."

Home. Neha had no idea what that would look like after this.

What anything would look like after this. The day after tomorrow, it might not look like anything at all.

———

DGS had been buzzing like a disturbed wasp's nest all week. All three stories of the brownstone were a hive of activity. Associates pretending to focus on cases. Paralegals walking on eggshells. The assistants trying to keep everyone on task, because that was just what good assistants did. The partners weren't happy. No, that was an understatement. The partners were *pissed*. The names had scheduled a vote for Monday—to fire Neha from the firm effective immediately, no matter that she might be floating facedown in the East River for all anyone knew. Nate wasn't about to enlighten Spencer Dickenson, Hannah Gould, or Michael Smythe on her whereabouts. He and Dustin had, however, done their best to rally the rest of the non-name partners and fight for Neha's right to return and face the music in person.

They still had all of tomorrow and the weekend to do some convincing, but Nate was just about rallied out now. He hurried through the foyer and down the brownstone's front steps with his head full of snide remarks and eye rolls and complaints that Neha's caseload had been divvied up among already overburdened junior and senior associates. *"I'm so sorry her being shot at and kidnapped and potentially murdered is such an inconvenience to all of you. Your compassion is overwhelming."* He'd held on to his temper for the most part but snapped back at Dickenson, who was doing his level best to live up to the first part of that name. *"Take a walk,"* the baby boomer had snarled. *"Or the next walk you take might be to the unemployment line."*

Nate had equity in the firm. They couldn't actually *fire* him. There would have to be a buyout. But he'd taken the advice. Made a beeline to the sidewalk. Fueled by equal parts rage and worry, he was halfway to the Brooklyn Heights Promenade before he even realized it. Someone fell into line behind him, their footsteps eerily mirroring his. Mugger? No. He knew without turning around who it was. Finn Conlan, the private investigator who wasn't a private investigator. The man who wasn't just a man. And who'd made himself so comfortable in Nate's home. He'd left with the same flourish with which he'd appeared…barely giving Nate time to process their conversation or Neha's cryptic text messages, but offering him plenty of frustrated fantasy fodder later that night. What did he want now?

Nate slowed his gait just enough so that they were even, taking up space on the sidewalk like asshole tourists. "To what do I owe this visit, Mr. Conlan?"

The vampire didn't bother purring pleasantries this time. He got right to the point. "There's a private party at Kamchatka tomorrow night. I would like to be your date." There was nothing romantic about the ask. His blue eyes were narrowed with focus, determination…ruthlessness.

Nate suppressed a shiver. "You're making a big assumption… that I can get on the guest list. That they'd *want* me on the guest list, considering what my client did to Vasiliev's men."

"That's precisely why they *would* welcome you. Curiosity, perversity, challenge, all wrapped in a tidy little bow. But not to worry: *I'm* on the guest list. I just need recognizable company. And I want witnesses. D'you understand? We need you there. A respected representative of the legal community. An advocate." Finn's intensity was startling. In such stark contrast to the flirtation he usually employed. It got the point across, though. Nate understood. The more people on their side in Vasiliev's club, the less the likelihood of the narrative playing out in the vor's favor. And the higher the stakes.

Still…Nate wasn't exactly raring to don one of his favorite bespoke suits and walk right into the lion's den. Bear's den. Whatever supernatural den Kamchatka was rumored to be. "Why do you think *I* need to be involved in this? It's a serious conflict of interest."

"So was keeping your associate's text messages to yourself," the vampire pointed out. "And you did that, didn't you? You didn't run straight on to the police with those texts after I left."

No. Nate had learned a long time ago, partially thanks to Dustin's friendship, that running to the police wasn't always the smartest option. But he didn't appreciate what Finn was hinting at. "So this is blackmail?"

"Nothing so pedestrian as that. It's a chance for you to see the real underbelly of this city," Finn said sharply. "The things that go bump in the night, and the creatures that eat those things. The people who allow it all, who fund it, who keep the dirty wheels greased. They're not just in your courtrooms, love."

"I don't know what you want from me." A lie. Because he knew at least *one* thing Finn wanted from him. "Or why I should put myself at risk for this."

Finn stopped below a streetlamp, shaking his head. As if he sensed the half-truths. "You know what it's like...walking amongst people, knowing you're different and they can't tell," he murmured, brilliant-blue eyes going distant with memory. "Unless you give something away. Then they turn on you. Pitchforks, torches. 'How dare you try and live amongst us like you're *normal*?'"

Nate's spine prickled with instant discomfort. "Are you comparing being Jewish to being a vampire? Or my being gay? Because I'm not comfortable with that, and it's not going to help your argument."

The Oppression Olympics were alive and well in this day and age, especially with supernaturals thrown into the mix. And as much of an advocate as Nate was, there were certain things he just wouldn't stand for. His grandparents hadn't fled Poland to have fang-laden predators perfectly capable of defending themselves claim some sort of kinship via shared marginalization.

Finn visibly paled. An impressive feat, considering he was pale to begin with. "I wouldn't dream of it," he assured. "I was speaking as a Catholic who'll shag your brother, your sister, *and* your mum without a second thought. As a thrice-damned slut who got shoved into seminary to try and hide my ills and chase out my demons. Didn't work, of course. Because I was a horny little queer who never believed in anything. Not until—" He cut himself off, as if realizing he'd revealed entirely too much about himself. "I contain multitudes, love," he finished cockily, as if that made up for the slip.

There were stories there. Narratives Nate didn't have a right to access. He didn't know what to make of any of it. "Sounds like you've 'shagged' multitudes, too," he said to try to maintain some distance.

"Is there a problem with that?" Finn crowded him against the lamppost. He leaned in—close, too close, close enough for Nate to consider doing something ludicrous like kiss him—before flinching back. "Oh. That's new," he observed with an odd sort of delight, frowning down at the singed flesh just below his collarbone. In the perfect shape of Nate's Star of David.

Nate understood very little about the pathology of the modern nonfictional vampire, but he had to laugh. "What do you mean 'that's new'? Did you really think it would only be crosses?"

Light glinted off the edges of Finn's canines as he bared his teeth in a macabre grin. "It's never just crosses, Nathaniel. They always find something to burn. Do you want it to be your colleague and your client?"

The shiver he'd experienced earlier broke out into a full blast of cold. It would be easy to blame it on something Finn was doing with his vampirical powers, but Nate was smarter than that. He knew what his conscience felt like, what his *fear* felt like.

"Okay," he said, finally. "Okay, I will go with you to this thing at Kamchatka. I'll be a witness to whatever it is you want me to see."

Finn's frightening, glittering intensity seemed to instantly dim to an attractive glow. "I'd say that you won't regret it, but I can't make that promise." He tilted forward, letting his full lips brush Nate's jaw. "I don't make promises to anyone anymore."

26

"NO. ABSO-FUCKING-LUTELY NOT." ELIJAH'S DARK eyes flashed gold with warning as he made the booming pronouncement.

It was the answer Danny had expected. Tossing and turning all night as he made his case to himself first. *I have to be there. I need to know Yulia is safe.* Flipping the arguments over and around in his head as he took the 7 train into Hudson Yards and then made the walk north to HQ. *I know I'm not qualified for away missions yet, but this is different.*

"It's not different," Elijah said when Danny made that particular point aloud. "In fact, it's even more dangerous. You're more of a liability than an asset. Vasiliev and his men *know* you. They can use you against Yulia and against us. Is that what you want? To be made the second you walk into that club?"

"That's the last thing I want." Danny squirmed in his seat. Elijah's public-facing office was equipped with all sorts of creature comforts—ergonomic chairs and everything—but it felt like he was sitting on a bed of nails. Like the heat was on full blast. Angry sweat was beading his skin. He felt petty and small and young. "Neha Ahluwalia's going in. She has no training whatsoever. How is that any less of a liability?"

Elijah leaned forward, interlacing his fingers on the gleaming granite desktop, looking for all the world like a principal about to give Danny detention. Hell, he'd taught school for a while; he probably had a lot of experience giving out detentions. "You have to look at the bigger picture, bruv. We don't let her go, she raises a ruckus. Or she goes in on her own, half-cocked. We can't risk that. We can't risk letting this get out of hand. Because more than just our mission is at stake. If this goes sideways, there could be global consequences."

Today was not the day to lecture Danny about the bigger picture. He was so sick of being reminded of that picture. "I know you care about everyone, Lije. You're always doing things for the greater good. But have you ever, *ever* done something for just one person? Risked it all for them? Have you ever loved someone that much? That's how I feel about Yulia." In the short time he'd been moonlighting at Third Shift, Danny had never heard Lije talk about his personal life, never seen him go out on dates or even *mention* interest in someone. Meghna Saxena-Saunders was the only woman who existed for him…and that was just a job.

"Point taken." Elijah accepted the direct hit with a curt nod. And because he was an exemplary boss, he didn't hit back. He just sat with the accusation for a long minute. His face was sober, his hands still gripping each other tightly. And then he circled back to something that Danny couldn't argue. "But if Yulia Vasilieva feels the same way, she'll want *you* safe. She grew up in the life. She knows how to handle herself. She's been doing it for decades. You're not there yet."

It was true. And it stung. He'd gone from beat cop to detective, but as far as 3S was concerned, he was still a rookie. And Yulia… Yulia had left her home, her job, a quiet life she'd loved—and *him*—all in exchange for safety. Lest Danny be killed or her bar burned to ashes. He didn't know who he was madder at: Elijah, himself, or the world at large. "I want to get there," he said wearily. "All I want is to get there so I can be there for *her*."

"I know," his boss said, untangling his hands so he could reach across and gently knock the back of Danny's. "I'm not so hard-hearted as all that."

But neither was he softhearted enough to fall for someone.

Danny didn't know whether to root for or dread the day he finally did.

———————

Danny's hand skated down her side, featherlight, before curling around her hip. She arched into him, welcoming his kiss, his dick, everything he had to give her. "Yulia," *he whispered, lowering himself into the cradle of her thighs.* "Yulia, I want to make this good for you. Safe for you."

And that was when the fantasy splintered, shattering like glass. Because there was nothing safe for her, was there? Not as long as she was bear and Danny was human. Yulia shook out of the ridiculous and ill-timed visions, willing the warmth from her bones and her sex. She gripped her smartphone, eyes once again darting across the street, watching the Brighton Beach MTA terminal for who might emerge.

Heard you have a staffing problem. Our agency will send over a sub ASAP, Danny had said. And that was more or less the end of all they'd dared say to each other. Brief. Impersonal. Somehow still as erotic as love letters. She'd deleted the messages immediately. Emptied the deleted messages box as well. She was not naive, not ignorant, despite so many impulses that might speak to the contrary. Bringing people into the club was reckless, dangerous. Effectively signing her own death warrant. But hadn't she already given up her life when she left the Confessional? She'd signed her soul over to her brother. Anything that happened now would happen to someone living a half-life.

A wave of people came down from the elevated train tracks, surging down the steps like a wave of insects. She knew almost immediately who Danny's people had sent. Tourists were easy to spot. Those who lived in the neighborhood, too. These women fell somewhere in between. Beautiful and brown-skinned, wearing their resting bitch faces so that they were largely unapproachable. And with carefully chosen accessories, they somehow managed to look like so many girls she knew from Eastern Europe. Animal-print jackets, garish blue eye shadow, stiletto heels. Perfect for the Pit. Anyone who wasn't looking for something suspicious would be none the wiser. But she was trained to look beyond the normal. To see which average New Yorker wasn't an average New Yorker at all.

They were humans, both of them. She detected no scent of a fellow predator. That did not mean they were prey. No, in fact, as they neared her, she could definitely say they were not prey. Like her, they were danger wrapped in deception.

"You are the girls from the agency, yes?" she said in lieu of a greeting, her accent just a bit exaggerated. Her best Boris-and-Natasha.

"Yes. We are to be helping you tonight and tomorrow," one of the women replied in an Indian accent that could've been lifted from *The Simpsons*. "It is a very big show, *hai na*?" Yulia struggled not to laugh at the glint in her eye. This had to be Neha Ahluwalia, the woman who had been in hiding with Aleksei's new guest.

"We'd like to start immediately. Get the lay of the land." Her companion was not as amused and spoke with no inflection in her crisp tone. She wore her eyeshadow and bright lipstick like weapons. One of Danny's colleagues, no doubt. "We don't want to make any mistakes when your guests arrive."

"Of course. We appreciate initiative." Yulia reverted to her natural voice and gestured them forward, walking with them in the general direction of the club. She could've called a car, but she hardly trusted drivers in the area. There was no telling who was on her brother's payroll. "Any phones will be locked in the employee safe for the length of your shift. Our patrons value discretion. No selfies. No cell-phone video. Nothing. You understand?"

"We didn't bring phones," the no-nonsense woman assured her, the lie nearly undetectable. She was taller than Neha and Yulia herself. Her curly ink-black hair was pulled into a high ponytail that only added to her imposing height, and her cheekbones were blade-sharp slashes in her striking face.

"What do I call you?" Yulia wondered.

"Maria," she said, providing the alias in a way that indicated it was best to not call her anything at all.

"Aishwarya, but you can call me 'Aish,'" Neha Ahluwalia added with another hint of laughter in her eyes. As if she was imparting a private joke. But her expression quickly sobered. "It's important that we do a good job. *Very* important."

Beyond important. Yulia felt the prickle of fur beneath her skin. The tease of extra teeth in her mouth and a growl building low in her throat. Her clan thought her weak, complacent, subservient. What happened on fight night, no matter which direction the wind blew, would change everything. There would be winners and there would be losers. There would be the living and the dead. Hope or the very absence of it. Aleksei's fall, or his continued rise. Were she and her two new friends all that stood between destruction and salvation…or the very force that would bring the roof down on all of their heads?

Yulia would find out soon enough.

27

"HEY. WE DON'T HAVE MUCH time. But I had to see you. I had to make sure you're okay."

It was fucking weird. Like something out of a dream. Neha but not Neha. She sounded like herself, but her hair was some funky shade of almost-blond, cut blunt at her jawline. The dress she was wearing barely hit her knees. It was some shiny, slick material like leather or PVC. She looked like a brown version of that spy chick from *Alias*. But her palms smoothing over him, her eyes cataloging his cuts and bruises, that was familiar. That was *her*. And it pulled him out of the haze of the tranqs.

"Neha?" He focused on her hands, on her face, letting those beautiful things bring on the rest of the clarity he needed.

Her wig brushed his cheek as she felt around him for something. "Yeah, Joe. It's me," she confirmed. "Yulia Vasilieva got me a half hour in here with you. We rerouted the security cameras. But it's not a rescue—not just yet, I'm sorry. Just some recon. You're not the only one good at that after all."

"You shouldn't have come looking for me," he said, struggling against the cuffs, torn between snuggling close and bucking her away from him.

Her hands closed over his wrists. For a second he thought she was trying—a futile effort—to hold him still. But no. She had a key or a pick or something. "Oh, Joe. You should know me better than that by now," she murmured as she worked the lock on his restraints. "I had no choice."

Bullshit. "Of course, you had a choice," he snapped. "I left you that phone number so you had a choice."

Neha rocked back on her heels once the chains were loose. The brief, beautiful light of victory at her achievement faded as she responded to what he said. "And you thought what…? That I'd just sit quietly in a corner and let people I don't even *know* handle it? Go back to my life like nothing happened? Do you really think it's possible?" she demanded.

"For you? It should be." Joe gingerly stood up, shook out his stiff limbs as best he could, knowing full well he was probably going to have to lock back up soon enough. Like she'd said when she let herself in here, no way could this turn into a rescue. It was just a temporary reprieve. Somebody would eventually notice the cameras were on a loop. If not that, the guards had a schedule. They'd be back to shoot him up full of their nasty cocktail of sedatives before too long. "You should be able to go back. To get back everything I took from you."

She cussed at him then. Lyrical and harsh Punjabi words he didn't understand but got the meaning of clear enough. And then she switched back to English with a frustrated huff. "And what about you? What about what's been taken from *you*?"

Nothing had been taken from him that he hadn't willingly given up. Joe knew that. He'd done this. Every decision he'd made in his life had led him right here. He'd enlisted. He'd said yes to Apex. He'd pulled the trigger over and over again. He'd literally bitten off more than he could chew. "I'm where I belong. In a cage with the other animals."

"Oh, *fuck* you." Neha blazed up in righteous rage, getting to her feet and socking him in the chest with a surprisingly powerful fist. "How *dare* you say that when there are thousands of people—hundreds of *kids*—in actual cages along our borders? You know you don't belong here. Just like you didn't belong in jail. You shouldn't have to pay for what the military turned you into! You shouldn't have to pay just because you're different."

Christ. She still didn't get it. *Refused* to get it. Like a Brave Little Social Justice Toaster. Of *course* he belonged in jail. "You want me to tell you they *made* us into killing machines. That they put this monster in me. Doc, it ain't nothin' that wasn't already there. I'm not *different*. I'm Death. And I *chose* this."

"I don't believe that." She stared at him, eyes full of fierce anger and unshed tears. All those weeks ago, she'd wanted him to use a PTSD defense. Maybe *she* was the one who needed it. Maybe the trauma of the past few days was finally getting to her. "I *won't* believe that. That is not the man I've gotten to know."

Joe barked out a laugh. "That's probably *every* man you know. Look at this world. Look at those cages on the border. People keep saying 'This isn't us' and 'This isn't America,' but it *is*. It's who we've always been. You know that even more than I do."

Neha didn't let it go. Wouldn't let it go. Wouldn't let *him* go. "But that's a cop-out!" she insisted. "Why can't I expect *better*? From America and from you?"

That was it, wasn't it? She didn't just expect better. She *demanded* better. She *deserved* better. Too bad she'd thrown in her lot with him. Joe growled, slamming his palm against the cinder-block wall. He already knew the noise would make no impact. He couldn't hear out, so they couldn't hear in. The room had been soundproofed. Probably so even the most sensitive shifters wouldn't pick up on the screaming if they were drinking upstairs in the club. "Maybe neither of us is capable of better. You ever consider that?"

"Never." Her reply was almost immediate. "If I considered that,

I wouldn't *be* here. Is that what you want, Joe? Is that what you really want? Me gone?"

No. No, it was the furthest thing from what he really wanted. He turned in one swift motion, whipping out one arm and hauling her bodily against him. Chest to chest. Thigh to thigh. Her curves against his angles. "What I really want…is you."

It felt like it'd been years since he'd kissed her. Too fucking long. So he did it now, lowering his head, taking her mouth. Swallowing whatever lawyerly argument she had lined up for him next. Inhaling her gasp of surprise and then the needy moan that followed it up. She wanted to blame every impulse on his wolf… but this was all the man. The man who'd wanted her from day one. The man who put her in danger because the need to fuck her was just that strong. The need to fuck her and have her and take her. To mark her with his teeth and his tongue. Sucking bruises into the column of her throat.

"Joe…" He felt her hands on him, her nails digging into his back. Urging him on instead of telling him to stop. *Why* wouldn't this woman tell him to stop? She was supposed to be the smart one, for Christ's sake. The one with sense, the one with limits. The one with a Taser and a .22 in her purse.

"Goddammit, Neha." He cursed into her soft skin even as he was baring it, yanking at the straps of her dress, tugging up her skirt. "I'm not better. I can't be better."

"Too bad," she murmured, tipping her head back like she was offering a vampire her jugular, like she was asking him to mark her throat. "You're all I want, too."

It was completely reckless to give in to this need. Just like they had in that alley what seemed like months ago now. Really just days. Now she was ready to take him against another wall, to spread her legs, welcome him deep. *Demanding* better from him. *Deserving* better from him. In the only way they could agree on right now. It was so risky. Letting her leave here smelling like him to go back out amid hostile shifters. But she'd already rubbed all over him. Already gotten his scent all over her. What did it matter if they made it worse? So, he made it as good as he could. Reaching down between them to stroke her clit through her panties. Kissing her until he was out of breath. He whispered all kinds of sentimental and sexy shit in her ear. Like how she was beautiful and how he'd never known anyone like her and he'd happily die in her pussy and wished he could right now.

"That...that would be traumatic for me," she laughed, even as she started to unravel. "I don't...I don't want you to die in my arms, Joe." The tiny little spasms against his fingers, the jagged sound of her breathing. Fuck, he loved how they were together. How she pushed up into him, trapping his hand, slamming their hips together, chasing her orgasm.

"I don't want you to die *at all*, baby." Joe stumbled away from the wall, one hand on her neck and the other gripping her ass, so there was nothing holding her up but him. So it was just *them* grinding up on each other, doing the work of getting her off. She locked her legs tighter around his waist, fucking herself on his fingers while his cock ached with jealousy. "That's it. Yeah. Use me. Use me up, Doc," he told her. "This is what I am. This is all I can be."

Her fuck toy. Her right now. Her future regret.

That wasn't what he said aloud, though. He was a colossal asshole who was absolutely going to break her heart, but he wasn't *that* cruel. When Neha moaned her release into his ear, panting the question "What? What's all you can be?" he told her the only thing that mattered in this moment.

"Yours. Just yours."

━━━━━━━━━

Yulia had promised her thirty minutes alone in the room, warning her that one of her brother's men would be coming in on the forty-five mark to tranquilize Joe again. Neha knew that time had to be up. She still didn't budge, except to set her clothing to rights.

"Baby, you have to leave," Joe whispered fiercely in the darkness that engulfed them, like he'd instinctively sensed part of the plan. "You have to go back."

"No. Not yet. Not without finishing this." Vasiliev was out there somewhere. The goon guarding the door, too. He probably had an entire clip with Joe's name on it—along with whatever they were pumping into his bloodstream every few hours to keep him from Hulking out and escaping. The last thing she was going to do was turn tail and run. She and Third Shift had already put too many things in motion. "Not without *you*."

"Not *with* me." There was a desperation in his voice she'd never heard before. And she couldn't see his eyes, but she knew it was mirrored there as well. "It can't end good with me. It *won't*."

"I'm not oblivious to reality, Joe," she whispered. For all her ideas of having DGS work things out with law enforcement, any chance of a plea had been off the table the minute they rabbited out of the courthouse. "Even if the people I brought in on this can get us out of this, I'll be disbarred. You'll land in solitary. That's assuming we don't get taken out by Vasiliev's guys on the way out of here...or some trigger-happy cop two blocks away."

"Then why won't you leave?" Joe still wouldn't look at her. He shoved ineffectually at the wall he'd just loved her against. Like he could push it away along with her. "Tell them I forced you. Tell them I kidnapped you. Tell them whatever. Just *go*. Get the fuck away from me."

"I can't." The confession tore from her throat. Badass Neha Ahluwalia, who was rarely afraid of anything and had a damn go bag full of weapons. And she was suddenly the most scared she'd ever been in her life. Scared of this moment. Scared of her truth. Scared of what would happen if she didn't speak it. "I can't leave you, Joe...because you're inside of me. It doesn't matter if I physically walk away from you… You're under my skin. You're in my head. I don't know where I stop and you begin. So we're going to get you out of here. Out of this. However we can."

Joe's shoulders shook. But he still wouldn't break. Even as he crouched to slip his cuffs back on and return to his position against the pipes that ran from floor to ceiling. Only when he was seated again, locked up tight, did he look up at her. And his eyes were hooded, hollow. "You think you can rescue me, Doc. Save me. But you can't. You never really could."

The three little words were right there. On the edge of her tongue. She knew better than to say them right now. So, she showed him instead. She joined him on the cold concrete floor, straddled his lap, and took his face between her palms. Forcing him to look at her. To acknowledge her. To acknowledge *this*. That he was hard for her—and soft for her—even with death right outside the door. "Tell me you're not here with me, Joe. Tell me I'm not your obsession after all."

But he couldn't, could he? Because that was why they were here in this place to begin with. All because he'd teased her across a table and then begged to hold her in his arms just once. *He* was the romantic, not her. *He* was the one driven by emotion. He'd killed six men because he wanted to. Because he needed to. And he'd kissed her because he wanted to. Because he needed to.

"Neha." He made a low, desperate sound. "Doc…"

"I can't leave you," she repeated, shifting to rub against his dick, wishing she could take its sweet, hot length one more time. "You're in me, Joe. You're *in me*."

He didn't try to argue. Not this time. Because there was no cross-examination to be made. She had him fair and square. He curved into her, as best he could with his hands restrained, buried his face in her throat, breathed her in. And she felt the damp warmth of his tears. Maybe he was crying for the little brother he'd lost and for the crimes he'd committed. Maybe he was crying for her, for them, for what they'd found together. He knew it just as well as she did: Neha wouldn't still be here if they weren't in love.

They didn't have time to waste, but they stole the minutes anyway. She held him close until the grief and the guilt abated and all that remained was pure passion, pure trust. And then she kissed him with *her* want, *her* need. It didn't last nearly long enough. Over before it began. Cut short by Yulia's sharp knock on the door… and by the inevitable weight of reality.

28

THE STAFF WAS SETTLED IN the kitchen for "family dinner" before the evening shift—none the wiser about the two new Pit waitresses who'd joined the table. Conversation flowed in English and various Russian dialects, and Yulia was not at all surprised to hear Grace's voice mixed in with the latter. She seemed formidable, more and more competent each moment. The same could not be said for Neha Ahluwalia…or for Yulia herself. Her knees shook as she made her way toward her brother's office, her skin still chilled with the memory of opening the "guest room" door to find Neha and her wolf lover in a desperate embrace. Foolish, foolish romantics. Taking such a risk. But she'd taken the same risks, hadn't she? Messaging Danny. Meeting with him. Kissing him recklessly where the drones and Aleksei's men could see. Bringing his people into the club.

And she wasn't done taking chances. Leading the woman not named Maria through the private corridors so she could do whatever she was here to do. Spying once again outside her brother's door. Pressing flat to the wall, slowing her heartbeat as if in hibernation, tuning her ears to the voices on the other side of the cinder blocks. She'd practiced such things as a girl. A child's game. Using her shifter skills to the best of her ability. Listening to her parents as they prepared for parties. Eavesdropping on Aleksei and Yuri as they played at being men and tussled like cubs. But there was no playing now. No game. What she heard now could be the difference between life and death.

"...I am ready, Sasha," Aleksei was saying in his most boastful tone. "After tonight, there will be no more distractions."

Sasha. She had a vague recollection of the honored guest from the other night in the arena. The man who'd smelled rank and strange. A representative of whoever held Aleksei's strings. His voice was higher than her brother's, his Russian accent stilted, as if he wasn't quite comfortable with the language. "You have assured us of this many times, and many times we've been disappointed. Aston won't be pleased if you fail him again."

Aston. This name, too, rang familiar. She'd heard it before, in whispers and other snatches of conversation not meant for her ears. What could, and would, this Aston do if Aleksei disappointed him once more? Take his territory? Take his life? What was worse? Yulia suppressed a shiver, concentrating on listening, on *remembering*. Anything that might help the operation. Anything that might get their prisoner out alive.

Their back-and-forth of threats and promises went on for a few minutes, like a kind of negotiation. And then Sasha laughed. "Enough!" he declared. "Either you will succeed or you will die, my friend. Now tell me of this grand finale you have arranged for us tonight."

And, oh, her prideful brother did just that, explaining with great relish how he was saving the best for last. "I will make an example of Joseph Peluso," he bragged. "He is fighting one of my best men, one of my best bears. Yuri will make certain he does not leave the cage alive...and all who witness the execution will understand that Aleksei Vasiliev is not to be trifled with. You cross me, you pay with your life."

Intellectually, she'd always known Yuri killed people for Aleksei. Such was their organization. When she'd moved to New York at eleven years old, she'd thought her elder sibling a successful restaurant owner, a simple businessman. Her illusions had shattered before her sixteenth birthday. But this? Seeing Yuri Medvedev murder a man in cold blood in front of dozens of witnesses? Yulia could hear no more. She wrenched away from the wall and scurried back toward the club proper. She ducked into the supply closet just off the kitchens, pulled her burner from the depths of her dress, and quickly summarized everything she'd learned. This was no time for cryptic codes and coyness about hotel accommodations. She laid it all it out in stark, simple words. The timeline for this evening's events. The name of her brother's superior. Danny wrote back almost immediately.

Good. This is incredibly helpful. Are you safe?

Was she safe? Had she *ever* been safe? Yulia choked on a lunatic giggle as she typed out a lie.

For now.

It was as if he could see her, hear her, through the cellular network.

That's not enough. I want you safe forever.

This time, she choked on a rush of tears. What had she done to deserve this sweet, caring human's affection and devotion? Served him a few drinks. Offered him a few truths and far more half-truths and not nearly enough kisses. And now he and his people were caught up in her world…where everything stank of death and destruction.

You're so funny, Danny. There is no assurance of forever.

Yes, there is. I'm coming for you. I'm gonna get you out.

But it was not her getting out that troubled her. It was, instead, a fear of dragging him further *in*.

———————————

Neha had watched professional wrestling. Ultimate fighting. Martial-arts movies. None of it compared to the Pit. To whatever *this* was. The air in the underground arena was rank with phero-mones, musk, something distinctly animal. The music piping in through the state-of-the-art sound system had long since been drowned out by a bizarre kind of white noise. It had taken her sev-eral minutes to figure out that the sound was growls. A chorus of vocal and subvocal sounds blending together. It was a struggle to hold on to her drinks tray—and her composure.

If Grace was similarly unsettled, there was no indication. She was gliding through the crowd with ease, just like Yulia. Bantering in Cantonese with a visiting businessman here, ducking a grabby hand there. She'd transformed from the scarily efficient operative who'd picked Neha up from the park yesterday to this bubbly, flirty beauty completely comfortable in terrifying surroundings. Whenever Finn showed up—which had to be soon—it would probably blow his mind.

Joe's match was the night's main event. Slated for some point after midnight. Three minor cage fights had already played out. Bear shifter versus bear shifter. Fairly evenly paired, but no less lethal for it. Neha wasn't sure she would ever forget the visuals. Fur and teeth. Blood slicking the floor. A random club employee coming in after each match to bleach the steel cage that sat in the center of the arena. It was a circular space, with tables situated in ever-widening rings around the fighting stage and a raised VIP area where Vasiliev and his goons could lounge within prime view of the blood sports. The walls and ceiling were painted a lurid bor-dello red, the floors easily washable terrazzo tile. The entire effect was terrifying in a way she'd never before experienced.

This was not Neha's world. She'd stepped through the Looking Glass when she crossed the threshold of Kamchatka. But she couldn't go back. She'd signed on for this. She'd *demanded* partici-pation. She was all in now. Because she'd made that call. Used the number Joe had given her...not to save herself, but to find her way back to him.

A commotion by the doors pulled her from her ill-timed reverie and her rote rounds of the arena. She caught a flash of familiar white hair. *Nate.* The quick meal she'd downed with the kitchen staff a few hours ago tossed in her gut like a laundry load. She hadn't seen him in what felt like years. She'd left him and Dustin twisting in the wind, throwing away all of their trust in her. He'd walked in with Finn, who was dressed to kill in a black leather jacket and skin-tight clothes beneath. He looked devastating and deadly. And that meant things were about to get serious. She had no idea how Nate and Finn even knew each other, but it was clearly part of whatever Third Shift had planned. Whether they were here to watch the proceedings or to help wreak havoc was anybody's guess.

Neha took care not to acknowledge the two new entrants to the Pit when they were finally given the go-ahead. Grace, ever the consummate operative, took no such pains. She made a beeline to her partner and his date, batting her eyelashes, swinging her hips, and offering them some high-end vodka. Even from across the room, Neha could see the lusty smile on Finn's lips and glinting blue in his eyes. Yeah, he *definitely* appreciated the performance.

Meanwhile, the bravado that Neha had slipped on like a Halloween costume from Ricky's continued to unravel. What was she doing here? She was a Punju girl from Queens, not a superspy. What could she even *do* to help Joe if shit hit the fan tonight? The doubt rippled across her skin, distracting her to the point where she found herself entirely too close to the VIP section where Aleksei Vasiliev was holding court with a slew of cronies. Doubt immediately turned to sweat. At first glance, the vor looked like his little sister. Fair-haired, pale-eyed, attractive. But a second glance...it was like that old TV show, *V*. When the lizard people peeled away their skin to show their true form. There was an icy monstrosity that pulsed in Vasiliev. In how he smiled at the men in the box with him. In the way that he threw his arm across the back of the banquette…with his hand partially shifted into a claw.

"The Bear Pit is a 'safe place,'" Yulia had warned her with a touch of mockery in her tone. *"Our people shift freely, not just to fight but also to watch. You must not show surprise or that you are afraid. To do so is to flag yourself as prey."* The heads-up hadn't actually prepared her for any of this. For half-shifted brown bears eating and drinking and trying to kill each other for sport. It was nothing like Tejal's father's side of the family…who only changed into their Naga forms for joy, for celebration, for prayer, and seldom did so in front of anyone who didn't share that identity. The first supernatural Neha had actually *seen* in their natural form—at least to her knowledge—was Joe, back in Auntie and Uncle's studio apartment. And now here she was…mere steps away from the man who'd ordered his death.

She suppressed a shiver and skirted toward the bar, hoping against hope that Vasiliev hadn't actually noticed her lingering, smelled her fear or whatever. And her luck held…because he stood, turning his attention toward the fighting cage in the center of the room. One of his pals handed him a wireless microphone. He hadn't acted as announcer for the earlier matches of the night. Those had been introduced by an older guy Yulia had called "Uncle Stanis." So, this could only mean one thing: It was already Joe's turn. So soon. Too soon. Was Third Shift even ready to move?

The whole team had agreed to go off comms for this mission, the risk of being caught with tech too great. *"We'll just have to rely on my profound psychic talents as a point of contact,"* Finn had cracked after the decision…admitting roughly two beats later, under the force of his bosses' glares, that he had no such psychic talents. *"Just my charm, loves."* Working with the vampire was probably as endlessly annoying as it was sexually frustrating. But at least they still had the surveillance hack in place, and the operatives back in

Hell's Kitchen monitoring as much of the club as they possibly could. Would the feed pick up Aleksei's low laughter, amplified by the mic? How his frigid gaze cut across the room, stopping first on his younger sister and then on Nate?

"Welcome." He drew the word out with a flourish, gesturing widely with the microphone. "We have very special guests tonight for a very special show. A Kamchatka exclusive. Our reigning champion, Yuri Medvedev, and an honored guest—Joseph Peluso. Two apex predators. One battle."

Two apex predators. Apex. Surely…surely, he couldn't *know*? Neha had to fight to hang on to her tray, to keep the brimming shot glasses from spilling over, as the doors at the back of the room opened. Joe's opponent strutted in first, on his own power. A dark-haired man with blue eyes. He was shirtless, revealing a sculpted chest and broad shoulders. Black athletic shorts clung to his massive thighs. Yuri Medvedev, according to Yulia. Classically good-looking, he wouldn't look out of place on the cover of a mafia romance novel. But the last thing he roused in Neha were romantic feelings. Just horror. Nausea. He was larger than Joe. Taller by at least four inches. *Without* shifting. It was not going to be an even match. Not by a long shot.

Joe was hustled in by two of Vasiliev's henchmen. Practically shoved into the arena and toward the cage. It had been half a day since she'd seen him, but he'd passed that time far less peacefully than she had. New bruises dotted his skin. There was a cut over one eye. Heaven forbid he be at peak health while facing off against a supernatural twice his size. But her lone wolf wasn't showing weakness. She saw in him that same swagger, that same curl of lip that he'd shown that first day in Brooklyn Detention. The sullen asshole with his shields up, not letting anyone in. He claimed a corner of the fighting cage and leaned against the bars, glaring across at Yuri Medvedev with "fuck you" in his gaze. A "fuck you" so emphatic that Neha could hear it from where she stood.

There was no way Aleksei Vasiliev didn't hear it and see it, too. And it delighted him. Energized him. Turned his crank. He threw his head back and roared. That was the only word for the sound. A reverberating howl of triumph that made the hairs on Neha's arms stand straight up. And when it died away, leaving only the uneasy murmurs of the audience in its wake, an eight-foot-tall brown bear stood in Yuri's place.

29

HE DIDN'T HAVE TIME TO think, to blink, to process—to *shift*—before there was a motherfucking giant bear barreling across the cage at him. So, all Joe could do was duck and roll out of the way, landing in a crouch in the next corner. His skin prickled. His jaw started to crack. *No. Stop.* He had to hold off the change. He couldn't show his cards this early. Not five seconds in. None of these fancy-ass mob people, gawking from their seats like tourists at a SeaWorld spectacle, knew what he was or what he could do, and that was his only advantage.

The bear charged him again, relying on brute strength. Like it was going to be that easy. Just trample him to death and be done with it. It wasn't really supposed to be a show but a slaughter. Too bad for him and Vasiliev, Joe was more than familiar with slaughter. He feinted to the side and then propelled into the next corner, the opposite side of the cage from where he'd started. Half-acrobat, half-Spider-Man, one hundred percent shifter agility. The Apex powers that be had a former Cirque du Soleil performer on staff to train their units. Leopard shifter or some shit. Helluva guy. Joe made a mental note to send him a fruit basket if he got out of this clusterfuck in one piece.

He kept the circus act going as long as he could. Ninety seconds. Two minutes. Three. Spinning and jumping from each corner. Rolling between the bear's legs and obnoxiously saluting the crowd after he hopped up without missing a beat. Until Medvedev was so pissed off he started to shift back. Still furry, fugly, but a few feet shorter. "Coward!" he spit out from a mouth that was almost human. "Face me. Face me like a man. Like a beast. Not this joke."

"You asked for it, asshole." Joe flashed a feral grin and let the change hit his bones. 'Cause now it was an actual fight.

He filtered out everything. The onlookers. The noise. Everything but the other man and his monster. Who couldn't possibly be a real match for his own. And this time, when Yuri charged him, Joe met him in the middle of the ring, stopping his momentum with their combined weight and then hooking one leg around his ankle and taking him down. Two twisted creatures hitting the concrete floor. Muscle against muscle. Snapping teeth and hooked nails. Grizzly Adams versus the Wolfman.

Joe was out of practice. Getting beat in the prison showers was nothing like this. And there hadn't been much hand-to-hand combat in the desert. If a quick kill with claws didn't do it, there was always a bullet to finish the job. None of the movies they'd made him watch at Apex compared to a real-time fight. Nothing was choreographed; nothing was staged. It didn't go on for fifteen minutes with fancy special effects. No, it was ugly and feral. A blur of limbs. Fists connecting, claws raking, teeth taking chunks out of flesh. And pain. So much pain. At some point, they were both on their feet again, locked together like boxers without gloves. Pushing and pulling, landing against the bars of the cage. The bear wouldn't stop until he was dead. There was murder in his eyes, in the rankness of his breath, steaming out of his pores with the sweat. And Joe felt the death dealer inside him rise to meet it. Bursting out of his skin and his borrowed clothes into a full change.

It was fucking fantastic. Like he was in the right skin again. In the right mind. The one that knew how to stalk and how to evade. The wolf went for the throat, snapping and biting and tearing. Twisting this way and that to avoid the bear shifter's flailing paws. The blood filling his mouth wasn't his own. And the hell of it was that it tasted fucking amazing. Like the hunt, like the kill. The beast was him. He was the beast. There was no end and no beginning. Not for him. But for his prey…? Oh, yes. He let the dance last a while. With nips at the bear's heels. A hunk of flesh torn from one haunch and then the other. Not to put on a show but to make the creature suffer. To make him pay. The end came with one final shatter of bone and rip of sinew. And then Joe was rising up on two legs with a corpse at his feet and the wild coursing through his veins.

His maw parted and he unleashed an unearthly howl, louder than Vasiliev's arrogant roar…and the entire place exploded into chaos. Screams and gunshots, even though no one was supposed to be armed. *Of course*, everyone was armed. With whatever they had. Bullets. Blades. Nails. Fangs. He wrenched the cage door open like it was made of balsa wood, wading down into the thick of it. Shoving people out of his way. He was bare-assed naked, wearing nothing but Medvedev's blood and tufts of fur from a partial shift. The nightmare of Helmand unleashed on American soil.

Joe could barely hear anything over the cacophony of the crowd and the cacophony of his rage…except for one voice. *Her* voice. Screaming his name from across the room while tears streaked down her face. Struggling as one of his lawyers and some woman tried to hold her back. *Fuck. Fuck.* She saw him. *All* of him. The merciless monster.

Someone grabbed his upper arm. Dark hair, light eyes, *vampire*. Joe snarled, and he snarled back, showing sharp, red-tipped canines. "Come on. We have to get you out."

It was hard to push human words through his half-morphed

jaw. He managed the only one that counted. "Neha." He couldn't go anywhere without knowing she would be okay.

"Don't worry about her." Irish accent. No scent but cold, like air in the dead of winter. "Gracie and Nate have got her. We have to go *now*."

The "now" resonated through him with a hint of power. Maybe he was getting whammied or something, but Joe pivoted and started moving toward the back of the arena, shifting fully back to human as he pushed past a few stragglers who hadn't made it to the front doors yet and were only interested in making it there alive.

The vampire shrugged out of his black leather jacket, urging it into Joe's hands. "I'm a firm believer in leaving the dance with the lad I came in with. You're lucky I make exceptions."

Oh, he was a goddamn *comedian*. Joe was in no mood to laugh as he shrugged on the jacket that was too tight across his shoulders and barely covered his dick. His brain was still a little scrambled, mostly animal and instinct, and it took everything just to get back through the narrow corridor that Vasiliev's thugs had shoved him through less than a half hour ago. *Out. Gone. Away. But not safe. Never safe.* He fought himself just as much as he fought anyone who blocked their path. Because he wanted to go back. The wolf wanted to go back to his mate. Tasting of warm flesh. Dripping with blood. Marking her with evidence of his kill. Traumatizing her even more than she'd already been traumatized. *Fuck.*

Joe took a left by the room where they'd held him, trusting the vampire to keep up. Not trusting himself at all. Not while the beast was still so strong and loud inside him. Maybe that was why he slipped up, lost focus. Why he walked into a fist and a 9mm. The blow to his temple stunned him, sent him stumbling back. He got the vague impression of blond hair and an ugly mug while his bell was ringing. And then all he saw was a bright spray of arterial blood and that ugly mug separating from the neck it was attached to.

The vampire grinned with satisfaction, wiping stained fingers against the fallen goon's shirt and then unceremoniously taking off his shoes and pants. He stripped the clothes with such efficiency that Joe had no doubt he'd done it before. Probably with just as many live men as dead ones. "You're a decent date," Joe huffed out as he took a few seconds to get right and get dressed. "Thanks."

A deep bow and an eyebrow motion that was probably illegal in half the world was the vampire's "you're welcome." And then Mr. Fanged and Flirty took it one more step. "You can call me Finn, lover," he added cheekily.

Joe had no intention of calling the guy anything except a ride to the nearest bus stop. "Let's go," he growled, stepping over the body in their way.

———

Neha wasn't sure how they got to the rendezvous point. Or even where it was. The past hour was a blur of sound and sensation and screaming inside her head that she couldn't silence. All she knew was that Nate hadn't let go of her hand since he and Grace had wrestled her into the back of a waiting SUV. Like he could will away what they'd just experienced with the warm squeeze of his fingers and his reassuring whispers that "everything will be okay." How? How could he say that? How could he be so calm? The memory of Joe and Yuri Medvedev's fight was tattooed on the inside of her eyelids. Brown fur clashing against black fur. Limbs that weren't quite human or quite animal. Two men stripped down to their very elemental natures, warring to the death. And Joe had won. He'd delivered that death without one hint of mercy or restraint.

He'd tried to tell her. A dozen times. A dozen different ways.

"Don't turn me into a saint. Don't look for something that ain't there."

"My backstory doesn't change what I did, Doc. Don't try to make it my defense."

"There was no insanity. No PTSD. I didn't shift. I didn't attack out of animal instinct. I planned it. I took out those motherfuckers because I wanted to."

And now she'd seen it for herself. What Joe became in his darkest moments, what he was so afraid to show her...and what had led to his outburst in court so many months ago. *"Yeah, I fucking did it,"* he'd said—wanting to *"get this bullshit over with."* Wanting to just go directly to jail and do his time and *pay.* No questions, no answers, no exposure to what he carried inside. Except he'd exposed part of himself to her, hadn't he? With all that crude flirtation. With that desperate need for connection that had called to something equally hungry in her.

"Neha...?" Nate nudged her gently with his shoulder. "We're here."

"Where's here?" She looked up with strangely bleary eyes, barely making out Grace in the front passenger seat next to a fair-haired driver she didn't know. The second time in a week she'd been carted off somewhere in a strange SUV. She had no idea how long they'd been parked.

"A playground off Canarsie Pier," Grace replied. "We took the Belt all the way from Brighton Beach. No tails. Finn knows where to find us."

"What if he can't? What if he...? What if *Joe*...?" She couldn't bring herself to finish the questions. And it made her feel ridiculous. The six victim profiles. The guard slumped over in the courthouse. The bear shifter in the cage. They'd all had names. They'd all had lives...lives she was so very well versed in rationalizing away the importance of. She'd been faced with death again and again, practically desensitized to it, but she couldn't even voice the possibility of Joe's out loud?

"How do I know I'm not losing myself?" she'd asked her mother what felt like a lifetime ago. And asked again, albeit not in so many words, when they spoke last night. Was this it? Was this the sign that she was already too far gone?

"I don't deal in 'what if,' Neha. I deal in facts, in science, in hard numbers. And I can tell you that Finian Conlan has escaped more impossible situations than you could even dream up. I'm sure the same could be said of Joe Peluso, given his military record. Given what you and he have already survived. They'll be here," Grace assured her.

"And after that?" This came from Nate, leaning forward to meet her cool gaze. "What happens to us?"

"We'll cross that borough bridge when we come to it," the driver responded with a soft laugh.

The joke wasn't comforting. But nothing could really comfort Neha right now, could it? Not when she had to reckon with both Joe's true nature and her own. She tried the back door of the fancy utility vehicle, surprised to find it unlocked, and tumbled out before anyone could tell her not to. She sucked in great big lung-fuls of cold night air and reveled in the chill on her bare arms and legs. Because she was burning up inside. Burning with confusion and shame and fear and guilt. And none of it would matter if Joe went and got himself killed. Everything she'd done, everything she felt would be completely meaningless. The last thing Neha wanted was to have loved in vain.

"Fuck." She swore first in English and then Punjabi, turning to stare at the playground equipment instead of at the three people spilling out of the car after her. Three people who'd risked their lives for her. She was so selfish. The antithesis of her Sikh upbringing and the lessons she'd been taught. *Meditate on the divine, work hard, and share with others.* Perhaps her parents had been *too* lax with their children when it came to respecting those tenets. Because she'd chosen the devil over the divine, abandoned her job, and…and what had she shared with others besides pain and peril?

Neha was thankful—hopeful—when the sound of a motor-cycle brought her spiral of self-recriminations to a halt. The engine wouldn't have been particularly loud on the average city street, but here, in the quiet dark, it sounded like the rumble of thunder...and Finn Conlan rode the storm right onto the grass with lightning on his back. *Joe*. He leapt off the bike like he was still the wolf, swift and graceful and dangerous...and he stalked toward her with such intensity that she felt Nate close in on one side of her. As if a human lawyer who'd spent his twenties devoted to GTL and his thirties and forties devoted to G&Ts could be any match for an angry shape-shifter wearing nothing but leather, ill-fitting pants, and a whole rack of muscles. Sweet, but so misguided.

So she wasn't prepared when Joe turned to him instead of her. When he snapped off "What's *she* doing here?" in the tersest of tones.

The words were like a slap back in time. To the very first day they'd met. A rude question asked *about* her instead of *to* her. Like she wasn't right there, worthy of being recognized, fully capable of speaking for herself. Neha stumbled back a step, teetering on her borrowed high heels as the breath rushed out of her chest in a whoosh. The fog she'd been in since they'd left the club was gone now. Replaced by sharp clarity. Joe was covered in cuts and bruises. Jagged claw marks across his bare chest still oozed with blood. But it was his eyes that had sustained the most damage. They were blank. Utterly devoid of warmth. "Joe..."

He ignored her, barreling on as his cold gaze swung like a lighthouse beam over Nate, Grace, Finn, and the man whose name she didn't yet know. "She was supposed to be *safe*," he rasped. "How the fuck is standing out here in the open *safe*? What the hell is wrong with you people? You're supposed to be skilled operatives."

Grace didn't even blink at the tirade. Probably her nerves of surgeon steel. "We *are*. That's why leading potential tails right back to our headquarters would be the weakest possible move. We regroup here. Neutralize any threats off-site. Then we close it up. If you don't like how we do things, Mr. Peluso, you're free to go back to Kamchatka's guest room."

The "guest room." That dark, dank space—not that much bigger than his jail cell—where Neha and Joe had held each other close, tasted each other's tears. Neha willed Joe to acknowledge her. To turn and face her, *see* her, like he had in that claustrophobic box. When that didn't work, she used her words. "I can take care of myself. You *know* I can take care of myself. So, what's this really about?" she demanded. "Why can't you look at me right now?"

His fists curled. His posture stiffened. And his head dropped along with his voice. "How can *you* look at me at all?"

That was easy. Because she'd never shied away. Even when he wore a prison-issue jumpsuit and handcuffs. Neha gave into the impulse that had been eating at her since he and Finn rode up. She went to him, slipping her arms around him, hugging him tight. Assuring herself that he was okay, here and with her and solid, albeit a little bit more battered than before. His hands stayed fisted. He didn't move to return the embrace. "Joe, let me in," she urged, swallowing the hurt, trying to be strong and calm and logical. "Don't shut me out."

But that was just what he did. Reaching up to grasp her shoulders…not to pull her close but to put inches between them. "I'm filthy with blood," he growled…genuinely a growl, like he hadn't quite shifted back to his full human form. "And not all of it's mine. You want that all over you? Do you want to taste it on my tongue? Because I don't think you do, Neha. I don't think you want to know what skin and bone feel like against your teeth. You saw me tear in. You saw me dig into the meat. It's not steak tartare, babe."

He was trying to disgust her, trying to scare her. Neha fought the queasiness his words evoked, and she fought Joe, too. Shoving at his chest, uncaring if her hands were stained red in the process. "Stop it. *Stop*. Don't act like I didn't already know who you were. Like I wasn't in your arms just hours before you stepped into that cage. I came with you knowing you'd taken six lives. You really think watching you take a seventh is going to send me running for the hills?"

"Seven? You think it's seven?" He laughed, turning to look at the Third Shift operatives. "These guys probably know. Bet they've seen the real records. I've killed hundreds, Neha. With bullets, with bombs, with fangs and claws. Boys barely old enough to shave. Insurgents who were fighting back after we fucked up their countries. People who looked like your uncles and your brothers. There is *so* much blood on my hands, and most of it didn't need to be there. But I chose this life. I made my own damn bed. You don't have to be in it with me."

They'd had this fight before. Back at the rental in Jackson Heights. Then they'd skirted around it at Kamchatka. Somehow, having it here, in the fresh night air with witnesses, made it a thousand times more painful. Because they couldn't fuck away the harsh truths, couldn't kiss the wounds better.

Fortunately, Neha wasn't exactly in the mood to kiss and fuck. No. She drew in a steadying breath, clenching her own fists in a parody of his, and tried to quell the ache his words had caused. He'd dealt her more than one low blow, but she'd be damned if she let him see how hard they'd landed. "You tried this already. Shutting me out. Pushing me away for my own good. And remember how well that worked?" He'd held her and cried against her neck. They'd almost said things it was too soon to say. "So, spare me your new bout of self-loathing man pain, Joe."

There was a choked laugh and a muffled "man pain?" from Finn at that, reminding her again that Joe was playing out this scene with an audience. The flush of humiliation hit her hard and fast. "I ran off with you without a single thought to my job, my family, my whole *life*. And I risked all of that again tonight to get you away from that club. And this is how you respond? By condescending to me in front of the operatives who helped? By throwing it in my face that you've killed people with brown skin?" As if she didn't already know that. As if that wasn't something she had to reckon with constantly, thanks to American patriotism and world-policing. "That's bullshit. You don't get to do that. You don't get to use who I am to ease your conscience and hurt me at the same time."

It was like she hadn't spoken, hadn't just worked up ridiculous amounts of nerve to call him out. Because Joe just shook his head, eyes blazing with emotion. "Goddammit! Why aren't you afraid of me? You should be! Take this fucking exit. Make these people get you as far away from me as possible!"

Neha felt Nate's hand on her shoulder. Still unnecessary...but, right now, totally appreciated. Her knees were wobbly, and rage tears—not sadness, not hurt, dammit—were flooding her eyes. How fucked up was it that this man who'd wooed her by wanting to hold her close now wanted nothing more than to put distance between them? He'd hedged it the first few times, in the alley and then again in Queens—couched it in hypotheticals. But there was no mistaking him now, no wiggle room, no blaming it on the dangers outside. He meant to leave her, to end this before it even began, and to make it as harsh and cruel as possible. Maybe this just confirmed her selfishness once and for all, but seeing Joe kill Yuri Medvedev hadn't rocked her nearly as much as this. As hearing him kill everything they'd shared leading up to it. "Only one of us is afraid, Joe. And that's you. I've seen every part of you, and I'm still here, and that scares the hell out of you. Well, tough shit. I'm not walking away."

A muscle jumped in his cheek. He stared at her, acknowledged her like she'd wanted him to just a few minutes ago, but his eyes were still hollow. "Fine," he said through gritted teeth. As if he had to force himself to speak. "If you won't walk away...then I will."

And he did just that. He turned and stalked off the playground, leaving all of them—leaving *her*—behind. Again.

30

NEHA WAS SHAKING. NOT WITH tears but with fury. Nate didn't know what to do for her. She'd long since shrugged off his comfort, pulled inward after Joe Peluso shoved his fear and his anger outward.

"I've got him," Finn had assured quietly. "There's a tracker sewn into the lining of my jacket, and I have the scent of his blood. Let me take care of this while you two take care of her."

Grace, who'd tersely introduced herself to Nate as such when they were hustling out of the nightclub, had nodded along with her partner. "We'll take her back to HQ and regroup from there."

The vampire's solemn demeanor had shifted for a second, back to his familiar flirtatious mien. "A group thing, eh? Look at you having all the fun without me."

After everything they'd been through tonight, and with everything that was still ahead of them, Nate didn't think he was still capable of blushing. Somehow, Finn's light quip—and the accompanying thoroughly filthy look from him to Grace—had done the trick. He'd felt heated all the way to his toes. He couldn't have said if Grace felt similarly warm, but her rail-straight posture had softened. So had her brisk tone. "Just be careful, Finian," she'd sighed.

"Oh, Gracie darling, I've never been careful in my life. Why start now?" With one last saucy wink, Finn had gone off to follow Joe's trail…giving leave for the rest of them to pile back into the SUV and head toward the city.

Neha kept her gaze averted, out the windows, and her hands clenched in tight fists on her lap. She'd only been gone a handful of days—not even a week—but it was like looking at a completely different woman than the one who'd worked alongside him at DGS. Not just because of the sparkly minidress and heels, or the messy hair she'd finally freed from a gaudy wig. That wig was somewhere in the back of the car now. Thrown there in a fit as she spat curses in multiple languages. Or maybe *he* was the one who'd changed. Today. Finally able to see everything around him for what it was. Everything Finn had wanted to show him. The reality of the different New Yorks that existed side by side. The reality of a coworker who was even tougher than he'd thought. The reality of vampires and werewolves and bear shifters, oh my! He'd defended supernatural clients, fought for supernatural rights just like he did for any other marginalized community, but tonight had opened his eyes in a different way. A far more personal way. Nate still wasn't sure how to feel about the chaos and the bloodshed. He just knew that what he'd seen couldn't be unseen. What he knew now couldn't be unknown.

The tricked-out SUV's comm crackled, breaking into the uneasy silence and his equally uneasy thoughts. "Echo Three, are you secure?" a male voice demanded.

"Aye, Echo Base," the driver, a white Australian operative named Mack, affirmed. "Go ahead."

Whoever was running the show at Echo Base, or Third Shift HQ as it more likely was, didn't waste any time. His no-nonsense voice came over the speakers like the *rat-a-tat* of a machine gun. "Bad news. Anton Sokolov intercepted Danny on his way to Brooklyn. From our surveillance, we know Sokolov's got both him and Yulia squirreled away at another location in the borough. Holding him for Vasiliev. Joaquin should have it pinpointed shortly."

Aleksei Vasiliev had fled Kamchatka during the crush, almost as soon as things got out of hand. Not sorry enough about his prizefighter's unexpected demise to stick around and do anything about it. Nate had spotted him vaulting from the VIP area in bear form along with a couple of his cronies. He assumed Third Shift had eyes on the man. Bear. Bear-man. *Whatever*.

"Do you want us to return to base or spin our wheels until we have the new site locked down?" Grace asked her boss.

Driving all the way to the west side of Manhattan if the threat was deep in Brooklyn didn't make much sense. They would just have to turn around and come back. Preferably after a bathroom break and a quick change of clothes. Not that they needed Nate's input on any of this. It was a first for him—keeping his mouth shut, letting others run the show. He'd always prided himself on being one of the smartest people in the room. On his and D's ability to out-lawyer lesser mortals. That didn't quite work when you were surrounded by superior mortals.

"HQ is too far. Impractical," the voice on the comm said. "Proceed to Safe House 13 and await further intel. Echo Base out."

Grace and Mack conferred quietly for a few minutes. They'd already turned the SUV off the Belt Parkway and headed north, but now they were looping back around. Getting back on the parkway. Wherever Safe House 13 was, it was obviously closer than Hell's Kitchen. Nate itched to call Dustin. To tell him what was going on, even though that was wildly irresponsible and would only drag D into a mess he was better left on the outside of. He just needed someone he understood and who understood him. Someone who wouldn't shut him out.

"You can stop staring a hole into the back of my head, Nate. I'm fine."

Neha's knee knocked into his. Her dark eyes, no longer fixed out the window, measured his with a mix of humor and sadness. When he arched his eyebrows at her in disbelief, she chuckled. "Okay, I'm pissed. Embarrassed. Probably a little self-loathing. But I *am* fine."

It was just enough of the truth to offset the lie. Nate still wasn't going to let her off the hook. "How can you even say that after everything you've been through?" Because he wasn't the one who'd been shot at, gone on the run with a wanted man, gotten intimate with said man, and then been dumped by said man in public, and *he* wasn't feeling fine. All he wanted was a stiff drink and a sympathetic ear.

Neha glanced up at Grace before looking back at him. "Because, right now, we don't have any other choice," she pointed out in a matter-of-fact tone. "You heard that call, Nate. Yulia Vasilieva put her safety on the line for me, and now she's in trouble. We have to help her. I can't afford to fall apart."

"There will be no falling apart for anyone," Grace agreed dryly from the front seat. "There's no time for that. Pencil a meltdown in for next Tuesday, because we don't have time to brief more of our own people on this...which means you two are invaluable assets and honorary Third Shift agents."

Oh, joy. Just what he'd always wanted. Safe House 13 awaited them in their immediate future, and Nate didn't feel remotely safe at all.

He'd imagined being close to Yulia thousands of times. Fantasized about finally feeling her body against his in the dark. Not like this. Never like this. Chained together back-to-back in metal chairs with zip ties around their wrists, immobilizing their hands. It wasn't Danny's idea of a romantic night out—certainly hadn't been what he anticipated when he left Third Shift HQ and headed downtown. And that had been a grave tactical error on his part. Proving why he was more rookie desk jockey at 3S than he was active operative. Proving that Elijah had been right to keep him on the bench. Because they'd *known* Anton Sokolov had dropped off the grid after being caught on surveillance footage in Queens. He'd stalked Joe Peluso and Neha Ahluwalia just long enough to bag one of his quarry…and then moved on to corralling new targets. And Danny hadn't considered that possibility.

He was a bird shifter of some kind. He'd flown above the drones. Danny only knew this because the guy had bragged while dragging him into the back of a van like all the old-school stranger-danger warnings. *"You humans and your technology. God gave me wings,"* Sokolov had boasted. Danny said something to the effect of *"Yeah, and God gave you a mouth so you could put a sock in it."* And then he woke up a while later in this warehouse with a splitting headache and a sore jaw. At least two of his teeth were loose in his mouth.

They'd brought Yulia in sometime after that. Struggling. Snarling. A beautiful, raging princess in a sparkly cocktail dress… who'd become a raging *bear* princess in scraps of a sparkly cocktail dress right before his very eyes. Sokolov and a few additional goons had moved quickly, jabbing her with a hypodermic filled with some kind of sedative. She was still out now. He could feel her head lolling against his, the deadweight of her still limbs. She'd reverted to human form while unconscious. Sokolov had emerged from another section of the warehouse with a hooded sweatshirt. And though Danny hadn't been able to see him do it, he'd gathered that the bird shifter had made sure Yulia was at least clothed again.

Aleksei Vasiliev's men were very, very afraid of pissing him off. That should've made Danny afraid, too, but he was strangely calm. Stuck in a chair watching the metaphorical clock tick until the big man showed up, he did what he did best. He analyzed, he researched, he weighed options and went over the facts as he knew them.

By now, Third Shift knew he'd been grabbed. They likely also knew that the Vasilievs were bear shifters—something they hadn't had visual confirmation on before, no matter how good their surveillance. Since Danny and Yulia were here, the probability was high that things had gone south with Peluso at Kamchatka and the organization needed leverage and another way to show their strength. Kidnapping a NYPD detective right off the street was a mark in the "win" column—again, Elijah had been right. Danny had proven to be a liability. Taking Yulia, too…well, he could only guess it was about teaching her a lesson in family loyalty.

As if she could sense him thinking about her—he was *always* thinking about her—Yulia moaned softly. Then she began to stir, her shoulders and elbows nudging his. Within seconds, probably due to her supernatural metabolism, she came fully awake. "Danny?" Her voice was hoarse. She coughed once, twice to clear her throat. And then she said his name again. "Danny, are you okay?"

She was the one who'd been down for the count, and here she was asking if *he* was okay. "Fine," he assured her. "They just gave me a free tooth extraction. It was really kind, given the state of health insurance these days."

"So funny." He could just imagine the weary scowl on her pretty face. "Anton should not have taken you. I don't know what Aleksei is thinking. Why he has done this."

"Maybe he knew we needed some time alone?" Danny could almost pretend he was bantering with her over the bar at the Confessional. Imagining that was better than thinking about how they might die here. In this dark industrial space with beams crisscrossing the ceiling and strange, malevolent shapes under tarps. A few tables were scattered about, both wood and metal, and they looked to be for sorting goods but could just as easily hold corpses.

He and Sarah weren't just Star Wars fans. They'd watched dozens of action movies. Where the Rock or Jason Statham got out of their ropes and kicked a bunch of bad-guy ass. Idris Elba, too. That was how his little sister had developed her massive crush. Danny harbored no illusions that he was going to be able to unchain himself and take on a bunch of henchmen. His personal speed was more dreamy K-dramas than martial-arts films. He could handle his service weapon and wasn't that bad in training sessions with Third Shift's various bits of hush-hush hardware. But he was no hotshot hero. He'd only ever wanted to be *Yulia's* hero, and he was failing miserably at that.

She struggled against the chains that bound them, huffing with frustration. "This was not how I pictured us being alone. I thought perhaps a movie theater. A nice dinner in the city. The Met."

Danny tried wiggling around, too. To no avail. His wrists were raw from the zip ties and his torso painfully constrained by the links of the metal chains. "The opera or the art museum?"

"Why not both?" Yulia suggested. "You could use some culture."

"Movies *are* culture," he defended automatically.

Her giggle echoing through the cavernous room was the best sound he'd heard in ages. The door swinging open was the worst. Because it heralded the arrival of Aleksei Vasiliev and his volcanic wrath.

31

JOE HAD NO IDEA WHERE he was. He'd been circling the ass-end of Brooklyn for an hour, ducking drones and avoiding residential areas. Avoiding himself was a lot harder, that was for damn sure. Everything he'd done to that bear shifter and anybody who got in his way after. Everything he said to Neha in that park. *"I don't think you want to know what skin and bone feel like against your teeth. You saw me tear in. You saw me dig into the meat. It's not steak tartare, babe."* It played on his eyelids in surround sound. No, IMAX.

It didn't help that he still had blood under his nails, and the dull coppery taste of it on his tongue. And he was wearing a dead man's pants. Couldn't forget that. *Wait.* Joe rifled through his memory banks for everything he knew about vampires—not all that much, Twilight movies and horror novels notwithstanding. 'Cause if vampires didn't count as alive, then he was wearing a dead man's leather jacket, too. Just fucking peachy.

The vampire in question didn't seem all that concerned with taking it back. He'd been following Joe this whole time. Not all that subtle about it either. Sometimes he was a block behind. Sometimes he dropped back a half mile. Sometimes he *whistled*. Joe had no idea a person *could* whistle "Achy Breaky Heart," but it was a passive-aggressive dick move he'd admire if he wasn't so angry about every damn thing.

"Can you at least pick another song?" he asked, not bothering to raise his voice since it was quiet enough on this industrial block to hear a mouse fart.

Just like he figured, America's Top Bloodsucking Model popped up next to him in short order. "Are you about done having a sulk, then?" he asked.

Joe glared. Threw in a snarl. "Bite me."

It didn't faze his shadow one bit. He just waggled his eyebrows—that ridiculous move he probably practiced in the mirror if he could see his reflection in it. "I appreciate your enthusiastic consent, but I've already had my supper and I've no desire to taste a temper tantrum for dessert."

Was it too late to go back to the cage? Because Joe would've rather faced a dozen bear shifters than be here for this impromptu roast. "Are you *trying* to piss me off, or is this your natural personality?"

"Bit of Column A, bit of Column B." Finn laughed at him, looking entirely too damn pretty for his own good, and then went serious. "We can't have you wandering around by yourself, Joe. Especially tonight. You must understand that."

Yeah, he did understand that. He was equally lost about his love life and his location, but he hadn't misplaced all of his training, all that military protocol, everything they taught you in black ops. Leaving a volatile asset to their own devices was not an option. "I was stretching my legs." He shrugged.

"Stretching the truth, too." The vampire chuckled. "And all that after breaking a lovely lady's heart. I think that's quite enough solo exercise for you for one evening."

Joe had no more energy for verbal sparring. And he was damn sure not discussing Neha with this wisecracking assclown. "So, what are we doing next?" he asked instead, slumping against the brick wall of the nearest building. "You locking me back up? Taking me from Vasiliev's cage to one provided by the United States government?"

Finn frowned and shook his head. "No. That's not my call to make. What *is* my call is getting us to a safe house and meeting back up with the team—because we're not quite done with Aleksei Vasiliev yet."

Christ. Yeah, it only figured they were not remotely finished with this goatfuck. There'd been no sign of the guy in the back hallways of the nightclub when they were fighting their way out. He'd probably slipped out using some secret tunnel or unmarked door. Right into a waiting getaway car. And Joe hadn't thought about that until now. Because his brain had been too full of one person and one person only.

"I ran off with you without a single thought to my job, my family, my whole life. And I risked all of that again tonight to get you away from that club. And this is how you respond?"

He'd yelled at her. In front of strangers. And then walked away from her. Tossed her away like so much trash…when *he* was the one who was garbage. But even with all of that, the question he'd asked her remained valid. It was itching at him like the dried blood and gore. Why the hell wasn't Neha afraid of him? She'd had a front-row seat for his ugly. She saw what he was really, actually capable of doing. And she still wanted his hands on her, still wanted him near her. It didn't make any sense. Stockholm syndrome wasn't a joke. Neither were the mind games they taught you in black ops. Apex's commanders and scientists had relied mostly on their supernatural strength…but also taught them how to fuck with people's heads. How to make people trust you. Had he done that to her? Made her *dependent* on him somehow?

The second he considered it was the same second Joe dismissed the theory. No. Not his Doc. There was no way she trusted him right now. And she'd looked at him with one hundred percent clarity, even when he was stomping all over her feelings. Like seeing that monster go to town in the cage was one thing but seeing him standing there alive was a bigger thing. More important. No one had ever looked at him that way before. Completely fearless and completely happy at the same time.

And he'd ruined it. Like he ruined all the good things in his life. He stripped that shine from her eyes and stole a dozen kisses off her lips. Because convincing her he was a piece of shit had been more vital to him than holding her tight and breathing her in and thanking god for this woman. Fuck, he was an ass. But this wasn't news. He'd been a complete fuckhead about women for as long as he could remember. Probably why he'd learned to eat pussy so good…to make up for everything else. And he had no idea how he was going to make this up to Neha. No clue if he even *could*, or if he even should.

Because she still deserved better than him. That was never gonna change, no matter how he felt about her. He could say he'd acted under orders, he could blame the animal he morphed into, but he'd made the conscious choice to *follow* orders instead of pushing back against them. He'd *welcomed* being turned into a wolf. As a result, he was always gonna be a killer, always gonna be a shape-shifter, always gonna have a target on his back. Thing was, Joe was pretty damn sure he was always gonna want Neha, too.

Maybe it was already over before it barely got started. Maybe he'd blown his shot with her once and for all back at the playground. And maybe he deserved that in exchange for every despicable act he'd committed in his life, for all the blood he'd spilled over the past two decades. But he'd be damned if he let Aleksei Vasiliev be the last shifter standing. *That* was one outcome he could be sure of.

"We getting outta here or what?" he asked the vampire, who'd been making a dramatic show of yawning and checking his fancy watch.

"I don't know. Do you reckon we commandeer another vehicle or use a ride-share app?" When he scowled, Finn nodded like it was an actual answer. "You're absolutely right. Good point. Who can get a car out here this time of night? Stealing, it is!"

Which was how Joe found himself, not ten minutes later, jimmying the lock on a Buick from the late 1980s. Then hotwiring the ignition. Misusing his vocational education while the vampire made himself comfortable in the passenger seat. He was an idea man, apparently. Not so much with the execution. And what was a little grand theft auto tacked onto Joe's existing charges, right? Luckily, doing the work meant he also got to drive. "Where we going, Irish? Directions would be helpful."

Finn stretched his arms over his head, bouncing his fingers on the slightly loose ceiling. "Second star to the right, straight on 'til morning."

Joe snorted, mostly so he didn't crack up and encourage the guy. "Thanks and fuck you, Peter Pan."

"Oh no, mate." Finn clicked his tongue and did that suggestive eyebrow thing again. "It's a pirate's life for me. I'm Captain Hook all the way."

This time Joe did bark out a laugh. "More like Captain Hookup."

"Brilliant. I'll be stealing that one for later use." Finn got with the program, though, and actually rattled off a decent set of directions, guiding Joe the rest of the way through Canarsie and Bergen Beach. Until they were pulling up to a huge-ass park just off the Belt, near the Mill Basin. Joe had never been out here before. Never knew any of this was here. Acres and acres of trees and grass with the ocean right there.

They pulled into the private drive of what looked like a ranch. A whole-ass ranch in South Brooklyn. With a fancy, old-timey, scrolled wooden sign that said 'Bergen Beach Equestrian Academy.' The gate was unlocked, rolled back for them, which couldn't possibly be secure. "*This* is your safe house?"

Finn looked up from his smartwatch, his megawatt smile dialed down to just a smug grin. "Never said it was an actual house, did I?"

Joe grimaced as he eased the car over a small speed bump and onto a long, narrow road. There were no markers and the light posts were all dark. The only illumination came from the Buick's headlights. "Let me guess… We're also not actually safe."

And if Neha was here, then she wasn't safe either. Not safe with him, not safe without him. So, what was even the damn point?

After a quick, scalding-hot shower and a change of clothes, Neha felt a lot more stable. And not just because she was technically *in* a stable. The riding academy also known as Safe House 13 had been a surprise to both her and Nate. Adjacent to protected parkland, it was a sprawling property with several resident horses, training fields, barns, the whole nine yards…and five hundred acres besides. Grace had refused to say how it was connected to Third Shift. It didn't exactly scream "secret spy base." Which made it the perfect secret spy base, she supposed. After tending to their immediate basic needs in the main facility, they all ended up gathering in a hidden room in the tack house—and it definitely didn't look like an equestrian center. There was tech everywhere—monitors for surveillance, computers, phones, a wall of weapons behind a locked glass pane—along with a mini-fridge, a microwave, and a few pieces of furniture.

"The couch folds out, if you'd like to sleep," Grace said, sliding into a leather office chair.

It was the first time Neha was seeing her dressed down. No dark suit. No cocktail wear and outrageous wig. Just the same sort of leggings and T-shirt that Neha wore and her curly black hair loose around her shoulders. But she still managed to look completely self-possessed. It was a posture Neha knew all too well. The armor you had to don when you were a woman of color in a white man's world. Be it in medicine or covert ops, Grace had no doubt dealt with people suspecting she wasn't qualified, people treating her as less than, people not respecting her authority. She couldn't risk showing vulnerability, couldn't ever let the mask slip.

Neha *did* respect her authority, but only to a point. "So you can leave me here the minute I start snoring? I don't think so." She sidestepped the cozy sitting area and joined Grace and the others at the conference table. "I meant what I said in the car. Yulia needs us. I don't abandon people in need."

That was the root of her whole predicament, wasn't it? If she'd only abandoned Joe at Brooklyn Detention, recused herself from the case the minute he stole that first kiss, none of this would have happened. As much as she held him responsible for flirting, for seducing, for setting up that clandestine meeting in the courthouse…she'd been the one to keep coming back, to say yes, and to stay by his side. Sure, he'd made his own bed with his choices, but she'd stolen the covers for herself with hers.

He'd tried to erase her culpability, her agency, by demanding Third Shift protect her and then storming away from her. And that had infuriated her. To make all that had transpired between them about fear and safety… That undercut and devalued every decision she'd made of her own free will. Being mad at Joe for that didn't mean she couldn't acknowledge one thing, though. She'd made some *bad* decisions. She couldn't afford to make any more.

She felt Nate's gaze on her from across the table. Quiet, assessing. She'd never known him to be so circumspect, without a single thing to say. He'd probably never seen her like she was tonight… emotional, out of control. They'd just been DGS colleagues before—senior partner and junior associate. Her decisions had changed that, too.

"I texted Dustin from a burner," Nate murmured when she made eye contact. "No location. Just that we're alright and our client is, too."

She winced. Dustin was the levelheaded one, the protective one, the partner at the firm who most of the associates went to with their problems. Now Nate and Neha *were* the problems. "He must be worried sick about you."

Nate shrugged, stretching the tight material of his borrowed black T-shirt. "He's my best friend. I couldn't not tell him."

Did Neha have anyone in her life she could call a best friend? *No.* She had Tejal and Toral. She had her college friends and some women from the DA's office she still got drinks with sometimes in the Meatpacking. But there was no one to text from a burner phone when her life was potentially in danger. She'd isolated herself in the pursuit of her career, put on extra armor over the top of what she already had to wear…just not enough to keep Joe from getting past it.

"Finn and Peluso just pulled up through the drive," the agent named Mack announced from the corner where he was banging away on a laptop. "ETA five minutes. I told them to swing by the main house first. Wash off. Get pretty."

She flattened her hands on the tabletop, barely hearing whatever Grace replied. Joe was still okay. Joe was *here*. All of the tears she'd washed away in the shower, let circle in the drain, threatened to flood her eyes. She had to fight them back, along with the twisting pain in her chest. *Breathe.* It hadn't even been two hours since he'd diminished her and the tentative relationship they'd forged. Now they were going to be in the same tiny room with the same people who'd watched them reveal some of their deepest feelings—and deepest insecurities—to each other. It was only slightly less daunting than being in the Pit at Kamchatka. Neha had to get it together—quickly. Like she'd told Nate earlier, she couldn't fall apart now.

"Do we know where Yulia and your operative are being held yet?" she asked Grace and Mack.

"We have the location and mission specs." Grace nodded, her

expression unreadable, a slight chill in her voice. "I'll patch in 3S HQ once Finian and Peluso arrive."

Neha was struck by the urge to apologize to the other woman, to explain. It was an odd impulse, considering she prided herself on never being sorry for asserting herself. "Would *you* want to be left behind if you were me?" she wondered, quietly.

A smile, or something like it, pulled at the edge of Grace's full lips. And her deep-brown eyes glinted with understanding. Even a little of the humor she'd shown back at the Locker. "For years, I was the only woman affiliated with Third Shift. I *was* left behind. Frequently. I hated every minute of it," she admitted.

"So, what changed?" Nate interjected.

"Assignment across the border." This came from the doorway. Finn's lilting Irish brogue. He didn't specify which border as he sauntered over the threshold of the secret room in a fresh set of dark clothes. Was there a never-ending supply of black T-shirts and pants stashed at the riding center's main building? The great thing about being in New York, at least, was that they all looked more like restaurant waitstaff than they did secret agents. "Jack and Lije actually let Gracie come along for that one. And she saved my life. After they fell arse over teakettle apologizing for being sexist gits, they cleared her for full active duty."

"Aren't you a vampire?" The word fell entirely too easily from Nate's lips, which were pursed with confusion. "How would that even work? I thought your kind couldn't die."

"I'm not immortal. Or only susceptible to fire and stakes. Though religious icons do sting quite a bit." A look passed between Finn and Nate that Neha couldn't interpret. But then he continued, addressing the room as a whole as if he were teaching Vampirism 101. "I have a slightly extended life span due to blood consumption. It keeps all the parts in working order and such. Makes me stronger, faster. Quite grand, really. Problem is, if I'm wounded, I can bleed out in seconds. *Then*, I'm in trouble."

"It's similar to how hemophilia impacts a human," Grace explained. "Since I had copious amounts of time to study my colleagues' medical histories while on desk duty, I had supplies on hand for each of their needs. I knew what needed to be done for Finian and that was that." There was no arrogance in her statement. Just the pure confidence of someone who knew they were the best at what they did.

Mack scowled from his little tech corner, pushing his laptop away from him. "Our young friend Danny was on desk duty. And look where he is now."

"We'll get him back, mate," Finn assured, stretching out on the couch with his arms behind his head. Deceptively relaxed. "Him *and* Yulia Vasilieva."

For the second time in as many minutes, Neha felt the threat of tears. It had to be the stress getting to her. The past week, the past *several weeks*, bearing down on her like a freight train. Or maybe it was just these people. Dedicated, deadly agents who looked out for one another no matter what. They really were a team. They trusted each other in ways that she'd never quite learned how to trust anyone. In the way that she'd *thought* she could trust Joe.

It was on the heels of that depressing rumination that the man himself appeared. Mack and Grace must have granted him access to the door, which was keypad-access only. Or maybe he'd just willed it open with the sheer force of his glower. Because, while he'd washed up and put on some actual clothes, Joe still wore that harsh, unyielding expression. The one that said he was here physically but locked away from her in every other way. He crossed his arms over his chest, another barrier, and stayed right by the door. As if he couldn't wait to leave.

"Finally. The elusive Joseph Peluso. It's about time we made your acquaintance." Jack Tate's voice came from the speakerphone in the middle of the conference table. She recognized it both from their meetings at the Third Shift offices and from the call in the

SUV. Had he been listening in on them, watching them all this entire time? Neha could only hope not. Because she was sure that her face, her posture, had given away entirely too much of what was going on in her head.

Joe seemed to recognize Tate's voice, too. Because he made a sound of disgust. "*You.* You were supposed to unfuck things. Seems to me you fucked them up even more."

His rudeness didn't seem to ruffle the Third Shift cofounder one bit. Tate maintained that even, neutral, morning-news-anchor tone. "Let he who has not killed six Russian nationals and brought us to the brink of political and bureaucratic nightmares cast the first stone."

The entire planet was a political and bureaucratic nightmare right now, Neha wanted to point out. But she also knew better than to get involved in whatever petty dick-measuring contest was going on at the moment. Joe chafing at authority. Jackson Tate resenting a wild card. The boys could figure it out themselves. She had enough to concern herself with. Like their next steps. And surviving those next steps. Like Joe. And surviving Joe.

Finn, who Neha had long since decided was the resident troll—figuratively, not literally—was the one who actually spoke up to cut the tension. "As riveting as this little tiff is, lads, can we address it later? Perhaps with a bit of Turkish oil wrestling?"

Grace smothered a sound that might have been a laugh against her palm, playing it off as a cough and then clearing her throat. "Finian's right," she said. "We have Mr. Peluso safe and secure. Everything else on that front can be sorted out later. What do you need us to do for Danny and Ms. Vasilieva, Boss?"

Tate spent the next few minutes briefing the group, sending digital copies of building schematics to all his agents' smart devices. But it all boiled down to a pretty simple plan. One that involved her and Joe being bait.

"Fuck no!" The words exploded from Joe like grenades mere

seconds after the implications set in. "Neha is not going back out into this colossal shitshow. There's gotta be another way to get your people out." Because, of course, he still wanted her wrapped up in a cocoon, kept out of harm's way. As if that could somehow make up for all the harm she'd already been put in the path of.

"It's not negotiable, Mr. Peluso." A second voice came over the comm. Lower pitched, with a thick Cockney accent. Elijah Richter. "You're not in charge here. We are. And this is the most efficient way to execute the mission and keep casualties to a minimum."

"I'm in," Neha said clearly and emphatically. "He doesn't speak for me."

"Nobody asked, but I'm in, too," Nate volunteered, which comforted her a great deal.

They traded rueful grins across the table. Maybe she'd been wrong about not having a team. About not having anyone outside family who she trusted like Third Shift's people trusted each other. Because here was Nate, as ride-or-die for her as he was for Dustin.

"Peluso?" Tate prompted from the speaker. "Does that change your position?"

"Yeah." Joe looked none too thrilled about giving the affirmative. He growled and slapped the door with one palm. "I'm not about to let my legal team go off and get killed while I sit here with my thumb up my ass, am I?"

They probably weren't going to be his legal team for very much longer. But Neha felt her chest tighten with a flicker of hope just the same. Maybe Joe believed in her, believed in *them*, after all. Perhaps Danny and Yulia weren't the only ones they would rescue tonight. Perhaps they could salvage this thing they'd built between them. And then he glanced at her…and Neha felt that tiny bit of hope turn to ash. Because there was nothing but sadness and regret in his gaze.

32

────

THE LITTLE MEETING BROKE UP pretty quickly once the boss man and his buddy finished the marching orders and got off the phone…which meant Joe had to stop leaning on the door. He moved to let the blond guy out while Grace—the woman who Finn would not shut up about on the drive over—went over and unlocked the weapons cabinet on the opposite wall. "Gracie'll cut you as soon as look at you," the vampire had said with admiration. Turned out she'd stitch you up, too. That didn't shock Joe at all. Because Neha was like that. Strong and take-no-shit but caring and compassionate.

If only she hadn't picked *him* to care about. Joe sighed and scrubbed his face with one hand. Watched Grace stock up on fresh weapons and issue two handguns to Finn. "One for you, one for Mack," she said. "Don't be selfish."

"Selfish? Me? You know I'm a giver, love. Or at least you would if you'd let me show you…"

The vampire somehow managed to leer at both his Third Shift coworker *and* Feinberg simultaneously. Only one of them blushed, and it wasn't Grace. *Great.* Joe's lawyer had a crush. Seemed like they were *all* a little bit fuckstruck. That couldn't be good for a mission. Look at him and Neha…how compromised they'd gotten. How compromised they still *were*.

She pushed her chair back and rose. Joe couldn't help but drink her in for a few seconds. Hair pulled back in a practical ponytail, long-sleeved T-shirt, skin-tight workout pants pulling his eyes down to the long lines of her legs. Not the most protective gear for an operation, but she would be able to run. And she looked beautiful. Beautiful and determined. "My .22 is at the office in Hell's Kitchen with the rest of my stuff," Neha directed at Grace. "I assume you're not authorized to give me a temporary replacement?"

That earned a brusque nod in response. But Grace pulled a few KA-BARs from the cabinet before swinging the door shut and turning the key. "How comfortable are you with knives?"

"How comfortable do you think?" Neha arched an eyebrow, effortlessly catching one of the blades the other woman slid across the table. Hilt first. "I'm Sikh. We're warriors and protectors by nature."

It was a great line. You'd never know she hadn't ever used a knife as a weapon. Joe didn't enlighten Grace to the truth, didn't ruin the totally boss moment. He had no clue about the exact words of whatever Neha had been taught, but he could guess the theme. Serving her people, helping others, no matter the cost. Too bad he'd learned just how high the price really was. And when the secret room started to empty for real, with Neha the last one out, he had to say something. *Anything.* "Hey. Hey, Doc. Can you wait a minute?"

Up close, her eyes were a little red. He could practically smell the salt of dried tears on her skin. But she would be damned if she let him see them fall. She did stop for him, though. One hand on the door handle, the other on the doorframe. "What do you want, Joe?" she asked, sounding so fucking exhausted that his own bones felt heavy.

There were a million things he could say in response. *I want you safe. I want for this day to have never happened. I want to rewind two years. I want to rewind twenty. I want to run into you on the 7 and ask for your number.* He picked the easiest one. The thing he'd never been afraid to confess, because it was right there in his pants, hard and obvious. "What I always want when I look at you."

Even without his supe senses, he would've heard her sharp intake of breath. Seen her teeth sink into her lower lip. And how her lashes fluttered as she blinked. But the way she drew herself up, shook off that instant physical reaction, was just as clear. She wasn't like him. She wasn't gonna let her inner animal take control. "Do you still regret everything? Do you still think I don't belong here?"

As much as he wanted to, he couldn't lie to her about this. He'd *never* lie to her about wanting to protect her. Even if it meant protecting her from himself. "Yeah. Yeah, I do."

She flinched. And then she just nodded, like she expected it. "Then we have nothing to talk about."

Bullshit. They had a million things to talk about. He would never run out of things he wanted to discuss. But first and foremost was the apology he owed her. "For what it's worth, I'm sorry for how I talked to you back at the park," he said softly. "I was an asshole. And that thing about killing people who looked like they could be related to you...that was really fucked up. I was wrong to lay that on you." So very, very wrong.

Neha nodded again, her posture tight, like she could uncoil and snap at any moment. "Yes, you were. It was an extremely shitty thing to say. I won't pretend it didn't hurt. Not this time." She exhaled in a huff, wearily rubbing at the creases between her eyebrows and letting her shoulders drop. "Would you kill my brothers if they were standing right here in front of us? Shoot my father or my uncle?" It was her shrink voice. Asking horrible questions that she absolutely had a right to know the answer to.

"Fuck no," he said without hesitation. "Of course not. But I killed a lot of brothers. A lot of sons. And for what?" The disgust crawled up from his gut and sat in the back of his throat. "Oil or some shit? So America could lord it over the rest of the world? I did ugly things for the worst reasons, Doc. Over there and over here. Right in front of you. *To* you. And it's not anything I'm proud of."

The expression that crossed her face reminded him of being across the table from her at Brooklyn Detention. Scrutinized. Studied. *Seen.* "It's not my job to absolve you for all of that, Joe," she reminded gently. With more grace than he'd earned. "I can't forgive you or the military on behalf of every brown casualty of war. You know that's unfair. That's impossible. Only you can make peace with what you've done. All *I* can do is believe you've changed and believe you'll do better going forward. Do *you* believe you? Do you believe in us?"

Now he faltered. No easy, immediate, response. "I…don't know." It wasn't enough.

He felt the anger in her when she brushed against him on her way out the door. She was vibrating with it like the third rail on the subway tracks. Like he'd get electrocuted if he touched her. He touched her anyway. Caught her wrist and took the current shooting up his arm. And maybe he sent it back to her in a closed circuit, because she shuddered and whispered his name. That one tiny syllable was all the incentive he needed to haul her in to him. To lean down and take her mouth. They'd almost died so many times, and the Reaper still had their number on speed dial. He couldn't *not* kiss her one more time.

Her hands came up, like she was going to shove him away—and god knew she should've—but she grabbed fistfuls of his T-shirt instead, anchoring herself as she arched up on her toes and gave as good as she got. A couple weeks ago, he thought he'd imprinted on her. That it was some animal thing, his wolf wanting to mate for life or some shit. And maybe it *was* that. But she'd imprinted on him, too. She needed him. She needed this. Just as badly as he did. She licked into him, battled and beat his tongue, nipped at his lower lip hard enough to open up one of the barely healed cuts. *Fuck*, it was hot. Joe groaned and cupped the back of her neck, holding her steady as the kiss burned hotter and wilder and practically blew off the top of his head.

He wasn't shocked when she chose that exact moment to stop it. To pull back just enough to stare at him with those big brown eyes that saw everything and too much. He wasn't shocked, but he wasn't prepared either. Scrambling to catch his breath and collect his spilled wits. Pushing back the wolf scratching at the door and willing away the erection that was still way too obviously tenting his borrowed jeans. And she just watched him. Her lips swollen, skin reddened by his stubble. Her palms sliding down his chest and then, finally, shoving at him like he'd expected her to in the first place.

When she spoke, her voice was as steady and direct as her hands. "Let me go or keep me, Joe. You can't do both."

"I'm a man and I'm an animal. You can't live with both," he pointed out almost immediately. 'Cause this tug-of-war…it was about more than just wanting to keep her. It was knowing he *couldn't*. And accepting how damn unfair it was of him to drag her into his life. To do this to her all because his instincts and his altered DNA said,"She's mine."

Neha just shook her head, the anger back in her expression along with disappointment. "It's not *your* call—what I can or can't live with. That's my choice to make. Even if it's a bad choice, it's still mine. You can't take that away from me out of some overprotective, sexist sense of obligation."

Joe got it and didn't get it at the same time…which probably summed up his entire forty-odd years of dealing with women. But understanding women, understanding *her*, had never been as important as it was right now. "So...what? I just let you put your-self in danger because it's sexist to stop you? I let you get hurt? I let you *die* when I could've prevented it? Look at what happened to Kenny," he reminded her. *The slab. The sheet. The waxy, cold skin riddled with bullet holes.* His stomach lurched with the memory... and at the idea of ink-black hair spilling across that coroner's table. "I can't go through that again. Not with *you*."

Neha dashed tears away with the backs of her hands. Maybe they were rage tears. Maybe they were for him, or for Kenny. "I ache for you, Joe. I hate that you lost him. I hate what it did to you. But what if I don't get hurt, Joe? What if I live? What then?" she demanded, raw and hoarse and one hundred percent on the money. "Can you go through *that* with me?"

Could he imagine their future? Could he promise her one? Did he think he deserved that? There were dozens of things wrapped up in that one intense question. Joe knew what she wanted him to say this time. Hell, it was what *he* wanted to say. But he couldn't make the one tiny syllable—the same number of letters as his name—leave his lips. It was too much. Too soon. Too terrifying.

And she wasn't surprised at all. "That's what I thought." She shrugged, sighed audibly, and again rubbed at the furrowed spot between her eyebrows. All signs of exhausted acceptance. What was worse than that, though, was how she glanced up at him and then out through the door. Like she was already looking ahead, because she had no other choice.

This time, when she walked away, he didn't try to stop her. But he followed. He would always follow her. Because he couldn't stop himself either.

———

Yulia's head felt like it was stuffed with wet wool. In reality, her veins were stuffed with some sort of tranquilizer. Something meant for large zoo animals. Her brother purchased such things in bulk from a black-market distributor. Mere minutes after her previous dose had worn off, Aleksei had waved one of his goons over to administer another injection. Heaven forbid she have enough strength to attempt a change, to attempt an escape...to dare to fight his authority. To dare dream of being more than his meek, dutiful rybka, content to swim in his personal fishpond.

Bears ate fishes, her brother had reminded her as the flunky jabbed the needle into her arm once more. *"We do what we must to survive."*

"Oh, yeah? And what part of kidnapping an NYPD detective helps your survival?" Danny had shouted at him. So brave, so foolish. *"'Cause from where I'm sitting, that's a really boneheaded move."*

She'd experienced the sting as Anton hit Danny for the insult, knocking his head into the back of hers. Aleksei had simply laughed, as if enjoying a theater production on Broadway. *"Where you are sitting, Officer Yeo, is in my chair, in my facility. Be thankful that you are not yet lying six feet underneath it."*

Was that a thing to be thankful for? Yulia did not know anymore. She'd spent so many years being told to be grateful for what Aleksei had given her. A home in the United States after Mama and Papa died. A place to be her true self. A steady job. A haven for their kind, both Russian and supernatural. But here he was, chaining her up, holding her captive, preventing her from shifting, preventing her from *loving*. He'd taken more away from her than he'd given...and he meant to take even more before the sun rose.

"Yulia?" Danny nudged her gently. "You awake?"

"Yes. Barely." She coughed to clear her throat. The sound echoed through the warehouse like a shot. Likely why Danny had not bothered to keep his voice down. Anything they said to each other would be heard in a place like this, and not just because her brother and his henchmen had supernatural senses. "I am sorry that I cannot...that I cannot be of use."

He somehow found the ability to chuckle. To make more jokes.

"Damn, because I was only interested in you because you're stronger than me. I need a rescuer. And someone to open all my pickle jars."

Yulia made herself laugh, too. "Liar. You did not know what I was when you used to come into the bar." Because that was true. Even if he had learned later what she was, who her family was, those first few visits were just of a man, a detective, patrolling his neighborhood.

Her Danny was not at all deterred by her argument. "I knew exactly what you were—a beautiful woman who fascinated me. And made killer manhattans."

She frowned even though he could not see the expression. As a bartender, it was her job to know her regular's preferences, and... "You don't drink manhattans. You like old-fashioneds."

He moved, his shoulders rippling against hers. "You're right. The last time we met up, I had an old-fashioned with Bulleit rye. I wonder how a manhattan would taste with Bulleit."

Yulia was no rocket scientist, but his implications were obvious. There was little chance Danny actually wanted to talk to her about cocktail recipes. Unless the knocks to his skull had begun to take a toll, he was trying to tell her something. Bulleit. Manhattan. His people, like the stunning woman who came to Kamchatka, were based in Manhattan...and they would come for him with guns.

Perhaps she should have been comforted by this news, but she wasn't calmed. No, it only replaced the sedatives in her system with dread. Yulia flexed against the chains, worked her wrists and hands against the zip ties, only to feel the reinforced plastic cut into her skin. Aleksei had been pacing the length of the warehouse in front of them—one ear to his mobile phone and the other attuned to his minions—before marching through a set of doors on the far end of the building. He would not be patient for much longer.

So many people thought the mafia or the Bratva—the Russian version—was glamorous, dangerous, an exciting concept from the movies. Few considered what organized crime did to families. How children were impacted. How sisters had to love and fear their brothers simultaneously. Yulia had not grown up wanting to betray her clan, had never considered turning against the organization. But they had betrayed *her*, hadn't they? Taking Danny…this was a slight she could never, ever forgive.

"You are a strange boy," she told him softly. "So obsessed with drinking when we may not even take another breath."

"Oh, Yulia." Danny's elbows dug into her sides. His body's motion shifted hers as well. "The only breath I want to take is while kissing you."

God in heaven. How many times in the past two years had she dreamed of kissing Danny Yeo until neither of them could function? But it was not practical to imagine that in the here and now. And she did not know when the people from his agency would arrive. It could be twenty minutes; it could be one hour. They could not rely on outsiders to save them when Aleksei was determined to have his revenge as soon as possible. And Yulia could not afford to wait until her brother returned to gloat.

It hurt. The cuts. The blood welling from the wounds. Yulia had felt worse pains in her life, but she was not so stoic that she could not acknowledge the agony of fighting against her bonds. The iron chains dug into her waist. The zip ties sliced through her wrists and down to the bone. But the fur rippling over her body… the teeth springing into her mouth…oh, that was bliss. It was like death and orgasm. Pain and pleasure hand in hand.

Danny's distress was plain. "Yulia…"

"Hush, my love." It was not a whisper so much as a scream. The bear took over, tumbling the chairs they'd been forced into, shattering the chains that had tied them. Yulia had not been her full self in so long—minutes, hours, months, years— that embracing her flesh and her skin and her marrow felt like coming home and being tormented all at once. Even with the blood pouring in rivulets from her arms, she was powerful and whole and strong.

She took the impact of the concrete floor gratefully. Because it was easier on her bulk than it was on Danny's frail human frame. She would heal. Her love…he could break. And that was something that could not be borne. He was quick, thank goodness, not relying on her ungainly paws to free him or help him stand. No, while she was still shaking off the pain and letting the beast take control, he'd grabbed two lengths of chain and was wielding them like whips.

"Ghost Rider meets Indiana Jones," her geeky detective said proudly, as if he was fluent in the growls that emanated from low in her throat. Perhaps he was. Danny had always known her, hadn't he? Always understood.

But the time for further understanding was not now. Not when Anton was sprouting talons and feathers and Aleksei's other goons were taking on different kinds of fur and fang. As for her brother himself…he was nowhere to be found. Always removed from the violence. Never dirtying his paws or staining his teeth.

That would end today. One way or another.

Yulia let loose a roar and sprang into the fray.

33

———

THE SETUP WAS SIMPLE. DROP a line to a low-level fence who worked on the outskirts of Vasiliev's organization. Have him "stumble" upon Joe and Neha. Follow the giddy goon to the warehouse even though they already knew full well where it was. Bait the trap. Spring it. The deskbound folks at Third Shift's headquarters had taken care of the first part of the plan. It was up to the rest of them to play out what came next. Nate hated everything about it. He liked facts. Arguments. Chains of evidence. Cases he could cite. And situations where nobody got shot at. He *really* liked those.

The team had split up, with Mack driving Joe and Neha to some drop-off spot. And *that* couldn't have been a comfortable trip. Joe had slid into the front passenger seat. Neha scooted into the back, hugging the far window right behind the driver. Nate imagined the temperature as something akin to a walk-in freezer and the interior quieter than the Reading Room at the New York Public Library. That had left him with Finn and Grace...which was weird and uncomfortable in a totally different way.

"*Selfish? Me? You know I'm a giver, love. Or at least you would if you'd let me show you...*"

Nate's pants were still burning from the look Finn had seared him with back at the riding academy. If Grace was similarly affected, she wasn't showing it now. Her hands were firm on the steering wheel, her eyes trained on the road ahead. The thing was, Nate wasn't self-involved enough, or clueless enough, to think she *was* unaffected. Sure, maybe she didn't flirt back…but what woman in a professional setting would? And in a black ops organization? There was too much at stake for a full-on office romance to blow up between them. Still, Grace had shown everyone just how much she cared about the inveterate flirt currently lounging against his side of the SUV when she told that story about saving his life in Mexico.

Nate had watched them both. How they held themselves. What they didn't say. All things he did in the courtroom or when deposing someone. Grace's white knuckles had belied her confident voice. Finn's careless pose against the doorframe had been at odds with the vulnerability in his eyes. And the guy could seriously not stop talking about her, praising her. Even while he was ogling Nate and reminding him of that moment beneath the streetlight. When his Star of David had sparked and sizzled against Finn's exposed collarbone.

Now was really *not* the time to contemplate whatever tangled sexual web the vampire was weaving. But he couldn't seem to stop himself. Because it was easier than thinking about what awaited them in their immediate future, just a few miles away. One of Aleksei Vasiliev's warehouses. More mayhem. Potential death.

So, what did it all mean? Was Conlan just a player who pursued everyone with the same vigor? Was it a deep-cover personality trait and not something he actually believed in at all? Did he want to thrall them into some kind of pansexual orgy? It certainly wouldn't be Nate's first dip into those waters. He was probably a 4 on the Kinsey scale. He'd dated women in high school, before coming out, and had some pretty wild exploits in undergrad and law school. He'd actually met Dustin at a kink party at Princeton—

Oh shit. Guilt replaced the lust and confusion milling through his brain. D had to be climbing the walls. He'd only given him a few details about how things had gone down tonight…and not nearly enough to ease his worries, which pretty much spanned the Manhattan Bridge. "Can I contact Dustin again? He should probably be updated before he hears whatever ends up on the morning news."

"Go right ahead, mate. Get in touch." Finn glanced at him over the back of the seat. Reminding him, strangely, of that night in his firehouse when the vampire had implied Nate and Dustin had been lovers. *"Is he touching you? Because that's an idea I will certainly wank off to in the near future."* But he made no further reference to it, accidental or deliberate. "The good Lord knows, at least one person's going to need a lawyer when this is all over."

"And the rest will need body bags," Grace said grimly as she punched some buttons on the dash and the sound of a dialing mobile phone filtered from the speakers.

Nate didn't ask how she had Dustin's number or when she'd programmed it in. Mostly because he didn't expect to get an answer. Fortunately, D *did* answer. He picked up on the third ring, his beautiful bass "Yeah?" like music to Nate's ears. Uncomfortably aware that this wasn't a private call, he didn't mince words. He told D that the operation wasn't done, that he, Neha, and Joe were still very much in danger.

There was silence on the line for a few seconds. And then the sound of a heavy sigh. "Are you telling me you might die, Nathaniel?"

Grace and Finn traded looks in the front seat. Looks that twisted something in the pit of his stomach. Was it strange that he didn't want to lose people he'd only just met? That he was already afraid tonight would be the last one he ever spent with agents of Third Shift? He'd questioned a lot of things in his life, a lot of the country's terrible, bullshit decisions. This was one thing he didn't question at all. "I'm telling you I don't want to."

Dustin's reply was sharp, fierce, and determined. "Good. 'Cause then you'll fight alongside those people. Just like you fight beside me in court. And I'm gonna be waiting to bail your ass out of whatever mess you make."

That was what Nate was counting on. D had saved him from countless messes over the years—starting with that orgy at Princeton. He was twenty years older now, but not that much wiser. It was entirely possible, before this was all over, that Dustin would have to save Nate from *himself*.

The man taking them to wherever Aleksei Vasiliev was holed up with his sister and Danny Yeo looked exactly like what you'd expect someone named Mickey Hands to look. Loud silk shirt, multiple gold chains resting on a thick mat of chest hair—open to the world despite the chill fall weather—and an equally thick mustache that was liberally streaked with gray. He'd worked Little Odessa for decades, he'd bragged as he slid into the car next to Neha, bringing a cloud of peppery cologne with him. *"Before Vasiliev was even born!"*

"Nice. Maybe you'll be lucky enough to outlive him," Joe had growled, tapping his fingertips impatiently on the dash, clanging the cuffs encircling his wrists. Not exactly the most reassuring thing to say to a criminal contact who could turn their whole operation sideways if he felt like it.

But there wasn't a script for these things, was there? No stage directions. And no end she could flip to in order to reassure herself that the good guys would win. Neha could barely sit still as they neared a series of dark buildings in Midwood...though the prop cuffs that secured her to the door handle were doing a decent job of keeping her in place. Her stomach was tight, her skin tingling. And her heart...it had yet to stop aching. Because, like a fool, she'd left it open when Joe's was clearly locked up tight. She was trying not to think about him, to lose focus when they had so much to do, but that was nearly impossible when he was just inches away.

She could still taste him on her mouth. That kiss she'd wrested from him while he was trying to wrest control from her. And his scent…that earthy scent of wolf beneath whatever soap he'd scrubbed up with in the riding-center showers. It somehow surrounded her even with the competition of Mickey Hands's eye-wateringly strong cologne. And with it came the memory of Joe's brutally tender hands and his cock and how he'd taken her with such passionate desperation over and over again. He'd whispered countless filthy things to her…but he hadn't made many promises, had he?

"Neha, I'll make a vow to you right now: I will do anything to keep you safe."

Except that one. It was the one he was determined to keep… even if that meant sacrificing her happiness and his own. That wasn't noble. That was selfish. And Neha almost wanted to tell him. To rail and rant at him again, Mack and Mickey Hands be damned.

Except the SUV was slowing. And Mickey was gesturing out the window at the street. "You'll want to park here," he said, as if being towed was a huge concern for Third Shift…or for the low-lifes they were pretending to be. "It ain't a bus lane or anything. No traffic cameras on the corners."

A largely Hasidic neighborhood, it was quiet for Shabbat. Lights were off, businesses closed, and not just because of the late/early hour. For Vasiliev to do business here seemed particularly evil, calculated. But that was the way of the world, wasn't it? Wickedness always wormed its way into places of peace. She'd wanted to keep her and Joe away from her gurdwara for that very reason…but there was no real respite, was there? The bad guys would always find you…unless you found them first.

Mack took the keys out of the ignition, slipping them into his pocket as easily as he slipped into the role of the random racist baddie who wanted to use his hostages and Mickey Hands as an introduction to the great Aleksei Vasiliev. He'd won the plum part not just because he was the whitest and most conventional of the operatives at hand, but because Finn and Grace had both been at the club and could be too easily made. *"Makes me feel like the Redshirt, honestly,"* he'd joked when the assignment was handed down. *"Please remember me well, mates."* There were no jokes now. He gestured Joe out of the passenger seat with his Glock and then got Neha out of her side of the SUV, quickly "relocking" her cuffs for Mickey's benefit. They were fake, Grace had explained back at the safe house. Magician's tools. Easy to snap out of at a moment's notice, but realistic enough to pass muster. After Aleksei's posturing at Kamchatka, it was a fair bet he'd be too busy crowing at getting his prisoner and a bonus back in custody to pay attention to how secure they were.

A fair bet. Because this was all a gamble. Neha suppressed a shudder as Mack and their new fence friend marched them toward a squat warehouse next to more structures of a similar shape. Joe's shoulders were thrown back, arrogant and proud, like he didn't give a damn about what he was walking into. It was a familiar sight. The cocky, angry bastard who didn't offer up an inch. But even more familiar was the man who smiled at her in bed. Who could rattle off his favorite restaurants and favorite books and debate the merits of Edward versus Jacob. That man had a softness in his eyes and to his mouth. That man's shoulders were a perfect fit for her head.

She had no idea if she was ever going to see him again. If Joe would allow that. If Aleksei and his men would allow that. One way or another, it would all end before sunrise. And even with that morbid thought in mind, Neha wasn't prepared when they were pushed through the warehouse door and met with a row of hulking mobsters holding semiautomatic weapons. Nine huge guns. Nine huge supernaturals. Plus their vor, standing several yards behind them—too confident to bother being armed at all. A quick assessment of the rest of the space revealed that Yulia and Danny Yeo weren't being held there...but they couldn't be far. Maybe in the next room or something.

Mickey Hands launched into his intro. His thick Brooklyn accent echoing across the cavernous, dimly lit space. Neha was only half listening to his patter and Mack's occasional interjections, too aware of the gun at her back. Sure, Mack didn't plan to do anything to her with it, but it didn't make it any easier to feel the muzzle against her spine.

"I can smell your fear, Doc. And if I can, these guys can, too," Joe said. Softly but not so softly that his voice didn't rumble over her like thunder. "See what you get when you get mixed up with me?"

They both knew people could hear them...and the more supes listening meant the more supes who weren't paying attention to their surroundings. Neha swallowed butterflies, throwing a scowl over her shoulder at Mack before glaring at Joe. "If now isn't a good time to be afraid, then when *is*? Let me know, because I'll pencil that in." It was equal parts improvisation and truth and a shout-out to what Grace had said to her and Nate barely two hours earlier.

They did not have time to second-guess things. To second-guess each other. But how could they trust one another in this when they didn't even trust themselves? Maybe Joe could smell that accusation on her, too, because he shifted subtly, keeping Aleksei and the goons in his periphery while meeting her gaze. "I know I got you into this. I swear, I'm gonna get you out of it. If it's the last thing I do."

I don't want it to be the last thing you do. I want it to be the first thing you do before promising you'll stay. Before saying you love me. She couldn't say that aloud for other people's benefit. She could barely think it for herself. Wanting Joe to love her...wanting to love him back...how had she even come to that over the course of a few weeks?

A single gunshot brought her inner turmoil to a swift end and sent her instinctively to the ground...and Mack hit the deck right beside her. His sightless eyes joined by a bloodred third one in the center of his forehead. A scream froze in Neha's throat as she crouched there, caught between scrambling away from the agent's body and not making herself the next target. Poor Mack. He'd called himself a Star Trek Redshirt, and...*ohgodohgodohgod*.

Aleksei blew on his gun like a stereotypical movie villain, looking too pleased with himself. "I grow tired of this brokering. Why make deals for what is rightfully mine?" he demanded of Mickey Hands. The elderly fence had no response to that except to scramble backward toward the door sputtering apologies. Neha felt more than saw the henchmen breaking formation to grab him. She still didn't dare rise off the concrete.

And that precise instant was when Joe snapped his cuffs and shifted. Fur burst through his clothes, his face rippled and elongated. A wolf on two legs. A man with a predator's teeth and sharp-nailed paws. He moved in a blur, knocking the gun from Aleksei's hand and claiming it for himself and then kicking out his legs from under him. Much like Joe, Vasiliev was shifting in an instant. Becoming a giant brown bear as he landed hard, scattering fancy suit buttons all over the place. Neha rolled out of the way as Joe squeezed off two shots at the men holding Mickey, breaking out of her own cuffs and grabbing Mack's Glock from where it had fallen just a few inches from his outstretched hand.

Jackson Tate and Elijah Richter had leveled very specific instructions at her and Nate during their briefing in the hidden room. *"You are civilians. You are humans. Your first priority is to get the hell out of the line of fire. Focus on evasion and defense. We don't need you hindering the operatives who are trained for this."* It had been on the tip of her tongue to ask them why more operatives who were more trained weren't taking their place. She'd kept the logical question to herself. Just as she kept her own counsel now, trying to shut out everything but the feel of the 9mm handgun in her fingers. It was heavy. An ill fit for her small hand. The kickback would hurt. And the huge henchmen, who were even now changing into their supernatural forms, weren't paper targets at the firing range. But the KA-BAR in the sheath beneath her shirt wouldn't do her much good right now. The unfamiliar gun was her only choice. She aimed, squeezed the trigger, and fired at one of the half-man, half-bear creatures. Blood bloomed at his kneecap, sending him stumbling. Mickey Hands took that opportunity to bolt out the warehouse door...and allow Grace, Finn, and Nate to rush inside.

Grace immediately dropped into a defensive stance, whipping two guns out of her shoulder holsters and opening fire. She finished off the man Neha had dropped and took out one more. Finn leapt at another, fangs flashing. Nate seemed to have Tate and Richter's edict well in hand, because he came straight for Neha, helping her off the ground and then practically dragging her out of the fray.

It was chaos. A swirl of sight and sound and pain. More people burst in through doors at the far end of the warehouse. An East Asian man and a bear being chased by some kind of bird man and a bunch of other hairy shape-shifters. Danny Yeo and Yulia had saved themselves...to a point. *Exeunt, pursued by a werebear*, she thought with a lunatic giggle. Because if you couldn't reach for your college Shakespeare when you were about to die, then what even was the point? As professional rescue plans went, this was a pretty shitty one. They were grossly outnumbered. Outmatched. Worst. Action movie. Ever.

And Joe was still battling Aleksei Vasiliev. He'd long since tossed aside the vor's gun in favor of his partially shifted claws. Doing Wolverine proud. They were grappling hand-to-hand, like he'd done with Yuri Medvedev in the cage. And just like then, it was horrifying to watch. But this wasn't a forced spectacle for a crowd. It wasn't for a show of the Vasiliev organization's strength. It was purely for Joe's survival, purely to put an end to Aleksei once and for all. His head was bleeding. Raw, red, scratches crisscrossed his chest. It sounded like Aleksei was laughing at him. Taunting him in growls. She didn't even realize she was trying to go to him—to stop him, to help him, to do *something*—until she registered Nate's strong grip clamping down on her upper arm and his voice in her ear. "You have to stop. Let him do this, Neha. You're only going to get in his way."

"Then why are we *here*?" she cried. "We can't just stay on the sidelines."

"We won't," he said grimly. He nodded toward Yulia and Danny, who were still fighting off the supes from the other room. "Come on."

Neha handed Nate the Glock and retrieved her combat knife from its sheath. They stuck to the perimeter of the warehouse, keeping their guards up and their attention on all of the skirmishes around them. She had no illusions about being able to take a shifter down in a fight. She'd greatly exaggerated her knife skills to Grace. But she could get a few cuts in, slow some of them down. Give Yulia and Danny some room. It was hard to believe the sweet, quiet young woman from the club was the glorious bear shifter swiping at the raptor man. She was powerful, furious, roaring at the bird of prey as she ducked his talons. The way she moved in a circle pattern made it clear that she was trying to protect Danny, who'd swept up a fallen semiautomatic to use against the other bear shifters around them but was missing more shots than he made. His ammo went wild, nearly hitting Neha and Nate as they closed in.

"And I thought *we* were bad at this." Nate grimaced, dropping into a crouch with a groan of protest.

Neha took Mack's Glock back from him. "We *are* bad at this. If we survive, I'm buying you Krav Maga classes for Hanukkah."

"Aw. I was going to get you Brazilian jiu-jitsu classes for...uh... Guru Nanakkah."

Guru Nanakkah. Inappropriate laughter for the win. Neha wiped ill-timed tears of mirth from her eyes with the back of her hand, gasping for breath. "His birthday's in November. Please do *not* call it that in front of any other Sikh people," she begged.

Their moment of levity was short-lived. An actual *polar bear*, with dirty white fur, wheeled away from his stalking of Danny and came barreling toward them at top speed. Neha raised the gun with shaking hands and fired three times in quick succession. It barely made an impact. Might as well have been thumb tacks. The bear shifter rose up on two legs, snarling, ready to pounce...

And then the ceiling caved in.

Actually, only a small part of the ceiling. As if it had been lasered open or blown with explosive charges. Tile and timber rained down on the floor...followed by a massive lion. Terrifying. Beautiful. He landed on all fours on top of a tarp-covered vehicle of some kind, shaking his tawny mane and whipping his tail. A white man floated down to the ground below him, and Neha easily recognized the tall, thin figure as Jack Tate. He'd barely touched the floor before he was conjuring huge fireballs that danced just above his palms, and he threw one at the polar bear like he was a starting pitcher for the Yankees. The bear howled, flickering from human to animal and back again, before throwing himself to the ground in an effort to put the flames out.

The cavalry had arrived—"You're on your own in Brooklyn" mission specs be damned—and Neha couldn't say that she was sorry. They'd been woefully out of their element with her and Nate on the team against so many supernaturals. They needed all the reinforcements they could get...and they'd received the very best. If Jack was throwing fiery fastballs, it was a reasonable assumption that the gorgeous and ginormous leonine creature leaping toward one of the werebears was Elijah Richter. Third Shift's leaders had come for their people.

34

HE WAS TOO DAMN TIRED and too damn old to be fighting like this. He'd already had his bell rung a couple of times by that bear shifter in the cage, and now he was on the defensive with Aleksei Vasiliev, who didn't have the decency to be at all winded. This furry motherfucker was a couple years older than him, pouring blood from several different wounds, and still coming back for more. He must've been running on some special supervillain juice. Or a full eight hours of sleep and decent health insurance. Joe couldn't remember the last time he'd had either. *No. Not true. You slept just fine in Doc's arms.* He couldn't think about that, though. Not right now. It was enough to know she was still up and moving somewhere in the warehouse. That was as much distraction as he could allow himself—occasionally clocking her location as he kept wrestling the Russian. They'd been going on five minutes. Maybe longer. It felt like the world's longest, most miserable prizefight.

At least the other thugs weren't his problem anymore. His new vampire pal and the scary surgeon had drawn them away. But there was no question they were still losing this fight. Too many supes, not enough people trained to take them down. Why was Feinberg here? What was Joe's *lawyer* going to do, for fuck's sake?

Argue a pissed-off shifter to death? But Nate had dragged Neha out of Aleksei's path, so Joe could spare a second to be thankful. The same second he spent ducking a paw. Then he rose up to slam his fist into the side of Aleksei's muzzle. He wasn't fully shifted, his human vocal cords still worked, so he growled out, "Would you just fucking *die* already?" like the vor might actually listen and drop dead on the spot.

That was when the roof fell in…and distracted Vasiliev long enough for Joe to swing upward and get in three more head shots in quick succession. *Bam. Bam. Bam.* He added claw to the last blow, ripping away a chunk of ear and cheek. The mobster screamed, his control finally snapping…forcing a shift back to his human form.

"You are a *fool*, Joseph Peluso," he hissed, holding his bleeding face as he staggered backward. "You really think this is the end? That my people will not keep coming for you and yours?"

"Look around. You're not the only one who has people." It felt strange to say that and realize it was true. To take a breath, too, for the first time in several minutes. Because a huge lion and some kind of sorcerer or warlock had joined the fray—on *his* side—and a polar bear shifter cornering Nate and Neha suddenly went up in flames like a campfire marshmallow. "You can keep 'em coming, Vasiliev. We'll keep stepping up. This city doesn't belong to you or your kind. You can't kill our brothers and sisters and neighbors and get away with it. You can't make us live in fear."

Kenny's body on that morgue slab. Mrs. C crying her eyes out. The four shifters in that back room. Neha screaming his name at the club. A dozen memories flitted through his brain like a movie montage. He had plenty *he* needed to pay for, too. *Just add one more sin to the tab.*

Joe charged forward with a bone-chilling howl, took Aleksei Vasiliev's face between his hands, and snapped his neck. But it wasn't like the movies…where killing the head bad guy brought a hush across the set and all the other goons dropped their weapons.

No. The only thing that fell was the vor's corpse. There were at least three hostiles still active. And as exhausted as Joe was, he wasn't done yet. So, he found the closest battle and waded in, grabbing a werebear by the arm and dragging him away from Grace, who was nearly out of ammo and cussing up a storm in every language she knew.

The sorcerer, or whatever the fuck he was, stunned the shifter with a spell, knocking him out cold. "Jackson Tate," he called to Joe, like they were at a cocktail party. "You can thank us later."

"You can fuck off later," he shouted back. It wasn't the most charitable response—especially after accepting that he had people willing to defend him—but Joe figured he'd earned some salt tonight. A whole damn truck's worth.

He did a quick assessment of the rest of the warehouse. The lion shifter was finishing off one last bear. One last *evil* bear. Because another seemed to be on the right side, and it took Joe precious seconds to realize it was Yulia, the girl who'd brought him food and smuggled in the operatives. *Hunh*. Who knew she was such a badass? And the avian shifter she'd been tangling with for however long finally figured that out, too. Because he changed targets. Swooping toward Nate and Neha. *Fuck*, it was like everybody in a ten-mile radius knew they were the most vulnerable people in the room. And Joe was too far away to do anything about it.

Finn wasn't. The vampire moved so fast it was almost impossible to see him. But he knocked the birdman out of the air, going in on the guy's neck at the same moment that Neha fired her gun at him. They both hit the concrete with a sickening thud. Joe was still only halfway there, but he was close enough to see the talons slicing into Finn's stomach before falling away. And the blood. So much blood.

Fuck. The big moment where the hush fell across the set? This was it.

It went from total chaos to complete silence in an instant. Too fast, too loud, too frightening…and then slow motion. Neha felt the Glock slip from her suddenly limp fingers. Her vision swam, full of feathers and thirty-odd years of her life flashing before her eyes, and Finn's body on the ground. *No. Oh, no.* For a split second, she thought she'd done it. Missed the raptor and shot the rakish vampire instead. And then she saw the blood-soaked talons. The slashes in Finn's belly. *It wasn't you, Neha. You didn't hurt him.* Relief and horror hit her in a double whammy.

Nate was already scrambling to the vampire's side, dragging the bird shifter's corpse off of him. Grace came up from the other direction at a near sprint. She was shaken. No, she was as undone as the woman probably got. Dark eyes stricken, hands clenched into fists…loosening only when she knelt by him and began prodding his wounds. "Finian Thomas Michael Conlan." The words were enunciated clearly, emphatically…and laden with a combination of fury and anguish. "I am *not* saving your life again. If you don't get your useless ass up right now, I will nail you to a cross at midday…and I don't mean a St. Andrew's one."

For a long stretch of seconds, there was nothing but quiet work. Grace demanding Nate's shirt. Using it as a field dressing. With nary a twitch from the supine form on the ground, soaked in the bird shifter's blood and his own, too. And then the vampire's foot twitched. His hand. And he moved his head on the concrete with a rusty groan. "The middle name *and* the confirmation name? For fuck's sake, woman. You could just say you love me."

"I can't stand you," she said automatically…but the tears choking the words revealed her lie just as much as the gentle way she put two fingers to Finn's throat to check his pulse.

"That actually works? You can get a heart rate?" Nate wondered softly. He still looked vaguely stunned from when Finn had knocked the shifter away from them and taken the brunt of the body blow. But not so out of it that he couldn't reach out and mimic Grace's motion, placing his fingers alongside hers.

Finn coughed violently, pale and bloodless, but still managed to choke out flirtation. "I'm full of surprises, darlin'," he assured with a half-strength eyebrow waggle. "Anytime you want a personal anatomy lesson, give us a ring."

The collective groan of relief/annoyance at his swift return to form was almost audible. And then Grace was lifting her wrist to his mouth, shutting him up by giving him the sustenance he desperately needed to heal. Neha instinctively turned away, as if that would give the trio some kind of privacy in the middle of all these onlookers. And the motion put her right in Joe's sight line. He'd stopped several feet away from the tableau, his features as grim as they were streaked with blood and dirt. His clothes were in tatters. His exposed limbs and fur not much better. He was still one of the most stunningly beautiful people she'd ever seen in her life.

It didn't matter that she was still furious with him. It didn't matter that her heart still felt as though it had been pulverized. Neha lurched toward him, polarized like a magnet, wanting nothing more than to snap to him, because as opposite as they were, they somehow belonged together anyway. Joe caught her before she could crash into his chest…and then he hauled her against it, crushing her in his embrace with the same frantic intensity that he used to bring his mouth down on hers. The kiss was like their first and their last wrapped into one explosive package. Everything tentative but also nothing held back. One hand palming her ass while the other tenderly cradled her cheek. He tasted like smoke and copper and light and hope.

Their completely reckless passions had brought them to this place, to this wild moment. Neha could only credit one thing with them surviving it. "Joe… I…" The words clung to her tongue, still unwilling to let go. To take that leap across the divide.

"Love you," he whispered, meeting her halfway. "I am a fucking asshole for not telling you that before. For not telling you a million times. For forcing you into all of these decisions without letting you know that I am *all in*. I am so damn in love with you, Neha. And if I'd lost you today…" He choked, unable to finish the thought, his brown eyes nearly black with emotion.

"You didn't. And I didn't lose *you*." Her heart hurt again. Not because it was pulverized but because it was knitting itself back into one piece. Neha relearned the harsh planes of his face with her fingertips. She reclaimed the hollow of his throat with her mouth. And she gave voice to the things she hadn't dared say before. "We never would've gotten this far if I didn't love you, too, Joe. That's why I made every choice I made. I wasn't forced. I did it willingly," she assured him fiercely. "I love you willingly."

That didn't solve their problems. Not remotely. It wouldn't erase the crimes Joe had committed or the ones Neha had abetted. It didn't make him any less of an ill-tempered chauvinistic asshat or her any less of an impulsive fool. But it sure as hell made it all worth it to hear the words spoken, to say them out loud. To *mean* them. She loved him. Had been in love with him for weeks now. She'd put her career on the line, put her *life* on the line, because of that mind-blowing, earth-shaking fact. Unprofessional? Sure. Lust-addled? Definitely. But all of it, everything, out of love.

Joe Peluso wasn't some movie-star handsome hunk. He had a filthy mouth and no boundaries. He clearly had issues with authority and impulse control. They'd have to work on the whole vigilante thing. As careers went, it was hardly a stable one. But she adored this man—flaws and all. His humor, his strength, his rage, and his vulnerability. The beast inside him, and the human, too.

35

DANNY WASTED NO TIME STRIPPING off his shirt and offering it to Yulia, who was shivering from what had to be the worst combination of shock, exhaustion, tranquilizers, and grief. Shifting back from her bear form had nearly sent her into a collapse...sinking into his arms like a deadweight. He hadn't minded. There was nothing he'd rather be doing than holding Yulia Vasilieva close. But now was neither the time nor the place for an extended version of that impulse. Once she'd covered up to her satisfaction, they slowly made their way to the rest of Third Shift and company. Leaning on each other, shoring each other up. Stopping every few feet to trade kisses that were too weary to be anything but chaste.

She'd betrayed her family, her clan tonight. For him and his. There was no going back from that. Wherever they went now...it was forward. Together.

He could feel the heat of Jack's glare from across the warehouse. Even though the man was rifling through a small backpack he'd brought and tossing clothes in Elijah's general direction, there was no doubt in Danny's mind that he was mad about how things had gone down. Once Elijah shifted—far less exhausted than Yulia by the effort—and tugged on a loose pair of track pants, his own baleful glare joined the "You're in trouble" party. Only he widened the searchlight beam to include nearly everyone.

"We done here?" he demanded, his rich and riveting voice echoing to the rafters. "Or does anyone else have any romantic declarations to make? More Russian vors to antagonize? I just want to get a sense of where we are."

"Hey." Joe Peluso looked just as dangerously angry. He stepped forward, still keeping an arm around Ms. Ahluwalia. "Back off, buddy. Unless you want to get a sense of my fist in your face. Nobody asked you and JC Penney over here to ruin your beauty sleep by showing up, okay?"

JC Penney. Danny had to stifle a burst of totally appropriate laughter. While Jackson did look like a catalog model, he'd probably never worn clothes off the rack in his entire life. His boss didn't bother making that point, though. "Technically you did ask me," he pointed out instead. "When you made that call to Third Shift. And where do you think you got that number? Where do you think the Apex Initiative came from? We were the first wave, Peluso. Phase One. Before they even had a name for the project. And we don't abandon our own."

Way to declassify. Danny's eyebrows skyrocketed into his hairline as he remembered everything Jack and Elijah had revealed back at the office, belying the patchy files they had on Peluso and his past. Heavily redacted for the likes of the Third Shift desk jockeys like himself and unceremoniously unredacted for literal regular Joes in a Brooklyn warehouse. Jack and Elijah really *were* aggravated about this whole situation. Danny cleared his throat, drawing their attention back over to where he stood. "So, what does this mean for all of us? What happens next?" *Will Yulia be safe?* That was his real question. The question that had sent him out into the night and gotten him held hostage when he was supposed to be following orders and maintaining a contact point at HQ.

He expected to be yelled at. To be met with the same attitude they'd dished back to Joe Peluso. But almost the near-opposite happened. Elijah brought over the small bag of clothes and gently offered it to Yulia. "There's another pair of sweatpants in there," he told her softly. "No such thing as 'too prepared' when shape-shifting's involved, yeah?" And then he turned to Danny. "I'm glad you're all right, mate. And I hate that Mack wasn't so lucky."

Elijah glanced across the warehouse to where Mack's body still lay. Along with so many others. Naked grief etched his features for a few seconds before he sighed heavily, scrubbing at his face with his knuckles. "But the rest? It's going to be a total shitshow," he assured. "There'll be a power vacuum in Little Odessa without Vasiliev's organization keeping things running. And the people he answers to… Well, the bright side is we hope this'll shake *them* up enough for us to nail them. I'll be assessing that operation in person soon enough."

Elijah had been prepping for his mission for weeks now. Studying up on Emeric Aston's girlfriend and other potential points of contact. This thing with Vasiliev and Peluso had simulta-neously thrown a wrench into that mission *and* made it more of a priority. Danny didn't envy him the task ahead. And the cleanup of *this* mess would be no walk in the park either. Scrubbing the ware-house, making arrangements for Mack, sorting out how much the NYPD would need to know about what actually happened…

The NYPD. Danny swallowed what tasted like bile in the back of his throat. Somewhere in the last few days, the police depart-ment had become a them instead of an us. He hadn't given a single thought to his precinct. To the calls he hadn't bothered to answer and the voicemails he'd deleted unheard. He didn't belong there anymore. Maybe he never had to begin with. The real justice work was being done bigger and better everywhere else. "City law enforcement's going to hate this," he said. Not just about the cleanup, but about the decision that was just starting to take root in his brain. "Be prepared for the local precincts to give you a ton of grief."

"We know. None of this is going to be a party." Jackson acknowledged him with a nod before looking around at the 3S operatives and civilians alike. "A cleaning crew is already en route for this location. Danny, you and Ms. Vasilieva should probably get checked out at HQ. Bunk down there, too, if you have to. Mr. Feinberg…as far as we're concerned, you were never here."

"I'm okay with developing a case of selective amnesia, but there are some things I won't be forgetting." The pale-haired lawyer was crouched by Finn, who still wasn't looking so great. The shirt pressed to his stomach was soaking through with blood, even though he'd fed from Grace to try to replace it. "Like how this is going to impact Joe's case. And Neha."

"I'm pretty interested in that, too," Neha said. By all rights, she should have been as exhausted as Yulia. After days in hiding, the infiltration of Kamchatka, and this supernatural showdown. But she stood tall in the circle of Peluso's arms. Her eyes were clear and the line of her mouth was sharp. "There are active APBs out for Joe right now. I have no idea what my family thinks of where I've been, but I do know that the New York State Bar Association isn't going to be thrilled when *they* are made aware of these circumstances."

"No one's going to be thrilled," Elijah responded drily. "Except maybe the *Daily News* and the *Post*. Hope we at least get some creative headlines out of this. But we'll get you two back to Safe House 13 while we enact the cover story and get all our ducks in a row."

Their ducks, their werebears, you name it. So much to do and so little time to do it all in. Somehow, Danny wasn't overwhelmed at the prospect. He looked at the brave, beautiful woman next to him…swimming in his shirt and a huge pair of drawstring sweatpants that were cinched as tightly as possible at the waist. They probably had a matching list of aches and pains. They would be able to compare bruises and scratches and broken teeth when they were in the med bay at HQ. And Yulia would cry and mourn at some point. And then cry and mourn some more. Because evil crime kingpin or no, Aleksei Vasiliev had still been her older brother. But Danny would be right beside her, holding her hand, giving her a shoulder, giving her someone to hit—and probably knock across the room.

He lifted her fingers to his cracked lips, brushing a kiss across her split knuckles. "Don't tell Elijah," he whispered, "but I have a romantic declaration to make."

"Later," Yulia said just as quietly, canting her body in to his. "First, you must take me on that date to the Met."

"The opera *and* the museum," Danny promised. "Because I need culture...but I also need you."

———————

It felt like hours before they got out of that godforsaken warehouse in Midwood. Before they were *alone*. Joe's head was a mess. Full of all kinds of shit. What-ifs. What-will-bes. What-the-fucks. But the only thing knocking around his brain that mattered was what Neha had said to him before those spy boys started lecturing. *"I love you willingly."* And what he'd said to her. *"I am so damn in love with you."* He heard the words over the sound of the fancy rainfall shower pounding his skin and pounding the tiles. Grace and the others had called it a locker room, but this was a fucking cabana or some country-club shit. Trust-fund kids got their horse-riding lessons in this fancy place. Now a blue-collar bruiser from Queens was taking advantage of the same perks. When he'd washed up before, it was quick, efficient. This time...this time, he sloughed off more than blood and dirt. He soaped away the courthouse. The cage. Vasiliev. All of it. He let everything but Neha's voice circle the drain. Her voice...and then the feel of her arms slipping around him as she joined him under the spray.

"Why waste water?" she murmured. "Besides, it was lonely in the other one."

Not lonelier than prison showers. Than the cell he'd spent months in. The cell he might be going back to. The cell he *should* go back to. *Jesus. Fuck.* Joe didn't know where the tremors come from, but all of a sudden, he couldn't stop shivering. The water was steaming hot, but he barely felt it. And the memory of Neha's *I love you*'s and her soft hands on his back didn't make a dent.

"Hey. Hey, it's alright. I'm here." Somewhere over the buzzing in his ears, he heard her comforting him. Whispering things in both English and Punjabi. And then she was shampooing his hair with the expensive-smelling stuff from the wall dispenser. Running her fingers along his scalp. Arching up on her toes, her front to his back, so she could reach.

Maybe it was what she said. Maybe it was the press of their bodies. Maybe it was just being *cared for*, because that had been such a foreign concept to him these past couple years, but he eventually stopped shaking. Braced against the tiles, bowing under the spray and under Neha's tender ministrations. She loved him willingly. And he loved her more than he'd ever thought he was capable of. If what was building between them only lasted as long as the next few hours, it was still more than he ever thought he'd have. So, he turned. And he tended to her the same way she did him. Burying his hands in the wet, thick ropes of her hair. Working a lather through the strands. After she rinsed out the shampoo, he went to work on the rest of her…soaping her feet and her legs and up her thighs.

"We're not in a rush now." She laughed softly, parting her legs in invitation. "You can take all the time you want. Do Aviation High proud."

He did them proud alright. *You better fucking believe it.* Sinking to his banged-up knees—healing just fast enough for him to do this properly—and pulling her onto his face like it was her custom-built seat. It had only been a day or two since they'd last had sex, but it was like tasting her new. The salt of her on his tongue. The warmth of her against his lips. It was so damn good. So damn perfect. The condemned's first meal and his last meal. He licked and took and sucked until she trembled with one orgasm and then another, crying out his name and scratching the back of his neck.

The water was cold by the time they got out. He wasn't footing the bills at this place, so he didn't spare it a thought beyond grabbing towels so Neha didn't shiver like he had. They dried off faster than they got wet. Dressing in fresh sets of spy clothes from a special locker hidden behind some modern art and then heading to the tack house and the safe room. "We've keyed in your print information, so your fingers should activate the biometric scanners on all the secure-access doors," Tate had told them before dropping them off. Which was creepy as hell. When Joe said this out loud during the short walk back, Neha slipped her hand into his. "I have a better use for your fingers," she assured him.

It was freaking weird and wonderful at the same time. Doing something as coupley as holding a woman's hand. He'd always thought the phantom bloodstains on his palms meant it wasn't for him. Guys like him didn't get walks in the park and love songs and happy endings, right?

Turned out he was wrong. Guys like him got to toe off their shoes and climb onto a fold-out couch and hold beautiful women in their arms. They got to breathe in her hair and her skin, and laugh when she admitted horses terrified her. "Seriously? I mean, yeah, they're kinda fucking scary…but you just faced down a bunch of bear shifters and some kind of hawk-shifter guy like you've been doing this supe thing your whole life, and it's *horses* that terrify you?"

Neha punched the thin pillows, huffing. "I had goat trauma during a visit to Punjab as a kid, okay? Goats, horses, cows. Things with hooves. It's all related."

Goat trauma. Joe cracked up. It felt real good to lose it, too. Like the world might actually be okay for a minute. "I promise to protect you from any goat shifters we meet," he said between wheezing chuckles.

"Oh my god. Are there *really* goat shifters?" She pulled back to gawk at him, her pretty face scrunched up with horror. "Don't tell me they actually exist? Like satyrs? Or centaurs?"

"Not that I know of...but I wouldn't rule it out, Doc." He'd learned a couple of valuable lessons since he'd been recruited into the Apex Initiative. Most of them in the past few weeks with Neha. But there was one that predated her: There was more bizarre, unexplained, and unexplainable shit on this planet than the average human could even dream up. He was living proof.

He was *living.* That, in and of itself, was unbelievably bizarre. He'd cheated death a thousand times in twenty years...hell, a thousand times in the past week. And all so he could be with this incredible woman. Those first couple days with her...he thought it was biological, chemical. Something his wolf wanted, something the scientists programmed into him. *Imprinting.* But it wasn't just the wolf now. It was the man, too. It was all of him. Together as one. Wanting her, loving her for exactly who she was. "Thank you," he told Neha, bringing her closer so she was tucked against his chest.

"For what?" He felt her curious frown on his neck. Her mouth tickled. It should've distracted him, but instead it just crystallized his answer.

"For seeing something in me." 'Cause god only knew most people didn't see beyond the surface. Beyond the battered mug and the scarred fists. "For hanging in there. For believing in me when I didn't give you a reason to."

"Unbridled lust isn't a reason?" she wondered, pressing a saucy, smacking kiss to his pulse.

Christ, he loved her so much. "'Unbridled,' huh? And now we're back to horses..."

"Oof! No!" Neha shuddered theatrically before settling in his arms. She stroked her palm over his heart in slow circles. Such a simple thing and it felt so good. So right. "I don't expect this to be easy. Just navigating your case in the wake of going AWOL is going to be a nightmare. To say nothing about how we're going to move forward *together*. And you should probably talk to a professional about your…anger management issues."

Joe couldn't help but laugh again. Not because the idea of talking to a therapist was so off base, but because she put the reason so damn delicately. "You can say it, you know. Because you're not wrong. I went off on a rampage. I killed people. And if you were in danger, I can't say I wouldn't want to repeat that. Hell yeah, my first impulse would be to play judge, jury, and executioner." He'd taken lives again tonight. Pushed to it, sure. But he'd done it knowing full well that killing was still something he was good at. He no longer wanted it to be the *only* thing he was good at. "I need to be the man you see, Neha. That guy. The one who makes better choices—whose first impulse will be to think of what *you'd* do."

"Hmm. What *I'd* do?" Neha rolled onto her back, staring up at the ceiling in the dark…but she reached for his hand, squeezing it tight. Like she didn't want to let him go even a little bit. "I try to help people. Sometimes I run off with questionable men who turn out to be perfect for me."

"I'd like to do that—help people," he admitted. Because, fuck knew, he had *so* much making up to do. So much penance to outweigh his sins. But… "I'm hoping the second thing's a one-time deal and only a you thing. 'Cause I don't know if I wanna run off with Finn."

His tough lawyer lady actually giggled. "I think there's a waiting list to run off with Finn. Or run *away* from him. Probably both."

Probably both. The vampire had taken a hit for her at that warehouse. Saved Joe's skin, too, back at the club. He was never going to be able to repay that. He was still going to give it a shot.

Thanking everyone at Third Shift—even those dicksmacks who ran it—for pulling his ass out of the fire. And for giving him one more chance with Neha Ahluwalia.

It was hard to speak over the sudden knot of emotion in his throat. He did it anyway. Because if you couldn't get sappy and sentimental at a time like this, what was even the point? "I love you, Doc. Just in case you forgot already."

"I love you, too," she mumbled sleepily, stretching to kiss his lips. "I won't forget."

He reminded her again. And kissed her back. A few times. Just to make sure.

They didn't get a whole lot of shut-eye. Three hours, maybe four. And they didn't manage much more than kissing before they finally passed out from exhaustion…mainly because they knew the room was completely wired and Third Shift had enough of a spy cam on their lives already. Pretty much five seconds after Joe awoke with that grumpy thought, still blinking the sleep from his eyes, the tech came online. The speakerphone crackled with static.

"We're on our way," Elijah Richter announced over the line. "You lot had better be decent."

"No chance of that…but we'll be dressed," Joe replied caustically as Neha sat up beside him, shaking off the fog of interrupted sleep.

"Guess they worked out the cover story already?" She grimaced while they put the sofa bed to rights and themselves, too. "A little more notice would have been nice. This can't be good."

It wasn't. At all. He understood that. But, thanks to her, he also understood what it *could* be. A fresh start.

Barely a half hour later, the secret room door slid back, revealing Detective Danny and his boss. Wearing matching grim expressions. But only one of them was wearing a badge and a gun. This wasn't Joe's first rodeo. Or even his second. He knew what the cop was going to say before the words even left his mouth. It was the only thing he *could* say.

Danny pulled a pair of handcuffs off his belt, looking at Elijah Richter for the go-ahead before turning back to Joe. His eyes were full of regret...but also something fierce. Strong. A little badass. "I just want you to know: This is the last time I'm ever going to do this. Or say this."

"Then you'd better make it good." Joe pressed a quick kiss to the side of Neha's head before he offered up his wrists with a flourish.

"Joseph Peluso? You're under arrest."

36

_____

THE MAN WHO SAT ACROSS from her looked like he wanted to eat her, and Neha Ahluwalia had no doubt that he could. In great big bites. Laying her to waste with swipes of his claws. Would it be kinder than what he'd done to land behind bars? *That*, she had no inkling of. But she did know he was guilty. Guilty and a killer. One was a legal distinction, the other largely genetic, and they were both equally true. It wasn't just the look in his eyes. Not just speculation or suspicion or her overactive imagination. It was the facts. And it was in her heart. Neha's wild, passionate heart. It had led her back to Joe Peluso time and time again, even to another visitors' room in another prison.

He'd been transferred to Sing Sing just days after his plea agreement, in a deal so sweet it was practically rolled in sugar. Sixteen years, with an option for parole in eight—thanks to the combination of an "extreme emotional disturbance" defense and some intervention from their new friends at Third Shift. It was air-tight, one hundred percent legal…and a sentence Joe never finished serving. He'd been extracted two weeks into the incarceration and furnished with a brand-new identity. Meanwhile, Joe Peluso had died in prison, the victim of a brutal jailhouse takedown—one last headline for the road. Neha had lived in terror that he'd die for real before they could fake it.

But he wasn't done paying. He would never be done making restitution for his sins. She stared across the conference table at him—at that face that she'd once thought only a mother could love—and she cataloged every new line, every new scar and scratch. The strong jaw now covered by a thick, soft beard—not nearly as impressive as her brother's, but it would get there eventually. His hair was already longer, too, brushing his neck and showing glints of gray. "Shifter genes," he'd admitted. "If I quit shaving, I'll look like Cousin Itt from *The Addams Family*." He had a different legal name now, but he was still just Joe to her. With a lightness to his once-sullen posture and a smile in his dark eyes.

"Doc," he chided, softly. "You just saw me ten hours ago. Ain't nothin' changed since then."

Everything had changed since then, a ridiculous part of her wanted to disagree. Everything was changing for them on a daily basis. But he was right. They'd been going along like this for weeks now. Grabbing a few hours together here and there between Joe's work assignments for 3S. He'd already logged a few frequent-flier miles to Eastern Europe, courtesy of Third Shift Air. Elijah and Jackson had decided it was just practical to keep Joe out of the country as much as possible. They were right. Even with his new look and new identity, the chances of Joe being recognized while he was on American soil were pretty high.

Her own family, at least, was none the wiser. They thought her new boyfriend was some kind of globetrotting secret agent. It was just soapy enough to suit Ma and Papa's TV tastes, and cool enough to keep Neal and Nitesh from busting her chops about not meeting the guy yet. Only Tejal and Toral knew the whole truth— because the twins were used to living with secrets they couldn't share with anyone else.

"I've missed you, that's all," she confessed aloud. She'd upended her world to go on the run with him, and it didn't make sense without him in it. Whenever he was gone, there was a Joe-shaped hole in her life. She was no longer a lawyer—she'd called the inevitable disbarment from a mile away—and was a veritable pariah among many of her extended family members. There would be no more studio keys from Aishneet Auntie, for example. Ma and Papa and her brothers had closed ranks around her. Tejal would always have her back. But she felt the sting of every "Chee!" from aunties, uncles, and other cousins, and she felt the chill when she stopped in to her old gurdwara.

The basic tenets of assisting people in need only went so far, after all. And she couldn't blame them for the judgment. Though most of the details of what had gone down with Aleksei Vasiliev had been kept out of the media, her name had still been linked to everything in the papers and on the local news. Joe had killed six men and apparently died in jail for the crimes…but as far as the public was concerned, *she* was alive to answer for being kidnapped, developing Stockholm syndrome, and speaking out in his defense after his "death." For their own purposes, Third Shift's connections had circulated through back channels that Joe's hits were part of a sanctioned operation. But murder was murder, even if the government found a way to justify it.

That was why Joe had thrown himself fully into working for Third Shift—not as a killer, but as an operative who went into problematic areas and *helped*. Sure, he fought if necessary, but he also used his wolf form to hunt for those who needed food, provided medical support, and advised green operatives from the safe confines of a comm and a van. He planned to do it for the rest of his life. He'd committed to saving lives instead of taking them, to choosing hope over despair and active restitution over passive guilt. He'd chosen her. And she loved him for it. More than she'd ever thought possible.

"Fuck. When you look at me that way, I just want to climb

across this table and have at you." Joe's laugh was strangled, and they both looked through the glass at the 3S people on the floor… all studiously pretending they weren't paying attention to the flirt-fest. Sure, they could secure the room, frost the glass, but neither of them were into sex in public places—that first time against the wall notwithstanding.

She grinned back at him. "When you talk to me that way, I just want to crawl into your lap and kiss your face off."

He tugged theatrically at his shirt collar, giving a low whistle. "Man, I hope you don't say that to *all* the jailbirds."

Thanks to Jack's connections, she'd secured two new positions. The first was moonlighting at Third Shift, providing an extra brain and an extra body during localized missions. The one she could actually admit to in public involved counseling recently released convicts, both human and supernatural, helping them transition back to the general population. So, yeah, it was safe to say she didn't talk to her clients the same way. She didn't have a prisoner fetish like she'd feared so long ago. She just had a Joe fetish.

"Remember how you talked to *me* when we first met?" she countered. "You're lucky I didn't punch your lights out."

"You *should've* punched my lights out." The mirth drained from him, leaving him serious. Contemplative. "I used to think…" He started and then stopped, the tips of his ears going red. It was oddly endearing. She'd seen so many emotions out of him in their brief and intense time on the run, but never such boyish embarrass-ment. The rest of his confession tumbled out in a rush of breath. "I used to tell myself, if they were gonna reinstate the death penalty and give me the chair, that I'd ask for one thing for a last meal."

"What? Popeye's? Junior's cheesecake? A Donovan's burger?" she teased.

"No." He smiled. "*You.*"

Oh. Neha seriously started reconsidering her stance on exhi-bitionism. Surely their colleagues had seen *worse* things? *Stop.*

In a Herculean effort to keep from melting through the floor in a puddle of lust, she turned to humor. "I had no idea you were a cannibal. Now I have to rethink our entire relationship so far."

His laughter this time was unguarded, boisterous. "Oh, she's got *jokes*."

Neha did have jokes. And hope and joy and a man who loved her. Their life would never look like a storybook marriage, never be a traditional happily-ever-after, but it was *their* life. This unconventional, unpredictable adventure they'd crafted together.

The conference-room speakers—really the man behind them—chose that exact moment to make their presence known. "Are you two finished flirting? Do I really need to institute a no-fraternization rule around here?" Jack barked over the comm, sounding downright ruffled, unlike his typical TV weatherman tone. "We've got a mission rollout in T-minus two hours, and I need all hands, feet, and laptops on deck. Lije and his team are counting on us for tactical support."

Shit. Jack was right. As much as she and Joe missed each other, craved each other, would always love each other, they also had plenty of work to do. They rose from their chairs in perfect synchronization as their coworkers rushed in off the floor with various bits of tech and half-empty cans of Red Bull. Danny looked a little guilty, as though the brand-new wedding band on his finger was the reason for Jack's ire and not Neha and Joe practically steaming up the windows. Grace and Finn took adjacent seats, bickering like the old married couple they refused to be. Joaquin was already laser-focused on their tasks, spitting commands into their wireless mic.

Neha glanced across the table at Joe and found him staring at her with something bright and beautiful in his gaze. It was excitement and adrenaline and love and trust. *This.* This was their adventure. Because the Third Shift was a shift that never really ended.

Enjoy this sneak peek at book 2 in the Third Shift series:

PRETTY LITTLE LION

COMING FALL 2021

1

────

THE VIP LOUNGE AT THE Manhattan Grand sat just below the hotel's trendy rooftop restaurant. Floor-to-ceiling tinted windows offered up near-perfect views of the city skyline awash in the neon lights of Times Square. Near-perfect because you had to ignore the periodic drone sweeps and the occasional ominous black helicopters...ignore them or lean fully into them, posting dramatic snaps with a drone in the background. Fortunately, Meghna Saxena-Saunders wasn't interested in anything outside. Unfortunately, what did hold her interest wasn't suitable for Instagram pics or Twitter updates.

Check out this view! #toomanykillersinthisroom. #criminalactivity. #relationshipgoals. Guaranteed to go viral? Sure. Also guaranteed to ruin everything. Just like the man across the room. A room with an ice sculpture of a naked woman—top-shelf vodka flowing down her breasts and painstakingly carved nipples. And scantily clad real women circulating with shots of the vile stuff. They'd signed ironclad NDAs to work the gig, knowing they'd walk away with hefty paychecks and tips besides. The hefty dose of fear was an unfortunate side effect. Not that you would know it from the way the three redheads strutted through the room in tiny bikini tops and leather mini-skirts. She wanted to salute them, to applaud. They were bold, breathtaking, brave, under the slobbering scrutiny of the drunken guests.

But *he* was still watching *her*. He'd been watching her all night, tracking her movements around the party with the focus of an apex predator stalking prey…but with the care and caution of someone who existed in a hostile world that needed no excuse to punish him. All of the guards in the room operated under the latter assumption. *Step one foot out of line and you die.* He knew the consequences of being caught paying her too much attention, of drawing too much attention to himself. And yet he tempted fate.

Meghna wasn't concerned by his interest so much as intrigued. She was used to the attention of men—counted on it, really. She wore bright red lipstick to draw their eyes to her mouth, picked curve-hugging dresses to pull their gazes to her tits or her ass… and she smiled *just so* while sliding stilettos between their ribs. The pin in her coiled up-do seemed to vibrate at that thought, like a sentient extension of her murderous impulses. Meghna shook off the tingle of anticipation, the burst of adrenaline, reminding herself that she was here to seduce not to slaughter. It would *not* do to leave bloodstains on Emeric Aston's carpet. Not tonight, at any rate.

So she returned the man's gaze, infusing it with an equal amount of focus and just a dash of sexual interest. It wasn't a difficult task. Not the challenge it had been when she inserted herself into Emeric's life, using all her training to tolerate his hands on her body and his cruel kisses. This man was as beautiful as he was dangerous. A black T-shirt and jeans, meant to help him blend into the background like the rest of the hired security, clung to his rock-solid body like a lover. His skin, darker than her own light brown, glowed with health. She doubted it came from any kind of product—none of the high-end brand names she'd shilled as an influencer. The smooth curve of his shaved head begged for hands to cradle it…to guide it down between her thighs. *Focus, Meghna. Observe. Find his weaknesses, not your own.* She took the mental reprimand like a slap, all the while tilting her head and laughing breathlessly at something that had made Aston's cronies chortle.

It was easy—pretending to be interested in what they were saying. They didn't expect real engagement, didn't expect her to actually *listen*. So, most of the time, she didn't. And the few times that she did…? Well, that was infinitely valuable. That was why she was here, with her arm looped through Mirko's, periodically blinking her heavily made-up eyes at him in vapid adoration while his right-hand man seethed. Sasha Nichols had never liked her, regarded her with barely veiled suspicion. Born of a Russian mother and an American father, with loyalties one hundred percent for sale. Dual nationalities and an utter lack of conscience was something he and Emeric had in common. He required careful monitoring, even in situations like this—where she was nothing but a pretty prop for his boss.

Her watcher was getting in the way, though. Splitting her attention. Sending prickles across every inch of skin bared by her bias-cut slip dress. He was as different from Emeric and Sasha as night from day, and not just because her fair-haired and pale-skinned "protector" and his equally Nordic-appearing henchman were the whitest of white men. And Mirko a white *human* at that. The stranger, who was very likely not a security guard at all, was a supernatural like her. Her instincts identified him as a shifter of some kind, the specifics of which she couldn't guess from this distance. Unlike Sasha, who had shifter blood but couldn't actually shift and resented the whole of the universe for it, this man didn't have any obvious insecurities. And unlike Mirko, who'd bought and paid for every companion in this room in one way or another, Mr. Shifter didn't have to demand the room. He already owned it.

Simply by standing in an alcove and spanning it with his gaze. Did that include her?

No. Never. Her kind belonged to no one. *Don't forget that, Meghna. Don't forget why you're here.*

As if that was a possibility. She scoffed at the warning voice. She didn't have the luxury of forgetting. Not in this world. Not in this life. Not after the Darkest Day, and the light that had been shined upon supernaturals afterward. Eventually, many humans had gone back to their idea of "normal." Work and school and leisure activities. The grocery stores had been restocked after the calamities that had plagued the past few years. The grief for those lost to sickness and violence had dulled to a throb, instead of the sharp, persistent, spike. The economy was slowly rebounding. The TV shows and streaming channels and podcasts were much the same as they had been…though perhaps a bit more patriotic and pro-government than before. Those who had never experienced oppression or an -ism lived as they always had: oblivious, privileged.

Her own upbringing should have marked her for that callous delusion that the only color that mattered was the green of money. A rich man's pampered daughter, born amongst the Washington elite, raised in her uncle's Bollywood and Hollywood circles. *Should have. Could have. Would have.* But she'd never had the chance to be simply that vapid socialite who voted conservatively because of her tax bracket. Because there was her upbringing… and then there was her heritage. Her duty. Her destiny.

Meghna gently slid her arm out from Mirko's. He barely noticed, caught up as he was in some outrageous—but no doubt still true—story about doing vodka shots in a Moscow brothel with the American president and the Russian prime minister. It was nothing she hadn't heard before. Nothing she could use. But the handsome supernatural watcher in the corner…? He was an unknown quantity. He could make or break what she'd come here to do, what she'd worked so hard for. All because he couldn't take his eyes from her.

Meghna saw only one solution. Well, one solution that didn't involve the stiletto in her hair. She had to fuck him. Tonight.

ACKNOWLEDGMENTS

───

Big Bad Wolf is a book that combines my politics and my passions. An idea conceived in a much simpler time came to fruition amidst a lot of anger and pain and confusion about the state of the world today. And fear. So much fear. But romance novels are what we turn to for comfort, right? So Joe and Neha helped me, held me, and healed me just a little. I hope some of you feel the same way.

This book would not have made it this far without my mama bear literary agent, Courtney Miller-Callihan, or Cat Clyne, who acquired it for Sourcebooks Casablanca. My Casablanca editors Mary Altman and Rachel Gilmer believed in this project every step of the way and helped me whip the manuscript into fighting shape. Thank you, too, to Stefani Sloma for marketing the hell out of my bonkers babies and putting up with my silliness on Zoom calls, and to Jessica Smith and Diane Dannenfeldt for shining *Big Bad Wolf* up. My deepest gratitude goes to Sandy Johal, Sonali Dev, and Nisha Sharma for their invaluable eleventh-hour feedback on Neha and her family. Kate Davies, Charlotte Stein, Jackie Barbosa, Jayce Ellis, Elizabeth Kerri Mahon and Melinda Utendorf deserve so many thanks for being the very first sets of eyes on the story and for assuring me it was good enough to be out in the world. Thank you also to Sarah Title for the writing dates, encouraging all the "danger boning," and answering important questions like "Is it okay to steal pants off a corpse?"

I wouldn't be here without friends like Melissa Blue, Regina Small, and Michelle Bell cheering me on during this journey. I owe a lot to the folks at 626 and RPS in Chicago for keeping me fueled and fed while I worked on *Big Bad Wolf* and its sequel, and to the businesses and people on Church Avenue in Kensington and Flatbush, who inspired the books in the first place. And Queens. . . how can I forget the borough that welcomed me to New York City? The references to Donovan's, the 7 train, Jackson Heights, and the bar with killer happy hour martinis all come from my years of living in one of the most vibrant, diverse, communities I've ever known. Thank you to my "nabe," and everyone in it. I also have to give a shout-out to the Jamaica Bay Riding Academy. Yes, there is actually a riding school right off the Mill Basin. No, I've never been there—and, as far as I know, it is not a secret spy base.

Lastly, thank you to my family. They're not allowed to read this book (I MEAN IT!), but I'm so lucky they let this creative cuckoo thrive in a nest full of academics. And, Dad, I miss you so much.

ABOUT THE AUTHOR

Suleikha Snyder is a bestselling and award-winning author of contemporary and erotic romance, whose works have been showcased in *Entertainment Weekly*, *BuzzFeed*, *The Times of India*, and *NPR*. An editor, writer, American desi, and lifelong geek, she is a passionate advocate for diversity and inclusivity in media of all kinds. Suleikha has lived in big cities like New York and Chicago, but her true home is the internet. Visit her website at suleikhasnyder.com and follow her on Twitter @suleikhasnyder.